Ginger and Me

Elissa Soave won the inaugural Primadonna Prize in 2019. She currently lives in South Lanarkshire and *Ginger and Me* is her debut novel.

Ginger and Me

Elissa Soave

ONE PLACE. MANY STORIES

HQ
An imprint of HarperCollins*Publishers* Ltd
1 London Bridge Street
London SE1 9GF

www.harpercollins.co.uk

HarperCollins*Publishers*
1st Floor, Watermarque Building, Ringsend Road
Dublin 4, Ireland

This edition 2022

1

First published in Great Britain by
HQ, an imprint of HarperCollins*Publishers* Ltd 2022

HB ISBN: 978-0-00-845841-6
TPB ISBN: 978-0-00-845842-3

MIX
Paper from
responsible sources
FSC™ C007454

This book is produced from independently certified FSC™ paper
to ensure responsible forest management.

For more information visit: www.harpercollins.co.uk/green

This book is set in 11.5/15.5 pt. Bembo

Printed and bound in the UK using 100% renewable electricity at
CPI Group (UK) Ltd, Croydon, CR0 4YY

For my boys, Luca and Sebastian, with love

Present, Polmont Prison

THEY KEPT ASKING ME why I was outside her house that day, and who was with me. I tried to say I would never harm Diane, I loved her. And I mean I loved *her*, not just the writing. Though I do love her writing too. The way she can squeeze the juice out of a metaphor, take you back to being eight years old with a sound, or a smell. Make you cringe. Or cry. It's genius, and I know because I'm a writer too. Just because I drive a bus, it doesn't mean I can't write. I'm even in a writers' group – though they don't always appreciate how good my stories are. One of the things I tried to tell the police was I'm a writer like Diane, that's what we've got in common, but they wouldn't listen. They arrested me and told me anything I said would be admissible in court, even though I loved Diane. I can't speak for Ginger, I can only tell you what I told them – I'd never hurt Diane. That didn't stop them putting me in a police car and taking me to Motherwell Police Station, practically via the same route as the 240, which was not my favourite route to drive at the best of times. I don't know where they took Ginger.

Next day, they took me to court. They woke me up at seven with a bowl of Cheerios and a cup of lukewarm tea.

'Do you have someone who can bring you some clothes?' It

was the same policewoman from the night before. She looked more feminine than I'd imagined female officers looked, even with the uniform. Her hair was tied back in one of those low buns but you could tell she would be pretty when she took it down. I wondered if she had a female sidekick, like Scott and Bailey, or whether she was more the lone wolf sort of detective, like Vera or maybe a brilliant female Morse.

'Wendy. Wendy!'

'Sorry, what?'

'You'll need clothes for court this morning. Is there someone we can call to bring you in some stuff?'

The only person would have been Ginger so I shook my head.

'Where are my own clothes? Someone took them off me yesterday but I don't have a lot of jeans so I'd like them back.'

She narrowed her eyes at me. 'Those are evidence now, Wendy. You won't be able to wear them. Look, don't worry, we'll find you something here.'

'What about my phone?' I called after her. 'They took that off me yesterday too and I really need it.' But I don't think she heard me because she didn't turn round.

I got changed in the toilet next to my cell while the police-woman stood outside. I wasn't too pleased with the skirt and sweatshirt combo she'd brought me but I wasn't in any position to argue, and at least they more or less fitted my long skinny frame. I washed my face in cold water, and risked a look at my morning-after self, surprised that it still looked like me. My forehead deep and broad, dominating over narrow eyes, still dull mahogany and revealing nothing. My pale skin remained so, though there was faint bruising on my right cheek, which must have happened the day before. My nose was long and straight, my dad's nose, but my smile was terrible, like I'd spotted someone across the room that I had to pretend to be pleased to see.

'If it pleases Your Honour this has all been a big misunderstanding,' I said into the mirror. I leaned in closer and turned my head to the left and right. My lank black hair was unaffected by a night in the cells. It was still in more or less the same style I've always worn it – a bob to my shoulders – though I had let Ginger cut the fringe a bit shorter recently. I wasn't sure about it but she said it would balance out my huge, shiny forehead and she was usually right about that sort of thing. I patted my hair down ten times on each side before smoothing it against the back of my neck. 'You can't make a silk purse out of a sow's ear Wendy,' I whispered to myself. They were my mum's words. Just as well I've never been the kind of person to put much store in looks. I left the bathroom counting backwards from twenty under my breath to keep me steady.

They put me in a small, windowless van with three other women and took us to Hamilton Sheriff Court. The skinny girl curled into the front seat raised her chin at me as I got on so I sat next to her.

'I'm Wendy,' I said. 'What are you going to court for?' But she didn't answer. I really wanted to tell her that these weren't my own clothes, I wouldn't have chosen a skirt for one thing, never mind pairing it with trainers. I could tell she didn't want to talk though and, to be fair, she probably thought I was some sort of criminal, so I just sat and bit my lips and tried not to think too much about where Ginger and Diane were now.

When we got to the court, I was assigned a duty solicitor called Mr Cameron. He was a small, V-neck jumper kind of man and I could imagine him cutting his grass on his weekends off, or going on mini-breaks to do nothing in Dunkeld. He shook my hand sweatily and told me we'd 'be up in five'. If you've watched as many courtroom dramas as I have, you might have the idea that a courtroom is an impressive place, dark wood lining the walls and men in wigs milling around with folders of important papers. The room they took me into was about the size of my living room, and the only people in there were me, Mr Cameron, another lawyer sitting across from us, and the judge. It was all over in a few minutes – they charged me, Mr Cameron said I made no plea and moved for bail, the other lawyer opposed it while they 'made further inquiries', and the judge said I'd be taken to Polmont Prison 'forthwith'.

The judge left the room and I watched as Mr Cameron got up and shook hands with the other lawyer. He walked back to me and said, 'We'll renew our motion for bail in a week but don't get your hopes up.'

'What do you mean? I can't go to prison – what about my house? My job? My passengers would miss me, they'd wonder where I was.'

'Wendy,' he said, frowning. 'I'm not sure if you realize just how much trouble you're in. These are extremely serious charges.'

'But it's a misunderstanding,' I said. 'Look, Diane and I are both writers, we've got a long history together. Ask her, she'll tell you.'

He shook his head, and told me he'd see me in Polmont some time during the week.

And that was it.

One Year Earlier: After Mum Died

1

IT'S HARD TO IMAGINE this now but there was a life before Ginger and Diane. After Mum died the most important person in my life was my support worker so I probably need to talk about her first because, in a way, she brought us all together.

Apart from work – and I didn't really count the people on my bus as friends, except maybe the regulars – my support worker was sometimes the only person I spoke to all week. I really liked her. Her name was Saanvi, and she always wore a sari, a different colour every time she came. My favourite was the red and gold one, it sparkled when the sun caught it, and she'd hoist it over her arm as she walked so she wouldn't get the hem dirty. Sometimes when she was speaking, I found myself staring at the blood-red spot in the centre of her forehead, mesmerized by it so that I wasn't really listening to what she was telling me at all. When she coughed, or called my name a couple of times, I'd bring myself back to the present and go, 'Yeah you're right,' or something like that so she wouldn't know I'd stopped listening. She'd sigh and say, 'There's only so much I can do Wendy. You're nineteen years old now, an adult, you have to try and help yourself too.' Or 'You know, social clubs and making new friends are open to everyone.' It's true, they are, but only in the same way that staying at the Savoy or jet skiing is available to everyone, and I won't be doing those things any time soon either.

In fact I hadn't been doing anything much at all since Mum died and Saanvi said that was one of my problems. Mum had died in August, and I'm not saying it was harder for me than anyone else who'd lost their mum but . . . I didn't realize how much I relied on her till she wasn't there. Maybe it was because I'd never had much luck making friends, and it had been just me and her for so long, living in our house in Birkenshaw. Before she got sick she was out working a lot of the time but, even when she wasn't at home, she left me lots of little notes, on the table and sometimes stuck to mirrors. In the kitchen they'd say things like: *Take the bin out Wendy. Remember to get milk on your way home. Put the stew on at three o'clock.* There was always a note about something or other. Up in the bathroom or my bedroom they'd say: *You're your own best friend. God made you perfect as you are.* And there was one that I kept stuck inside my wardrobe that just said: *Love yourself.* After she was gone, I missed those scribbled notes pasted all over the house. Suddenly there was no one to care if I got the milk or not, and I realized she hadn't told me *how* to love myself.

I didn't go to work or eat or even take a bath for weeks after she died. I was finding it really hard to know what I was doing all those things for when Mum and me weren't going to Tunnock's for our tea, or into town window shopping at the posh shops, or even just talking over dinner about what had happened on my bus that day. With Mum gone, I didn't think anyone would notice or care if life caved in on me, and I just stopped being part of it all. But Mr Laverty came round to see why I wasn't at work and called in social services as soon as he saw my house and the way I was living. I was angry about that at the time, he may have been my boss but he didn't have the right to get strangers to come to my house and judge me. I refused to go to hospital but it turns out if you're not coping as well as other people say you should be they can slap a section on you and make you go to hospital anyway. They seemed surprised I hadn't spoken to a counsellor before but why would I need that when I always had my mum to help me through life? I didn't agree with most of the stuff they said, like how I had to make peace with Mum dying and be grateful for the life I had; and that the way to happiness was to strike a balance between the terror that is life and the wonder that is living, but I nodded and pretended to agree with everything. They lifted the section after a week, but it was another four months before they said I was well enough to leave the hospital and come home.

Saanvi came to see me every Wednesday because it's important to establish a routine. That's one of the first things she told me. She said to start small, and I did find that small things became important, ways of eating up the hours till the day was over, then the week, and then a month had passed.

I went back to work in the February, and I loved my job on the buses so that helped a bit. My favourite was the 255 – that's the hourly service from Birkenshaw bus bay, through Mossend and up to Bellshill. A lot of the other drivers don't like doing the local services – you do have to go back and forth over the same route a lot of times in one shift – but I liked it, especially before I knew Ginger and Diane, when my regulars would keep me going. I'd start off in front of Naf's in Birkenshaw, not far from my house in fact, then head up Old Edinburgh Road towards Viewpark. I'd fly along the top road past the Viewpark Community Centre, where the pre-school children all went to Rising 5s, and loads of kids from my own school had gone to basketball and karate and that sort of thing. I didn't go to any clubs but my dad once took me to see a pro wrestling show in there and a block-jawed wrestler called the Dynamite Kid signed a gigantic foam finger for me. There was a stop outside JR's Tyres, and The Ashley was just opposite. It didn't matter what shift you were on, the drunks would be slumped outside, gulping down nicotine like oxygen, or standing about gabbing the way they say women do. No one ever called it The Ashley, it was always known as The Flying Tumbler, I don't know why. I knew it well though as it was one of my dad's favourites when he first got made redundant. A young guy that Ginger told me later was Wee Eddie would be running on the street somewhere, either on his way to Coral or heading back to The Olde Club, as we drove by. Beyond St Columbas and a couple more stops took you to the memorial garden with the bronze statue of Jimmy Johnstone, and then round the corner past The Laughing Buddha and The Rolling Barrel, the pub my dad went to after The Flying Tumbler wouldn't have him any more. 'I've changed my allegiance,' was how he put it to me as Mum snorted from the kitchen beyond. By the time I pulled up in front of the Spar in Bellshill the bus would generally be full, no matter the weather. The laughter and chatter from Irish Mary, Terry, Myra and the rest of my regulars would float down the bus, so it was just as though I was part of the conversation myself.

I finished early on Thursdays, so I'd go home and change out of my uniform, have a hot shower and put on my jeans. If I stayed a while in the shower, that could use up almost an hour. It took about twenty minutes to walk from my house in Birkenshaw, down the Holm Brae and across the motorway bridge to Uddingston proper. The village, as Mum used to call it, though it's hardly a village now with all the new houses they've built, there's even a sushi restaurant. Sushi in Uddingston! Main Street's always busy, in the early afternoons you've got the mums and the prams, usually walking three abreast so you can't get by without one of them tutting and saying 'excuse *us*'. You've got the rich old folk coming back from Bothwell Golf Club to have a drink at Angels or the new wine bar they've opened, Rosso's or Rossi's I think, I've never been in. My dad wouldn't recognize Uddingston these days, I don't think he would've liked it. He certainly wouldn't have been seen dead drinking in a wine bar.

At first it felt strange going into Tunnock's for my steak pie because me and Mum used to go there together every Thursday. We'd have a cup of tea and a scone in the café at the back and then pick up the large pie the ladies behind the counter would have all packaged and ready for us on the way out. Mum would ask the woman handing over the pie about her daughter who'd gone to university, and check with the woman at the till how her uncle who'd had a stroke was doing. And she'd been at school with the manageress so they used to joke about not getting any younger and how old age doesn't come alone. She always knew the right thing to say, and made it easy for me to hang back and say nothing, which was what we were both used to.

The first time I went in after was a bit awkward. The ladies knew Mum had died and felt they had to say something but I couldn't talk about it – another issue according to Saanvi. After one of them said, 'So sorry to hear about your mum,' I looked past her into the chilled cabinet and said, 'A steak pie please.

A small one.' She must have thought I hadn't heard because she said again what a shame Mum had died, and I said, 'Will you wrap it up for me and I'll get it after my tea?' and left the three women behind the counter looking at each other in surprise as I headed to the back of the shop. I could tell I'd handled it all wrong because of the way they huddled and whispered together behind me, and I was glad Saanvi hadn't been there to see it. I wasn't trying to be rude. After Mum died, I realized it was just another thing I hadn't learned – how to talk to people about little things, like family, or what cakes they liked, or whether it looked like rain. And even after my stay in hospital, I still didn't know what people wanted from me when they said they were sorry she'd died, tears maybe, or some other emotion. I never knew the right response, better just to say nothing.

Friday was my day for the library. I've been going to Uddingston library since it was in the old sandstone building at the far end of Main Street. That's a podiatrist's clinic now and I think they also offer massages, so you could get your feet and neck done at the same time if you wanted. The new library is round the corner from the Tunnock's factory, right next to the Baptist church. The librarian's called Linda, she's really nice, and sometimes even stops what she's doing to talk to me for a while about books.

Once I saw a poster behind her desk advertising the local book club.

'Can anyone go to the book club?' I asked, following her as she carried a pile of books to the big red box in the children's section.

She put down the books and said, 'Yes, of course. Are you interested?'

I shrugged. I wasn't sure if I was interested or not but I did know the evenings were long with no one to talk to and, though I'd never be as good at talking to people as Mum was, I thought maybe even I could join in if we were only talking about books. Also, I knew it would make Saanvi happy.

'It's on the last Wednesday of every month,' Linda said. 'We all take turns hosting the discussion evening, and—'

'Wait, you have to have people to your house?'

She nodded.

I wouldn't have wanted anyone seeing my house far less have to offer them tea in cups that matched so I just told Linda I would think about it, and watched as she tidied up the *Mr Men* books.

I usually tried to stay in the library for a full hour before walking back up the road. Sometimes when I passed the Baptist church, I was quite tempted by the signs outside that said things like *We Welcome Everyone* or *God Loves All His Flock*, but I knew Mum would turn in her grave if I actually went into a non-Catholic church so I never did.

Weekends were more problematic, especially if I couldn't get any extra shifts. I tried to keep busy, maybe read, and I did a lot of walking. If you walk down Station Hill, and go across the roundabout by Anne's Pantry, there's a wee lane, half hidden by trees, which takes you to a path that leads straight to Bothwell Castle. It's kind of boggy and overgrown but I love the quiet, and the trees overhanging the river make it dark and private. On your right-hand side as you walk towards the castle is the River Clyde. Lots of kids from my school used to go there in the summer, hang a tyre swing over the water and swing from the bank over the river and back again. I used to hear them talk about the buzz it gave you, it sounded great. I could easily pass a good hour or two walking there and it usually lifted my spirits. Sometimes I became a bit focused on the dog walkers, in pairs, or the couples with their arms twisted round each other, or the young families in their brightly coloured woollens and wellies, and I understood what it was like to have people in your life by my own lack of it.

Once I saw a woman, a bit older than me maybe, wearing a Ramones T-shirt and purple Doc Martens. She was pushing a white-haired woman in a wheelchair, and they were headed towards a group of three ducks paddling at the water's edge.

'Take some bread Mum, they like that.' The woman handed her mum some chunks of bread from a small plastic bag then placed the bag on the ground beside them.

I hesitated, then remembered Saanvi telling me that if I wanted to make friends I had to be more confident and take the initiative sometimes, and the Ramones woman did look really nice and I hadn't spoken to anyone the entire weekend except Naf at the corner shop. I shut my eyes tight and muttered, 'Come on Wendy,' opened them and shuffled over to where they were standing. 'Hi. Hello,' I said, in a loud voice in case the old lady was hard of hearing. Neither woman replied though the younger woman smiled at me.

Encouraged, I tried again. 'Looks like rain.'

The younger woman looked up at the clear blue sky and said, 'Maybe.'

I leaned closer to the woman in the chair and shouted, 'You'll be alright in there anyway' and smiled. I picked up some bread from the bag on the ground and started to throw it into the water, thinking maybe Saanvi was right and making friends was easier than I'd imagined.

'Do you come here often?' I said, turning again to the younger woman but she was already taking the brakes off the chair and pushing it back to the path. I stood and watched them hurry off, shouting after them, 'Wait, you've left your bread!' but they must have been too far away to hear as they didn't turn back. I fed the rest of the bread to the ducks, wondering if I'd said the wrong thing. The ducks left too as soon as the bread was finished, and I headed back up the hill to my house, to wait for the week to begin again.

The highlight of the week was Wednesday when I saw Saanvi. At first, I was annoyed social services thought I couldn't look after myself – I definitely could – but after a while I started to look forward to Saanvi's visits, practise what I was going to say beforehand, and try to impress her with how well I was doing. I thought if I did everything she told me I might learn how to make friends and be as good at life as she was.

She usually opened with the same question. 'Tell me about your week Wendy, what's been happening?' I remember she was really impressed when I told her I'd made the effort to go to the cinema.

It had been a good day. I'd taken the 63 to Hamilton, it wasn't a driver I knew so I just sat at the back, looking out the window. As we got closer to the town centre, I swivelled my head as we drove by the spot where my old school had been. It's not there any more, it's been replaced by a housing estate of tiny houses for new families, and I certainly hope they'll be happier there than I was at school.

The cinema was practically empty so it was bad luck that one of the three other customers was sitting in my favourite aisle seat, row 12, seat D. I stood over him and coughed a couple of times but, when he didn't move, I took the seat next to him. He tutted as I struggled out of my jacket, looked for the best spot to place my rucksack so it wouldn't be under my feet, and then had to pick it up again when I remembered I'd forgotten to take out my snack. I could feel him tense next to me as I started peeling my orange and sucking the juice from it – you'd think he'd never seen anyone eat an orange in the cinema before. The way he was huffing and puffing and shuffling round in his seat, honestly I'd be amazed if he saw anything of the film at all. Not that he missed much – I should probably have checked what was on before I bought my ticket because to be honest, I didn't enjoy the film that much. I watch a lot of movies and nobody likes a good twist more than me but I do think you need at least some basic structure to follow. The story was told looking backwards for one thing – never easy – and for another we were seeing everything from the point of view of the main character but he had problems with his memory so you couldn't be sure if what he was telling you was right or not. I couldn't tell who was responsible for killing his wife, or even if she was dead at all. Still, it got me out of the house for almost four hours so that was most of the day gone. And I could tell Saanvi was pleased with me.

'That's great Wendy,' she said, checking her watch, then bending down to put her folder in her bag. 'Little steps forwards, going to work, going to the cinema, you're on the right track now.'

I wasn't sure doing all the things Saanvi suggested was making me any happier but at least we had stuff to talk about every week. And maybe she was right – I was on the right track, and I could have stayed there too, if it hadn't been for Ginger and Diane.

2

I WAS ALREADY FRIENDS WITH Diane when I met Ginger. Twitter friends anyway, which still counts, maybe even more so because you have to squeeze so much into your 280 characters and then send them out into the world like Post-it notes in a hurricane, hoping they'd reach their target.

It was funny because, in just a couple of months, I'd gone from having no friends at all to meeting my two best friends and also being in the writers' group. I think Saanvi was pleased. It was her that suggested the writers' group in the first place. I'd been telling her about a book I'd been reading from the library and she asked if I'd ever thought about joining a writers' group and trying to write some stuff myself. Secretly I thought maybe I could write something that would speak to people like me but, as for a writing group, I shook my head and told her I wasn't the kind of person that joined clubs and I didn't think I'd be any good at them because I never knew the right thing to say.

'Wendy, everyone can find a club that suits them. You don't need any special permission to join one, you know.'

I wasn't convinced but when she explained that a writers' group was just a place for people who loved reading and writing to meet up and talk, I thought it might be a club even I could go to and maybe make some friends. Plus I didn't want her to think I wasn't taking her advice on board when she was trying so hard to help so I joined the group. She was pleased with me for doing that and I was glad I'd impressed her.

The group met every Monday night at The Drury, a pub near Central Station. We'd always sit in the same place, commandeering the biggest table at the back of the bar, underneath the print of that cool woman with the bob from *Pulp Fiction*.

Henry was the chairperson, and he was born to be one. At the start of every meeting, he'd shout, 'Order order,' like he was in the House of Commons, and we all had to stop talking and listen to his spiel about trigger warnings and respecting the work of others and blah blah. Same every week. Sophie would gaze up at him hopefully, twirling her hair and taking her glasses off and on so he'd notice her. He was never going to of course, or at least not in the way she wanted him to, because Henry was too busy gazing the same way at Joseph. For someone who wanted to be a writer, Sophie wasn't very observant.

Reginald was about ninety and wrote poems about nature and trees and that sort of thing. They were quite boring and, to be honest, sometimes I didn't even read them before the meeting. When it was my turn to give feedback I'd just say stuff like, 'Very evocative' and 'I found it calming,' and that seemed to keep him happy. It's a shame but his puffy red eyes and the way his teeth slipped out from under his top lip and just sort of hung there for a bit when he was concentrating could be off-putting to new members, I thought.

We'd get a lot of new members, people who'd come for a week and then never come back. I really liked the look of one girl who had a Liam Neeson fan club badge on her cardigan and one of those hats with drinking straws attached so you don't even have to go to the bar for a drink. I didn't know Ginger then but she would have loved that hat. Seems this girl thought we were a special needs group but she was mixing us up with the group that meets at the GOMA library on a Tuesday, so she must have gone to that one instead because we never saw her again. Henry suggested to me I might fancy it for a change but I said I was quite happy with our group. He gave me a very wide smile, it practically split his face in two, so I think he was relieved not to lose another member, even if it was only me.

Henry's right-hand man was Joseph. He was my least favourite of everyone who came to the group, and not just because of his man bun and unlaced Converse. Henry might have been Mr Punch, dealing the blows front of house, but it was Joseph who was pulling his strings. I don't think either of them liked me much although I did overhear Joseph say to Henry once that I was the thinking woman's Jackie Collins. Or it may have been unthinking, I can't recall now but I found out later that Jackie Collins was a Hollywood superstar so it was clear they secretly rated my writing more than they let on.

The other regular was Muriel, who I liked even though she was in her forties, at least. I think she liked me too, didn't not like me as much as the others anyway. Maybe I reminded her of her dead daughter. I know she's dead because I overheard her telling Joseph about her one night – how she'd committed suicide by gassing herself.

'Was it in an oven?' I asked, but she didn't answer. I was going to tell her that's how Sylvia Plath had done it, and she was a very famous writer. Joseph gave me one of his looks though so I sat back and just waited for my turn to read out my poem. Of course I knew they wouldn't get it, much of my writing seemed to be over their heads. It could be infuriating to listen to their critiques, which were never very positive. I tried to bear in mind that a) they were used to agreeing with whatever Henry and Joseph said, and they were complete amateurs, and b) lots of people think they can write when they really can't. There were certainly several people in this group that fell into that category, so it wasn't surprising if they didn't appreciate sensitive poetry when they saw it. I don't know why I kept going, really, except they were the closest things to friends I had at the time. Before I knew Ginger and Diane that is.

I think it was my third week or so at the group when I first heard Sophie telling Henry about this brilliant novel she was reading. She was all breathless and excited, like she got when she was talking to Henry, but she did sound convincing so I leaned in a bit closer to catch the name. *Out of Sight, Out of Mind* by Diane Weston. I liked the sound of it, and was intrigued that it was written by a local woman, someone just like me. I decided to give it a go, thought maybe then I could join in the conversation.

I asked Linda at Uddingston library to order it for me.

'No need to order it Wendy,' she said, strolling over to the contemporary fiction section. I watched as she knelt down to the Ws, ran her finger along the bottom shelf, said, 'There we go,' and held up a thick hardback book, covered in the library's clear plastic wrapping. 'If we can't keep our local celebrity's books, it'd be a sad day wouldn't it?' she said, stamping it and handing it to me.

'Thanks,' I said, placing it carefully in my rucksack.

'No problem, I think you'll enjoy it, I loved it so let me know what you think.'

I started reading the book as soon as I came off shift that evening and I stayed up half the night finishing it. It was the first time I'd ever read a book about a girl like me, someone whose life I could recognize and whose problems I could understand. She was called Gillian and she lived in the East End of Glasgow in the eighties. She never met her dad but she lived with her mum and her wee brother, Sean, in a tenement flat on Duke Street. I couldn't believe it when I read that – I'd been to Duke Street, and to the Parkhead Forge and the People's Palace, which were all mentioned in the book. I didn't know you could write about people like us, from here, not from London or abroad. 'Gillian gripped Sean's hand and half dragged him the length of Duke Street back home to face their mother's wrath.' Duke Street! 'Gillian's mum sat on the edge of her bed. Smoothing the hair away from the crying girl's forehead, she said it didn't matter what anyone else thought of her, she'd always be Mum's special girl. Gillian smiled, not caring any more what the others thought.' I took a sharp breath when I read that bit, and repeated it to myself over and over, until I knew it like a prayer.

I never really got the chance to tell everyone at writers' group I'd read it in the end but it didn't matter. That book made me see how crap their writing was, in comparison to mine and Diane's, I mean. But it was more than just the brilliant writing, that book really spoke to me. Maybe because it was still only a couple of months after I'd got out of hospital. But the thing is, there are things in that book that no one could possibly know unless they'd been there too. So I knew before I even met Diane that we had loads in common. That book changed my life.

As soon as I'd finished work the next day I googled 'Diane Weston' on my phone to find out what I could about her. There wasn't that much considering she was such a brilliant writer, I thought she deserved to have much more written about her. But then I saw she was on Twitter and my hand was shaking a bit as I tapped in her name and her page popped up on my screen.

Award-winning Scottish writer · Books include: OUT OF SIGHT, OUT OF MIND; ELIZABETH; THIS GIRL'S LIFE; EXPRESSIVE EXPRESSIONISM · ONE WORLD and PONDLIFE coming soon · #WomensWriting #WorkingClassWriters #WordsMatter

Then:

Location: Citizen of the world

Citizen of the world? I loved that! I realized she was more famous than I'd thought. She had thousands of followers – 9,392 when I first started checking and more every time I looked. Her Pinned Tweet had 992 likes, and it deserved to have even more in my opinion.

Words matter. Word after word, sentence after sentence, page after page, a book is born. Your story matters – only you can tell it.

My mouth fell open as I read that. It was as though she had written it directly to me. My mind was whirring with possibilities as I kicked my trainers off and pushed myself further up the bed, impatient to read everything Diane had to tell me.

Reread Kelman's masterpiece, 'How Late It Was How Late' and am reminded of why we must fight to write our own stories. 'My culture and my language have a right to exist and no one has the authority to dismiss that right.' Never a truer word.

I opened a new tab and searched for 'Kelman' and was surprised to see he's written quite a few books, almost as many as Diane in fact. I don't think I'd heard anyone mention him at writers' group, which only confirmed my suspicions that they didn't know what they were talking about. Not like Diane.

Is any man capable of writing about women without telling us how firm her breasts are? Do better.

I looked up from my phone for a bit to think about that. Personally, I wouldn't mind if anyone described my breasts as firm – though no one ever has – but maybe Diane had a point, it wasn't the sort of thing men should be writing about. After all, who really cared about their opinion on breasts and surely there were other more interesting things about women they could focus on. I pressed the love heart button to like the tweet, along with 239 other followers.

If you wouldn't ask a man who happens to be a father how he manages childcare while he writes, don't ask a woman who happens to be a mother.

I hadn't considered that before but, when you think about it, people do expect women to fit in everything round their children, whereas men can just go and do what they like. There's men out drinking in The Flying Tumbler all hours of the day every day, and who's looking after their children? If women were allowed to spend even half of the time writing that men spend in pubs, think how much great work they could produce. Diane's right about that – there'd be a lot more books by women if they weren't spending all their time changing nappies and doing pointless activities with their toddlers like sticking wee coloured squares of paper onto bigger pieces of paper. I put a heart beside that tweet as well.

Every so often she posted pictures too, and I zoomed in on them to make sure I didn't miss any detail. One was titled, 'Spring has sprung at Bothwell Castle', and was a close-up shot of rough, red brick contrasted with feathery spikes of heather. I looked a bit closer and recognized the crumbling remnants of the Great Hall, facing the Clyde. The idea that Diane had walked the same path as me, thinking about storylines and characters maybe, looking at the same trees swaying over the same river, was awe-inspiring to me. I kept scrolling.

Every time she tweeted something, it would get at least one hundred likes, sometimes more. You could tell people really liked what she was saying, probably because she was passionate in her opinions and wasn't just tweeting for the likes, or to raise her profile, or to sell more books, or any of the other reasons writers are generally on Twitter. She tweeted about women writing and why weren't there more books published by working-class women, black women (women of colour she called them), old women in their forties or fifties even. She thought everyone deserved to be heard, even people like me, stuck at the back of the room, not fitting in, and clinging to the wall hoping no one would see them. Apart from Mum, she was the first person I'd come across who thought people like us should be pushed forwards and listened to, that our opinions mattered.

And I could see straight away that we had lots of similar opinions on things. She was saying things I didn't even know I thought until she said them.

Good literature is not about heroes and deities. It's about people like us with our own stories to tell. As Ishiguro tells it: It's how we say, this is how it feels for me, is this how it feels for you?

I had to put my phone down for a bit and catch my breath after I read that one. When I looked up, I realized my bedroom was pitch black and I'd spent the whole evening in Diane's company. Just one more, I thought, before I get some sleep. And that's when I read the tweet that made me see there was nothing stopping me from being a writer like Diane.

We all have a story to tell. Women matter. Working-class voices matter. Your story matters.

I was a woman and I had loads of stories I wanted to tell. I'd never really thought about what class I was – Dad didn't work for a long time but Mum always worked, sometimes three jobs at a time. And I loved my work, so that was probably enough to qualify me as working class. So yes, I was all of these things, and Diane said that meant my story mattered.

As soon as I got up the next morning, I found an old notepad in Mum's odds and sods drawer in the kitchen, and started making notes for a new story to take to writers' group. It was amazing how close to Diane I felt as I was writing. I could almost feel her presence at my shoulder, her breath on my cheek, willing me to write the best story I could, because my story mattered and I was the only one who could tell it. I wrote until my neck ached, and when I closed the pad and stretched out my arms, I thought how good it felt to be on the right track at last.

3

I'D BEEN TO writers' group the night before I met Ginger, and I was still a bit annoyed about it, maybe that's why I didn't notice her right away. That night, they'd been talking about films and that's something I do know about since it was just me and Netflix most nights, and I watched lots of different things. I kept trying to edge my way into the conversation but they were sitting in a tight circle and speaking fast so it was hard for me to say anything. It reminded me of lunchtimes at school when the girls I wanted to talk to would stand shoulder to shoulder, flicking their hair and looking everywhere except at me, and that was before Nuala Brennan called me Weirdo and it stuck. At writers' group, Henry and Joseph were the top dogs whose rules had to be followed by the rest or else. At one point, Henry was going on about how they'd ruined the Bond movies by giving 007 insecurities and I shouted over Muriel's back that most people had things about themselves they didn't like if that's what he meant, but he kept on talking to Joseph as though I hadn't spoken at all.

When we got down to business, I was excited to hear what they'd made about my piece inspired by Diane. I don't write a lot about love because, unlike books and films, it's not a subject

I know much about. I mean, I sometimes look at couples on my bus in the mornings and wonder if they've tasted each other's genitals the night before and, if so, how it is they can sit next to each other on my bus and talk about the rain, or what they've put in their sandwiches for lunch. I don't understand how they're not too mortified to look each other in the eye. How does that work? People say love's different to sex but I would definitely have to love someone before I could let them see me in my pants or hear me peeing, never mind puncture me with their . . . anyway, that's a whole other thing. This piece I wrote was definitely about love, about the kind of beauty I like – warm, honey skin and soft hair that floats in loose curls, sometimes coppery and other times gold. Diane's a warm beauty. Not like me. You wouldn't describe me as warm. Well, you wouldn't describe me as a beauty either – I'm tall and skinny, like a beansprout. Even thinner since Mum died and there's no reason to cook anything and no one to stop me having toast for dinner. You wouldn't have dreams about me, or not good ones anyway.

I took a deep breath when it was my turn and began reading:

For Diane

Take me to your heart, and I'll show you a sunset
I'll paint you the skies in shades of emerald green
If you promise to be my friend till after forever.

If you stay with me till dawn
I'll make the moon appear mid afternoon
And light up the river like a flaming human sacrifice.

I'll stand naked by the cherry tree while the blossoms
dress me
Telling you my secrets, and listening to yours
I'll let you see my darker side.

I'll confess my weaknesses and bathe you in my
humility
I'll swallow my pride and give you my all
If you let my secrets lie within you till it ceases to
matter.

By Wendy

My piece was so different from the usual crap we heard in the
group, they weren't even sure how to critique it.

'It's a love poem about best friends,' I said, into the silence.

'Thanks for that Wendy,' said Henry, clearing his throat and
fixing his salmon pink tie although unlike him it was already
straight. 'Any . . . comments from the group?'

The others shuffled round the table, shifting their drinks and
moving jackets out of the way. Finally Sophie raised her hand,
blushed to her hair roots and said, 'I mean, it's very personal
so . . .'

'I've got another poem too,' I said, rooting about in my rucksack.

'Erm, we might keep that for another week Wendy. We've

quite a few submissions to get through,' said Henry, shuffling a pile of papers to emphasize the point.

Then he just moved on to the next piece, yet another extract from one of Joseph's detective novels. They were all based on Islay, really a phenomenal number of murders took place there for an island of 3,000 people. Nobody dared to point that out to him though, because he had a tongue like a blade and a look that could flay you. I once told him that the body contains eight pints of blood so there's really no way to drain a corpse in the back seat of a Ford Fiesta without making a helluva mess, which was what he'd suggested in his opening chapter. He just gave me one of his looks and said, 'Wendy. We don't all need to be as literal as you are, the writer is permitted a little artistic licence.' I was quite chuffed as that was the most anyone had said to me directly at any of the meetings so I didn't press the point – even though I knew I was right because Diane said it's the job of the writer to convey exact truths to the reader, and if that isn't saying writers should be literal then I don't know what is.

I didn't bother listening as the others gave their feedback on Joseph's latest submission. The chatter weaved its way around me as I thought back to an article I'd come across that morning while I was searching on Diane's name. I'd been thinking about it all day.

Perhaps the thing that strikes you most on meeting Ms Weston is the absolute conviction she holds that we all have a story to tell. Nothing is above her notice as a writer – from the most mundane (critics would say inconsequential) to the almost aggressively political (one can be in no doubt as to where her sympathies lie after even a few paragraphs of her Women's Prize-winning novel, *Out of Sight, Out of Mind*). 'We have to ask ourselves what the purpose of literature is,' she says. 'Do we want to feed the fantasies of the privileged white few, or do we want to interrogate the meaning of life in all its brutality and beauty?' Therein lies the question.

And what a great question! So, between the group and the article and Diane's latest tweets, my mind was full of all this writing stuff and I didn't notice Ginger get on the bus. It was a May morning but no one had bothered to inform the Scottish weather because the rain was bouncing up from the pavements and pelting the windscreen so hard I could barely see the road ahead. I was running late because the seniors' dance club was on at the old library in Bellshill and the bus was like the departure lounge for the September flight to Benidorm. But I did see her tiny figure curled up in the back seat somewhere between Lidl in Mossend and before we reached the Citizens Advice Centre in Tannochside. We were on the 255 to Bellshill so a lot of the route was through the schemes, which meant a lot of stopping and waiting for the old folk to get their shopping trolleys on and sometimes lowering the platform at the door so the young girls and grannies could get their buggies on without waking up their toddlers, whose little wellies poked out below their plastic pram covers. The windows were steamed up all along the bus and my windscreen wipers were screeching in their efforts to keep my own window clear. I could smell the damp from my passengers' anoraks and umbrellas as they made their short trips to Rani's in the arcade or the Mecca Bingo or the café at Tesco, just to get away from their own four walls for a bit and see the outside world, even if it was only Bellshill.

The damp and the rabble of voices and the constant juddering of the bus stopping and starting didn't seem to bother Ginger, though. She spent the day riding on my bus and I watched as she sprawled herself out across the length of the back seat, or sat up and pressed her nose to the window, her finger tracing the swirls of condensation in front of her face. I don't think people realize how much the driver can see through the rearview mirror. I've seen all sorts. Once I watched this couple all the way from Glasgow to Cambuslang and they must've fallen out before they got on because she sort of flounced into the seat in front of him rather than sitting next to him – childish – even though they were clearly together because he'd paid for two singles. They didn't speak to each other the whole journey but I knew by the way he kept glancing at the back of her neck that he loved her. He couldn't take his eyes off that vulnerable spot at the top of her spine where the knobbly white bone eases its way into the hairline. I wanted to tell him to get off at the next stop and run and run till the wind lashed his cheeks and made a mop of his hair. Till he forgot all about the girl on the bus. Run and never look back because she didn't love him, not the same way anyway, and not the way you should love someone.

Ginger was thin like Audrey Hepburn, but she dressed differently. The day I met her she was wearing faded blue Lonsdale sweatpants. The cracked Adidas on her feet looked about two sizes too big for her judging by the space between her sports sock and the edge of the shoe. Her hair was the orange of Lucozade and, when the bus bounced over road bumps, it moved and fizzled about her head. It was a shame she had a small bald patch just at the point your forehead goes into your parting. It was a slightly different colour from the rest of her hair, and she told me later she rubbed carbon paper on the fuzz that was left there to try and colour it darker than her scalp. 'It camouflages the bald bit,' she said. It didn't really work but I never told her that, even when we were close enough to tell each other lots of stuff. When she smiled up at me, I was surprised to see teeth that were straight like a comb. If you'd asked me her age then, I would have said about twelve, maybe thirteen or so, but the next time I saw her she was eating a whole jam roly-poly which she said was to celebrate turning fifteen, so I guess she was older than she looked.

I woke her up when we got to the circle in Birkenshaw.

She started, quickly sat upright and gave a huge yawn, at the same time running her hand over the front of her hair so that the bald patch was covered. One of her cheeks was red where it had been squashed against the rough, woollen seat cover.

'This is the last stop,' I said. 'You'll need to get off now.' I bent down and wiped a circle in the window. The rain was as heavy as it had been all day, the sky dark as December.

'Where's your jacket?' I said, as she got up to leave. Her shoulders were up at her ears and she was wiping her nose with the back of her hand.

'I didn't bring one.' She sniffed. 'It wasn't raining when I left. Anyway, I'm only going up to Viewpark.'

'Why didn't you get off at the community centre then, that's closer?'

She yawned again even though she'd been half asleep all day.

35

'I'm in no rush to get home,' she said. 'Anyway, I was sleeping. You just woke me up.'

'Sorry,' I said. She did look tired and I felt sorry for her having to walk home in that rain.

'Wait a minute.' I ran back to the front of the bus and reached under the driver's seat for the umbrella one of my regulars had left behind. 'Here.' I handed it to her. 'You'll need to give me it back though because it belongs to Irish Mary and she'll be looking for it next time she gets on.'

'For me?' she said, taking the pink brolly and twirling it like a baton. 'Thanks. Doesn't really match my hair, does it?' She smiled for the first time and I saw her perfect teeth gleaming up at me. 'How will I get it back to you though?'

'Well, you could just get back on my bus?'

'But how will I know when it's you driving and not another driver?'

I was still thinking when she spoke again.

'Why don't you give me your number and I could see you in the park in Uddingston to give you it back? If you want, I mean?'

'We could, I suppose . . .'

'I could meet you there? Tomorrow lunchtime maybe if the weather's okay?'

I looked up and down the empty bus, not quite sure what was happening. But I was on a late shift the next day and I did need to get the umbrella back and there didn't seem to be any reason not to so I said, 'Okay,' flicking my fringe a lot so she would think I was used to making arrangements to meet new people. She smiled again like she was really happy I'd agreed and copied the number from my phone into hers, and said she'd see me tomorrow then.

36

She got off the bus and I watched her struggle for a bit with the umbrella in the wind and then disappear along the top road, the pink umbrella and her orange hair a little burst of colour in the grey. I remember thinking, 'I bet that's the last I see of her and Irish Mary's brolly.' Of course I often think now how much better it would have been for both of us if I'd been right.

The Beginning of Ginger and Me

4

I HARDLY SLEPT THAT NIGHT, I couldn't stop thinking about meeting Ginger the next day. I lay there watching the shadows on my wall as the sun rose slowly behind the thin curtains, and checked the time on my phone every half hour or so in case I'd slept past the alarm. At three I was excited about getting to know Ginger, by four I was terrified that as soon as she got to know me she wouldn't hang around because I wouldn't know the right things to say. By five I was trying to think of all the things Mum used to talk to people about. There was the weather of course – people were really interested in the weather – or their various family members. I didn't know anything about Ginger's family so there were loads of questions I could ask about that, though I wouldn't be able to say much about mine in return. Maybe she'd talk a lot and I wouldn't have to. Something else occurred to me too, Saanvi would be really pleased with me for taking her advice and making new friends. And maybe this was just the start. Maybe Ginger would have other friends that she'd introduce me to and we'd all go round together in a group. Maybe we'd even have a nickname for ourselves, something only we knew that would make us laugh when we said it. At six I suddenly thought maybe we'd have our own WhatsApp group and I couldn't sleep another wink after that so I got up and put the hot water on so I could have a bath before I changed into my clean jeans.

We'd arranged to meet in the park beside the Tunnock's factory in Uddingston. It was further away than the playing field behind my house but I was glad Ginger had suggested it because, being down in Uddingston proper, it was better maintained than anything round our way. It even had an outdoor gym as well as the usual swings and roundabout. In our play park the council had removed the seats and even the chains from the swings and the place was littered with dog shit and drained MD 20/20 bottles. Besides, I liked the walk down the hill and noseying at the big houses behind Main Street.

Ginger was already sitting on the swing when I got there, her head tilted to one side and resting against the chain. She was wearing the same blue sweatpants she'd had on the day before, and a grey hoodie with Adidas splashed across the front in white letters. Even though I was early, she was even earlier than me. Her long orange hair was draped over one shoulder and she was plaiting it as I walked towards her. When she looked up, she smiled and waved. I looked behind me to see who she was waving at before I realized with a start it was me. I smiled and waved back at her, hurrying over to where she sat.

'I didn't think you'd come,' she said, as I took the swing next to her. 'Otherwise I'd have kept you some of my jam roly-poly.' She gestured to the empty packet lying next to her on the ground, beside Irish Mary's umbrella. 'It was for my birthday.'

'Happy birthday,' I said. 'What age are you?'

'Fifteen.'

'I'm nineteen.' I wondered if she'd still want to be friends.

'You look older.'

'Do I?' No one had ever told me that before.

'Maybe because you're so tall.'

'Maybe.'

There was a pause and I panicked a bit, trying to remember all the stuff I'd thought of to talk about but it turned out I was worrying about nothing because Ginger was very good at making conversation. We talked about loads of important stuff even that first day.

'Do you like Chinese or Indian best?' she asked, sitting back on the swing and pushing the dirt with the toe of her trainers.

I thought about it then said I didn't like either. My dad was never a fan of foreign food and my mum had insisted on cooking most meals from scratch so we never had takeaways at our house, except fish and chips if they were feeling flush, or we had something to celebrate.

'So how do you know you don't like it then?' said Ginger, smiling at me from behind the swing chain, her perfect teeth shining white between her chapped lips. 'I love chicken korma the best. Sometimes Uncle Tam brings me back mixed pakora after he's been out. That's chicken and mushroom and . . . fish, I think. I always keep the chicken bits for last, they're the best. Though sometimes it's hard to tell which bits are chicken and you bite in and—' She screwed up her face.

'It isn't chicken?'

'Exactly.'

'Do you see a lot of your uncle Tam then?'

Ginger sniffed and looked towards Scotmid on the other side of the park. 'I live with him. We live in his house in Viewpark.'

I was going to ask why she didn't live with her mum and dad but she was speaking again.

'He's all right. He's out a lot.'

'Will he not mind you're not at school today?'

'He won't know. He's always sleeping during the day so I can do what I like.'

'Does he not work?' I asked.

'He's . . . a businessman.'

'What kind of business does he do?'

She shrugged. 'He buys and sells stuff. The flat's always full of it, I'll show you if you ever come over. If you want a TV or anything, there's always loads in the hall and the back bedroom. He wouldn't even miss one.'

I gave a low whistle. 'He must be doing well if you've got more than one TV.'

She didn't reply but sniffed again and reached up to rub her bald patch, which seemed to be getting bigger. Maybe because she was always touching it. She lifted her gold heart locket to her mouth and sucked on it. I'm not sure if it was a comfort thing but I noticed she did it a lot. Unlike most red-haired people, she had no freckles blotching her pale skin but, close up, I could see it was dry and flaky, especially round her mouth. Her green eyes were much bigger and rounder than mine, and the left one had tiny gold flecks surrounding the pupil. She had beautiful eyes, it was a shame about the purple scoops underneath them, like she didn't sleep much. Her nose was like a button, as they say in books, though it was nothing like a button except that it was small and round with two holes. Actually maybe not unlike a button after all, though I'd never describe any characters' noses like that in my stories, Diane would say it's a cliché and I agreed with her on that.

'Have you read anything by Diane Weston?' I asked Ginger, pleased with myself for remembering one of the questions I'd rehearsed.

But she shook her head and looked away, her locket in her mouth.

'Oh, you should, she's brilliant. You'd love her books, they all take place here in Scotland. She's a famous writer, even though she's Scottish.'

Ginger shrugged.

I carried on, happy to be talking about Diane, even though Ginger didn't seem that interested. 'She tweeted something brilliant yesterday about the writer's tools. I agree with her that the most important thing is making time to write. Space, we call it.'

Ginger didn't answer. I thought she probably didn't read much since she never went to school. Just as well her uncle was such a successful businessman because I couldn't see any employer taking on someone who didn't read books, and that was as well as going bald.

'I'd have thought paper and pen were the most important tools,' she said.

I laughed. 'Well, everyone writes on computers now of course. Though actually I don't because I don't have one.' I turned to face her. 'Do you know what I'd really love – one of those wee tablets that you can take places with you so that whenever inspiration strikes' – I clicked my fingers – 'you can just take out your tablet and write it all down. Diane has one of those, I bet.'

Ginger swung back and forth a bit longer then got up and shook out her hair. 'Come on, let's go into Aladdin's for a bit.'

I was on a late shift so I had hours to pass before I had to start getting ready for work. 'Okay,' I said, picking up Irish Mary's brolly and putting it in my rucksack. 'Race you.' We both ran across the park and back up the hill towards the shopping arcade in Viewpark, Ginger's hair streaking behind her like laces and her feet pounding the grass.

We bought a bag of chips each – I soon discovered that Ginger was always hungry, I don't know how she stayed so thin – and ate them as we wandered through the arcade. I looked in the window at the Shelter shop and pointed out a wedding dress to Ginger. The price tag said seventy-nine pounds.

'Who'd buy a second-hand wedding dress?' I asked Ginger, licking the salt off my thumb and looking round for a bin.

'Not me. I'll be buying mine from New York or London and it'll cost over a thousand. At least. And that's without the veil even.'

'Oh yeah? How are you going to afford that?' I laughed.

'I'm marrying someone rich.' She looked at me. 'That's the only reason to get married. That, and to get away from Roddy and Tam.' She examined a fat chip before putting it in her mouth.

'Who's Roddy?' I said. 'Another uncle?'

'He's . . . I call him Uncle. Sometimes. He's . . . my uncle's friend. I hate him.' She hissed the last three words, and screwed up her face as though there'd been too much vinegar on her chip. I was about to tell her she was lucky to have family around but she waved her hand suddenly and said, 'It's only when he's been drinking. It's nothing. Where can we dump these?'

46

We binned the greasy chip papers and headed into Cash Converters to look at the phones. I wiped my hands down my jeans and told Ginger to do the same. She tutted but did as she was told.

The shop was quiet at that time, and the piped music and clammy heat of the place lulled me into a trance. The giant TV screens on the back wall showed a football match in lurid colour. Ginger headed towards the laptops, and I could see her orange hair bobbing up and down between the aisles. I was wandering through homewares and wondering why anyone would choose a bright blue kettle when sparks of a heated exchange at the counter caught my attention.

'Look, I want my money back, simple as that.' I could tell by the woman's unrelenting, high-pitched voice and the aggressive way she kept heaving her reusable Tesco bag up her arm that she meant business.

The acne-ridden manager, who was surely the same age as Ginger, tutted and rolled his shoulders. 'As I've explained to you Madam, it doesn't matter if you've got your receipt. The store policy is that once you've used the item—'

'How do you know I've used it? Have I said I've used it?'

She had him there. I moved a bit closer and waited.

He tipped the small, stainless steel toaster upside down and we all watched as the crumbs fell onto the counter between them.

The woman said nothing for a moment but soon rallied. 'Well, obviously I had to try it out. Obviously. How else could I have known that it did the toast too hard?'

Something about her willingness to stand her ground, even in the face of the young man's disdain and the clear ridiculousness of her situation, reminded me of my mum. I remembered all the times I'd stood beside her, gripping her firm, rough hand as she argued the toss with the bus driver over not having the right change, or the Saturday girl at the café we sometimes went to for a roll and sausage when the rolls were definitely not fresh, or the man from the council who wasn't happy about where she'd left the bins. She was tiny my mum, not like me at all, but she always stood her ground. Most of the time, anyway.

'Can I help you Madam?'

I started, as I realized they were both looking at me, the woman glaring in a way that also reminded me of my mum.

'No, I'm just . . . thanks, no, I'm just looking.'

I wandered away then, leaving them to their negotiations. I suddenly remembered Ginger was with me and I was looking round for her when she sidled up to me from nowhere and whispered, 'Leave now, I'll head out first and you follow me as quick as you can.'

'What? Why? We've as much right to be here as anyone else, it's—'

But Ginger had already turned and run out the store. I heard a shout from behind the counter and clocked the security guard dashing from the back of the shop where he'd been standing watching the football. His eyes leapt from the door to me, and I ran for it, as fast as I could. I hesitated in front of the shop, not sure which way to go, then took a right towards the exit. I couldn't see Ginger but I kept running till I'd left the arcade and the security guard far behind me. I stood behind the old fountain, bent forwards with my hands on my knees, trying to get my breath back.

As I stood up, I caught a glimpse of Ginger's tiny figure

peeking out from behind the bushes. She beckoned me over and I ran to join her.

'What the hell?' I said, my voice shrill and my heart still thudding like it was going to break through my chest.

She flashed me her perfect smile, her cheeks brilliant pink and her orange hair all over the place like a street urchin's.

'Ta-dah,' she said, pulling out a small rectangular box from inside her jacket.

'What is that? Ginger, did you nick that?'

She was holding up a sleek black tablet, exactly the model I'd had my eye on for ages.

'It's for you,' she said, waiting for me to take it.

'I can't take that. What if someone saw you? What if we get caught?'

'Don't worry about it,' said Ginger. 'If we were going to get caught, they'd have done it by now. It's yours, take it.'

I took the tablet from her and turned it over in my hands.

'How . . . Why did you do that?' I said, still trying to work out what had happened.

'You said you wanted one,' she said simply. 'And I wanted you to have it.'

I sighed and wondered what on earth her uncle would say if he knew she'd been stealing. She said not to worry about that, and come on, there was still time to go back down to the swings before the schools came out and the place was overrun by kids.

We spent the next hour or so with me reading out the instructions to Ginger and her pressing buttons and working out what the tablet could do. I watched as she pushed her hair back from her face, seeing two red spots bloom high on her cheeks when she'd been laughing – we laughed a lot that day. I watched the way her skinny legs crossed and uncrossed at the ankle as she lolled back on the swing, her green eyes wide and shiny. She was charismatic and fun, that's what people forget when they focus on what happened later. I mean, if you read a book and your favourite character did something terrible on the first page, they'd never get the chance to become your favourite character, would they? No, you have to get to know them a bit first, learn what they like and what it is you like about them. Later when they do things you can't agree with, well, it's too late then because you're committed to liking them regardless. Anyway, there we were – we'd just met and she'd already turned us into Bonnie and Clyde. The way things ended wasn't too far from them either but, of course, I didn't know that then.

5

I SHOWED SAANVI MY NEW tablet the following Wednesday. She was impressed and asked me if I'd bought it on interest free.

'How do you mean?' I said.

'Well, did you take out a payment plan at the shop, or had you saved up for it for a while?'

I thought about it for a moment then said I'd saved up for it since I knew what that meant.

'That's great Wendy, but you know, maybe now you're back at work you should think about using some of your wages to brighten the place up a bit?' She gestured round the room with her hand, taking in the worn carpet and the fireplace that was leaning against the wall but wasn't attached to it. I suppose the house was a bit dingy, but it's hard to care what your house looks like when you're the only one that sees it.

She must have been worried she'd offended me because she said quickly, 'But little steps Wendy, that's what we're all about. I'm so glad that the writing group is working out for you, it seems to have really sparked your interest. You definitely seem brighter?'

I nodded but to be honest, even though I'd only been going for a few weeks, I was beginning to wonder if I hadn't already outgrown the group. Their writing just seemed so amateurish most of the time, compared to mine and Diane's. At the last meeting Joseph had written a death scene featuring a woman with a brain tumour. I know better than most that that isn't a reason for comedy, but still, I think most stories can benefit from a degree of humour. When Henry finally let me give feedback, I said, 'Joseph, I know she's got a brain tumour but the way you've written it, all the reader can see is her lying in some flea-ridden camp bed in the old Royal, ga-ga, peeing her pants, with her worst fears gathered together by her side. I can't think of anyone who'd want to read that, can you?' I looked round the rest of the group but they were all busy with their glasses or fixing their shoes and stuff. Joseph pulled a few strands from his man bun and gave me one of his looks.

'What would you suggest Weeeendy?'

That's how he said my name, as though it had four 'e's in the middle rather than just one.

'Can I suggest you watch some films by the Coens? They're two brothers from America who—'

'Yes, I do know who the Coen brothers are.' He slid a look to Henry who smiled and raised his left eyebrow at Joseph to show him exactly what he thought of my comments.

I carried on anyway. 'Right well, you should think about the way they write about sad things and bad stuff. Really, the way they write about death is brilliant, but funny too. There's a scene where Walter and The Dude are trying to scatter Donny's ashes but they keep blowing back in the wind, right into their faces. I couldn't stop laughing so I finished the movie feeling happy even though one of the best characters had died, you see? You should try something along those lines I think.'

I sat back, exhausted at having said so much, but Joseph looked at me and said, 'Thanks for the information Wendy,' so I was hopeful he'd taken my advice on board. But, the thing is, it was really very tiring being the one to pick up on all the errors in their writing all the time, and I wasn't sure how much benefit I was getting from their feedback on my own writing. Even Muriel kept saying how I needed to show things not just tell them, but how can the reader pick up anything at all if you don't tell them what's happening, honestly. This was exactly the kind of thing Diane would laugh her head off at if I told her. I didn't want Saanvi to think I was being negative though so I said something about enjoying talking to other writers. I waited till she had made some more notes before I told her my big news.

'Oh, and something you'll be pleased about,' I said, blushing a little as I made my offering. 'I've made a new friend.'

Saanvi raised her eyebrows. 'Right. And is this someone you work with or . . . ?'

'No, she's called Ginger. That's her real name, it's ideal for her because she's got long ginger hair, all the way down her back.' I swivelled round and placed my hand at the small of my back to indicate how far down her back Ginger's hair reached.

Saanvi smiled. 'She sounds very pretty Wendy. Where did you meet her?'

'She was on my bus. I gave her Irish Mary's umbrella because it was raining and she didn't have a jacket. We met up at the park the next day and spent the whole day together. We had loads to talk about.'

'You see? Being with friends makes you feel good, doesn't it? We all need that connection. And do you think you'll be seeing her again?'

'I already have.' I couldn't stop the smile spreading across my face. 'She spent the whole of yesterday afternoon riding on my bus. We went to Cambuslang and back four times.'

'Oh, is that allowed? While you're working I mean?'

I hadn't thought about that. 'It's a public bus. Anybody can ride on it.' I plucked the arm of the sofa and bit the edge of my lip.

'No, I'm sure you're right, Wendy,' Saanvi said quickly. 'That's really great. You need to do more of that – meeting up with people, making connections, it's a lot easier than you think to make friends, you'll see. Now, how about self-love generally, are you managing to practise that in your daily routines?'

I looked up. This was the first time she'd brought this up, or perhaps I just hadn't been listening before. I was quite surprised she was being so open about it to be honest but I thought it was a good thing, nothing to be ashamed of I suppose. I told her I usually did it in the shower because then I could be absolutely sure my fingers were clean afterwards. Her pen stopped on the page and she took a few seconds before she looked up.

'No Wendy, I mean, are you taking care of yourself, baths and so on?' Her pen hovered above the page.

I couldn't see why a bath would be better than the shower, after all, don't they say you just end up bathing in your own dirty water and if that also includes, well you know, how is that better for you than doing it in the shower? I wasn't sure this was the best advice, although she had been right about joining the writers' group and making new friends so I was willing to try it.

'No,' she said. She looked hot now and her beautiful peach sari had a wet patch blooming under each arm. 'No, Wendy,

I meant, have you been looking after your personal hygiene and so forth?'

'Personal—?'

'Look, never mind, I'm going to tick that box as I can see you're looking better.' She started gathering up her bag then and didn't stay for a cup of tea which was just as well as I realized I'd run out of milk again. It was so difficult to remember all the little things that were necessary to reassure people I was living properly – like always having milk and bread, doing up the house, and making friends. Thank goodness Saanvi hadn't stayed for tea because I didn't want her to think I wasn't coping.

Later, I had a bath as Saanvi had advised, and my head was still spinning with all the things I had to get better at. I picked up my phone to see if Diane had tweeted anything to distract me. I was pleased to see she'd written a whole new thread and I settled back into the hot water to read everything she had to tell me.

It's not enough to identify the under-representation of working-class writers as a challenge; the real challenge is to do something about it. #WorkingClassWriters

That had fifteen likes so I added my own before I read through the replies. One of them, by another blue-tick writer, annoyed me.

If a writer is talented enough, they will rise to the top and get published regardless of their background. #NoExcuses

That had more likes than Diane's tweet so I went back to hers and tried to like it again but it wouldn't let me do that. I think Twitter is missing a trick there because if you could like something several times that would be like emphasizing your point, wouldn't it, and showing whoever wrote the tweet that you really, really agreed with them. Diane had replied.

> The publishing industry is controlled by white middle class men so of course the writing that reaches the public reflects this. To think otherwise is pure naiveté.

I liked that immediately and was pleased to be the first heart. I waited but no one else liked that tweet and I was worried Diane would think no one agreed with her. I'd never actually replied to any of her tweets before but I felt I had to reply to this one since no one else had and she might think she'd said something stupid. As the water cooled around me, I concentrated on my 280 characters. Eventually I wrote something that had been bothering me for a while and which seemed relevant to Diane's tweets.

> Fed up reading about girls called Tillie or Cassie who share a flat in London with other girls they met at university, and they all go on to work in PR or publishing. What even is PR?

In less than a minute, two bells appeared at the bottom of my screen and I jabbed it with my finger. Diane had liked my tweet and replied with a love heart! Diane had read something I'd written, agreed with it, and replied with a beautiful red love heart. A minute or so later, another bell appeared to let me know I had a new follower. Diane was following me! I lay back in the bath with a huge smile on my face. I stuck my leg in the air and covered it in lukewarm bubbles. Maybe that was something else Saanvi was right about – making new friends wasn't that hard after all.

6

I THINK IF YOU READ books, it calms you down. And it makes you realize there's a place for everybody, no matter how weird. It's like, there's a whole world out there and no one can stop you from entering, it's open to anyone who wants to be part of it, even me.

Linda at Uddingston library was great at getting me all the books I requested, even the ones that had just come out. I started buying some as well after I was back at work and I was building up reassuring piles of them on the floor beside my bed. One pile was dedicated entirely to Diane's stuff. Not a lot of people know this, but she's written several biographies, as well as her novels and short stories. They're all of creative types like her, people whose work she's admired, whatever their field.

I finished *Elizabeth* in two days. Even took a sickie, which is something I never do because why would I want to sit around the house all day on my own? It wasn't so bad before Mum died but afterwards it was just me, the four walls and the smell of disinfectant from her room still raging through the house. I couldn't get rid of that smell – and it reminded me of her, a skeleton in that downstairs room, the tumours burrowing into her like rats. She couldn't speak in the end. It was in her brain by then. Losing your hair, that's one thing, but losing the power to speak? They both make babies of you but if you can't speak, you might as well be dead. Just like Elizabeth most of the time. It was her dad that forced her to take acting lessons, though he did try to save her from that travesty of a marriage to Burton. Old drunk, no idea how to treat a woman. Trust Diane to let Elizabeth shine when everyone else was interested in the husband. That confirmed for me what I already knew – Diane was a genius. The more I read her books, and the more I read what she had to say on Twitter, the more connected to her I felt. After I'd finished *Elizabeth* I tweeted how much it had meant to me. Within half an hour, she'd liked it, retweeted it, *and* replied with a smiley face. I loved the way our relationship was developing.

Most weeks I tried to turn the conversation at writers' group round to Diane but I could tell the others weren't that interested, even Sophie who had introduced me to Diane's books in the first place. They didn't seem to be able to stick with one writer for more than a book at a time before they jumped on the next bandwagon. The thing you've got to understand about my writers' group, maybe all writers' groups, I don't know, is that mostly they've got no idea what they're talking about. They all think they're suffering for their art, like that makes them bigger or better versions of themselves. It's crap because anyone that's really suffered knows it just makes you smaller, turns you into a helpless puppy or something, and not the cute kind. When Mum was sick, I mean really sick, she would mewl like a lamb or howl in the night with the pain of it. It hacked into her till she was almost cut to nothing by the suffering. Sometimes I'd go to her, other times

I'd get right under the duvet and howl a bit myself. There's nothing clever about suffering but they couldn't see it, that's what I mean when I say they were a bunch of amateurs. That was part of it anyway.

Just as well they were no longer my only friends. In fact, I think even Saanvi would have been surprised at just how many people were coming in and out of my life at that point, and that's not including the regulars on the bus either.

I first met Ginger's uncle Tam not long after we became best friends. It wasn't planned, I mean, he hadn't invited me for tea or anything, he just happened to be in the house and out of his bed that first time I went round.

It was my day off and we were down in the park. It was empty at ten o'clock on a Wednesday morning and Ginger was slumped at the top of the slide, her hands at her temples and her middle fingers touching her bald patch. We'd known each other for about a month by then and I knew already that you couldn't predict what kind of mood she'd be in when we met. That day, she looked paler than usual and even her electric hair was colourless. The lilac half-crescents under her eyes were swollen, lending her normally thin face a bloated look. I thought about asking her if she was okay but my experience of being very much not okay after Mum died – and not being able to tell anyone how I was feeling or why – made me worry Ginger might feel the same way and not want to talk about whatever was bothering her. I waited.

She gave a big sigh, starting from a deep intake of breath through her nose and reaching all the way down to her belly and out through her mouth again. She looked at me from the side of her eye.

I said nothing and tapped my fingers on the edges of the slide where I was sitting at the bottom.

She sighed again, this time the end of it was a low whistle.

I ran my hands over the smooth, rubbery tarmac underneath the slide, and glanced at the big houses opposite, wondering about the families who got to live in houses like that. I looked up at the sky, which was patchy blue as though the sun might come out later and give us the weather we should have been having in early June.

'Are you not going to ask me what's the matter?' Ginger sounded annoyed with me and I looked up at her, surprised.

'Sorry, have I done something wrong?' I said, noticing the yellowish skin across her cheekbones looked more stretched and thinner than usual.

'Not you, no, but I'm not feeling great this morning. I didn't get much sleep last night.'

'Were you busy?'

'No, I wasn't *busy* Wendy, I . . . Roddy came round, well, a whole bunch of strangers were there, loads of people, drinking, and partying. The music was so loud I couldn't sleep even with my head so far under the pillow I could hardly breathe.'

I wasn't sure what she wanted me to say but she looked like she was going to start crying and I didn't know how to deal with that. When I was away getting better after Mum died, there was a girl in the next bed who cried all the time. I don't mean a bit of gentle sobbing, I mean full on, from the gut, ugly crying from morning till night. After a couple of days sitting next to her, saying nothing, I asked her if she was okay, and she jumped across the floor between our beds and grabbed me by the hair. She stuck her thumb up my nostril and made my nose bleed before one of the nurses came through and pulled her off me. So I was keen to stop Ginger's crying before it took hold.

'Why don't you go home now and go back to bed then?' I cocked my head to one side and did something with my mouth that I remember the nurses used to do to express sympathy or something. It must have worked because she dropped her locket from her mouth and gave me a smile.

'I might. Would you . . . would you maybe want to come with me?'

I stayed still.

'I don't want to be on my own and it is your day off, and, well, what else would you be doing? We could make toast and jam and watch something?'

She was right that I didn't have anything else to do, and nobody to do it with. This was one of my main problems, Saanvi said, too much time on my own and living inside my own head – although Diane says all writers have to experience life second hand and one step removed in order to be able to write about it, I'm paraphrasing but something like that, so it's hard to know how much time alone is too much. But what Ginger was suggesting sounded nice.

'Okay,' I said, hardly able to believe what was happening. A friend was inviting me to their house to hang out, the way the popular girls at school had done with each other. I jumped up and started marching towards Viewpark before she could change her mind.

'Hang on, wait for me,' she shouted, sliding down the squeaky slide and catching up with me.

We headed up the Holm Brae and past the old Smurfit factory where they were building all the new houses. We didn't speak much as we turned right on Old Edinburgh Road and towards Viewpark. We circled the drunks smoking outside The Olde Club, and ignored the cheers of a group of younger guys, vaping so hard they'd become phantoms behind the clouds. One of them said, 'Alright?' to Ginger but she ignored him and carried on walking. A guy bolted out the front door of the Club, and dashed past us and into Coral a bit up the road. It was the boy I often saw when I was driving the 255 towards Bellshill, and he'd be running up and down the street between The Olde Club, Coral, The Ashley, and back again, whippet thin with all the running. I asked Ginger who he was.

'That's Wee Eddie Miller,' she said. 'He's the bookies' runner.'

'What, that's a job?' I said. I'd never heard of it.

'Well, kind of. He doesn't get paid, he puts bets on for the guys drinking in there and they buy him a drink, or maybe give him a fiver if their luck's in. He's a bit . . . you know.' She put her finger to her head and twisted it.

'Do you know him then?'

'Everybody knows Wee Eddie,' she said. She was clacking her locket against her teeth and glancing up at me every so often as we crossed the road at the community centre and walked down the hill deep into the scheme.

'What?' I said. She was making me nervous, I hadn't been to anyone else's house since my mum made sure I was invited to her cousin's daughter's party when I was fifteen. I didn't even want to go but she marched me round there in my cord skirt and the brown leather, heeled boots she'd bought me for my birthday. I spent half the party eyeing the other party guests at the opposite side of the room, who were whispering together and avoiding my eye, and the rest in the kitchen with my mum's cousin while she tried to find a number for my mum so she could come and take me away. I think maybe I'm not a party person. I kept waiting for something to happen, but it seemed like the highlight was if one of the boys came and tapped you on the shoulder and took you to the middle of the floor to sway in time to some crap music playing too loud on one of the boys' speakers. I was quite capable of dancing myself without the permission of some boy, thanks very much.

Ginger lived in one of the gas flats at the end of a narrow road at the very bottom of the scheme. Although Birkenshaw where I lived was only ten minutes' walk away, I'd never been this far into Viewpark before. My mum always said it was too rough, with its pubs and bookies on every corner and the young team hanging round looking for trouble. She said to keep away, even though it's where my dad's family was from originally. He used to say Mum was talking rubbish, there was nothing wrong with it, that people make a place and the folk from Viewpark were as good as any you'd meet anywhere else.

Whether the area was rough or not, I thought the street itself was quite pretty. There were trees and bushes opposite which must have been nice to look out on, even if the bin beside them was overflowing with smashed cans and bags of dog shit. We passed a shop called Al's Conveniences but it was boarded up and the boards were covered in red paint with the North Roaders slagging off the Mossend Young Team. There was a black bin bag outside, half full of clothes that streamed across the pavement. We had to pick our way over the old coats and jumpers to get past.

Ginger said nothing as she pushed open the main door at the bottom and the musky smell of cat pee hit us.

'Someone loves their cats,' I said, wrinkling my nose.

'Yeah, me,' she said. 'She's ancient but I absolutely love her. How did you know about my cat?'

'Just a guess,' I said, and followed her up the stairs to their front door. The number beside 1 was on its side so the flat could have been 16 or 19. There was a frayed welcome mat in front of the door, half covered by a white paint stain that started on the wall and ended up on the mat so that it now read 'COME'. We didn't bother wiping our feet on it.

As she turned the key in the lock, I stopped her suddenly and said, 'Ginger, this is all right isn't it?'

'What is?'

'Me being here I mean. Your uncle Tam won't mind when he sees me? I haven't . . . brought anything.' It occurred to me that this was what people did when they visited other people – brought them grapes or flowers by way of an entry fee.

Ginger laughed. 'Don't be daft. Anyway, he'll be sleeping it off. I told you – they were at it till four this morning, he probably won't see the daylight today.'

The scent of a party still clung to the air, but it was sour and heavy, like a hangover. We walked through a haze of smoke, and the smell reminded me of how my dad had smelled after a session at the pub. Ginger kicked away odd shoes and a stained old donkey jacket that littered the gloomy hallway, and I followed close behind her. There were cardboard boxes piled high against the wall all the way through to the kitchen, and I jumped as a skinny cat, streaked orange and white, darted out from behind a box.

'There she is,' cooed Ginger. 'There's my wee Nina.' She stooped to pet her but wasn't quick enough, the creature sprang down the hall and disappeared.

It was very dark in the kitchen too, although it was daytime, and she turned on the strip light overhead. I don't know if the place was worse than usual but Ginger didn't seem fazed as she pushed back the crunched-up cans and overflowing ashtrays against the sticky tiles so she could reach the kettle. Her hand hovered above it for a few seconds then she turned to me and said, 'Come on, let's just go up to my room. It's depressing in here.'

We stopped on the small landing as we heard the sound of the toilet flushing followed by guttural coughing and expunging of phlegm. The door scraped open on the lino.

Ginger's uncle Tam was a lot younger than I expected. He wore light blue jeans that were so tight I could make out the shape of his skinny calves, his knees were poking through a rip in each leg. His scrawny torso was bare so I kept my eyes above his neck, noting a face that was thin and sallow, with lips pouty red like the models on magazine covers. He wore his hair long over one eye which I thought at first was just naff, but later I saw he had a scar that ran the length of his left cheek, from temple to jawbone, and I understood the long flick of his fringe. His jaw seemed to be moving, like he was chewing something all the time. He was handsome I suppose, if you like that sort of thing. He wore those trendy glasses with plastic rims but I soon learned they were not just for show, he was half blind without them. Once, I saw him coming out of the bathroom in his dressing gown with no glasses and he had to screw his eyes up so tight they practically disappeared behind his scar. 'Ginger?' he said. 'What are you up to, sneaking up on me like that? Make us a cup of tea will you, a strong one.' I had to cough behind my hand to stop laughing out loud because I'm much taller than Ginger

66

for one thing and look nothing like her. When I told her, we laughed so hard we were holding each other up. I stopped long enough to tell her she'd better make him a cup of tea. Strong.

The first time I saw him, though, he had his glasses on and he could see me just fine. He looked me up and down and said to Ginger, 'Who's this you've brought home then?'

Ginger stubbed her toe along the hall carpet and pushed her bottom lip over the top one.

'This is Wendy. We were just . . . I thought you'd be in bed.'

'What day is it? Is this not a school day?' He shook his head. 'Christ, my head's banging. Get us a cup of tea. Get one for Fran too.' He looked at me again and said to Ginger, 'Roddy's coming tonight. We've got business so she'll need to be out by then.' Ginger muttered something about Roddy always being there but Uncle Tam cut her off, saying, 'Zip it Ginger,' and walked into the room at the end of the hall, closing the door behind him.

'Who's Fran?' I asked Ginger as we went back to the kitchen and she pulled two mugs out of the sink, rinsing them pointlessly with cold water.

'Frances. She stays with us sometimes. With Uncle Tam.'

'Is she your aunt?'

Ginger shrugged. 'Sort of.'

'Your uncle Tam seems nice.'

'He's all right. It's just . . . Roddy's always here, and then there's . . . this.' She gestured round the wrecked kitchen, the greasy surfaces, the coffee rings, the cooker off its hinges and the fridge whose door didn't close properly.

Saanvi would have said Ginger and Uncle Tam weren't very good at taking care of themselves but I understood because sometimes I forgot to put things away or clean the surfaces the

67

way my mum used to do, or make sure there were eggs in the fridge. It was one of the reasons Ginger and me got on so well, we both knew how hard it was to get everything right all the time.

'I'll help you tidy up,' I said, grabbing an empty biscuit packet and a saucer full of used teabags and taking them to the bin. It was already full so I sat them in an unsteady pile in front of it, and told Ginger not to put too much milk in the tea, men didn't like it milky.

7

Diane Weston retweeted:
Local author @diane_weston will sign copies of her latest
novel One World @WaterstonesGla on 12 June at 11am.
Free but ticketed. All welcome.

I'D JUST POURED SAANVI'S second cup of tea and we were
chatting about what I'd been up to when I showed her the tweet
about Diane's event.

'I'd love to go to that,' I said as I tore open the red and gold
foil on my caramel wafer.

'Well why don't you then?' she said, smiling as she handed
me back my phone.

I'd thought of little else since the tweet had popped up on
my timeline a couple of evenings before, but there was no way
someone like me could go to a literary event – I hadn't even
been to university.

'I can't go. Not to something like that.' I scratched my head
and looked at Saanvi. 'Can I?'

She laughed. 'Of course you can. You've been telling me for
weeks how much you love her books, it'd be great to go along

and meet her in person, get her to sign a copy of her novel for you. Why not?'

She made it sound so easy. 'But . . . I can't go on my own. I mean, I wouldn't know anybody, I wouldn't know what to say.'

'What about your writers' group? Is there not a friend there who'd like to go with you?'

'I don't think so.'

'You won't know till you've asked, Wendy.'

So I did and, to my surprise, Muriel said right away how much she'd loved Diane's first novel and that she'd love to go, and then Sophie shrugged and said well why not.

'I'm always in town anyway on a Saturday so I'll nip in,' said Joseph, and Henry almost dropped his drink in his rush to say he'd go too.

I couldn't believe it. Saanvi was right – all I had to do was ask and suddenly I had friends to go places with. I wondered if I should get my hair cut and maybe get a leather jacket too, like the one Sophie sometimes wore to writers' group. I didn't have time in the end and I was glad I didn't spend the money because it turned out that none of them could make it after all.

First, Henry and Joseph showed how little they knew about how the writing world worked when they took offence at a review Diane had written that had blown up on Twitter. I didn't know the writer she was talking about and I certainly won't be reading his books after what Diane had to say.

There are some writers, and Mr Booth is one, whose own life story gets in the way of their writing. Booth's latest offering purports to be a novel but is in fact just the story of his own over-privileged life – consisting mainly of sleeping with lots of famous women, competing with his father, slagging off other writers, and writing loads of books about other boring, middle-class white men like himself . . . Never one to work too hard when there was a Hampstead bash to attend instead, Booth was not above begging, stealing or borrowing material from other writers of the same ilk – but the less said about that the better since this is a review of his current novel, not a tip-off of past rip-offs . . . Of course Booth loves to shock, and the inclusion of the final scene with the cucumber – yes, sadly it is exactly as you are picturing – is but the latest in a long line of scenes written with the express purpose of exceeding what he perceives as the limits of acceptability and good taste. The trouble is, at the ripe old age of seventy-six, there does come a time when such antics are less likely to be put down to the vagaries of genius, and more likely to be attributed instead to the meanderings of a misogynistic and sad old letch.

It was a bit cruel I suppose, but anyone who knows Diane knows she speaks her mind, and that's what they pay her for – to say truthfully what she thinks of the books she's reviewing. But then the author threatened to sue her for calling him a plagiarist and she had to take it all back, even though everyone else was saying exactly the same thing. It was in all the papers, and even got a mention on *Newsnight*.

I was late to writers' group that night because I got caught up in the Twitter debate about the writer's freedom to say what they liked. Of course I stood up for Diane, and had to be quite aggressive towards some of the people on her feed who were saying really hurtful things. Mostly it was men who were annoyed and this is something I've noticed – that men don't like it sometimes when women speak their minds, it makes them angry when they step out of line or something. My mum would have had plenty to say about that, I think she would have admired the way Diane stands up for herself, and I did too. I was learning so much from her.

Henry was already pontificating on the subject when I sat down next to Reginald with my Diet Coke. 'I mean, it's hardly a review at all when all the reviewer wants to do is be downright nasty.'

Joseph nodded. 'Exactly. After all, this is a man who has won every literary prize going. Except the Booker and we all know the politics that goes into that. Basically this Diane Weston was just being an absolute Karen.'

'If you ask me, that's just a shorthand way of dismissing women whose opinions you don't agree with,' I said. Diane had tweeted something along these lines a couple of weeks back and it had got over 150 likes.

Sophie giggled nervously, and I glared at her before turning back to Henry and Joseph. 'Anyone who knows Diane knows she's nothing like that.'

Henry sighed grandly in Joseph's direction. 'Time to start going through the submissions I think,' he said, raising the palm of his hand in front of my face and saying, 'Order order,' which I was beginning to think was just his way of shutting me up. I was about to say more when Reginald woke up with a start, shouting, 'Whatsit?' and toppling sideways onto my shoulder. I dropped my glass, the Coke spilling all over Henry's chinos, and the moment was lost.

Soon after Henry and Joseph changed their minds about going to Diane's signing, Muriel said she had to babysit her niece's twins and wouldn't be able to come after all.

'Just me and Sophie then,' I said but Sophie suddenly remembered she had a doctor's appointment and couldn't make it either. It must have been something serious for her to have an appointment on a Saturday – my doctor isn't even open at the weekend – so I told her that was fine, I was used to going places on my own anyway. She said, 'Oh Wendy,' and sort of looked down at the table so I think she was as disappointed as I was that she had to miss it.

But maybe it was just as well there was no one else there to distract me because Diane and me had this connection from the start.

The event started at eleven so I set my alarm for six so I could get up early to rehearse all the questions I wanted to ask Diane. I'd planned to get the ten o'clock train into town but I just couldn't wait any longer for the day to start and was in town and meandering around the tables at Waterstones by half nine.

I still had only a vague idea of what Diane looked like, from the author photographs on the back of her books, and most of those were black and white artsy shots where she's looking away from the camera. There was a surprising lack of books about her in Uddingston library, and no more pictures of her online. It was as though she didn't want her face to be seen. Even her Twitter account had a grainy sketch of a woman huddled under a glass dome instead of a photo. I thought maybe she was afraid someone would take her personal information and use it against her – not an issue for me since anyone who stole my identity would give it straight back – or maybe she was one of those writers who believed the words should speak for themselves. Either way, she seemed like someone who preferred to keep herself under wraps so it was a huge surprise to see her in real life.

The day we met, she was wearing a pink and red swirly skirt, paired with a bright red cardigan over a white T-shirt that was cut low enough for me to see the freckles on her chest. She had a soft pink scarf covered in red poppies tied loosely round her neck. Even though she was sitting down I could tell she was petite, certainly much smaller than me, but her clothes and the way she laughed with her mouth wide open and swung her hair about made her seem larger than life. She had freckles on the backs of her hands too, and a pair of little, round glasses that she took off and on depending on whether she was signing the book or looking up at the person buying it. Her hair was as beautiful as it looked in her photographs, an impossibly sleek and shiny copper cap that flowed around her as she shook her head or raised her chin. I knew she had to be quite a bit older than me but her lipstick and eye make-up made it hard to guess her exact age.

'Next,' called the shop assistant, dowdy and everyday next to the glittering Diane.

I moved forwards, and my eyes locked with Diane's. When I gave her my copy of *One World* to sign, she asked for my name and wrote, 'For Wendy, Hope you enjoy it, Diane Weston'. *For Wendy*, not *to*. You maybe don't grasp the difference if you're not a writer, but I knew.

'I'm Wendy from Twitter,' I said as she was writing in my book. 'You follow me, we . . . follow each other.'

She looked up and smiled. 'Right. Well, thanks for coming to my signing.'

'I've loved all your books,' I said, 'but I especially loved *This Girl's Life*. It was really important to me to read about someone else that had gone through those sorts of things.'

'Thank you. I think it's important too. We should all be able to see ourselves reflected back in the books we read, not just middle-aged, middle-class white men. They've had their day, don't you think?' She laughed.

'Definitely. Thanks very much for writing your story.'

She hesitated then said, 'Well, it's fiction of course, but yes, it's important for all voices to be heard.'

I nodded, happy to play along with this idea that it was pure fiction if that's what she wanted. It was all going brilliantly and I could feel the connection between us like the live wires on the circuit boards we used to study in chemistry.

'Do you prefer writing short stories or novels?' I asked the question I had been rehearsing in my head all morning.

'Great question,' she said, glancing at the shop assistant who was hovering at my left shoulder. 'I do love being immersed in a totally different world, which can only really be achieved by the novel. But then again, I've always had a soft spot for the short story – a little glimpse into someone's life, just a fragment.'

I nodded vigorously and told her I'd just read a collection of stories by this writer I'd discovered called Raymond Carver that I thought she might like too. I couldn't believe it when it turned out she already knew about him and his writing – we even had the same taste in books!

'Well, he's the master of course. So glad you enjoyed it. And great to meet you Wendy.'

She would have talked more but the shop assistant coughed and said there was quite a large queue, so Diane had to move on to the next person even though we were getting along great. I wanted to tell her how much I admired her for sticking up for herself and not letting anyone tell her what she should think, and how much I was learning from her, but the assistant said, 'Move along now please,' and Diane had no option but to end our conversation and sign the next person's book.

As I turned to leave, the wee, fat woman behind me dropped her book and I turned round and picked it up for her. Diane said, 'Thanks, Wendy.' She remembered my name, out of everyone in that crowd – she's dead popular in Glasgow – she called me by my first name. It was with us both being writers, I think.

I waited about at the front of the shop for ages afterwards so we could carry on our conversation but her bodyguards must have rushed her away through the back of the shop so the fans couldn't mob her. Like I said, she's very famous in Glasgow, so I didn't blame them but unfortunately it did mean she couldn't see her fellow writers either. After I'd been staring in the window for an hour or so, the store manager came and asked if he could help me. I told him I was a writer and I was waiting for Diane so we could carry on our conversation. He said she'd already left but there were loads of signed copies of her book in the store if I was interested. I could tell he thought I was just a fan myself so I didn't waste any more time talking to him.

If I was writing a memoir, I would say the real story of my life started that day, the day I met Diane. I'd never found it so easy to talk to someone as I did with Diane, we just really understood each other, probably because we were both writers. I knew even that first time we met that we had the kind of connection Saanvi was always on about. I just met Ginger at the wrong time. Her story threw me and Diane's off track and made it all messy. Ginger used to say that everybody gets what they deserve in the end, but I don't think that's true. I think me and Diane deserved much more and even though I loved Ginger, I'm still angry with her for ruining that.

8

AFTER I GOT HOME FROM Waterstones that afternoon, I decided to reread the book Diane and I had been talking about – *This Girl's Life*. It's her fourth book, not one of her best known but like I told her when we met, I think it's one of her best. I don't want to drop Diane in it if she says it's not about her, but I can tell you something – it's definitely about me. The alcoholic father squirming under the mother's tyranny, the blistering tempers then the silence, the parents' break-up and just the generally crap childhood guaranteed to make lonely children like us writers. It was like reading my own story, honest to God. I would say the second time I read it, after I'd actually spoken with Diane, that's when it all slotted into place. I knew then – Diane and I were more than just fellow writers. We were soulmates.

I agreed with Diane that the worst thing about having an alcoholic for a parent was the uncertainty of it. Never knowing whether the dad you're coming home to is the one that admires your shoes and asks how your maths test went, or the strange man whose coat and hair leave a smoky trail as he stumbles past you up the stairs, mumbling things you don't understand. Not knowing if the dad that's coming home to you is the same one who left to 'get a few things' a couple of hours earlier, or the wobbly, sour-smelling stranger who screws his eyes up when he comes across you in the kitchen and doesn't say hello or stroke your hair. I knew not everybody had dads like that because once, when this Italian girl called Carla came to our school in primary six and the teacher gave me the job of being her buddy, I was invited to her house after school a few times. Her dad taught Italian at the university and he shook my hand when he saw me and asked me what my favourite books were. When he came home, he kissed his wife and daughter, and winked at me. Sometimes, he kissed me too. He didn't always do that but when he did, I loved the feel of his rough cheek against mine and the faint smell of spicy aftershave and clammy classrooms that clung to his skin. Sometimes, I wished he was my dad then I felt terrible when I went home and saw Dad slumped in the armchair, his own skin rough too but, I guessed, smelling of something completely different from Carla's dad's face.

Mum's endless rants and screeching were almost worse than Dad's drinking. She seemed to think she could make him stop by screaming at him how awful he was all the time. Once I was coming home from school and I could hear them shouting at each other from the end of our street. My face was all red and I was shaking as I carried on walking right past our house so anybody watching wouldn't have known they were anything to do with me.

So nobody understood better than me what it was like to sit on your bed with the blankets over your ears so you couldn't hear what was going on downstairs. Diane described it better than I ever could, the shame that burns and marks you out as different from the others, the fear that they'll fall out in front of your teachers at parents' night or in the audience at the school play with all the other parents watching and smirking. And how hard it was to make friends that wouldn't judge you by your parents' standards and find you lacking. In Diane's book, everything was told from her character's point of view, it was supposed to be fiction, but if she was fooling all the other readers, she certainly didn't fool me.

I could understand why she wouldn't want to admit it was all real of course. Like me, she had that hard, secretive way about her that adults who have been unhappy children often have. Years of bearing up and shutting up make us stoic, and a bit aloof from everyone else. Ginger could be that way too and I sometimes wonder if it's more to do with being women than being brought up in difficult circumstances. It's like, we're not supposed to say anything's bothering us because that's our job – to put up with the shit, make sure everyone else is fine and just carry on.

There was so much more I'd wanted to ask Diane that first day we met and I was still annoyed by the way the shop assistant had cut our conversation short. I told Ginger about it when we had breakfast in the View the next day but I could tell she didn't understand.

'But she could have just said she was enjoying talking to you and carried on,' she said, picking at something crusty on her sleeve. 'If she'd really wanted to, I mean.'

'No, that's what I'm telling you. She couldn't because the shop assistant made her talk to the next person in the queue,' I said. 'Diane definitely wanted to talk to me, we had this . . . connection.'

Ginger dropped her locket from her mouth. 'She could have told the shop assistant to leave her alone, she was talking to you, if she'd wanted to though. Or she could have said she'd see you after the queue went down. If she'd really wanted to.'

She was lolling against the table, playing with the remains of her scrambled eggs in a way that would have driven my mum mad. The soft skin beneath her eyes was dark and one of her sleeves had a large brown stain the shape of Africa down almost the entire length of it, which annoyed me for some reason.

Sometimes, the four-year age gap between us really showed and I found it impossible to talk to her about anything serious. She was just too young to understand how things worked yet I suppose. I decided to change the subject. 'Have you read that book I gave you?'

'The book?' She put her head on one side and wrinkled her forehead so that the fuzzy hair at her parting dropped down into it. She looked about twelve, I thought, and tried to be patient with her.

'Diane's book. Her novel that's set in Motherwell.' I was sure Ginger would love it if she gave it a chance – the book mentioned places close to where we lived, it talked about people like us, people like the ones getting on and off my bus every day, people even Ginger could recognize.

'I haven't had time to start it yet,' she said, her fingers reaching up into her hair.

'What do you mean, you haven't had time? You've got nothing but time, what else do you do all day, apart from watching those cat videos?'

Ginger took her hand from her hair and said something about hardly looking at her phone at all, and how not all of us wanted to waste our time reading fantasy books, some of us had real things to worry about. She dipped a teaspoon in her tea and then into the sugar bowl, and licked the damp clumps off the back of it.

I was silent for a bit then I asked her if everything was okay with her uncle Tam and Fran, etcetera.

'Uncle Tam and Fran, *etcetera*' – that's how she said it, sort of emphasized it, if it had been written in a book it would have been in italics – 'are all fine. It's just . . .' She looked around the café and shrugged. 'I don't know, it's just . . .'

I waited.

The whites of her eyes seemed more pink today, and the skin was stretched taut across her cheekbones. I was conscious there had been no one at Waterstones who looked like her, and I hoped that I was more like the other people in the bookshop than like Ginger. I batted the thought away quickly, and wiped my hand across my forehead, as though erasing the betrayal. Ginger was my friend, and I was worried about her.

I had a sudden thought. 'Do you . . . do you need money?'

Her chin came up. 'No. Why would you say that?'

'I just thought . . . maybe with me working and . . .' I trailed off because I could see her lips getting thinner till her smile was barely a scrape across her face.

'Why would I need money? Do you think we're friends because I want you to pay for things?' She spat the words out like they tasted bad.

'No, I just—'

'I thought we were friends Wendy. I've told you stuff, stuff I haven't told anyone else. You've been to my house.'

She was right – she hadn't asked anything from me, and she never did. In fact the only thing she seemed to want from me was the one thing that no one else wanted – my company.

'We are friends Ginger,' I said, realizing suddenly that it was true. I liked Ginger, I liked being in her company – most of the time, anyway – and for some reason, she seemed to like being in mine. I half reached out to touch her knee, then, seeing the skin crinkled between her eyebrows and her lips shut tight, I drew back and scratched my head instead. 'It's just that . . . sometimes I feel like you're . . . I don't know, hiding something from me. Something that makes you unhappy at times maybe?'

Her hand was fluttering about her face. She seemed to be chasing an itch across her cheek and the constant scratch-scratch was annoying me but I tried not to show it. Something was bothering her, I knew it, but I didn't know how to help her the way friends should. I wished Mum was there to tell me what to say.

We both spoke at the same time.

'It's Uncle—'

'Shall we go and—'

She stopped talking. 'Sorry.'

'No, what were you going to say?'

'No, nothing important.' She waved it away. 'You go first.'

'Well, I was just going to say, do you fancy coming with me to Dunelm and helping me to choose some coasters?'

'I thought you had to go home and write your story after we'd finished here?'

'That can wait.'

She brightened a bit and threw some sugar at me across the table. 'So we're going to Dunelm to buy bits of coloured cardboard for you to put your mugs on?'

I tutted. 'Do you want to come or not?'

'Course I do,' she said. 'What else would I be doing?'

I was really pleased I asked her to come along because we ended up having a great laugh and it turned out there was nothing wrong with her after all. I made a mental note to tell Saanvi how well I'd been able to read the situation and what an understanding friend I'd been to Ginger. It felt good to be making progress.

9

GINGER AND ME WERE supposed to be meeting in the park the next day at eleven but when I got there she wasn't sitting on the swings, or lounging by the roundabout, or perched on top of the metal slide that was so slow it made a high pitched squeal as you slid to the bottom of it. I wandered aimlessly round the damp play park, waiting for her to show up. The smell of boiling chocolate, sickly sweet, wafted over the park from the Tunnock's factory and made me queasy at that time in the morning. As usual, I'd forgotten to eat breakfast and there'd been no milk left for tea. Well kept and tidy as it was, the park was a depressing place to be on your own so, to be honest, I was a bit annoyed with Ginger for not being there. It was drizzling down and miserable and I'd left the house early so I'd be on time, meanwhile she hadn't even bothered to turn up. I sat on the swing she normally took, my legs dangling on the wet sand in front of me. I felt a bit self-conscious as other people passed through the park on their way to Scotmid, or the young mums pushed their prams past me and thought better of stopping and letting their toddlers out to play when the only other person in the whole place was me, loitering by the swings. One actually tutted at me and said to the wee boy gripping her hand, in a loud voice meant for me, 'No Fraser, we'll need to wait till after playgroup today sweetie,' before dragging him away.

I saw two boys saunter down the hill and walk into the park, the elder couldn't have been more than twelve but he was holding an unlit cigarette. They came closer than anyone else, one sitting on the next swing along, the other standing behind him, leaning against the wooden frame. They said nothing for a bit but I could tell by the way they were eyeing me that they were thinking about it.

'Got a light missus?' said the older one, indicating the cigarette stub that I could see had already been lit then nipped.

'Sorry,' I said. 'I don't smoke.' I paused then I said, 'You shouldn't either, it's bad for you.'

They both looked at each other then laughed. 'Fuck off, hanging about the park. Fuckin' weirdo. 'Mon Jamesy.' This was the smaller boy, who looked the more vicious of the two, with his pinched, yellow face and his hair scraped back to his scalp. Both looked like they could do with a wash.

'You should be at school,' I called after them as they ran across the park in the direction of Main Street. The older one turned and spat hugely through the air mid run.

I sighed and shook my head, wondering what I was doing here when I could be at home, writing, or reading Diane's tweets, or doing . . . something, and I took one last look round the park before I headed home.

It was eight o'clock that same night and I was wondering what I should do next. I'd spent the whole day at home, wandering in and out of Mum's room, tormented by images of her in there when she'd been ill, lying still in the narrow bed, or bent over and shouting at me to make her more tea. I was going to do some writing but I remembered Diane saying everyone had their own story to tell and I wasn't sure I wanted Mum's illness to be mine so I didn't write anything in the end.

Ginger came to the back door which nearly gave me a heart attack as no one ever went round the back. I mean, the only people that ever came to the front door were Saanvi and the postman, once in a blue moon. So when I heard the knock, I sat rooted to my chair for a bit, looking round the room for a heavy object to grab. There was another series of small knocks and I didn't get up. Then I heard her.

'Wendy? Wendy, I know you're there, let me in.'

I got up and opened the door and there was Ginger, standing on the bottom step, leaning against the wall.

'Ginger? What are you doing here?'

She pulled at a long grey thread trailing from the pocket of her hoodie and didn't answer. She looked pale, like all the colour had drained out of her. Even her dazzling hair was listless, the fuzzy patches, where downy hair was growing in again, were spreading across her head like moss.

'Are you going to let me in or what?'

I stood to the side and she came up the back steps and into my house. We both stood in the kitchen, me not knowing what to do with my visitor, and Ginger with her arms folded tightly across her body, staring at the grimy floor tiles.

'Has something happened?' I said, as I showed her into the living room next door. 'Sorry about the mess. I don't get visitors. Usually.'

She waved her hand and we sat down. She looked round the room and I shut my eyes so I couldn't see her take in the stained carpet, the drab olive wallpaper, peeling down at the corner behind the TV, and the tape on the edges of the coffee table keeping the Formica in place. I could smell damp rising from the floorboards. I would need to do something about this place, I thought, if I was going to have visitors. I was about to say this out loud when Ginger dropped her head and started to cry. I sat, glued to my seat, as her shoulders shook and the room was filled with the doleful sound of her crying. I saw for the first time new bald patches at the back of her head as she leaned forwards and her hair tumbled down almost to the dirty carpet.

'Ginger, I . . .'

The sobbing grew louder then stopped as suddenly as it had begun. She sniffed and wiped her face with the back of her hand, pushed her hair back, and reached her fingers into it to make sure the bald patches were covered.

'Sorry,' she said. Her voice was rasping, and her breathing heavy like she was gulping for air. She crossed and uncrossed her legs, her jeans bagged at the knee like she'd been wearing them for weeks. She'd sweated through her clothes as though she'd run all the way from Viewpark.

'It's nothing, don't even know what I'm crying for. Have you got a tissue or something?' She sniffed and looked round the room.

'Wait a minute,' I said, and ran upstairs, two at a time, coming back with a wad of toilet paper. 'Here.'

I waited till she'd blown her nose and wiped the remaining tears from her cheeks. 'Did something happen?'

She tutted. 'Not really. It's just . . . Mum came round.'

'Your mum? I assumed, I mean, I thought . . .'

'She's not dead Wendy, if that's what you thought. I only see her a couple of times a year. Sometimes not even that. She's . . . Uncle Tam's her wee brother, she left me with him when she went off with, Christ, I can't even remember his name, he's long gone now anyway.' She paused and sniffed again. 'I must look a right state.' She half laughed.

'Yeah,' I said. 'You do.'

I don't know why that made her smile because it was true but I was glad she'd cheered up a bit. 'She came to see you at least, is that not good?'

She waved her hand. 'Don't be ridiculous, she didn't come to see me. She only came because she needed money. That's the only reason she ever comes. And I gave her all the cash I had but she said it wasn't enough and I was an ungrateful wee bitch. Like I've got anything to be grateful for! She was totally out of it, and Uncle Tam came home and he wouldn't give her any more money either, said she'd only use it to get wasted and to get the fuck out his house and . . .' She started crying again.

I bit my lip then went over and sat beside her on the sofa. I hadn't sat on the other cushion for ages, I always sat on the one closest to the TV that Ginger was sitting on, so when I sat down, the whole sofa sort of collapsed over to one side and we both fell to our knees. I almost landed on Ginger and I was embarrassed by how bad my house was but then I was glad because it made her laugh. Soon, she was laughing so much her hair shook and it took us ages to get up off our knees and try to sit right on the wonky sofa.

'Sorry,' I said again. 'My house . . . I didn't keep up with things when Mum was sick and I . . . went a bit crazy after she died, I couldn't bear to see her stuff all round me, things she'd

89

chosen and had to leave behind. I . . . got rid of most of it.' I felt stupid admitting that but Ginger wasn't laughing at me. 'I wasn't thinking straight,' I said. 'I need to get new stuff I suppose.' I raised my hands and dropped them again, not knowing how else to explain that it hadn't always been this way.

'At least it's yours Wendy,' she said. 'No one can get you here.'

I looked at her, I'd never thought about it that way before but she was right.

'I'm sorry your mum's visit didn't go well,' I said.

'It's fine, lot of fuss about nothing. Who needs her anyway?' She pulled her locket up to her mouth and said, 'Do you want to go to the park?'

'What, now? No, it's too late.'

I looked out the window and saw that it had started to rain again.

'Did you bring a jacket?' I asked her.

She got up abruptly, shaking out her hair. 'I'm just leaving Wendy, don't worry.'

I stood up quickly. 'No Ginger, I didn't . . .'

She looked at me, waiting.

I curled and uncurled my fingers by my sides.

'Did you . . . do you, I mean, do you want to stay? Are you hungry? I've got fish fingers. I think I have anyway. Would they be okay?'

She smiled at me and said she was starving. We went back into the kitchen and I rooted about in the freezer for the half empty pack of fish fingers and she put the kettle on, humming something under her breath.

She ate quickly, spooning up the beans then stabbing the fish fingers with her fork and shoving them whole into her mouth. After she'd eaten, she got up and wandered back into the living room.

'The coasters look nice,' she said, looking at the little pile of four coasters we'd chosen, two with black Scottie dogs and two with white.

'Yeah, but . . .' I was about to apologize again for the state of the place when she walked over to the fireplace and picked up the only ornament that was left there, turning it over in her hands.

'Do you know what that means?' I said, pointing to the inscription on the Wallace clan shield she was holding.

She went bright red and said, 'Of course I can read it.' She passed it back to me. 'Sorry, I shouldn't have picked it up.'

'No, it's fine,' I said, 'that's my clan shield my dad brought me back from . . . one of his trips. My mum hated it so I used to keep it in my room but now, I mean, I can put it anywhere I like can't I?'

'It's your house,' she said. 'You can do what you like in it.'

'It means "For liberty". It's Latin,' I said, in case she didn't realize.

'Oh,' she said. 'Latin. No, I can't speak Latin, that's why I couldn't read it. The tartan's nice though, red and yellow.'

Ginger wandered off to look at the rest of the house and left me holding the shield. Dad had brought it back for me as a present after the first time he went off on his own. He was away for two days and didn't come back till very late on a school night. I'm not sure how long ago it was but he didn't have that methylated spirits smell that hung about him in later years, this must have been before that. He'd been to Stirling, to think about things, he said, glancing through to the kitchen where Mum was giving her biceps a workout wiping down all the surfaces with lemon bleach. He told me 'For liberty' was the Wallace clan motto and said next time he'd take me to the monument with him. We both heard Mum snort from the kitchen and I looked through at her but he ignored her. 'I will take you next time, I promise,' he said. He never did take me but at least I've still got the shield. I placed it carefully back on the mantelpiece and went to see what Ginger was up to.

She was in my bedroom, looking out the back window but it was so dark by then that all we could see were our own images reflected back at us.

'How long have you had your own house Wendy? It's brilliant.'

'Me and Mum moved here when I was thirteen,' I said. 'I can hardly remember living anywhere else.' Even if I thought about it really hard, I couldn't remember much about the house I lived in before that, when Dad still lived with us, but I could still see those flashes – jagged little episodes like the day he disappeared and came back with the shield. I remembered how Mum and Dad were with each other.

I didn't mind telling Ginger a bit about my childhood, and how things were with my mum and dad because I thought that would make her feel better about living with Uncle Tam. But even though Saanvi said it was good to talk, I found when I spoke about Mum, even months after she'd died, it gave me this gnawing feeling right at the bottom of my stomach, like I was empty, or hungry for something but I didn't know what. It was better for me to keep the ache of missing my mum all covered up like a bandaged wound.

I realize now that one of the reasons Ginger and me hit it off as well as we did, despite the fact she was four years younger than me, was because she'd lost her mum too. I mean, she might not have been dead but having a mum that only visits once or twice a year when she needs money isn't really any better than having a dead one, is it?

'Tell you what, maybe you could help me,' I said. 'I've been thinking for a while that I need to do more to brighten this place up a bit. I haven't looked after it at all since Mum died but you're right – it's mine now and I'm lucky to have it. I just need to make it more . . .' I looked round the room, trying to think of the word.

'Homey?' suggested Ginger.

'Yeah, homey. Exactly.'

'Uncle Tam sells quite a bit of stuff at the Barras. I've been with him a couple of times and they've got some great beanbags and big pictures and all sorts of weird knick-knacks and things that would go lovely in here. We should go.'

It was only the next morning when Ginger left that I wondered how she'd known where to find me. I asked her next time I saw her but she was acting like she'd never been to the house at all, and everything was fine.

'You make a lot of fuss about nothing Wendy, you know that?' she said, as she drew circles in the sand at the back of the swings with her heel. 'Fancy some company on the bus today?'

And that's how she put up with most of the stuff that went on in her life. Whine a bit then shrug and put up with it, move on to the next thing. I said to her once I should put her in one of my stories but she looked at me from under her orange eyelashes and said why would anyone be interested in reading about her.

I can't help thinking now that a better friend than me would have seen the signs and spotted there was something wrong with her. Maybe that's why I'd never been any good at having friends, because when Ginger said she was okay, I just believed her.

10

WE WENT TO THE Barras the following Sunday, though Ginger was in such a bad mood when she came round, at first I thought she must have changed her mind.

She rapped on my back door at half nine, just as I was finishing my cornflakes.

'You're early,' I said, as she slumped into the seat opposite me, her body curled in on itself like a mollusc shell.

'Sorry. I left in a rush. My phone ran out of charge. I couldn't call you. Let you know I was on my way.' Her words were strangely disjointed, like it was too much effort for her to string a sentence together. 'It's not a problem is it?' She raised her chin up at me, daring me to tell her to leave. Her face was pale, except for a dull red mark across her cheek. She saw me looking at it and put her elbow on the table so that she could rest her cheek against her palm, covering most of her face.

'Any cornflakes left? I'm starving.'

We ran down to the station and made it in time for the half ten train into Central. She didn't say much on the way there but by the time we got into town and she saw all the people milling about the station with their backpacks and wheelie cases, and felt the buzz of the city centre atmosphere, she cheered up a bit.

We walked the length of Argyle Street back towards the East End. Most of the shops were open and there was even a queue at the hot dog stand in front of Marks & Spencer. A small crowd had formed around a guy whose whole act was to stand still and pretend he was a statue for hours. I'm not sure what they were expecting to see.

'Mum used to work in there,' said Ginger, as we passed Clinton Cards. 'She took me in with her once and I got to sit behind the counter eating Galaxy Buttons, and help her move the boxes in the stockroom.' She lifted her locket to her mouth and sighed. 'She got the sack after a few weeks though because she was always late. The manageress was younger than she was but she acted like she was her mother or something. Told her to come back when she was responsible enough to hold down a job.'

'When was that?' I asked, keen to keep the conversation going as this was the most she'd told me about her mum in the time I'd known her.

She shrugged. 'We'd already moved in with Uncle Tam so a few years ago now. Just before she left for good with that English guy she met. "The love of my life."' She mimicked her mum in a stupid high voice and rolled her eyes. 'I liked him better than the others mind you. Never wanted me though, just her.'

'I'm sorry,' I said, but she brushed me off.

'No skin off my nose. I never wanted to move away from Viewpark anyway, I'm fine where I am.'

We'd reached the Trongate and the traffic was getting busy. As we waited to cross at the lights, I spotted several posters advertising the Write Now festival happening that September stuck on the wall of the Tron.

'Diane's doing a session at Write Now this year,' I told Ginger. 'It's a book festival on at the CCA. That's the Centre for Contemporary Arts on Sauchiehall Street,' I added, since Ginger shrugged as though she hadn't heard of the festival or the CCA.

We crossed the road and I carried on over the rumble of the traffic. 'I was thinking of going. After we got on so well at Waterstones, there's a few other things I'd like to ask her about my own writing, stuff she might be able to help me with.'

Ginger pursed her lips but I didn't rise to it because I knew by now that she wasn't interested in books, and she definitely wasn't interested in hearing about Diane. It was as though because Ginger and me were friends, I wasn't allowed to be friends with anyone else. But writing and books, especially Diane's, had become too important for me to give them up to please anyone else, even Ginger.

We reached the market and I remembered how much I'd loved it when Dad had taken me there as a Sunday morning treat while Mum was doing the chapel flowers. We'd spend hours looking through the outdoor stalls and the indoor pitches, all filled with weird and wonderful stuff so that you never knew what you might come across next. We'd buy a punnet of strawberries from Davy, the fruit and veg guy, and share them as we perused the stands. Dad's favourite was the store that was filled with combat gear – military style jackets, long green capes and a rack of kilts, complete with fusty old sporrans like mouldy ferrets. He'd spend a long time chatting with the owner, Military Bob, who may have been related to Tool Bob who sold all the saws and screws three stands along.

He also knew Big Peter who ran the carpet stall, next to the glassmaker. 'He's not that big, Dad,' I whispered as he pushed me forwards to shake hands with his old classmate. Then Big Peter started speaking and the force of his personality left me in no doubt about how he'd got his nickname. I don't know why they didn't stay in touch after Dad lost his job and Big Peter hit the big time with his carpet company and was even doing adverts on TV.

Once I remember we spent ages choosing a new ornament for Mum and eventually settled on a dimpled brass plate that you hung on the wall. It said 'A Round Tuit' on it and we both thought that was hilarious and would make a great present for Mum. She didn't like it though and said what did she want with someone else's tat, she had enough of her own, and shoved it in the cupboard at the back of the kitchen.

The smell of whelks and mussels from the Loch Fyne Shellfish Café brought all those memories back to me, and even though the market wasn't as big or as busy as I remembered, they were still selling the same kind of stuff when Ginger and me went. Randall's Antiques was still there and we rif-fled through their collection of dusky silver jewellery, faded pouffes, guitars with missing strings and chipped wooden necks, and an array of old records. Ginger was interested in the clothing stalls but mostly they contained racks of clothes that grannies would wear, like skirts with elasticated waists that you could have fitted Ginger and me into twice, and beach shirts huge as sails. I nearly bought a mug at the Braw Wee Emporium that said 'Wee Yin' on it but I couldn't choose between that and one that said 'Big Blether', and the stallholder was getting annoyed about how long I was taking to choose. Ginger pulled me away saying, 'Why should we give the cranky old bugger our business?' so I didn't get one in the end.

Ginger insisted on going into Glickman's for a quarter of aniseed balls and she sucked on the fiery little sweets for the next half hour. We spent ages looking through all the stands and eventually I settled on a red rectangular photograph frame and a little silver one in the shape of a love heart. Ginger tried to talk the man selling them down from a fiver each to three pounds but when he told her to sling her hook, I stepped in and apologized and asked if I could have both of them for fifteen. He agreed right away and I made a mental note not to let Ginger do the bargaining in future, I was obviously so much better at it.

As we were leaving the market and heading on to London Road, a crowd of people streamed out of St Alphonsus and we had to step off the pavement to allow the family groups of four or more to pass. The doors of the church remained open and Ginger said, 'Fancy going in for a sit down for ten minutes?' I hadn't been in a church since my mum's funeral, something I did feel guilty about at times, and it was Sunday, so I agreed.

It was cold and a bit damp inside but there was something very comforting about being in the quiet half-light with the candles flickering on the altar and the acrid smell of incense lingering in the air above us. Out of habit, I genuflected before the altar and crossed myself. Ginger watched me with interest.

'Do you believe in God then?' she said as I sat down next to her.

'Ssshhh, keep your voice down.' I looked all round to check no one was being annoyed by her loud voice.

'What? There's no one here but us.' She picked up the hymn book from the ledge in front of her, flipped through it, then put it on the seat next to her. 'Do you though?' she whispered, looking at me intently.

'Yes, I think so,' I said. 'I mean, I was always brought up to believe in God so . . . How else do you explain how we all got here?' I played my mum's trump card.

Ginger shrugged. 'I don't know but I know I don't believe there's a big bearded man up in the clouds. That's just stupid.'

'Ginger! Remember where we are.' I waved around at the thick red candles still burning brightly at the front of the church, the huge framed pictures of the stations of the cross, and the altar itself draped with a gold and white cloth. 'You can't say that. He's . . . God's listening.'

'Ppff. Well, he's not listening very hard then. What's he doing for me?'

'He's looking after you, he looks after everyone.'

Ginger turned round and stared at me, her lips stained deep red from all the aniseed balls. 'Do you see God looking after me? No one's looking after me. No one – except me.' She poked herself in the chest as she said this.

'And me,' I said.

'Yeah well.' She looked down at the floor and drummed her fingers against the wooden pews on each side of her legs.

'And I bet your mum looked after you too when she was around.'

'I suppose so, sometimes anyway. She made sure we always had a place to stay. She made Uncle Tam take us in when we got chucked out our last place. He didn't want to because he didn't have the room he said and he was right. Me and Mum used to share my bedroom when she was still living with us. If you think I'm messy, you should have seen it when she was there. I don't know how she had the nerve to bring guys back.'

'What – she had men in the room? When you were there?'

Ginger laughed. 'Most weekends. I had to keep my head under the covers but I could still hear them. *Bang bang oohh oohh oooohhhh.*'

I couldn't stop myself from laughing even though we were in church. 'Ginger!'

'At least I got my own room when she left.'

'That's true. I'm sorry I didn't meet her though. She sounds a lot more fun than my mum. At least when she was, you know, sober I mean.'

'Well, maybe. But one of the things you need to learn Wendy, is that not everyone's as nice as you are. You always see the best in everyone. I worry about you sometimes.'

I didn't know what to say to that because no one but Mum, and maybe Dad, had ever worried about me, and it did feel good even if I didn't need her concern.

Ginger was speaking again as she looked up at the altar. 'People can take advantage you know. Like this Diane Weston woman you're always on about.'

I swung round to face her. 'What? That's rubbish. She's taught me so much, and she's lovely. We had a brilliant talk at Waterstones, we've just got this—'

'Connection. I know,' said Ginger. 'She's not your friend though Wendy, not like me.' She looked away, her cheeks flushing beneath the thick waves of her hair.

'You and me are friends Ginger, it's been great having you to hang out with these last few weeks. But . . . Diane and me are friends too. It's just . . . different.'

Ginger said nothing but I could tell she wasn't convinced.

'Okay, well tell me this. What do I have that she could possibly want to take advantage of? Think about that.'

'Maybe she likes being, you know, hero worshipped. Maybe it feeds her ego or something, I don't know. Anyway,' she turned to face me again. 'I'm just saying be careful who you trust because not everyone is as nice as you. That's all, don't get your knickers in a twist.'

Knickers in the house of God was the last straw and I stood up and told Ginger it was time to go. She smiled at me like the conversation hadn't taken place at all and said, 'Let's go by the Val D'Oro and get a roll and sausage before we get the train.'

Later that night, I took out my tablet and checked Twitter for the first time that day. I whispered, 'Come on, come on,' as it refreshed but Diane hadn't tweeted anything since her last tweet two days ago.

I ate my toast in the dark, not even bothering to put on the telly, as I wondered what Diane was doing, and who she was spending her evening with. I wondered if I should have invited Ginger back to mine again, it would have been better than sitting here alone, even if she was in one of her moods. I could feel the tears threatening and knew if Mum had been there she'd tell me to stop feeling sorry for myself and find something positive to do.

I sniffed as I remembered the photo frames we'd bought and went through to the kitchen to get them out of my rucksack. I had the perfect photo for the red one. I went into Mum's old room and carefully opened the drawer of her bedside cabinet. The photo was just where I'd left it – Mum on her way to a St Patrick's Night dance at my school hall. She was wearing a shimmering green dress and her hair was mostly pinned up, with just a few long curls hanging loose over her ears. She'd been so pretty once, I'd forgotten that beside all the images I'd stored up of her wasting away and in pain.

The photograph was a perfect fit for the red frame and I sat it on the fold-up table beside my bed, next to the empty silver one. It occurred to me I could put a photograph of Ginger and me in that, or maybe even one of Diane if I ever managed to get one.

I couldn't wait to show Saanvi the room on Wednesday. It was true what she said – doing a little bit of décor and adding a few personal touches to your house did make you feel better about things. And Diane's belief in me – she'd actually said that the world needed stories from women like me – was starting to make me feel I deserved that.

I was grateful to Ginger too because if it hadn't been for her, I'd never have gone to the Barras and starting buying nice things. I thought about what she'd said in the church about no one looking after her, and I suddenly thought of something that I could do for her. I sat on the bed with my tablet and ordered Ginger a pair of trainers from Very. They were bright red with an orange stripe up the back almost the exact colour of her hair and I knew she'd love them.

I put the tablet on charge, got under the covers and turned out the light, thinking how lucky I was to have friends like Ginger and Diane.

11

THE STORY OF HOW I'd found out where Diane lives was quite funny. This would have been a month or so after I'd met Ginger but she wasn't riding the bus with me that day. I was driving the 63 from Hamilton town centre to Motherwell – and just before I got to the big S-bend on Glasgow Road, who did I see crossing over the road but Diane! I couldn't miss her to be honest because although it wasn't quite July yet, Diane was making the most of the watery sunshine in a floaty summer dress, mostly orange but with some white patches, and a huge straw hat with a ribbon streaming behind her as she marched across the road. I nearly drove into the old dental practice that's offering Botox now, I was that surprised to see her. She didn't wave or anything – she didn't see me, wouldn't have been expecting me to drive a bus either I suppose, she only knew me as a writer – but I slowed down and watched her put her key in the front door of one of those big sandstones, across from the train station. That's how I knew it was her house. It was a really nice house, I mean, the paint was peeling a bit and there was mould round the windows, but that was because her mind was on other things. She certainly wasn't bothered about what the neighbours thought of how she kept her house, was she? The garden was surrounded by a low wall so you could see right in. It was big but not too regimented or set out like a public park, not like some of them down that road. No, hers had a few rose bushes down each side of the path, pinks and yellows, bright and summery like she often was in her swirly skirts and stripey sweaters. There was a kind of stooped, old tree – maybe an oak? – right in front of her window. I think I saw her shadow on the threshold after she went in but I had to drive on then, some of my passengers were getting narky. I wasn't bothered – I knew I could go back any time.

Although Diane's house was nothing like mine of course, she actually lived quite close to me. That's the way Uddingston is – it's small enough that you're never far away from anyone else but depending on which side of the motorway you live, it can be a very different place. Down at the bottom of the village where Diane lived is Uddingston proper, and that's where all the massive red sandstone houses are. 'All tapas and *Telegraphs*,' my dad used to say, he had no time for the ones that did all the complaining when they wanted to build Aladdin's just beside Tunnock's. They put up petitions and all sorts and they won in the end because they built the arcade at the top of the hill between Birkenshaw and Viewpark instead. Diane wouldn't have complained though, even if you didn't know her, you can tell by her books that she's down-to-earth and would love a good Subway as much as the rest of us.

I walked past her house every single day for the next week. I mean, it was just as easy to walk that way to the library or to Tunnock's for my steak pie on Thursday as it was to go by any other route. Once when I walked by, she was just leaving in her wee red Fiesta so I dawdled for a few minutes till I was sure the house was empty then I walked up the path and took a peek into the large bay window at the front of the house. The room I looked into was massive, big enough to take three large brown leather sofas comfortably, and a well stocked bookcase on the left-hand wall. I drew a breath as I took in the huge work of art facing me on the back wall. Not a picture of anything in particular, just daubs of paint – but the colours! Beautiful rose pinks and chubby yellows all swirled round the canvas in a fury of colour. I couldn't explain it but looking at Diane's picture made me feel like crying. Not out of sadness, well maybe sadness that it wasn't mine, but more awe of the beauty, the patterns and the colours. And to have the taste to choose something like that, and the space to hang it up in. It wasn't like any picture we'd ever had in our house.

The next time I walked by she was standing in her garden, leaning on a spiky rake, and surveying the freshly cut grass. I think that was the only time I ever saw her in trousers, they were tucked into big green wellies and she had flowery rubber gardening gloves on, making her hands look enormous.

I was going to put my head down and keep walking but then I remembered everything I'd learned about taking the initiative and making connections, and I really wanted to make Saanvi proud of me. I told myself, 'You can do this,' and patted down my hair and ran my tongue over dry lips.

'Hello,' I said, walking towards Diane's garden and waving my hand at the same time. I stayed where I was on the other side of the low wall and she squinted to see me better. She half smiled and said hello back but sort of half-heartedly like she wasn't sure who I was.

I walked further along the edge of the garden so she could see it was me. I was standing directly opposite her but with the wall between us. Even her gardening clothes were in her usual bright colours, her top a vivid red and covered in tiny pineapples. But without her make-up on, and outdoors like that, she was older than I'd thought. I was surprised by the two deep lines between her eyes, and the others round her mouth. Her hair, normally round her shoulders, was gathered in a messy low ponytail, and held away from her face with an old-fashioned Alice band, the hair underneath the band and round her forehead a sort of yellowish grey. Probably writing all those books had aged her a bit, but not in a bad way, you could tell she had experience.

'It's me, Wendy,' I said, pointing to my chest like I had a name badge on.

'Oh, yes, Wendy,' she said, glancing at the house behind her then back at me. 'Do we . . . have we met?'

I laughed, incredulous. 'Yes, we met at Waterstones. At your book signing? I'm a writer too. We know each other on Twitter. Wendy,' I repeated. I was surprised she didn't seem to know me but, afterwards, I realized it was because her mind was on other things, plotlines and so on. What a lot of people don't understand is that social niceties are not the priority for writers, the way they are for other people. Of course she knew who I was, it was just my name had slipped her mind and she wouldn't have been expecting to see me at her house either.

'Right,' she said. 'You're a writer.' She dropped her rake and walked closer to the wall.

'I loved *One World*,' I said quickly as she came towards me. In fact, it had been my least favourite of all her books I'd read so far. It was about an old man who taught at Edinburgh University, who was having some sort of crisis over a love affair that had gone wrong, and losing his job, and his children not wanting to visit him. I'm not saying they weren't serious problems but, overall, the book didn't seem to chime with everything else she said about working-class women taking centre stage and all that sort of thing. Mind you, she did give him a nervous breakdown at the end and there was a scene where he acknowledged he was nothing without his wife, but still, I was a bit disappointed. Of course I didn't tell her that. 'I loved the way you described Edinburgh as the Athens of the North. Very original.'

She laughed. 'Yes, my editor chided me for that too.'

'Well, she's wrong,' I said, shaking my head. 'It was brilliant.'

'Right,' said Diane, smiling her huge smile. 'I'll tell her that next time.' Her hands, now she'd taken off the gardening gloves, were small and neat, like a little girl's hands. Like most people, she was much shorter than me even though the bright outfits and the way she waved her hands around and laughed a lot gave you the impression she took up more room than ordinary people.

'Wendy?'

I tried to concentrate on what she was saying. 'I'm sorry?'

'I was just asking what sort of things you write. You said you're a writer?'

'Oh yes, yes, I am. Poems mostly, sometimes short stories. About people like us, you know.'

She smiled again and tapped the wall twice with her hand. 'Well, keep at it Wendy, the world needs your stories too, remember that. Nice to speak to you.'

She was walking away! I called after her, 'Yes, it was nice to speak to you too. Your garden's lovely. Do you have to water these a lot?' I gestured to the pink rose bushes thriving on the other side of the wall, asking the first thing that came into my head so she would have to come back and talk a bit more.

'Yes, it does take quite a bit of work but it's worth it – I get a lot of inspiration from my garden,' she said, turning back and smiling at me. 'Just marvelling at the beauty of my roses, you know? You should try it. Being at one with nature is so helpful for letting the ideas flow, I find. Anyway, listen to me harping on, I'm sure you have plenty of things to be getting on with.'

'No,' I said. 'Nothing at all.'

'Right, well . . .' Her smile faded a little and she looked away and back at her roses.

Just then, the front door opened and an old guy, at least forty, walked out. He had a pot belly and a head like a peeled potato. He started to say something to Diane then stopped as he saw me.

'Hello?' he said to me.

'This is Wendy,' Diane called to him.

'I'm a writer too,' I said quickly.

The man smiled and said, 'Good stuff,' then turning back to Diane, 'That's almost time for us to get going.'

'Right, I'm just finishing up here,' she said, walking away from me again and picking up her rake. 'Bye Wendy,' she called over her shoulder. 'Nice to meet you, and keep writing.'

'Thanks,' I called from the other side of the wall. 'Thanks, yes, I will. I'll see you at another reading soon no doubt.'

She was too far away to hear me. I stood watching her for a few more minutes then realized the man was still at the door, watching me. Diane walked into the porch and the man stood aside to let her in. He waved at me and followed behind her, shutting the door with enough force to make the stained glass panels wobble a bit.

I stood at the wall for a bit longer admiring Diane's beautiful garden before I headed back home. I thought a lot about our conversation later that night, and I've been over it hundreds of times since then, trying to remember exactly what she said, and how I responded. It's important because that was our first proper talk alone together, until *he*'d appeared. I do know Diane and I had made a real connection over our respective writing careers and she enjoyed talking to a fellow writer as much as I did. I realized Saanvi was right as usual – if you just made the effort to get to know someone better, it wasn't that difficult to make them your friend.

12

MY MIND WAS STILL racing the next day with all the stuff Diane and me had been discussing but I had to go to work. I was driving the 255 to Bellshill. The bus was filling up by the time we got to the big Tesco and I had to ask the pink-haired girl waiting at the bus stop to fold up her buggy or there wouldn't be room for it on the bus.

'But they're nearly sleeping,' she said, looking down at the near identical toddlers lolling against matching blue blankets in the buggy.

'I'm sorry,' I said, 'but there's no room on the bus for a double buggy. Here, I'll help you put it down if you like?'

'Don't worry missus,' said a blond boy wearing a Cardinal Newman blazer, looking up from his book. 'I'll help her.'

I waited while the girl faffed about with the sleepy children, making sure they were propping each other up on the seat behind me before she took her shopping bags off the handles and let the boy fold up the buggy and pack it away under her feet.

'Check out Mummy's little helper,' called out one of the boys sitting further up the bus, his stripey, red and black school tie unknotted and one end draped over his shoulder like a scarf.

The blond boy blushed and sat down, dipping his head back into the book.

I said nothing but shot glances at them in the rearview mirror. Gorgeous Kevin was in his usual seat three rows from the back, on the opposite side from me, his left cheek pressed tight against the window. I knew his name because I'd heard groups of kids walking past calling out to him as he got on the bus, so I'm guessing he must have been really handsome before . . . whatever happened to him. I saw him flinch when the schoolboys got on but they hadn't said anything. The schoolkids could be rowdy, especially boys sitting three or four together, but I don't think any of them would have joked about poor Kevin's burnt face. Still, I was keeping my eye on them to make sure.

Their high pitched voices and the volume at which they were conducting their conversation meant that everyone on the bus was party to it.

'Here's one for you,' said the bigger lad, his tie loosely knotted and swinging low down his chest. 'What do Mr Thompson and Mr—'

'What, that poofter from Art and Design?'

'. . . Mackenzie have in common?'

'Dunno, surprise us.'

'Easy,' said a third boy, the sweat patches under the arms of his pale blue shirt visible from where I sat. 'Mr Oswald would do them both.'

All three boys fell back laughing against the seats, one of them almost toppling into the aisle. I didn't think it was that funny but maybe I just didn't get the joke, or maybe you had to know the teachers they were talking about to get it. But it was quite a talent, I thought, to be able to make people laugh like that at something you said, and I wondered if that was the difference between the group of boys shouting and slapping each other on the back, and the boy in the blazer, sitting on his own. Maybe there was a story there – the quiet boy that nobody likes but who triumphs in the end when he becomes the first man to land on Mars or something. None of the others at writers' group had written anything like that and it might make a nice change from the bloodbath on Islay. As I signalled left by the new housing estate, I remembered Diane had tweeted once about inspiration striking anywhere and it made me smile that she was right, as usual.

I was glad when all the schoolkids got off at McDonald's. Kevin could relax, and the bus was quiet enough for me to think about Diane again and how pleased she'd been to talk to another writer.

I meant to start writing the schoolboy goes to Mars story as soon as I got home but ended up scrolling through Twitter instead. I was disappointed to see no new tweets from Diane and nobody else had tweeted anything worth reading. I still had a couple of hours to fill before I had to leave for writers' group so I was happy to see Ginger when she appeared at my door.

She hadn't been in the house very long before she started driving me nuts, pacing up and down my living room like she couldn't bear to sit still. The air held the aftermath of a quarrel though we'd hardly spoken. I sat with my book on my lap and watched as she put her locket in her mouth and sucked on it, the thin gold chain resting against her cheeks. Her hair was all over the place, a great mop of orange, with the darker patch at the front. She was wearing some new sweatpants, they were billowing round her midriff and didn't quite reach her ankles. I could see flakes of dry skin gathered at the corners of her mouth.

'What?' she said, stopping suddenly in the middle of her pacing as she became aware of me staring at her.

'Nothing. Why don't you sit down, maybe read a book?'

She batted away my suggestion and walked over to the fireplace, running her hand idly along the mantelpiece till she spotted the miniature Grecian urn at the end.

'Careful with that,' I said, as she picked it up.

'This is new,' she said, turning it over and running her fingers along the smooth gold leaf markings.

'No, it isn't. I've had it for ages.' I kept my eyes on my book and tried hard not to let her annoy me.

'No, it definitely wasn't there the last time I was here,' Ginger persisted, throwing it now from one hand to the other, waiting for my reaction.

I stood up and snatched it from her. 'That's because I found it in my mum's drawer the other night and only just put it out. My dad brought it back from a business trip.'

She snorted. 'A business trip? I thought you said your dad didn't work. You said that's why your mum left him.'

'That's not why she left him, I never said that.' I was getting flustered. 'He used to work. He used to work in distribution for a newspaper company and they sent him on business trips abroad all the time. Conferences and . . . and sales trips, all the time.' I placed the little vase carefully on the table in front of me, wishing Ginger would just go home.

She shrugged and walked towards the window.

'Don't touch—'

Too late, the curtain fell from the rail and landed in a soft heap on the carpet.

'Oh sorry Wendy, I thought you were going to get that fixed?' she said, picking up the curtain and hanging it over the sofa.

She perched herself on the other end of the couch and looked at me from under her thick hair.

'What are you doing?'

I indicated the open book on my lap.

She sighed and started sucking on her locket again.

I put my book down and said, 'Why don't you read that book I gave you? Here, you left it, come on, try it.'

'I'm not a reader Wendy, I told you.'

'You should read though.'

'Why?'

'Why? *Why*? Because it can take you places, let you experience stuff you don't usually do.'

She tutted, and picked at the threads hanging off the curtain. 'But it takes you away from what's real.'

'Exactly,' I said. 'Or do you love your real life so much you can't bear to be parted from it?'

'No,' she whispered. 'But sometimes it's worse to dream then wake up and have it all snatched away than not dream at all.'

I didn't know what to say to that so I opened my book again and carried on reading. A thought struck, and once I had it, I couldn't believe I hadn't realized before. I put down my book and went through to the downstairs bedroom that Mum had slept in at the end. I knelt down in front of the tiny bookcase she'd kept from when I was a child and leafed through the children's books there. I picked up one on telling the time with the jam pandas and took it back through to the living room.

'Ginger,' I said softly.

She didn't reply.

'Ginger, you can't read, can you? No, don't answer, it's fine because I'm going to teach you. I'm going to teach you the way you would have learned at school if you'd had parents who made sure you went to school, right?'

I couldn't see her face under her orange hair, her head was bent almost as low as her lap. But she hadn't marched away, I noticed, so I opened the book and started to sound out the words on the first page. Her head moved a little to the side and I could see she was looking at the page with my finger moving underneath each word.

'I'm not stupid Wendy,' she said in a quiet voice. 'I just wasn't there often enough, and after I'd missed a few weeks and went back, the others could read and there was never any time for the teacher to help me catch up. The less I went, the more I fell behind. I was catching up when I went to high school, there was this teacher, Mrs McHugh, she liked me, used to get me to come in early and go over stuff before the other kids got there. But then, Mum left and everything, and what was the point of school anyway.' She sniffed then held her head up. 'But yeah, if you wanted to teach me, I wouldn't say no. Might even give us something to do, eh?'

I smiled at her then, and thought how great it was to be the one offering help for a change. We spent about an hour going over the book that first day and when I had to go and get ready to catch the train, Ginger asked me if she could take the book home with her.

★

At writers' group that night, Sophie had hardly finished reading out her story when Joseph raised his hand and, before Henry even gave him the go-ahead, he practically shouted, 'You can't describe someone's eyes as almond shaped.'

Sophie's face fell and she dropped her paper onto the table. 'Oh, I didn't know that,' she said, her eyes darting over to Henry and back to the floor.

'Why can't she?' I asked.

Joseph tutted. 'It's racist,' he said smugly, looking over to Henry who was nodding in agreement.

'Why?' I said again.

'Sorry?' he said.

'Why is it racist?'

'Because . . .'

We all waited.

'It's . . . culturally insensitive. It's like describing them as slanty.' He guffawed at this last word and raised his chin in Henry's direction, inviting him to join in.

'She didn't say they were slanty, she said—'

'Wendy,' Joseph said. 'Everyone has to take the critique. You cannot use racist terms to . . .'

I looked at him carefully, taking in his greasy chin and the strands of hair that hung loosely round his face. His eyes were an opaque grey and he had this way of half closing them so that it seemed he was constantly appraising you, and finding you lacking. It struck me that he had probably never helped anyone in his life, definitely not to read, or stop them being lonely, or even just noticing that maybe they were in pain, and needed to talk, or be hugged, or just acknowledged as another human being, with as many hopes, ambitions and needs as he had. I had the sudden thought that if Diane had been there she would have agreed with me, and that gave me courage.

'Shut up Joseph,' I said in a voice that was louder than it needed to be to be heard in that company. 'I thought that was a great story, Sophie, your best yet, in fact. Right, who's next to read?' I said, dismissing Joseph and looking round the group, who were all staring at me open-mouthed.

'I . . . I think it's me,' said Reginald and put on his glasses.

I glanced over at Joseph and saw his face was red and his man bun drooping almost to the nape of his scraggy neck. I thought maybe I'd gone too far but then I felt Muriel's hand on my arm and she winked at me. I glanced at Sophie and she mouthed, 'Thanks,' to me. I nodded and sat back to listen to Reginald's piece, my pen poised to make notes for my critique. Joseph slumped in his seat and Henry avoided my eye.

13

I'M NOT SURE IF it's because he was still annoyed with me the following week but I did notice something funny had happened to Henry's face after he asked me if I wanted to come to the night out. He'd been smiling at first but his smile had dropped to his boots when I said I'd love to go.

He cleared his throat and his hands reached up to smooth his tie.

'Are you sure Wendy? I mean, it'll just be the regulars—'

'I'm a regular,' I said, glancing over at Sophie and Muriel who were both engrossed in rereading the submissions we'd already dealt with.

'I'm a regular,' I repeated. 'I've been coming to every meeting since March and it's July now so that's . . .' I thought about it, 'well, months now. That makes me a regular, doesn't it?'

'Well yes, of course. It's just . . . We won't be talking about writing or . . . stuff. In fact, it'll probably be quite boring. I'm sure you have plenty of other things you'd rather be doing than going out with us.' His upper lip was twitching and he kept glancing over at Joseph, who was glaring back at me.

'Look Wendy,' said Joseph, coming over finally and taking the seat next to me. 'If you want to come, come, okay? Just don't . . .'

'What?' I said.

'Don't act all . . .'

'She'll be fine,' Muriel called over. 'Won't you love?'

Sophie nodded in agreement. 'Of course she will.'

Don't get me wrong, I'm no fool and I knew that Henry and Joseph weren't keen for me to go along on their night out. They knew by now my writing was so superior to theirs that we were basically on different levels. After I'd finished reading my new story a couple of weeks before, Joseph said something about Hilary Mantel having to watch her back and I think even Muriel was jealous because she glared at Joseph and muttered something under her breath about there being no need for it. Sometimes I wondered if the real problem was that I was a woman and better at writing than they were even though they were men and thought they were naturally better at everything. This is something I noticed a lot at work. Oh there's a lot of talk about equal opportunities and women being just as good as men and all that but if they really believed it they'd pay us all the same wouldn't they, and they'd promote us to managers more often than they do. Not that I was yearning to go up to the office. I loved my job, seeing my regulars, helping people out, and they liked me too. I think the other drivers like Big Alex, with his belly hanging over his trousers, and Jim, who's never been seen without a fag hanging out his mouth, and all the rest of those guys were jealous of the relationships I had with my customers. Some people actually waited on my bus you know, let another one run by them so they could come on mine. I could see why that might annoy some of the other drivers, make them jealous, but it's not like I asked anyone to do that, and it's not my fault if I was good at my job.

Ginger wasn't happy with me going to the group night out either. She'd turned up unannounced, which she'd started to do pretty often, sometimes I wasn't sure why as she didn't seem to want to talk to me when she did appear. She sat on my bed as I got ready, locket in her mouth as she pretended to scroll through her phone between sighing and shaking her hair.

'I would have thought once a week with them would be enough. Didn't you say they were a bunch of amateurs?'

'Did I say that?' I stopped brushing my hair for a moment and thought about it. 'Well yeah, maybe they are. But just because they can't write like me and Diane doesn't mean I don't want to go out with them. Muriel's all right, I can talk to her. And Sophie's quite nice too once you get to know her. But anyway, it's important for me to go out and meet people. Everyone needs to do that, you know,' I added, quoting one of Saanvi's usual pieces of advice.

'Hmph,' said Ginger, plucking at the blanket and staring out of my bedroom window. The back of my house looked onto Birkenshaw Sports Barn and the playing field. We could hear the sound of the football thudding against the walls of the barn and the boys swearing and egging each other on as they kicked the ball up and down the pitch in the early evening sunshine.

Ginger turned back to me and said casually, 'I could just wait here for you. Till you get back I mean. If you wanted?'

I looked at her. We'd known each other about three months by then and she'd been staying over more and more. Often she would arrive at odd hours of the day or night, with some story about how she'd mislaid her phone, or it was out of charge, and did I mind if she stayed because there were so many people at hers. It wasn't that I minded exactly, though often she was really grumpy, or so tired all she wanted to do was sleep, and it would have been better to be on my own properly than to be with someone who was no company at all. But I did wonder sometimes what was happening at her own house that she couldn't even sleep there.

'Are you not planning on doing anything yourself tonight?' I asked her, as though it was perfectly routine for either of us to be going out with friends for a night on the town. She harumphed in a way that suggested she knew exactly how disingenuous I was being and heaved herself off the bed.

'So shall I wait here for you then? Maybe we could watch a late-night movie when you get back?'

'Will your uncle not wonder where you are?'

She snorted and said, 'As if. The only one who would miss me at all is wee Nina, and she's not bothered as long as someone feeds her. That's how cats are, they look after themselves. Same as me. We don't need anyone to look after us.' She ran her hand over her hair, and rested it over the bald patch at the front. 'Roddy's coming round tonight.' She spat out his name, the first time I'd heard her mention him for weeks. 'They're planning . . . some business.'

I could understand her not wanting to be there if they were discussing a business deal so I said of course she could stay. I leaned against the wall and watched her back as she flounced downstairs headed for the TV in the living room.

'There's crisps,' I called over my shoulder as I left the house and ran down the hill to the station.

I made the earlier train with seconds to spare.

'Where are you headed?' the ticket guy said to me as he towered over my seat.

'Well, I'm going to Glasgow to meet my friends,' I said. He said nothing so I thought more was required. 'We're in a writers' group together and this is a night out. We're going for a pizza and then—'

'Everyone's a joker,' he said to the schoolkids opposite who were looking at each other and smirking. 'Central or Queen Street love? I haven't got all day.'

I walked round from Central to Buchanan Street, thinking what a beautiful night it was and how lovely the city centre looked in the haze. It's a shame more writers don't write about how Glasgow really is – the pavement cafés and the House of Fraser and the rich folk that come through from the West End and how we were City of Culture once. Most of them only want to talk about the drinking and the fights and the tartan. Not Diane of course, I mean she is Scottish but she doesn't make a career out of it.

Glamorous people passed me, in couples holding hands and fawning over each other, and in small groups of four or five, girls in make-up and high heels and boys pushing each other and showing off for them. I felt a bit of a pang and wished I was like them but then I remembered I was going on a night out too, I was meeting friends in town just like them. I swung my rucksack a bit higher on my shoulder and strode on.

I was about twenty minutes early in the end so I stood outside the door of the pizzeria, engrossed in writing then deleting texts so anyone passing by would think I had loads of friends. Muriel and Sophie arrived first, and after they'd said hello we all went inside.

'You look different,' I said to Sophie who was wearing some sort of ruffled skirt, very short, and heels so high she clicked and clacked her way unsteadily across the wooden floors to the booth Henry had reserved for us.

'Um, thanks?' she said, glancing at Muriel. 'I really haven't made much of an effort, hardly at all.' She plucked her skirt in a this-old-thing gesture and took in my jeans (clean) and my long-sleeved top from Tesco Extra and said, 'Your . . . hair looks nice too.' I had washed it but I was beginning to think I should have made more of an effort, maybe put on some of Mum's old lipstick or a top that showed my shoulders or something, but it was too late now.

'I envy you in a way Wendy,' she said. 'You're so . . . low maintenance.'

'Thanks,' I said, pleased the night was getting off to such a good start.

We ordered some drinks and settled back to wait for the others.

'I love your nails,' said Muriel, taking one of Sophie's hands in hers and admiring her glitter-tipped fingers.

'Thanks,' said Sophie. 'I'm trying to grow them long enough to get a French manicure. That's my life goal.'

I mean, I'm not the most ambitious person in the world but a trip to France to get your nails done seemed a pretty low target.

'Yeah,' she said. 'I want to get a classy French manicure.' She blushed as she added, 'Might even get Henry's attention.'

At least one of those goals was achievable, I thought, and was about to say as much when Muriel said in a loud voice, 'Oh and here's the man himself,' as Henry and Joseph walked in.

Muriel and Sophie were sitting close together on one side of the table so there were an awkward few moments when Henry and Joseph both wanted to sit next to me, and neither wanted to sit at the edge of the table with their back to the room.

'Please Henry, you were here first,' said Joseph, a thin, red ribbon tied round his man bun for the occasion.

'No, not at all Joseph, I insist,' said Henry, indicating with his outstretched palm that Joseph should take the seat next to me.

Joseph did not sit. He cleared his throat then said in a different, very low voice, 'Sit down Henry. I insist.'

Henry looked round the table, at the empty place next to me, then sighing, took it. Finally, we were all sat down.

'Shall we order some wine for the table? Red everyone?'

I usually stayed away from wine, especially red, as I found when I drank it, it made my vagina feel tingly. Not that that was unpleasant, not at all, just I wasn't sure if I wanted to feel that way while I was sitting next to Henry. I didn't say anything though and made up my mind to take only small sips from the glass of Chianti that the waiter placed in front of me.

Muriel waited till the waiter had left then lifted her glass and said, 'Cheers everyone.' We all clinked our glasses together then Henry said, 'So, should we eat?'

'Phew, what's that smell?' I said, as he leaned across me to pick up a menu.

Henry sniffed the air. 'I can't smell anything,' he said then turned his attention back to Joseph. 'So I said to him, well, if you don't know how to differentiate between the objective and the subjective, there's really no point—'

'No, it's really strong,' I insisted. 'It's like a mix of granny flowers and pine air freshener. It's . . .' I sniffed the air next to Henry and said, 'It's you Henry, the smell, it's . . . really quite overpowering.'

He sighed dramatically then said, 'Is it my aftershave Wendy? Is that what you're referring to?'

'Yeah, actually, might be. Phew, that's a lot of poof juice Henry.' I stopped. 'Sorry, I meant, that's just another name for aftershave, it's not . . . I didn't mean—'

'Are we having starters?' said Muriel brightly from across the table.

By the time we were on to desserts, Henry's face was flushed with so much food and wine and the excitement of sitting close to Joseph and having his full attention all evening.

'Of course he is very talented, perhaps the most talented actor of his generation?' I heard him say as I came back from the bar, as Joseph nodded and reached up his hand to fix his man bun. Sophie was sitting directly opposite Henry, her head cocked to one side as she tried to join in the conversation.

'Who?' I said, putting my Diet Coke down next to Henry's strawberry gin. I leaned across him so I could join in the conversation, even though he had been twisting his back away from me all evening. Henry looked at me, and swatted his hand in my direction like I was an annoying fly buzzing around his ear.

I ignored him. 'Who's the most talented actor of his generation?' I said, taking a sip of my Coke.

Henry sighed again and did an exchange of raised eyebrows with Joseph before answering me.

'We were talking about George Clooney. His acting is superb, and of course he's very handsome too.'

I looked pointedly at Sophie as Henry went on and on about George Clooney's big brown eyes and full lips and the way his hair sort of swept back from his forehead as though it had a natural wave rather than being gelled but she was too busy nodding her agreement with Henry to notice.

'Of course he started out playing a doctor on daytime telly,' I said, sitting forwards so Henry would have to acknowledge my contribution to the conversation.

'Who did?'

'George Clooney. That was before the crap films, though I believe the TV series was just as bad.'

Henry's top lip twitched as though he was about to taste something he didn't fancy eating then he said, 'They're not all crap. Some of us rather liked—'

Joseph interrupted. 'None of them are crap. Henry's right – George Clooney is one of the finest actors, and now directors, of his generation.'

'Oh really?' I said. 'Are you telling me you loved *The American*? What about *Solaris*? I mean, did anyone stay awake till the end of that turkey?'

Henry spluttered his pink drink down his front. 'Well, what about *Gravity*, or *The Monuments Men*? Or . . . or . . . *Ocean's Eleven*?'

'Ppff. Or *Ocean's Twenty-Nine*? Or *Sixty-Five*?' I was on safe ground there.

'Well, anyway,' said Muriel, joining in the conversation and throwing me a glance. 'I think we can all agree he's a good-looking guy. Though I am more of a Ralph Fiennes woman myself. Pre-M and before he started changing into Leonard Rossiter obviously.'

'Who?' asked Sophie, her eyes still on Henry.

'Ralph Fiennes. He plays M in the Bond movies. You must have seen *Spectre*?'

'No, I meant who's the Leonard Rossiter guy he looks like now. Was he in *Spectre* too?'

Everyone laughed at poor Sophie. It was all going great, I was really involved in the conversation so I seized my chance to jump in with a brilliant joke. 'Here's one for you,' I said. 'What do George Clooney and Ralph Fiennes have in common?'

Henry and Joseph exchanged glances and Muriel said finally, 'I don't know Wendy, what do George Clooney and Ralph Fiennes have in common?'

I waited a few seconds for full effect then grinned. 'Easy. Henry would do them both.'

'What the hell do you mean by that?' said Joseph, swinging round in his chair to face me, while Henry looked at Joseph, his mouth hanging loose.

'It was supposed to be funny,' I said, wondering again if maybe they just weren't that smart, the boys on the bus had been killing themselves laughing at that joke. I didn't bother explaining it to them. 'But they were both in *Hail, Caesar!* which was not a very good film by the Coen brothers, way below their usual standard, and I really hope not the beginning of the end. Though you might like Laurence Lorenz, Henry?'

'And is Leonard Rossiter in that?' said Sophie.

Henry recovered himself and banged his hand on the table, causing everyone to reach for their drinks to stop them from falling over.

'Order, order,' he said as though we were at a writers' group meeting and not on a night out. 'I think we've heard enough about everyone's opinions on films for one night' – he glared at me – 'why don't we change the subject for a bit?'

Joseph couldn't help himself. 'But if I could just end the

discussion about fine actors? Nobody, and I mean nobody'
– another dirty look at me – 'could deny Clooney's ability to
convey emotion. Remember when he had to give that poor
woman the news that her only son is never going to wake up
from his medically induced coma, and there he was in his white
coat with his chiselled cheeks and his stethoscope round his
neck. I was *crying*.'

'Indeed,' nodded Henry. 'You'd have to be living in a cultural
wasteland not to appreciate some of the fine work by George
Clooney. And Ralph Fiennes,' he added.

'Yeah,' said Joseph. 'You'd have to be a complete weirdo.' He
picked up his pint and drained it without looking at me.

'Total weirdo,' agreed Henry, sitting back and smiling broadly.

I sat very still then and said nothing as memories of that
word 'weirdo' tumbled into my brain from wherever they'd
been lurking, knocking against the sides and thumping their
way back into my consciousness after all I'd done to bury them.

I met Nuala Brennan in our first year at secondary school.
I stuck out like a sore thumb, I was so much taller than
everyone else. Most of the other girls were petite and round,
their hair swinging, all matching with their Nike schoolbags
and Converse trainers, in contrast to my satchel and lace-ups.
People called me String Bean or asked me what the weather
was like up there, and I never got picked to be on any teams
at gym. I don't know how I managed to have no friends at all.
I did have friends at primary school and I don't think I had
any real problems there. At one point the school counsellor did
call a meeting with my mum and told her he thought I could
be autistic, but Mum said why couldn't they just let people be

themselves and why did they have to put a label on everyone. Afterwards, her and my dad fell out because Dad said she was only annoyed that we weren't middle class enough for me to have Asperger's. Mum said I was easily distracted maybe, but fine just as I was and, after all, you couldn't make a silk purse out of a sow's ear. I did spend a lot of time on my own, reading and writing secrets in my diary, but I definitely had friends too. I have vague memories of writing school magazines with a little blonde girl called Patricia, and tumbling over the climbing frame in the playground with freckled twins, whose names I can't remember now. But at the big school there was just a sea of indistinct faces – spotty, pale, pretty – all much smaller and gawping up at me.

Nuala was in my English class. I usually sat next to a stout German girl called Ulrike, with thick ankles and limp hair greased over in a side parting. She was as unpopular as me, I think because of the way she smelled, but that day, we all had to swap seats and work with a partner. Mine was Nuala. Our assignment was to write about our favourite club and it turned out me and Nuala were the only ones in the class who didn't go to any.

'What about gymnastics? Or Guides?' Miss Gray couldn't believe we had no hobbies at all.

'No Miss,' said Nuala. 'Does that mean we can't do this essay Miss?'

'Absolutely not, Nuala Brennan,' said Miss Gray, clicking her tongue and scowling. 'Write about the club you'd most like to attend then,' she said finally, going back to the front of the classroom with a swish of her skirt.

We wrote a short essay about being the only members of

Nick Cave's songwriting club, and were still laughing at our own genius when the bell rang to end the period.

Nuala wasn't one of the popular crowd but she did have her own tribe, girls who, like her, dressed entirely in black or deep purple, with clumpy boots and black braids wound round their wrists, their hair long and straight, hanging over their make-up-whitened faces. I don't know why she let me hang round with them but I was too happy to be part of something bigger than myself to question it.

Of course I never invited Nuala back to our house because of Dad and the way he was by then but I went round to her house a few times. Her mum worked backshifts putting the strawberries on the strawberry flans at the cake factory in Bellshill so there was no one there but me and her, and sometimes Julie or Daz would join us. We sprawled on Nuala's bed, eating ginger snaps and listening to music on her iPod. I kept wondering when they would notice I wasn't like them and throw me out.

One afternoon, it was just me and Nuala at her house. It had been one of those weird Scottish spring days that start off freezing then unexpectedly become so warm, you don't even need your jacket.

Nuala hopped on the bed, throwing off her shoes.

'Are you not going to sit down?' she said, then watched as I slid my schoolbag off my shoulder and perched myself on the edge of her bed.

'What do you want to listen to?'

I shrugged and flattened down my fringe with my hand, wondering if my hair looked okay. I still knew nothing about music though I'd been trying to research the stuff Nuala liked so I could like it too. I didn't recognize the song she put on her iPod, though, sort of melancholy and slow, the singer's nasally voice vaguely familiar.

I asked Nuala who it was but she didn't answer as she jumped off the bed and swished her black blinds down, giving the bedroom a dangerous, nightclub feel.

'That's better,' she said. She looked at me in the gloom. 'Are you not too warm?'

I shrugged as though I was neither warm nor cool, even though I could feel the sweat gathering at the waistband of my skirt. I felt awkward sitting on her bed, her knee almost touching mine but not quite.

'Here, move up a bit,' she said squashing herself back against the pillows and patting the cover next to her.

My knee banged against her thigh.

'Sorry,' I said, drawing back to the edge of the bed.

'It's okay,' she said. 'You just knocked against a bruise. I bruise really easily. Look.' She lifted up her long skirt and pulled her tights down far enough for me to see a small, greenish bruise on the outside of her thigh. Her skin was white and covered in tiny, blonde hairs, unlike the dyed blue-black hair I associated with her.

'Yeah, I bruise all the time,' she was saying. 'But the weird thing is, they're not painful to touch. Here, try it.' She took my hand and pressed it against the bruise on her thigh. I held my breath as I felt the warmth of her skin. We were both looking intently at the bruise.

'I'm going to take these tights off altogether,' she said suddenly, fiddling about under her skirt and throwing her tights off the end of her bed. 'That's better,' she said, wiggling her toes, her toenails painted navy blue. 'Whose idea was it to make us wear those tights? They're so hot and scratchy aren't they?' She paused. 'Why don't you take yours off, it's warm in here.'

'I . . . don't think . . .' My face was flushed and I felt confused. I wanted to take my tights off and be bare-legged and relaxed like her but that desire was mixing with other, stranger desires, to do with Nuala's skin and her wiggling toes and the way strands of her hair were curling at her neck.

She patted the bed next to her again. 'Lie beside me.' Her voice was soft and the music continued to wail in the background.

I got back on the bed and lay facing her.

She stroked my face then rested her hand on my neck for a few seconds, her eyes on mine. The music stopped and I felt her hand reach into my shirt. I drew in a shallow breath but didn't move away as her fingers found the tip of my newly rounded breast, making tiny circles there until the skin wrinkled.

The downstairs door banged open and Nuala and I leapt back from each other. She jumped off the bed while I tried to quickly button up my shirt and tuck it back into my skirt.

Julie's face appeared at Nuala's bedroom door, and her eyes narrowed immediately as she saw us.

'You said just to come up . . .' She trailed off, eyeing me with suspicion. 'Why's your shirt undone Wendy?' She looked over at Nuala's bare legs.

Nuala laughed. 'Because she's a total weirdo, that's why.'

I swung round to look at her for the first time since she'd touched me. 'Me?' I said.

'Yeah, look Wendy, we've not really got anything in common have we?' She turned to Julie. 'She asked me earlier who the Cocteau Twins were.'

Julie laughed, and they both watched as I grabbed my school-bag and fled.

Next day, it started.

I walked into English class first period and the class fell silent. I kept my head down and made for my seat. There was no one else sitting beside Ulrike but there was no other chair at the table either. I looked round the room, and found everyone sitting there, staring at me. A low murmur set off round the room, starting small but increasing in volume. 'Weirdo, weirdo.' I stood in the middle aisle, my bag falling off my shoulder and taking my jacket sleeve with it. I pushed it back up and wondered what to do.

Miss Gray walked into the room.

'Sit down Wendy, please.'

'Miss, there's no seats, my chair's . . . missing.'

Miss Gray looked up, clocked the atmosphere in the room and, like so many teachers, chose not to fight against the rabble.

'Then come and sit next to me Wendy, instead of holding up the whole class. The rest of you, sit down, quiet down and get out your textbooks. Page 127.'

I stayed where I was for a moment then made my way slowly to the front of the class. Miss Gray had pulled out a low stool from under the desk and patted it. I laid my bag down next to the desk and perched myself on the edge of the stool. Tall as I was, I could barely reach the top of the desk to write in my jotter. I was aware of the eyes of the class upon me, a joined intake of breath as they waited for me to complain. I reached into my bag for a pen and began to take notes as the teacher read, my arms stretched and cramping by the end of the lesson.

This continued for the rest of the day, and into the coming weeks. It got so it was accepted that I would not be with the body of the class but, depending on the teacher and how willing or otherwise they were to conspire with the majority, perched at the edge of the teacher's desk, hunched up against the radiator or even, on occasion, just outside the room by the open door.

I stopped going for school dinners, even though I got them free, preferring instead to walk up the street, away from my tormentors for the duration of lunch. Even then, as I wandered up Muir Street, or along Cadzow Bridge, I could hear the whispers of 'Weirdo' and 'State of that' streaking behind me in the wind.

Of course I suspected the whole campaign had been started by Nuala but she was always careful to be at the back of the action, rather than fronting it. Only once when Daz spat on a chair in Modern Studies, and pushed my hand into the still warm bubbling phlegm, did she step forwards and say, 'For Christ's sake Daz,' and bite her lip as she looked at me.

Mum came into my bedroom one Saturday morning and told me to get dressed, she was taking me to Tunnock's just the two of us.

'Are you not working?' I said, because she always worked on a Saturday, I didn't usually see her at all till after six.

'Not today,' she said. 'Come on, let's treat ourselves to tea and a scone.'

The café was quiet and we took a table at the back. Mum sat opposite me and asked me what was wrong, was something happening at school because I wasn't myself. She waved a chapped hand at me as she spoke. She used her hands a lot, even when she wasn't shouting or angry. I remember that used to annoy me but now I'm not sure why.

I looked into my mug of tea then across at Mum's face, the irises of her eyes surely paler than they should be, and her eyelids pink at the corners. She looked tired and there was a shiny patch of red skin across her nose. There was a stripe of grey at each side of her parting, and the odd crinkly hair sparkled as the overhead strip light caught it.

I thought about telling her what had happened that Friday. How everyone had been on their phones, passing them around in small groups, smirking and digging each other in the ribs when I passed. At lunchtime, one of the third years I didn't even know had sneaked up behind me and asked me if it was true I sucked women's tits.

'Leave me alone,' I said, focusing on zipping up my schoolbag, and trying to walk on.

The boy stood in front of me, his feet placed wide apart and his hands on his hips.

'I heard it was. In fact, I know it's true because there's proof.'

He grabbed me by the shoulder – he was slightly shorter than me I noticed and I considered pushing him out of the way, but he could probably run faster than me, and I knew he was strong because his grip was tight on my upper arm. He thrust a phone directly under my eyeline.

It took me a moment to process what I was seeing. The image seemed to be of my face but most of it was hidden under a pillow of pink flesh, I couldn't make out what it was. I bent my head to the side to get a better view and realized, too late, it was my picture Photoshopped to make it look like there was a huge breast in my mouth. The word 'lezzer' was flashing in red across the screen.

I pushed the phone away and told the boy to get lost.

He laughed. 'Lezzer. Weirdo,' was his parting shot as he ran off to rejoin his friends, who were standing waiting for him outside the deli on the corner.

I couldn't tell Mum that even though she was waiting for an answer, stirring more sugar into her tea, her forehead wrinkled with concern.

'It's nothing Mum,' I said. 'Just school stuff.'

She waited till the woman in the headscarf and bulky, red coat had scraped past with her shopping trolley then she leaned across the table so her face was close to mine. Her Cinnabar made me want to sneeze. 'I'm going to tell you something Wendy,' she said. 'People don't like it when girls are a bit different because then they can't fit them into the only image they have for them.' She looked at my hand resting on the table and I prayed silently that she wouldn't try and hold it in public. She was still talking. 'But it's important to always be yourself whether they like it or not because that's the best person you can be. It's a good thing to be weird – it doesn't mean you're autistic, or on the spectrum, or any of those other labels they're constantly throwing about these days – it just means you're not kowtowing to anybody else's version of what it means to be a woman, always remember that.'

I didn't think she was right about that but I nodded and finished my teacake. I've been thinking a lot recently about what she said that day, and sometimes I wonder how things would have been if Mum hadn't got sick, and also if I'd listened a bit more to the things she'd tried to teach me. I think if I'd told Mum about Nuala and Julie and all the rest, she would've told me to ignore them and rise above it, and that I would have the last laugh. She was like Ginger that way – she thought everyone got what they deserved in the end.

★

'All right Wendy? You're miles away there,' said Muriel, snapping me out of my daydream and replacing the memory of Nuala Brennan's half formed face with her own sympathetic one. I sighed in relief as I remembered I wasn't twelve any more but an adult with friends on a night out. 'Where are the others?' I said, as only me and Muriel remained at the booth and Henry, Joseph and Sophie were nowhere to be seen.

'Sophie's in the ladies, and Henry followed Joseph to the bar to help him carry back some more drinks. Listen, Wendy, don't mind them. They don't mean to be nasty, it's just, that's the way young men are sometimes, you know?'

I looked at her and assured her no one had offended me and to please excuse me, I was going to the toilet myself. She looked like she was about to say something more then thought better of it and stopped herself so I got up.

I made my way downstairs to the ladies and spotted Joseph and Henry outside the gents. Joseph's face was brick-red and he was jabbing a finger in Henry's chest.

'I'm not like you, do you hear me? Nothing. Like. You.' Each word a jab in the chest. 'So keep your filthy suggestions to yourself,' he sneered, before swinging his jacket over his shoulder and taking the steps out of the restaurant two at a time.

'Are you all right Henry?' I said, because even though we'd never got on, I couldn't bear to see him looking so dejected.

Henry jumped when he realized I'd been watching him and Joseph. His face contorted into a nastier version of itself and he hissed, 'Why don't you just fuck off, weirdo, and do whatever the hell you usually do on a Saturday night?'

He pushed past me and made his way up the stairs and out of the restaurant.

I stood with my back against the wall for a few minutes, trying to get my breath and looking round to check no one had heard what he'd called me. I shook my head and decided I'd had enough. Going out and meeting people was all very well but I'd done what Saanvi had advised and what a waste of time that had turned out to be. If the choice was between going out with a bunch of talentless wannabe writers or not going out at all, well . . .

Muriel and Sophie insisted on walking me home from the train station, and it turned out Muriel's house was only two streets away from mine. We stopped off for chips on the way. I bought some chicken pakora for Ginger and parted company with Muriel and Sophie at my front gate.

'Sure you'll be all right now then?' said Muriel as she and Sophie turned to leave.

'Fine Muriel,' I said. 'Thanks for walking me home.' I watched them stagger along the street to Muriel's, Sophie propped up on the older woman's shoulder then, as an afterthought, shouted after them, 'Thanks for inviting me. See you next week.' Muriel raised her hand in goodbye and they disappeared out of view.

My house was in darkness and I knew when I opened the front door there was no one there. I called up the stairs anyway, 'Ginger? Ginger are you upstairs?' I walked through the house to check if she was sitting out in the back garden, which she liked to do, sometimes till late into the night. She said she loved how the garden was so quiet you could hear the motorway in the distance roaring like a waterfall. But the garden was empty. I clicked the door shut, locked it, and ate the cold pakora myself, the familiar silence of my house echoing around me.

14

I DIDN'T SEE OR HEAR from Ginger for a couple of days after the night out so I spent all my time trying to improve my writing. Diane was such an inspiration and gave me so much support, she had this way of tweeting exactly what I needed to hear.

Stories are how we learn about ourselves. And also how we learn about the world around us. #WomenWriting

I thought that was brilliant. I had a lot to learn, about myself and especially about the world, so I was trying to spend at least an hour a day on my new story. You'd be amazed how hard it is to do that once you've started making friends and joining clubs.

Ginger showed up unannounced when I was leaving the house to start an early shift. I locked the front door and, when I turned round, there she was, sheltering under the tree in my garden. Scotland was doing its own version of July weather and the whole garden was sodden. Ginger stood there shivering in the drizzle, her jumper pasted onto her shoulders, and her hair flashing red and dripping onto her face.

'Surprise?' she said but like 'Is it okay for me to be here?' rather than the way people say it at surprise birthday parties.

I knew her well enough by then to know that I had to respond with a smile or else she would take the huff and run off.

'It's awful early,' I said. 'What are you doing out here in the rain?' Then I added quickly, 'You should have come into the house when you've no jacket.' I was getting good at this people stuff, Saanvi would have been proud of me.

'My phone's out of charge again but, anyway, I wasn't sure if you'd be up yet. I thought I'd wait till you opened your curtains.' She sniffed and wiped the back of her hand across her face. 'But then I remembered you don't open your curtains in case they fall off the shoogly pole so I just waited till you came out the house.'

She was right, I had to sort those curtains.

'I'm working today,' I said, indicating my dark grey trousers and regulation windcheater jacket.

'Can I ride with you?' She said it without looking at me, as though she wasn't bothered if I said yes or no.

'No problem,' I said. 'I'm on the 255 so wait at the first bus stop and I'll pick you up, okay?'

Her face lit up momentarily then she remembered she wasn't bothered either way and said, 'Fine, see you outside Naf's,' and walked off, her shoulders still at her ears against the downpour, and her gangly legs trembling.

It was mid-week and business wasn't bad, considering the rain. Ginger was sitting diagonally behind me on the front seat, her legs curled up underneath her. Her teeth were still chattering and I told her to take off her jumper and hang it on the back of her seat so it would dry out but she said she only had a T-shirt underneath so she couldn't. No wonder she was cold. I could smell the damp on her clothes and in her hair as I drove.

I picked up the first group of regulars at the bus bay, they were heading up to their seniors' dance club at the old library.

'How you doing Myra? Alright Irish Mary? Morning Terry,' I said as they filed past me, flashing their free bus passes.

'Not so bad love. Could do without this weather though, eh? Flaming July, I don't think.'

'We'll not melt Myra, get yourself on.'

'Oh, you've your wee helper with you today, that's nice.'

I waited till they'd got themselves settled in their usual seats at the front, their plastic bags with their slippers, and sodden umbrellas resting at their feet. I glanced at Ginger in the mirror and saw that her eyes were already heavy and drooping. I knew she'd be asleep before too long.

I picked up Mad Sadie outside The Flying Tumbler, she was already crying and apologizing at half ten in the morning.

'It's only the vodka doll,' she breathed at me, her glasses fogged and her hair flat to her head on one side but sticking up like hedgehog spines on the other. She staggered up to the back of the bus, her huge hips bouncing off Irish Mary who tutted as she passed by.

'God's sake, the state of her. Drunk as a monkey and not even lunchtime yet.'

'Aw leave her be Mary, she's not doing you any harm.'

I pulled away again, flashing the guy in the Ford Focus behind me who let me out on the top road.

A couple of stops later and I'd picked up the old lady in tweed who gets the bus every Tuesday to go and play chess with her sister. The bus went silent for a bit as two shy nuns from St Clare's got on and sat in silence, their heads bowed till they got off again at the chapel house, and the bus breathed a communal sigh of relief.

The rain was lashing off the windows by then, the bus looked like a steamie and the chatter levels had risen to match. Ginger was asleep, her head resting against the window so that her face was squashed.

'Are you all going to Marjory's on Friday?' asked Irish Mary.

'Yeah. Our Sandra's not going but our Debbie is, and I spoke to your Agnes at the gala day, she told me her lot were all going, and your cousin Sylvia's going too. What are you wearing?'

'Oh, I'll be wearing my green again. No point in buying anything new. Why do you ask – are you going to be done up like a dish of fish?'

'Not me,' said Myra. 'I'm just wearing whatever I feel comfy in. Probably my sparkly top, you know the one I had on for St Patrick's Day? You know what I'm like – with this chest and these arms, if I'm not careful, I end up looking like a wrestler.' She jigged up her enormous bosoms with her forearm and sniffed.

'You're all woman right enough, Myra,' said Terry.

'Jealous,' said Myra, and they all laughed.

I drew up at the next stop, and lowered the platform to let on two young mums and their prams.

'Thanks very much, driver,' said the first one, tall and lean like a stick of celery, and not much more than a kid herself.

'Come on Tracey,' she shouted back at her pal, 'the bus'll be leaving without you on it.'

I waited as she manoeuvred the buggy up the bus, laden with plastic shopping bags and a huge wooden sword poking out the back.

'Come on you wee bugger, I told you there was no time for that,' screamed the second girl, face red, and wet with either rain or sweat, as she held her hand out for her grubby toddler, who came running from the patch of dirt at the side of the bus stop.

'I told you, didn't I? That's it, no more Fruit Shoot for you. Ever,' she added, her finger pointed in the boy's face.

The boy started crying, hot, dirty tears at the injustice of being dragged away from his game, compounded by the threat from his mother. Somehow, his pudgy baby brother managed to keep sleeping through the noise in his buggy. So did Ginger.

Another tut from Irish Mary as the pram bashed her leg and the girl gave her a look that dared her to say anything.

'Come on Charlton, keep moving up the bus, son.'

I set off again, looking up at the sky towards Bellshill, where the cloud seemed to be lifting. The next stop was just outside the Spar and I slowed down but there was no one standing there. I looked up the bus to check no one was wanting off either and I was just about to speed up again when the girl ran out of the shop, spotted me, and rapped on the door for me to open up.

'Hurry up,' she was mouthing at me through the glass, though I couldn't have opened the door any faster.

'All right,' I said. 'What's your hurry?'

'The security guard's after me but I didn't do anything honest to God I didn't. Please just drive away quick and he'll not see me.'

'What?' I said. 'Look, I'm not wanting any trouble—'

'Please. Pleeeeeaaase. Just drive, I promise you, I didn't steal anything, honest to God.'

Ginger was roused from her sleep by the shouting and said to me, 'Just drive for God's sake Wendy.'

I looked at her, then back at the girl who'd just got on, my nose twitching at the smell of drink and cheap soap coming off her. She had grainy blue initials and a love heart tattooed onto the knuckles of her left hand. She wasn't much older than Ginger.

I was about to tell her to go back into the shop and explain they'd made a mistake when she spotted the security guy running out of the shop, the chubby manager in his shiny suit following on close behind. She panicked.

'Right, I didn't want to do this but . . . right, I'm going to have to command you. Drive away now.' She looked at me, eyebrows in her hair and mouth gaping in a giant O. 'I haven't stolen anything but they won't believe me. Drive,' she said again. 'Please.'

I glanced into the rearview mirror and saw the two men eye the bus, and do a double take when they saw her standing in the doorway.

'That's her, quick,' cried the older one.

I pushed the bus into first gear and started to drive, keeping my eye on the girl who was wobbling near the door as the bus picked up speed.

'What are you supposed to have stolen?' Ginger said to her, patting the seat beside her so the girl could sit down.

'Blackcurrant and liquorice out the pick-n-mix,' she said.

'What? You're holding up a bus for the sake of a quarter pound of liquorice and black?' called Irish Mary from behind me.

'Ah but I didn't take them,' said the girl. 'I mean, who would? They're bogging,' she said to Ginger, who nodded and said, 'Who's going to steal blackcurrant sweets when there's caramel cups and Everton mints on offer?'

'But you didn't steal anything though, did you?' I said,

glancing back at her to see if there was any loot concealed about her person.

'No, no I didn't, not me. I'm honest as the day's long, too honest for my own good sometimes, folk take advantage . . .'

'Right, sit where you are then and we'll get you out the way.' I glanced in my mirror again and saw the two men pushing past a couple of schoolkids and knocking over a bin in their rush to catch up with the hot felon on my bus.

She waved at them through the window, a cheeky wave and a thumbs up sign, guaranteed to make their blood boil. They gave chase, following the bus right down the hill.

'What did you do that for?' I shouted up the bus to her.

She shrugged. 'Serves them right. Those pigs are always after the likes of us am I right?' She addressed the two young mums sitting a few rows behind her.

'You're not wrong doll. Last week, they accused my wee Charlton here of nicking a Ben 10 toy from Rani's in the arcade. He might not be an angel I said but he'd never nick anything.' She sniffed. 'Course his dad said later I should have taken it right back, as soon as I found it, but he never knew it was stealing did he? Anyway, the prices they charge in that arcade, it was hardly stealing at all, more like payback. Here, have a cheesy Quaver.'

As she offered the girl her crisps, I took the corner by the library a bit tight and the bus swerved, causing the girl to fall sideways across the aisle into the woman in tweed.

'Sorry missus,' she said as she straightened up.

'It is you isn't it, Theresa McGonigle?' said the old woman, steadying the girl at her side.

'It is, aw shit Miss Harker, is that you? I can't believe you're still alive.'

'Very much alive Theresa, and still waiting on that last piece of homework you never bothered to hand in. What sort of state is this you've got yourself into?'

'Aw Miss, I didn't do it, honest!'

'Is that the same not doing it as when you didn't steal the stapler from my desk and use it to staple poor wee Willie Donaldson's homework to the back wall? Or the same not doing as it as when you didn't take Noreen McPhilemy's brand new iPod-thingummyjig and accidentally smash the screen?'

The girl looked sheepish. 'Aw Miss, that was a long time ago, I've changed. I didn't steal those sweets, honest.'

Suddenly, Irish Mary shouted from the front of the bus. 'You'll need to hurry up Wendy, they're catching us.'

I looked in my mirror and saw the security guard refusing to give up as he weaved in and out the traffic queuing behind the bus, his hair plastered to his head and the shoulders of his shirt sopping.

'What a tosser, sorry Miss Harker,' said the girl, dipping her head so she could see the guard's progress out the window. 'Can this bus not go any faster?' she shouted to me.

We lost them just before the big Tesco in Bellshill and the girl got off at the roundabout in front of the school. 'Thanks very much ladies,' she said as she got up to leave. 'We've got to stick together, they're a bunch of tossers, men, aren't they? 'Scuse my French Miss Harker but they are aren't they?'

Miss Harker said nothing but smiled at the girl as she got off the bus. Just as I was about to shut the door and breathe a sigh of relief, she turned round again and pulled a large plastic bag from under her sweatshirt.

'Here,' she said, handing me the bag of blackcurrant and

liquorice. 'Share these between you. You lot deserve them more than me, honest to God you do.'

We were still laughing by the time I dropped Ginger off at the top of Viewpark so she could walk down the hill to her house.

'Is it always as exciting as that on your bus Wendy?' she said, her face flushed with excitement and her voice hoarse after all the laughing with Irish Mary and the others at the girl's cheek.

'Yeah,' I said. 'Yeah, being a bus driver's a brilliant job.'

'Do you want to go down to the park later? After you've signed off your shift?'

I shook my head. I felt really proud I'd been able to give Ginger such a great day that she didn't want it to end but I had something else I needed to do after work. Something far too important to give up for a mooch round the park.

''S'alright,' she said, lifting her locket to her mouth. 'I'll go home and spend some time with wee Nina. Cats are always there for you when you need company.' She sniffed.

'I'll see you tomorrow though,' I shouted after her so she wouldn't think I didn't want to spend time with her. 'I'll bring that new book I got from the library for you and we can practise some reading if you like?' She raised her hand as she headed down the hill but didn't turn round.

The evening was muggy and the grass on the hill next to the train station smelled musky sweet after the rain. Diane's house looked peaceful, the garden radiant, even in the dimming light, after its day-long watering. I spread out my mum's old picnic blanket and took up my watch.

I sat there for around an hour, admiring Diane's roses and

her stripey, well maintained lawn, and waited for inspiration to strike. My eyes might occasionally have strayed up to the house itself, scanning for movement behind the curtains, but mostly I was enjoying the view and the fresh air, and thinking about writing, as Diane had advised. I was about to pack up and go home when the front door opened a little. I strained forwards to see who would come out – and it was Diane! She was wearing her red mac over a white shirt, with her beautiful pink scarf with the poppies floating behind her. She called back to someone in the house – I would fret about who was in the house with her later – before stepping onto the path. She was carrying an adorable pink and red striped umbrella which she swung to the sky then down again as she walked. I drew a deep breath and her name escaped from my lips unbidden, as she got into her car. I was distracted by movement inside the house, just a shadow moving in the gloom but enough to make me miss seeing which direction Diane drove off in. No matter, I thought, as I folded up Mum's blanket, I'd seen Diane, and my heart was full as I headed back up the road. It had been a good day.

15

MY BOSS AT THE depot called me into his office before I clocked on the following Monday.

'The thing is Wendy, we have to take such complaints seriously, and look into each one carefully. Do you understand?'

I nodded, looking round Mr Laverty's office, eyeing the calendar with a half dressed model staring down at me from the wall behind his desk. Miss July was called Kelli – a spelling mistake surely – and she enjoyed boxercise, water aerobics and long walks on the beach. It certainly kept her trim.

'Wendy?'

'Sorry,' I said, turning to face him again.

'You're entitled to have union representation, you know that don't you?'

'I don't need anyone else to speak for me,' I said, leaning forwards so that my face was closer to the manager's own bristled and pock-marked face. He really was an incredibly hairy man. Hirsute, I'd have called him if I'd been putting him in one of my stories. Like most Scots, summer didn't suit him and he was having to mop the sweat off his forehead and upper lip with his hanky as he spoke. His tie was loosened and the words

'Uddingston and Bothwell Golf Club' were hanging down somewhere near his belly.

He coughed then shuffled his chair back a little.

'Look Wendy, you've been back with us for a few months now and I've been really happy to see how you've got over . . . what happened with your mum and everything. You've been an excellent employee while you've been with us.'

'Passengers love travelling on my bus,' I said. 'I talk to them, ask them where they're going, how they are. Sometimes nobody else talks to them all day, that can happen with some people, and I should know.'

Mr Laverty coughed again, and glanced out of the window at the pigeons pecking at the remains of the drivers' elevenses in the yard outside. The midday sun was directly in his face, the damp stain where his shirt met his waistband spreading as he spoke.

'I know that Wendy, and that's why I'm only giving you a verbal warning this time but please,' he leaned his elbows on his desk and lowered his bushy brows. 'Please do not allow your friends, whoever they may be, to ride along with you on your shift. You're working Wendy, not having days out with your pals, understand?'

I nodded, and waited.

'That's all Wendy, you can go and pick up your bus now.'

I scraped my chair back and made for the door.

'Wendy?' he called after me.

'Yes?'

'You seem . . . erm, much better now. Is everything okay? At home and so forth?' He was looking at his desk as he spoke.

I thought about it for a few minutes then answered honestly that yes, everything was going well for me.

'That's good Wendy. I know it's not been easy for you at home since your mum died.'

He was right in a way, but things hadn't been easy at home for a long time before that.

'It'll be fine Wendy. Honestly, it will. Everything will work out for the best.' Mum carried on folding my jumpers and school shirts and placing them neatly in one of the three suitcases sitting on the bed they'd shared.

'But what about Dad?' I said, biting my thumbnail and watching the fold, fold, twist of the clothes as they landed in the case.

'What about him?' she replied curtly, snapping down the lid of the case and easing it onto the bedroom floor. She stopped what she was doing for a moment then brought her face level with mine and said, 'The truth is Wendy, the way he's been recently, he probably won't even notice we're gone.' She smoothed down her skirt and lifted the second case onto the bed, ready to begin the whole folding and filling process again.

The taxi driver heaved the last of the suitcases into the boot of his car and we drove away from the house we'd lived in for the whole of my twelve years. I didn't get to say goodbye to Dad before we left because he hadn't come home yet.

The new house had been – still was – cold, and there was something subterranean about the dampness and the gloom. It was still in Birkenshaw but further into the scheme and closer to Viewpark.

Mum stood in the kitchen, taking in the cracked tiles behind the cooker and the slow spreading darkened patches creeping along the skirting boards.

'Not what we're used to Wendy but we'll make it work. Now,

let's get a bit of Simon and Garfunkel on, roll up our sleeves and get to work.'

Even though we'd only moved a few streets across the scheme, the council's arbitrary boundary lines meant I had to change school and I started my new school about a week later. I was glad about that at least, thought a new start and getting away from Nuala and the rest of them would help me turn things round. I'd forgotten I couldn't leave myself behind though and they didn't take to me at my new school either. They soon realized I wasn't the same as them and, like Mum said, people don't like that. I don't know how it happened, or what I did, but it seemed that just trying hard not to be noticed was enough to get me noticed and once Louise Valente and her gang of popular girls started calling me Weirdo, I knew it was all over.

The real trouble started when Mikey Sanderson asked me out. I think he did anyway. I hadn't paid much notice to him standing at the bus stop every day after school. I knew him a bit from being in the same registration class when I'd first started at the new school but that was before he became Mikey and started wearing black leather and badges and stuff, he'd still been plain Michael then. But he started creeping closer and closer, smiling at me when I glanced in his direction, before finally standing right next to me and talking about school stuff. One afternoon, he asked me what I was doing on Friday night. I told him either maths or English but probably English since I was a bit behind with that. He gave me a funny look so I thought maybe he'd forgotten to do his. Or maybe he wanted to copy mine. I narrowed my eyes and waited. He sort of coughed then said no, he was asking me out with him.

'What – on a date?'

'Well, yeah, I suppose.'

I looked around then to see if his pals were watching, if they'd put him up to it as a sort of dare or something. There was no one at the bus stop except us and a bunch of first years bashing each other over the head with their badminton racquets.

Mikey's face looked hot as he waited for me to answer.

'Well, no,' I said. 'I don't think so,' and opened my bag to take out my book, hoping he'd go away. He carried on standing next to me but, when the bus arrived, he walked past where I was sitting and took a seat at the very back.

The next day after school he came over again. He wasn't smiling when he said, 'Are you one of those girls who just says no to everyone who asks you out, or what?'

I didn't know what to say, as nobody had ever asked me out before, so I took my book out again and stared very hard at the words dancing along the page. A couple of the younger boys spotted us and sidled over, laughing and saying, 'Mikey fancies the weirdo,' banging into one another and egging each other on.

'I said no,' I shouted, without thinking, desperate to be left alone to wait on my bus.

Mikey was startled, his cheeks fired up and he tossed his bag over his shoulder. 'As if,' he called out to the boys, then turning to me, hissed, 'Weirdo,' as he stalked off.

At the end of that week, I was doing my usual circuit round the edge of the playground and eating my crisps, when Louise Valente's sidekick, Ruth, appeared at my shoulder. I wiped my hands down my skirt and said hello, and waited. She told me there was a party at hers on Saturday night and I should come.

'Why?' I said, narrowing my eyes as I knew she and her friends despised me.

'Look Wendy, do you want to come out and have a bit of fun or don't you?' she said, turning on her heel, and heading back to Louise and the others, with a flick of her hair.

I wasn't sure that I did want to go out and have fun with those girls but it felt more like a command than an invitation. Also, something in me wanted to be part of their gang, however much I told myself I despised them. I needed some sort of connection, something that I could be part of. I was never going to say no.

On Saturday, I knocked on Ruth's door, already feeling out of place in an avenue full of big houses, with driveways as long as our street, and each housing at least two cars. I was relieved to see Ruth's house was not as imposing as those on the opposite side of the street. It was tall and narrow, made of blond sandstone, but I was to discover when I went in that the house was like a Tardis, far larger inside than it appeared from the street, its long narrow hallways stretching as far back as I could see, its high ceilings making the rooms spacious and echoey. From outside, I could see two large balconies overhanging the street. I leaned back to try and make out what looked like a statue or something on one of the balconies when I heard footsteps inside approaching the door. I tucked my warm plaid shirt further into my jeans and bit my lip as I waited for the door to be opened.

I was surprised to see loads of people from school already gathered there, not just our year but some sixth years too, who wouldn't usually be seen dead hanging out with third years like us. They were all standing in a semicircle in Ruth's living room as though anticipating a show. Whether because they were all whispering or because no one was meeting my eye, I don't know, but I could feel the atmosphere was charged with hostility and I stumbled a bit as I made my way into the room. I wished I hadn't come but then I saw a girl I'd been in the choir with in second year, who'd been quite friendly, and I made my way over to where she was standing. Suddenly the air changed as Mikey, black clad and cool, made his entrance. He made straight for Louise and placed his arm loosely round her shoulders. I watched as Louise pushed some of Mikey's hair back from his forehead tenderly.

Mikey stared at me. 'Who invited Weirdo?' he said, addressing the crowd while stroking Louise's neck and pulling gently on the silver charm dangling from her ear.

Everyone else laughed nervously, looking over to see my reaction. I was wondering whether to just leave straight away but that seemed more embarrassing than staying, so I remained rooted to the spot.

Mikey moved slowly to the balcony and drew back the heavy, velvet curtain to reveal a tower of around half a dozen different types of chairs loosely stacked this way and that, balanced on top of a small glass table. He turned back to everyone waiting inside and said, 'What do you think – can Weirdo stay if she completes this one small dare?'

Louise put her hand to her throat and giggled. 'Why do you want her to stay?'

Mikey ignored her and turned back to me. 'Well?'

'I don't understand. Do you want me to lift the chairs, or . . . ?'

Mikey laughed, and indicated that I should come and join him on the balcony.

'No, it's simpler than that Weirdo. All you have to do is climb to the top chair and sit on it. Prove yourself so to speak, then we can get this party started. That's it.'

'That's it?' I said, knocking against the chairs as I stepped round them and looked up. 'They don't seem that stable. I don't think . . .'

Mikey shrugged. 'Up to you Weirdo. Entirely up to you.'

I scanned the room in panic. Ruth was smirking, Louise was looking at me with a look I couldn't interpret but it certainly didn't seem friendly, and everyone else in the room appeared to have stopped breathing as they watched the drama unfold. I pulled my already damp checked shirt away from my skin and rubbed the wet patch on my top lip with my index finger. I didn't want to be at the party any longer but I couldn't walk away from a dare and have everybody know about it.

'I'll do it,' I said. The others watched as I placed my hand on the wooden chair leg closest to me. The rest of the stack quivered against my touch. I started to climb. I reached the seat of the first chair and already the chairs higher up were trembling. As I took a breath and considered my next move, Mikey started to clap his hands, motioning to the others to join him as they chanted, 'Climb, climb, climb,' as one mocking voice. I wiped my lip again then climbed another chair. I could feel the sweat gathering beneath my arms, pooling around my armpits and back. I tried counting backwards to keep myself steady but I couldn't concentrate enough on the numbers. I told myself it would soon be over, I could do this. I was nearly at the top, but I sensed the chairs were in real danger of toppling. As I raised one arm, panting with the effort to stay balanced, I could see two of the prettiest girls nearest to me, pointing at the white skin showing between my shirt and jeans. One was laughing but the other, a cool girl caked in make-up and hair flowing down her back like she was going to a music festival, was frowning at my ridiculous appearance. Flushing deeply, I reached down to tug at my shirt and the chairs lurched dangerously.

'That's enough,' shouted Louise suddenly. 'Let her come down now.'

Mikey's face darkened with anger at Louise's attempt to save me. He started to clap louder. 'To the top was the deal,' he shouted, marching in front of the others, a tyrant exerting his authority over the crowd, making sure they carried on clapping and jeering.

I grunted as I climbed to the topmost chair, breathing in sharply as I swayed precariously against the slippery leg of a formal dining room chair. Oblivious now to the clapping and the taunts inside the room, I was aware instead of the braying car radios from the street below and the lights glowing from the warm, safe houses opposite. Deeper inside my head, I thought I could hear the swishing of the wind through the trees outside.

'That's far enough Wendy,' cried Louise, and this time, she walked towards me to help me down. Mikey grabbed her roughly by the arm to pull her back and she screamed.

'Who do you think you are, telling me when it's enough?' he shouted at her.

Something snapped in me and I half climbed, half fell back down the stack of chairs to the floor. I lay there in a heap for a moment while the shouting and clapping and mayhem went on around me, then I got up and fled from the party. I heard later that Mikey had slapped Louise hard across her face and her parents were thinking about bringing charges. The party ended as soon as I left.

But the most surprising thing about the whole episode was that that Sunday, Louise came round to my house. I couldn't work out why she looked so different to her usual self, the popular girl at school, then I realized it was because she wasn't wearing her usual ten tons of thick foundation and masses of gooey, shiny lipstick. There was a flicker of a bruise on her right cheek as she turned to face me but otherwise her naked skin shone with beauty, there were no dark shadows like mine under her eyes and her lips looked soft and damp. I dragged my eyes away from her lips and focused on her calm blue eyes while she was talking. She was asking if I was okay. 'After last night.'

I stared at her.

'At the party I mean? I'm . . . we're all sorry about making you do that, climb those chairs. It was dangerous, I don't know what Mikey was thinking. He can be . . .' She shrugged and raised her hands in the air.

'Was it his idea then?' I asked, though I already knew the answer.

She nodded and looked away into the street, avoiding my eye. Then she turned back and said in an urgent, low voice, 'I'm not like them. I just . . . it's important to me that you know that.'

Before I could respond, she'd turned away and started walking back down our path.

'Louise,' I shouted after her.

She turned at the gate.

'I'm not like them either,' I said.

'I'm sorry I called you, you know . . .' She dug her toe into the grass verge. 'Weirdo. I'm sorry I called you that.' She gave me a half smile and hurried away.

Louise didn't speak to me, or even acknowledge me at school on Monday, but to my astonishment, she was waiting for me at the bus stop after school.

'Fancy a Costa?' she said, her lip gloss gleaming.

I looked around to see if Ruth or Mikey were waiting in the wings, ready to laugh at me if I said yes, but it was just Louise, asking me to spend time with her. We went to Costa after school quite a few times after that and I'd watch as she took the froth off her cappuccino with the back of her spoon, and licked the sugar from her shortbread before crumbling it in her mouth. She'd ask me about my day and tell me how she hated her wee brother and how she was going to be a beauty therapist when she left school and what was I going to be and, once, when we were sheltering from the rain under her oversized North Face jacket, she left me breathless as she leaned in and kissed me, full on the lips. She never spoke to me again after that but it didn't matter. Louise made me realize why I hadn't wanted to go out with someone like Mikey; it was because I wanted to go out with someone like Louise instead.

Mr Laverty cleared his throat noisily, breaking into my day-dream about Louise and reminding me I was in the middle of a conversation with my boss. He started speaking again, his cheeks red underneath his morning shadow, his dark beard already threatening a reappearance, and his eyes not meeting mine.

'So all I'm saying is that no one can help what happens to them when they're growing up Wendy, you can't choose your family. But you can choose not to be affected by it when you're an adult.' He coughed and stood up. 'Anyway, listen to me, what do I know? Go and pick up your bus Wendy, you're very good with the passengers, I know that.'

'Thanks,' I said. He really was a nice man and I appreciated him taking the time to talk to me. I knew he meant well, even though he didn't know what he was talking about.

Not like Diane. She knew exactly what she was talking about. She writes brilliantly about unhappy childhoods in *This Girl's Life*. She calls it fiction and that's fine, I understand that, I really do, but reading that book helped me so much. It made me understand that I wasn't the only one who felt lonely and different all through school, and that I could even use some of my experiences in my writing. I'm not sure yet whether I'll follow Diane's example and pretend it's fiction, we'll see.

I said goodbye to Mr Laverty and left the office, already planning my visit to the hill opposite Diane's beautiful garden after my shift.

16

THE WEEK HADN'T IMPROVED any by Wednesday and I wasn't looking forward to Saanvi's visit. I put her tea down on one of my new coasters, and said, 'Sorry there's no milk. I meant to go shopping but . . . I forgot.' I sat down opposite her, crossed my arms and pressed my chin down against my chest.

'Black tea's fine, thanks,' Saanvi said, smiling. She took her folder and pen from her bag and said, 'How's your week been? What's been happening?'

I shrugged, and looked at the carpet.

After a pause, she said, 'The house is looking better. With your new coasters, and I don't think that rug was there last time I came?' She indicated my mum's old plum-coloured rug which I'd rescued from where I'd dumped it under her bed. It was a bit mouldy but surprisingly soft and I'd been happy with it when I unrolled it.

I bit the side of my lip and said nothing.

Saanvi tutted and said, 'Look Wendy, I can't help you if you don't talk to me.'

I shook myself then because I didn't want her to think I wasn't trying. 'Sorry, I'm just a bit . . . tired.'

'Can you try to tell me what's bothering you specifically?'

I shrugged again because I wasn't sure how to explain to Saanvi why I felt so bad. It was a mixture of a lot of things – the night out with the writers' group and the way Henry had treated me when I was only trying to help, the fact that Ginger hadn't been in touch all week again, though I'd called her three times and even gone round to her house and shouted up to her bedroom window – she was probably fed up with me already. And then there was the trouble at work – I hated to disappoint Mr Laverty and I didn't know what I'd do if I didn't have my job to keep me sane. And, most importantly, Diane hadn't tweeted all week and though I'd sat on the hill most days and walked past her house four times, I hadn't seen her, not even when I'd peered into the window at the back. There was some washing hanging on the line and I ran my hand along the newly washed towels and bedding, so clean and fresh, billowing in the wind. What was it like, I wondered, to live in a house with freshly laundered towels, and clean, lemony sheets for the bed?

I didn't know how to explain all that to Saanvi so I said something instead I knew she'd understand. 'I wish my mum was here.'

'I know you do Wendy but you must realize that she isn't coming back. Life is all about change, constantly moving goalposts, you've got to try and accept that.'

'I suppose so. I mean, I do. It's just . . . I thought if I did all the things you said, you know, doing up the house, making friends and going out and stuff, I'd feel better. I thought I'd be good at life like you are, but . . . I'm still rubbish at everything.'

Saanvi sighed and put her folder down beside her. She leaned forwards and put her hand on my arm and said in a softer voice, 'Wendy, all the time I've known you, you've been beating yourself up about something or other, you're not good enough for this, or you need to try harder at that. Have you ever thought about trying a different approach?'

I sniffed. 'What do you mean?'

'Well, how about trying to pamper yourself for a change?'

'Pamper myself?'

'Yes, you know, be good to yourself. Maybe treat yourself to a new haircut, or—'

'What's wrong with my hair?'

'No, nothing, that's not what I meant. I mean, you're nineteen years old Wendy, you should be having the time of your life. Getting dolled up for a night out every once in a while, treating yourself to new clothes maybe, having nice things planned to look forward to. Just being kinder to yourself and enjoying life. Do you know what I mean by that?'

'Not really.' I shook my head. 'I mean, maybe . . . Ginger's mentioned going out a couple of times. We could, I suppose.'

'Yes, definitely. Life is so short Wendy, well I don't need to tell you that, but it's also filled with wonderful experiences and when you're nineteen years old, the world is your oyster Wendy, it really is.' She leaned back and looked at me again. 'Will you think about what I've said anyway, between now and next week? Really think about how you can turn this difficult corner in your life and start enjoying yourself a bit more.'

My head was throbbing with an ache that had started at the base of my skull, a buzzing electrical current working its way towards the top of my head. I was desperate for Saanvi to stop talking and let me go and lie down in the dark so I just nodded and stood up, hoping she'd take the hint.

She looked surprised as I usually offered her a second cup of tea but, to be honest, trying to persuade someone who's paid to care about your wellbeing that all is well is really almost as exhausting as trying to make sure it is. I leaned against the door after I'd closed it on her and let out a long sigh.

I lay in bed that night, still awake as the room turned from deep purple to milky grey. Saanvi's words were going round in my head and the more I told myself I had to enjoy life, the more panicky I became and the more convinced that no matter how hard I tried, I was never going to be any good at it. I reached across the bed for my phone to see if Twitter could distract me. And that's when I saw Diane's tweet.

Writers without rejections are just not trying hard enough. We need courage to keep writing and, more than that, to try new things, push ourselves, take chances, change, learn, love, live. #LifeInEveryBreath

I gasped as I read it then read it again, out loud this time, so I could capture the meaning of every word. As usual, Diane had got right to the nub of the matter – I did get things wrong sometimes but maybe other people did too, and maybe if you didn't get stuff wrong it meant you weren't trying hard enough, not that you were perfect. And I think that's what Saanvi was trying to say too. I had to start enjoying life more, maybe pampering myself – whatever that meant – and going out, having fun like other nineteen-year-olds were doing.

A streaky orange sunlight crept into the room as I took

a screenshot of Diane's tweet and saved it as the new home screen for my phone. I lay back, my headache lifting at last, and Diane's words lighting up the phone on the pillow next to me.

Life in every breath, I thought as I drifted off. That tweet marked the start of the best summer of my life.

Ginger and Me and the
Best Summer Ever

17

IT WAS AS THOUGH Ginger had been struck with the same realization that life was for living and that we should be enjoying ourselves more because she arrived at my door the following morning, pink and smiling, and fizzing with energy. I watched her spin round, pulling her Lonsdale hoodie over her head and peeking out the head hole like a toddler playing hide and seek.

'Has . . . something happened?' I asked, but I was pleased that she was in such a good mood and delighted she still wanted to be friends.

'What? No, nothing. Sorry I wasn't around last week. Things were . . . but guess what? I've got the house to myself for a couple of weeks! They've all had to get away for a bit, Fran went too.'

'On a business trip?'

'Yeah, something like that. There was no one there when I got home yesterday and the house was so peaceful all night. I was going to call you and ask you round but it was so quiet and I was so tired that I fell asleep on the couch about half nine. I slept the whole night and only woke up when the sun was coming in the front window and wee Nina was miaowing for her Whiskas – it was brilliant.'

She joined me in looking into my mean fridge then back

at me as though I could suddenly magic up bacon and eggs. I looked at the empty shelves and made up my mind.

'Right Ginger,' I said. 'Life's too short to be eating toast and lemon curd for breakfast on a day like today. Put your jumper back on. We're going out for breakfast.'

She punched the air and said, 'This day just gets better.'

'Actually, wait a minute, I've got something for you.' I ran up to my room to get the trainers which had finally arrived.

She looked at the square package I handed her. 'For me?' she said.

I nodded and watched her rip open the sellotape.

At first I thought I'd got it wrong as usual because she looked like she was going to start crying when she saw them.

'Is it the colour?' I said. 'Because I can easily change them to blue or even just black if you'd rather?'

'No Wendy,' she said, looking up at me. 'They're perfect, honest. I love them.'

I watched as she pulled off her old trainers and slung them across the kitchen, slipping her feet into the shiny new ones. She got up and walked with her hands on her hips, turning at the back door and going, 'Ta-dah,' like she was a supermodel.

'No one's ever got me anything as lovely Wendy. Thank you.'

'You're welcome,' I said, amazed at how easy it was to make her happy.

After we'd had breakfast at The View, we headed along to Aladdin's so that I could buy some of the spicy sausages I liked from Dino's. As we wandered past Paddy Power, I saw the reflection of three young women, two of them arm-in-arm, strolling past New Look on the other side of the walkway.

'Quick,' I said, pulling Ginger's arm. 'Stop here and pretend you're looking in the window.'

'Of the bookies?' she said, craning her head to see who we were avoiding.

'Don't look,' I hissed, and we both studied the odds on the afternoon's match between Dunfermline and Rangers. I waited till the group had passed by then said, 'Okay, they've gone.'

'Who was it? Those girls over there?'

'Yes, they were at my school – Louise, Ruth and Geraldine. The popular group. They didn't like me much. No wonder,' I gestured towards my limp bob and down at my old wind-cheater. 'They're gorgeous, always were.'

Ginger's eyes widened. 'You must be joking. Those three? The Blob Fish Twins, and the hips on the other one – Christ! You're way better looking than them Wendy.' She stopped and looked at the ground, sliding her foot along the concrete floor.

'What?' I said.

'Well, I mean, you *could* be better looking than them, if you, you know, made a bit of an effort.'

'What do you mean – made an effort?'

'With your clothes, I mean. And your . . .' she waved up in the direction of my head. 'I mean, do you wear your hair like that on purpose? All flat like that?'

I touched my hand to my fringe. 'I've always had my hair like this. My dad used to like this style.'

It was true. A long time ago, I used to lie on the floor next to his armchair and he'd stroke the palm of his hand from the top of my head all the way down to the tips of my hair. My hair was like silk, he'd say, as we watched David Attenborough, or one of those other nature programmes we liked.

'Well, it's fine of course,' said Ginger, 'if you really like it like that. What about make-up? We could do something like this.' She brought up a picture on her phone of an actress who was wearing far too much make-up in my opinion, you could hardly see her own features. 'No, really,' said Ginger quickly, seeing my face, 'we could open your eyes right up with some eyeliner and mascara. You know Wendy,' she said, standing on her tiptoes so she could look into my face directly, 'with your lovely dark eyes, you could be really pretty. With my help. And your cheekbones are amazing.'

I was about to say that you can't make a silk purse from a sow's ear but I stopped myself and touched my hand to my cheek instead. I'd never considered my cheekbones before. 'Are they?' I said.

'Definitely. Okay, we'd have to work round your huge fore-head and your shiny nose, but honestly, I could make you look gorgeous Wendy.'

Her enthusiasm was infectious and I laughed as she did a tap dance with her new red trainers on the concrete floor, although two skinny pensioners, anoraks zipped up to their chins and trailing a tweed shopping trolley each, were not happy when she backed into them.

'Oops sorry,' she said, then, when they tutted and swerved away from her, she shouted after them, 'It was an accident you know.' She turned to me and said, 'Some people just don't know how to have fun do they?'

I was working the five to ten shift that evening so I couldn't go round to Ginger's till the following day.

'Wow, someone's been busy,' I said. The hallway was clear and much wider than I'd thought now that it was bereft of all the electrical goods, boxes and rolls of carpet that usually cluttered it. The cat scuttled past us, leaping the first two steps and slinking upstairs to curl up on her spot on Ginger's bed.

Ginger had clearly been making the most of her time because the kitchen was as tidy as I'd ever seen it.

'It looks bigger like this doesn't it?' she said, running her hand proudly along the clean, empty surfaces.

'Here we are then.' She'd set a chair in the middle of the kitchen, facing one of the worktops. It had a thin red towel hanging down the back and there was a large mirror propped up against the kettle. Sitting in front of the mirror were a little make-up bag with the words 'Hello Kitty' blazoned across it, and an array of sparkly eyeshadows in a box marked 'Glambusters'.

'Welcome to the spa Wendy,' she said, waiting for my reaction.

'This looks great,' I said. 'I take it everyone's still away.'

She nodded, told me to take a seat and put the towel round my shoulders.

I hesitated. 'You won't make me look too different will you?' Saanvi did say I should pamper myself but I wouldn't want my regulars not to recognize me.

'Don't worry about that. Come on, put your bag down and let's get started.'

That reminded me. I reached into my rucksack and brought out the book I'd taken out of the library that morning especially. I tapped on it and told Ginger, 'It says here it's important to remain as natural as possible and let your inner beauty shine through. I'm paraphrasing but something like that.' I leafed through the book, looking for the exact quote.

'We don't need books for this Wendy, I know what I'm doing.'
She rolled up the sleeves of her sweatshirt.

'Well,' I said, unwilling to give up my book just yet. 'We should maybe check a few chapters first.'

'What book is it?' she said, glancing at the cover picture of a half naked woman lolling on a satin sheet.

'It's *Britt Ekland's Book of Natural Beauty*. Maybe we could try reading it together after you've finished *The Tiger Who Came to Tea*?'

'Oh yeah, very educational.'

'Exactly,' I said, 'the more books you read the better. Here, listen to this,' I started reading from one of the opening chapters. 'Always remember to shave your big toe when you are shaving your legs. Hair on the foot is not sexy.' I paused. 'Well I don't know why you're laughing, that's perfectly true,' I said huffily, as Ginger took the book from me and placed it on the work surface behind her.

'Yes but I don't think we need an eighties porn star to tell us that.'

'Porn star – was she?' I looked at the reclining woman on the cover again with interest.

'God Wendy, I don't know, I've never heard of her but I'm guessing she's not starring in movies with Leonardo DiCaprio if she's writing books about hairy toes, is she?'

She had a point.

'Right. Lift your head up and look straight ahead.' She started by squeezing some peachy-coloured cream from a tube that she dabbed on my forehead, cheeks and chin. She used the tips of her fingers to rub it all round my face. I held my breath as she bent down in front of me. Her face was very close to mine and

I could feel her breath on my cheek as she applied the foundation. I could smell the freshly washed smell that I always associated with her happy days. The touch of her fingers on my face was soft and I could feel the hairs on my arms rise and prickle.

'Am I really spotty?' I said, suddenly conscious of her gaze and the fact that I only used soap to wash my face and never used cream or beauty products on it at all.

'Ssshhhh,' she said. 'I'm concentrating on blending.' She leaned across me to get the next magic wand from the bag and I felt her breast rest on my shoulder for a split second. I tried to focus on what she was saying.

'You don't need much mascara Wendy, you're lucky because your eyelashes are already thick and black. You've got the eye-lashes I want.'

I didn't answer as she moved on to my cheeks, brushing them lightly with a thick, soft brush, working swiftly and with a confident touch.

'Where did you learn to put on make-up?' I asked, waiting until she'd finished using yet another pencil, this time it seemed she had drawn round the shape of my mouth.

'From my mum. I used to watch her getting ready to go out. Putting on the war paint she called it. I was always sad when I saw the red lipstick because that meant she was going out and leaving me.' She sniffed. 'Mind you, it also meant I'd be getting Monster Munch and Fruit Shoot for dinner so it wasn't all bad. Right, what do you think?' She swivelled me round in the chair to face the mirror.

I stared at the strange face looking back at me, surprised by how different I looked. My skin was smoother than usual and there was a shimmer across my cheeks, my eyes were heavy like the setting sun, my mouth obscenely soft and large, suggesting things without words. I looked . . . grown-up, like the nineteen-year-old Saanvi said I should be – the one who went on nights out and did things in the world. Maybe she was right, and I could do that stuff after all.

'Do you like it?' said Ginger. 'I've given you a smoky eye. That means you wear it at night rather than during the day.'

'It's great,' I said. 'Now it's your turn.' I couldn't apply make-up so I offered to paint her nails instead. She had two bottles of nail polish – one silver, one blue. I held them up and she chose the silver. She sat down and held up her hand. The sleeves of her sweatshirt were still rolled up and as I took her hand in mine I caught a flash of colour just below the crook of her elbow. Inked onto her skin in tiny blue letters, were the word MUM and a little blue rose beside it.

'Stupid,' she whispered, looking up at me from beneath her eyelashes, before snatching her hand away and rolling down the sleeve of her sweatshirt.

Later we ordered in some food from the Amran and sat with our feet up on the sofa, me in full make-up and Ginger with her silver nails, eating pakora and chips with curry sauce. When I got home I posted a picture of myself all made-up on Twitter then sat up for an hour waiting to see if Diane liked it. She didn't, but on the plus side, a man I'd never even met before called xxxStudManxxx@SaturdayNight DMed me to say I was a very pretty lady and he'd love to get to know me better and to please send him more photos, which only goes to show the power of a good lipstick.

18

IT WAS GINGER'S IDEA to go on a night out, she said we might as well show the world – Viewpark anyway – what we looked like dolled up. I wasn't sure when she suggested it but Saanvi had said I should go out and enjoy myself, and I think that was the kind of thing she had in mind.

I knew The Rolling Barrel from when my dad used to drink there but, apart from that, I'd only passed it on the bus. At lunchtimes, it was mainly older women going in and out, maybe about Terry and Irish Mary's age, tempted in by the pensioners' specials and as much tea as you could drink. On the backshift, I'd see the younger groups streaming in, straight from their shifts at Direct Line or one of the furniture showrooms in the industrial estate at the back of Birkenshaw. I envied the girls in their navy blue skirts and smart coats, their day's work done and out for a glass of wine with their pals. There was an ocean between their lives and mine.

But then I found Ginger, or she found me, and there we were getting ready for a night of our own, just like those office girls. Ginger's house was still quiet and tidy with Uncle Tam and everyone away, and we toasted each other with the whisky she'd found beside Uncle Tam's bed.

'Urgh, that's disgusting,' I said, shaking my head as the hot liquid stung my throat.

'Isn't it? Totally rank,' she said, as she poured us both another. 'One more then we'll do our make-up.'

And then we had to go through the whole make-up charade again. Honestly I don't know how some women do it all the time – the eyeliner, the eyeshadow, flick flick, smudge it here, smooth it there, sparkly stuff to highlight your cheekbones, creamy stuff to shade out pores, it goes on and on. Imagine being Britt Ekland and having to do that stuff every day just to look natural, and that was as well as shaving her feet.

I don't know if it was because we were going on an actual night out or because of the whisky, but Ginger seemed to be putting a lot more make-up on me than the time before. I stopped her as she dipped the brush into the bright green eyeshadow.

'Green? Are you sure?'

'Trust me,' she said, 'you can get away with bright green Wendy,' and started to smear it on my eyelid.

'Can I? Why?'

'Well, because . . .' she burst into a fit of giggles and I wondered if she'd been drinking the whisky before I'd arrived, 'because you're tall, that's why.'

That didn't seem right but her mum had taught her about make-up so I suppose she knew what she was talking about.

'Did your mum wear green eyeshadow?' I said, taking a sip of whisky as Ginger bent over the Glambusters box to select her next colour.

'No, she didn't wear eyeshadow. She used to draw thick black lines with liquid eyeliner on the top of her eyelids. Like this.' She drew an imaginary line across her own eyelid, pulling it up at the end like a big tick. 'You need a lot of skill to do that properly though, I couldn't do it. My mum was . . .'

I waited, but she flapped her hand suddenly. 'Anyway, never mind her. Ta-dah, you're finished, now go and get your glad rags on.'

Glad rags was pushing it a bit. I did get changed into a different top I'd brought with me but I kept on the same jeans since they were still clean and perfectly serviceable. When I went back into the kitchen, Ginger let out a low wolf whistle and told me I looked like a different person. That made me happy because I'd wanted to be a different person for as long as I could remember. I wished Diane could see me but that felt disloyal to Ginger so I tried to forget about Diane and concentrate on our night out instead.

'You look nice too,' I said. She did, her eyes looked bigger and greener now they were framed in thick black lashes, her lips were shimmering pink and she'd pinned her hair up at the front to hide the bald patches, and that made her look taller. She was wearing a black crocheted cardigan over a black strappy top that revealed the pale skin of her chest. I was thinking maybe I should have worn something more exciting than my cream pullover from Matalan but it was too late now.

They must have changed the décor in The Rolling Barrel from when my dad used to drink there. It was done out in white and silver, with lots of blingy mirrors everywhere you looked, and dimpled steel-topped tables. I looked up at the huge chandelier dangling over the bar area, and couldn't imagine Dad there at all. It wasn't busy when we first went in, only three of the tables had people sitting at them, and I didn't feel as conspicuous as I'd thought I would. Maybe my bright green eyeshadow was helping me blend in.

Ginger said, 'I'll get us a seat and you go to the bar, Wendy. Just in case anyone spots I'm underage.'

I nodded, though she looked at least eighteen with all the make-up and bare skin. She certainly looked as old as the other customers in the place, who were mostly teenage girls, all wearing even more make-up than we were. I stood at the bar, waiting for the blonde girl wiping glasses to serve me.

By the time I got back to our table with the Bacardi Breezers and crisps, the place was starting to fill up a bit and they'd put on some loud music.

'There you go,' I shouted to Ginger, putting the drinks down on the slightly shoogly table.

'Cheers,' she shouted back and raised her glass to me.

I took a sip and sat back to look around me. I don't know what I imagined people were doing in bars and clubs on nights out but I suppose I thought it would be more exciting than this. All that fuss with the make-up and getting changed just to sit in a room done out like a brothel and shout at each other over the loudspeakers?

'This is great isn't it, Wendy?'

'Yeah,' I said. 'Great.' I watched Ginger, tapping her feet and sipping her drink, looking all round the room, her face glowing through the powder and blusher. It was as though putting on the mask of colour and getting away from home had freed her from whatever it was that so often affected her mood. With her mass of red hair and the make-up accentuating her green eyes and wide mouth, I saw for the first time that she really was quite striking. It wasn't long before she'd attracted the attention of the men in the place. I saw a few of them looking over, nudging each other.

Eventually two guys, a bit older than we were, approached our table.

'Can we join you ladies?' said the smaller one, a stocky barrel of a man, his hair shorn to the scalp at the sides but longer on top and greased over to one side. He was wearing a small gold sleeper in his right ear and carried a blue Berghaus jacket over his shoulder.

Ginger gave him a wide smile and said, 'Of course,' as she moved her own jacket from the seat next to her.

The taller one in the black polo neck sat next to me.

'I'm Doc,' said the one sitting next to Ginger, 'and this is Marcel.'

Marcel raised his chin but said nothing, and Doc turned to Ginger. 'I know you. You're Tam's girl, aren't you?'

Ginger stiffened. 'He's my uncle,' she said.

'I was at school with Tam. A few years below him but I knew him. Well, everybody knew Tam. He was always cock of the walk, him and his henchmen − Roddy was it? − and all the others. They were going places, you could just tell, especially Tam.' He took a swig of his pint. 'Where is he now?'

'Viewpark,' said Ginger.

'Right,' said Doc. He turned to me, trying to bring Marcel into the conversation. 'Now you need to be gentle on Marcel here, he's just back from a long stay at the Heartbreak Hotel, if you know what I mean?'

I didn't know what he meant but I could see Marcel wasn't happy at what Doc was saying.

'Shut it Doc,' were the first words he spoke.

'What man? You were dumped, happens to us all.' Doc elbowed Ginger and she laughed, head back, showing her perfect teeth. She seemed to be shaking out her hair even more than usual. Doc was lucky not to get smacked in the face with it the way she was whooshing it all over the place.

'I wasn't dumped. Exactly,' said Marcel. 'It was more of a mutual parting of the ways.'

'Marcel, buddy, she said she wouldn't want to see you again if she was on fire and yours was the only piss in the western hemisphere.'

'That does sound like she dumped you,' I said, putting my hand on his arm to sympathize, like Saanvi had taught me.

He looked down at my hand and said, 'Oh well, Maxine's loss. I can go out with whoever I want now.'

'That's the spirit Marcel. And let me tell you girls, he's a man worth holding on to. He drives a Honda Civic. Brand new.'

'Big deal,' I said. 'I drive a bus.'

They all laughed, including Ginger.

'I mean it. I could give you a free ride on my bus if you wanted.'

Doc laughed even louder and said, 'A free bus ride. That'd be one to cross off my bucket list.' So I think he was impressed.

'Anyway, are you buying us another drink or what?' said Ginger. 'Mine's a Bacardi Breezer. Watermelon. What about you Wendy?'

'Um, same,' I said, though I wasn't sure I wanted them to buy us drinks, as I was worried that would mean we owed them something later.

'Bacardi Breezers it is girls.' Doc went back to the bar, giving the thumbs up to Marcel as he left.

'And crisps,' Ginger called after him.

As the night wore on, the bar filled up, the music got even louder, Ginger got giddier and I wondered what on earth I was doing there. I kept watching Ginger and the way she was cosying up to Doc, laughing hard at everything he said and doing this weird thing with her eyes every time she looked up at him. Did she . . . like him? We'd never talked about boys and whether she fancied them or not. I always thought she hated men, but she certainly didn't seem to hate Doc.

Marcel kept trying to get my attention. He'd brought me over another bottle of pink Bacardi Breezer, I'd lost count of how many I'd had by then but perhaps it was enough to make him handsome. He leaned towards me and I tried to listen to what he was saying. His eyes were really quite a nice, deep brown, and if I just thought of the large hairy mole above his lip as a beauty spot, I could almost imagine myself kissing him. He was also taller than me which was a plus. Maybe I did like him after all, I thought, and I leaned in towards him too, doing that closing my eyes then opening them really wide thing that I'd seen Ginger do. I pretended to be fascinated by the Celtic score and how they'd been robbed, and how the petrol consumption of a Honda Civic is far more economical than people give it credit for, and how anyone who thought they were getting more functionality in an iPhone than a perfectly good Samsung was a mug for the marketing plain and simple, and . . . Oh. My. God. My eyes glazed over and I knew it was no good.

I stood up and found myself stumbling after all the Bacardi I'd had.

'Watch yourself Wendy,' said Ginger, taking a break from being enthralled by Doc for a few seconds.

'I'm going home Ginger. I've had enough.' I grappled with my jacket, trying to force my arms through the sleeves.

'Do you not want to come back to mine for a coffee?' said Marcel. 'And when I say coffee, I mean coffee.'

That seemed an odd thing to clarify as what else could coffee mean, but I wasn't persuaded. 'No, I'm going home.'

'Wait, I'll come with you Wendy. Can't have you going home yourself in that state.' Ginger peeled herself away from Doc and started putting her own jacket on.

'Wait a wee minute girls,' said Doc. 'Don't be hasty now. Why don't we come with you?' He half stood and Ginger pushed him in the chest so he fell back into his seat.

'No, we're going home ourselves. Thanks for the drinks.'

Doc's smile vanished and was replaced by a scowl. 'What the fuck's wrong with you two? We've been buying you drinks all night.'

'Yeah, and we're grateful but now we're leaving. In fact we're going back to Tam's house, okay?'

Doc got the hint. He stood up and pushed over Ginger's half empty bottle of Bacardi so that the pink dregs sloshed across the table and just missed Ginger's feet. 'Fuck off then, cockteasers the pair of you.'

Marcel chimed in. 'What is it – you two lezzers or what?'

'Yours definitely is,' said Doc. 'Come on, let's check out the rest of the talent before last orders.' As they headed off in search of fresh prey, I heard him say to Marcel, 'Tell you what though, I wouldn't mind being a fly on the wall when those two get home.'

Ginger stuck her tongue out at Doc's back as he and Marcel stalked off and said to me, 'Let's go to mine.'

A thick, unseasonal fog had descended and Ginger put her arm through mine and cuddled up to me for warmth. We decided to walk rather than get a taxi, despite the weather, because Ginger said the fresh air would sober us up.

We walked along the top road in silence for a bit then I said, 'Sorry, you seemed to like yours.'

She waved her hand and said, 'Ppff.' She waited until an old guy and his German shepherd had passed us then she turned and said to me, 'Do you though?'

'Do I what?'

'Like girls?'

I laughed and jabbed her in the arm. 'I like you,' I said. She didn't say anything, and the silence between us was the time for honesty but instead I added quickly, 'You're the best friend anyone could want, honestly. And I've had a brilliant time tonight, thanks for taking me.'

'But—'

'Come on,' I said, and took her arm again. 'Let's go home, I'm freezing out here.'

We turned into Laburnum Road where the houses were coated in thick mist.

'This is amazing Wendy! Look, you can hardly see your hand in front of your face.' Ginger was laughing and spinning like a Catherine wheel, a brilliant spark in the gloom. 'Come on, let's get to mine and order a pizza. You should stay over and we can stay up all night!' I could hardly keep up with her.

The fog was worse at the bottom of the scheme and we couldn't see anything when we heard the screaming. I felt Ginger stiffen beside me but we kept walking and the noise grew louder. The sounds of women screeching, rough shouts of 'Fuck' and

'It's all a load of shite,' and the boom boom boom of house music coming from a few hundred yards in front of us.

Just as I stopped her to say did she want to go to mine instead, we had to step back from the pavement as something glowing orange came hurtling towards us in the dark.

'What on earth?' I pulled Ginger further back as a burning pram came careering towards us, a flaming blue blanket hanging off the back of it. It was quickly followed by a blur of young guys in their Mera Peak jackets, shrieking and flinging empty Buckfast bottles after it.

Ginger peered up towards her house, every window lit up, the walls pulsating with the thudding music, and the front door hanging open. She'd stopped laughing, and stood at the side of the road, all the energy and light gone from her, like a firework doused in rain.

'They're back,' she said flatly, lifting her locket from her chest and putting it into her mouth.

19

GINGER STAYED AT MINE that night since she said she'd never get any sleep with all those people at Uncle Tam's. For the next few weeks we saw each other most days, and she'd stay over quite often too, it was like she didn't want to go home. I gave her a back door key so she could come even when I wasn't there. I loved it when I finished work and there she'd be, lying on the couch flicking through the channels. She looked so happy and relaxed, as though she belonged there. Sometimes when I got off a backshift she'd be sitting at the kitchen table, with two bowls piled high with her speciality mincey pasta in front of her, waiting for me to come and eat. More often I'd bring in something for us both.

'What's on the menu tonight Wendy?' she'd say, her hands already outstretched for the boxes or plastic cartons. If it was chicken pakora, or pizza from Enzo's, her eyes lit up like I'd gifted her diamonds.

'Oh Wendy,' she'd say, 'you're brilliant, you know that?'

And after we'd eaten, I'd persuade Ginger to pick up whatever book we were working on and read me half a dozen pages from it. She was still embarrassed about reading children's books but I was proud of the way she kept at it, she could be pretty determined when she wanted to be.

It wasn't all about me helping Ginger though, she helped me too. She was the one who said we should make a project of doing up my house. I knew she was right. Doing up the house and making it feel more like home the way it used to would make me feel better, so we went round the house making a list of all the things that needed to be fixed or replaced, painted over or covered up. It was a long list.

'I think we should start first thing tomorrow – with the living room,' Ginger said. Apparently new coasters and the resurrection of Mum's mouldy old rug didn't quite cut it as far as she was concerned. I could see her point, and I was off the next day so I said, 'Okay, let's do it.'

Next morning, she knocked on the back door at half past ten. I stopped at the door when I saw her. She had her hair up in a high ponytail like a girl heading out to her exercise class. Her neck was thin and delicate, her cheekbones – normally covered by the thick waves of hair – were revealed to be high and prominent.

'Something wrong?' she said.

'I . . . no, nothing,' I said, dragging my eyes away from her jutting collarbone, and looking at what she was holding.

She grinned at me, and raised the two soft paintbrushes, their handles looped through two huge tins of paint she'd brought with her.

'Uncle Tam comes in handy sometimes,' she said, as she dropped them onto the kitchen floor.

'I didn't know he was also involved in the decorating business.' I shook my head, and hunkered down to check what colour of paint was in the tins. 'Cool chartreuse? What colour's that?'

'No idea, but it's got to be better than what's on here, hasn't it?'

I nodded, taking a last look at the dull olive walls and the plaster blistering behind the TV. I rolled up my pyjama sleeves.

'Wait a minute, you can't paint in your PJs. Go and get dressed in something old, and I'll get started.'

We ran out of paint before we finished the last wall but Ginger said not to worry, there was loads more in Uncle Tam's lock-up.

'Are you sure he won't mind us taking all this paint? Maybe I should offer to pay him something for it?'

'Don't be daft. He's got so much stuff in that lock-up, he won't even miss it.'

I was going to say I hoped she hadn't been in there messing around with Uncle Tam's stuff but she was in such a good mood, I didn't want to spoil it. 'Come on then,' I said instead, wiping a streak of paint across my cheek. 'Let's go and get it.'

I stayed in the back yard while Ginger nipped up to get the key to the lock-up. I was thinking that the squat, grey lock-ups, filled with other people's treasures, might make a great backdrop to a story. Maybe there could be a robbery and the loot got stashed in one of them but then the leader of the gang loses the key and the others—

'What the fuck are you hanging round here for?'

I jumped, as Roddy pulled down the metal door of Uncle Tam's lock-up with a bang, and came towards me slowly.

I'd met Roddy once before, coming down the path as we were heading into Ginger's house. He'd been at an afternoon business meeting with Uncle Tam and it must have gone well because he was really happy, he was even singing. He was shorter than me with a fat belly hanging over his jogging pants. His hair and skin were very dark, and his uneven teeth glowed almost greenish against them. I was staring at his teeth when he asked me if I had a boyfriend. I shook my head. He looked me up and down, laughing, and said of course I wouldn't, I was the type who'd stay at home and flip the bean, so I'm not sure if Ginger had told him I was some sort of vegetarian.

'He seems nice,' I said to Ginger later, but she tutted and said, 'He was just drunk. But there you go again, seeing the best in everybody. Even the most evil people on earth can seem nice if they pretend hard enough and no one stops them.' Which I thought was a bit dramatic, even for her.

But the day we met him going to get the paint, I could see her point. Ginger came round the corner, swinging the key from her fingers, but stopped short when she saw Roddy. He put his head to one side when he saw her and raised his eyebrows.

'And here's your sidekick,' he said, wiping his chubby hands down the front of his sweatpants.

'Uncle Tam's in,' Ginger said quickly, standing close and slightly behind me.

'So?' said Roddy, looking from Ginger to me and back again. 'Stay. The. Fuck. Out. The. Lock-up.' That's how he said it, as though there were full stops between every word. 'It's private, got it?'

Ginger kicked the dirt and refused to look up at him. 'It's up to Uncle Tam,' she mumbled. 'It's his lock-up.'

Roddy reached behind me and grabbed Ginger's upper arm.

'Don't,' I said and tried to prise his hand from her but he was too strong for me.

'Why don't you mind your own business? You've suddenly got a lot to say for yourself haven't you?'

I looked at the ground and said nothing.

Ginger licked her lips and said, 'Look we won't go into the lock-up again but can you go and get us a tin of that yellow paint then? Uncle Tam said we could have it,' she lied.

Roddy stared at us for a moment longer then said, 'Wait here.'

He pushed the tin of paint towards Ginger and said, 'Stay out of the lock-up, understood?'

Ginger nodded, and clutched the paint to her chest as we both watched Roddy go back into the lock-up and slam the door down behind him so that it rattled against the concrete.

'Tosser,' whispered Ginger, then to me, 'Come on, let's get out of here.'

She was quiet as we walked out of her street and I thought Roddy must have upset her.

'Was your uncle Roddy in a bad mood today or something?'

'He's always like that. I told you. Now do you see why I prefer staying at yours?'

I did. 'Don't let him ruin your day Ginger. Come on, we'll get takeaway tonight and you can stay over again.'

She brightened at that and before we'd even reached the community centre, she was laughing and joking like we hadn't met Roddy at all.

By half past four that afternoon, my living room was transformed. Chartreuse, it turned out, was a colour halfway between green and yellow. Ginger may have been pushing it a bit to say anything was better than it was before.

'I mean, it's clean at least,' I said, standing back to survey the whole room.

'It is,' agreed Ginger.

We said nothing for a bit till Ginger started laughing. It started with a snigger which she tried to hide with a cough then ended up coming from deep in her belly, a raucous, loud guffaw that I'd never heard from her before.

'What are you laughing at?' I said, a smile playing around my own lips.

'Nothing, it's . . .' She carried on laughing, supporting herself on the edge of the sofa. Breathless, she said, 'It's really very nice Wendy. Just one thing I'm thinking . . .'

'Yes?' I said, laughing myself now.

'Have you got shades? Because you'll need to wear them if you want to sit in here with these walls.'

'Very funny,' I said and threw the old sofa cushion at her so that she toppled off the sofa altogether, landing in a laughing heap on the floor.

We had fried rice and curry sauce for dinner and, after I'd thrown away the greasy cartons, I flopped back onto the couch with my legs curled beneath me, and flicked through Netflix in search of something for us to watch. Ginger came and sank down next to me.

'Other sofa's even worse,' she said. It was true.

She slipped off her trainers and socks and wiggled her toes against the soft couch. Her toenails were painted shiny pink except the big toe of her right foot, which was bruised and nail varnish free. Most of her hair had come loose from her ponytail so that half of it was streaming round her neck and down her back. She reached up for her hairband and handed it to me.

'Here, put my hair back up for me would you? My hands are all dry and raw with the paint.'

So were mine but I didn't say so. She turned her back to me and leaned lightly against my chest. I could feel the warmth of her back radiating into me. I put my hands in her hair, it was soft like cotton wool and that day it smelled of coconut shampoo. I spread my fingers so they worked like a comb against her scalp.

'Mmm, that's nice,' she said, shifting further down into the sofa and snuggling closer to me. I could feel my heart beating against her back, wondered if she could feel it too, and I started stroking her scalp slowly then moving my fingers all the way through her hair down to its tips.

'Your hair's growing in again, you know in the . . . patches.' I was careful as I said this because sometimes she became annoyed if I mentioned them, embarrassed I suppose.

'Yeah,' she said. 'They only get worse when I'm stressed. Things are going okay just now. I'm here a lot so I don't have to see Roddy much. Well, you saw what he's like.'

I nodded.

'It's been good not having to worry about him. Not that I can't handle him because I can.' She turned her face to the side and I could see her chin raised in defiance.

'Of course you can. That's good though,' I added, twisting the band round her hair now so that her ponytail bounced high on her head again. 'All done,' I said. She looked at me like she wanted to say something.

'That's not the only reason I like staying here though. It's been great spending time with you, you're always fun to be with.'

No one had ever said that to me before. 'Am I?'

She laughed. 'Now you're fishing for compliments. But yeah, it's been brilliant.'

And it was. Ginger and me were best friends that summer, she was the first best friend I'd ever had. I wish we could have stayed that way for ever.

20

SAANVI CAME TO SEE me a few days later. She was wearing her blue and yellow sari and my eyes were drawn to the pointy gold beaks of the little birds that danced all over the fabric. It was beautiful, like having the sunny weather from outdoors brought right into my living room. I looked at my own nondescript jeans and jumper, exactly the same as half a dozen other pairs of jeans and jumpers that I rotated between my wardrobe and washing machine, and wondered if I should make more of an effort. Diane really suited the colourful clothes she always wore, though maybe she could get away with them because she was older than me. But even if my huge forehead and limp hair meant I'd always be closer to a sow's ear than a silk purse, that didn't mean I couldn't try a bit harder to improve my appearance. I'd already made some changes and I could tell by the way Saanvi was staring that she'd noticed something different about me.

'Is that . . . um, a new lipstick Wendy?'

'Yes,' I said, running my finger over the waxy slick of my top lip. After I'd let Ginger put make-up on me for our night out, she kept saying how I should wear it more often and make the best of myself. Now that I was going out more and doing stuff, I thought maybe she was right and I should smarten myself up a bit. Ginger bought me the new lipstick. Deep plum from a shop called Christian Dior, which I'd never heard of.

'How much do I owe you?' I said, because I didn't think Ginger should be subsidizing me when I was earning good money on the buses and she wasn't working yet.

She waved away the three pound coins I had in my hand, and said not to worry, lipstick wasn't expensive.

I wasn't sure if I liked it or not really. It certainly made an impression when I wore it to work. The lads all winked and shoved each other, and Wee Rab who was there doing his work experience for the summer whistled so long it hurt my ears, so I knew they liked my new look.

'Do you like it?' I asked Saanvi. 'It's from Christian Dior, some shop in the arcade,' I added, in case she hadn't heard of it either.

'Really?' she smiled. 'Yes, it's . . . a very strong colour Wendy, it suits you. You seem . . . different recently. Things seem much better with you?' Her pen hovered over her notebook and she looked at me kindly.

Things were better, and it was mainly thanks to Ginger. Even though she wasn't always in a good mood, for the rest of the summer she was more often in a good mood than not. We did lots of things that friends do. I told Saanvi about our day out at Tollcross Park.

'Why Tollcross?' Ginger had said, picking at the skin round her mouth. 'Why don't we just head down to our usual park?'

'Because it's good for us to get out of our comfort zone.' I was repeating the words Saanvi used to say to me when she wanted me to join clubs and things. They sounded sensible when I said them to Ginger.

'I'm comfortable in my comfort zone,' Ginger said huffily, but she sloped off to the bathroom to get changed and, after an unpromising start, we ended up having a great day.

A light drizzle pattered against the windows of the bus as we rode to Tollcross. We got off just before the big Lidl and walked past the leisure centre at the entrance to the park and through to the trees at the back.

'Look Ginger, the river.' I pointed towards the scummy water, the dirty yellow waves lapping along the sorry looking banks as the smell of sewage wafted by and pigeons hobbled towards us on their wonky legs. Ginger was not impressed.

'Let's go up to the Winter Gardens,' I said. 'We can get a coffee in there. And cake.'

She shrugged and trailed behind me as I marched up the hill.

There was a big sign up on the conservatory saying the Winter Gardens were shut for refurbishment. I'm not sure how long the place had been shut but it looked derelict. I was disappointed and turned to Ginger. 'My mum and dad used to bring me here when I was really young. There was a soft play and a coffee shop where they bought me giant Smartie cookies.'

I walked further round the glass building, sighing at the shattered panes and the wooden boards covered in graffiti. 'And there was a big wooden bench that was carved from a tree trunk.'

'Aren't they all?'

I tutted. 'You know what I mean, it still looked like a big bit of a tree.'

'Mmmm.'

I could tell she wasn't interested and, to be honest, her lack of enthusiasm was starting to annoy me. I was about to suggest we just called it a day, when she spotted the giant spiral slide and started to run towards the swing park. I hesitated, I was nineteen years old, playing on slides and swings was not how I wanted to spend my time, but as I saw the muted fire of Ginger's hair streaming behind her, and her feet pounding the grass in her bright red shoes, I relented. Friends had to do things their friends wanted to do at times, I knew that, so if hanging out at the swing park made her happy, that's what we'd do. Ginger and me stayed in the park till the light softened into evening and even later, till it got too dark to see properly.

'That's great Wendy,' said Saanvi. 'You seem to be spending a lot of your free time with Ginger? Is she the one who's been helping you do up the house?'

I nodded. We were at my house a lot, decorating mostly – the whole house had a freshly painted smell which made me feel on top of things.

We still spent some time at Ginger's house too, mostly because she wanted to check up on her cat. It was usually just us, I rarely saw her uncle Tam. Often, Ginger said, he was still asleep in his bedroom, other times he was at Fran's, and we had the place to ourselves.

She wasn't as proud of her uncle being a successful business-man as you might think she'd be. I once counted six giant television sets – I mean giant like you'd see on the wall of a pub, like the huge screen at the back of The Drury, for instance – lined up along the wall in their hall, and propped up against the sofas in the front room. I asked her why they needed so many and she said they were part of a deal her uncle Tam and Roddy were doing. I don't know what a TV like that would sell for but it certainly wasn't a small deal.

He came back early one Thursday, just as Ginger and me were cutting the mouldy bits off a block of cheddar to try and make some sandwiches. The cat was wandering between our legs, rubbing its skinny body against our ankles and miaowing for attention.

The front door slammed like a warning bell, and the cat leapt into the hall, avoiding Uncle Tam as he stomped into the kitchen, surprisingly heavy on his feet for someone so wiry and slight. As before, the hair on one side of his face swung low and it was only when he turned round that I saw the fresh slash opened on his cheekbone, framed by patchy, seagreen bruises on each side.

'What happened to your—' I began but Ginger took me by the arm and pulled me away.

'He might seem nice,' she said when we were back in her bedroom, 'but . . .'

'He isn't?' I asked.

'Well, you just have to be careful around him, that's all,' she said. 'Tell you what, let's go to yours and think about tackling your bedroom next.'

Back at mine, I lounged on my bed while Ginger paced round the room, running her hand across the walls and throwing out colour suggestions. She kept fingering the bald patch at her crown.

'Is that new?' I asked, gently because I knew by then how sensitive she was about it.

She shrugged. It seemed to me she was saying less these days, shrugging more.

'Has your mum been back?'

She glared at me. 'As if. I told you, she only comes round when she needs money. She has to be desperate.'

She joined me on the bed and told me to put out the light so we could look at the stars. I flipped the switch by the door and she pulled the curtains across the window. On the ceiling above my bed, Ginger had stuck half a dozen neon stars so that when we looked up in the dark it was like lying under a starlit sky. We spent hours lying there watching the stars, it was one of my favourite things we did together.

I watched her staring at the stars in the dark. The yellow light bounced off her skin and made her look ghostly. I knew what it was like to have a desperate parent, so I knew it wasn't easy.

'And is there anything else you want to talk about? Anything else you've been up to?' Saanvi was still there, asking me questions and writing her notes.

I hesitated, wondering if I should tell her about my visits to Diane's. After I'd realized there was a certain spot on the hill that lets you see almost directly into her house, I'd been going there quite a lot. I could have knocked on her door and told her how much her advice on writing, and life generally, meant to me, how she was helping me, and how much we had in common because I think she would've been chuffed to know the impact she was having on a fellow writer. But I knew she was really busy and I didn't want to bother her; I just felt this need to see her, to drink her in, that's all. And anyway, she was the one who'd told me I should spend time outdoors and let nature inspire me. I'd take a flask of tea and Mum's old blanket and enjoy the fresh air on the hill opposite her house. I managed to go two or three times a week even though Ginger and me were busy doing other stuff as well. It felt so calming, watching the flowers in her garden sway in the breeze, and that huge oak tree in front of her window standing there tall and permanent. I'd watch as she came out of the house in her beautiful red mac, swinging her bag, or looping her hair behind her ears. A couple of times I saw her with a little boy, once helping him keep his balance on a bright blue scooter, another chasing him down the path as he wore an imitation hard hat and a tool belt like he'd just come off a building site. That was typical of Diane, looking after other people's children even though she was so busy with her own life. Often, she'd get into her little red Fiesta and drive off to do her business. She'd be going to the library, or maybe for a doctor's appointment. Sometimes she might be going to sit in a coffee shop alone, to people watch and write stories. Or maybe to the hairdresser to get just the very ends snipped off her beautiful soft hair. I'd hold my breath till she drove out of her driveway and then sit and sip my tea for a couple more hours, hoping to catch another glimpse of her when she came back home. The hours flew by and the trains would come roaring in and out of the station, groups of people coming and going, trips into town, or to meet friends maybe. I'd sip my tea and sometimes hum to myself as the light afternoons turned to dusk. My shoulders would be cold by then, my flask empty, and my knees a bit stiff. I'd pack up my stuff, go home and see what Ginger was up to. I wasn't doing anything wrong but I wasn't sure Saanvi would see it that way so I said nothing, and made a sort of sucking noise with my teeth against my bottom lip, tasting the artificial waxiness of the lipstick. It beat me how anyone could want to kiss that and get a mouthful of chemicals.

'What about your book group? Are you still going there?'

'Writers' group's been cancelled for the last few weeks,' I said truthfully, although nobody had told me and the first time I'd sat in The Drury on my own with a Bacardi Breezer for almost an hour before I'd given up. I hadn't seen or heard from anybody from the group since the night out when Joseph had walked out on Henry. Muriel had posted something on the WhatsApp group the next day about Henry being unavailable for the next couple of weeks. She'd ended the message with 'Joseph?' but whether that meant Joseph was going to take over as chairperson if Henry retired, I wasn't sure. I hoped not – total amateur.

'Oh dear,' said Saanvi. 'Well, let's hope it's back on soon after a summer break, it's been so good for your confidence, hasn't it?'

'I couldn't go next week anyway. Ginger and me are going to a tribute night at The Flying Tumbler. That's where a band nobody knows pretends to be a famous band and people go and drink and watch them,' I added, in case, like me, she hadn't heard of a tribute night before.

'That's great,' she said. 'Who's on?'

'A band called Mamma Mia. They're coming all the way from Sweden apparently. I hope they like Viewpark.'

Saanvi laughed. 'Oh, you're a card sometimes Wendy, you know that?'

'Am I?' I said, but I smiled because I could tell she was pleased with me, and I was really happy to be getting things right at last.

21

IT WAS ALMOST THE end of summer when Ginger had her idea for our big day out.

We were painting my downstairs hall, the paint this time a more acceptable shade of deep yellow. It was giving my house a summery feel, which made me happy.

Ginger was humming along to Lewis Capaldi as she reached up to slap yellow paint high on the wall next to the front door. She looked across at me suddenly and said, 'Hey, you know what we should do?'

'What?' I was perched halfway up the stairs doing a difficult bit near the stair carpet and didn't look at her.

'Go to the seaside.'

I laughed and carried on painting. 'Ginger, it's nearly September in Scotland, it's far too cold to go paddling.'

'Please Wendy. I'd just like to see the sea, and we could get an ice cream, and maybe go looking for crabs. We could walk for miles along the beach and there'd be no one else, except us.'

She came over and pushed her shoulder against mine. 'Come on, we've worked so hard on the house, we deserve it. And you've got the day off tomorrow, what else are you going to be doing?'

She was right – thanks to her my house was starting to look really good. She was a tireless worker, insisting we finished stuff when I couldn't be bothered, endlessly trailing round Dunelm, or B&M, or the Barras, searching for the perfect posters or ornaments, or bedspread. Just the day before we'd gone over to Sofa King in the industrial estate and put down a deposit on a gorgeous new leather couch and two chairs. I'd never have done it all without her, I owed her a day out at least.

That night, we packed raspberry jam sandwiches, mini bottles of Irn-Bru and some salt and vinegar crisps into one of my old rucksacks. We Googled the route to Ayr, and I made sure my mum's old Micra still started.

'All those times we've waited on buses and trains and you never said you had a car,' said Ginger, using the back of her hand to wipe the thick dust off the dashboard as I checked the mirrors and adjusted my seat.

'It's my mum's,' I said. 'I haven't been in it since . . . she died.'

'Do you miss her?' she asked me, reaching over to pat my arm awkwardly.

I shook my head because sometimes, I could hardly remember what Mum had been like before the illness took hold. When we still lived with Dad she was always shouting at him, even if they were in the same room, she'd practically scream at him to make sure he understood just how disappointed she was with him not being able to get a job. I didn't think that was fair because he'd worked in newspaper distribution, and as anyone who'd been following current affairs would know, people were not buying newspapers any more. So how could he get a job distributing them? And he was willing to do most things. For a while he worked in the Chunky Chicken factory in Coatbridge. Mum didn't like that either because he always stunk so badly when he came home she made him take off his clothes on the front porch before she let him into the house. Once, he took off his shirt in front of me and a chicken fillet fell onto the floor as he bent over. He stuck it out till the factory shut down and he got his redundancy. Mum said that was the worst thing that ever happened because then he had enough money to go out and drink every day. Nothing to do but drink, he would say.

But then later, when it was just me and Mum, it wasn't like we suddenly spent loads more time together just because it was only us sharing the house. Unlike Dad, she had no trouble getting work. Seems like there's always work for women to do. As long as people want their toilets cleaned, or their papers filed, or their kids looked after, or their pints poured for them, there will always be work for women. Amazing really she still had time to look after me and the house and write all those notes telling me what to do.

'Wendy!' shouted Ginger, as the car jolted forwards in the dark. It was getting late by then and I hadn't switched the headlights on.

'Sorry,' I said. 'I was miles away. Stalled it.' I laughed at Ginger's frowning face. 'Were you scared? Don't worry, I used to do that all the time when I was learning.'

'Who taught you to drive?'

'My mum, mostly.' I've thought about that quite a bit since she died. How she wanted me to drive as soon as I was seventeen, insisted on it in fact. Even on the days she'd come back from her second job, she'd have a quick something to eat then it'd be straight back into the car.

'It's freedom, Wendy, driving,' she'd say. 'You can get into the car and drive, no need to wait for a man to take you anywhere, hear me?'

At the time it was just annoying, having to go out and spend time with her, but now I see she was right. The world was full of people trying to restrict girls' behaviour – don't wear skirts that are too short, don't wear red lipstick, don't walk anywhere on your own, don't stay out too late – all for our own good of course, but the focus was always on what you couldn't do. Mum wasn't like that, she was all about what you could and *should* do. I see that now.

She'd been right about the driving lessons too. I'd passed first time thanks to her making me go out and practise every day, and keeping on at me till I got it right. Maybe we needed her to shout at us sometimes, me and Dad.

'She sounds brilliant,' said Ginger, fiddling with the volume dial on the radio and rubbing the dust off the handbrake with her sleeve.

I stopped checking the gearstick and looked at her. 'Why would you say that?'

'Well, I'm sure there was plenty of stuff she'd rather have been doing than sitting with her heart in her mouth while you mastered the gears and all this.' She gestured towards the dashboard. 'And did you not say she had about sixty different jobs, she'd have been tired with all that.'

'I suppose,' I said doubtfully.

'And she never left you with anyone else Wendy. She always stayed and looked after you while she could. Before she, you know, died and everything . . .' She trailed off.

'Yes Ginger, I know what you mean. I just never thought of her like that before. I suppose she was really good to me, in some ways anyway.'

'What did she die of?' Ginger was still asking questions.

'Cancer,' I said curtly, turning off the engine and getting out of the car. I didn't want to talk about that. Not yet. I knew Ginger would expect me to be sad, but grief is more than just one thing. I was sad, sometimes, but I was also angry – she'd taken me away from Dad, she hadn't helped him through bad times, what kind of love was that? Also, I felt guilty. For all the times I didn't go to her when she shouted in the middle of the night, and the many days I wished I could have just stayed at work and not had to go home to care for her. People don't want to hear about these things, though. When they ask you how you feel after someone close to you has died, they expect sadness, that's all they want to hear, it's as much as they can understand. I didn't want to go into all that with Ginger.

We stayed up far later than we'd intended, watching a full season of some Norwegian detective drama I'd heard the others talking about at writers' group. It was good but not as groundbreaking as they'd made out. I've noticed this before, when people get together to discuss programmes or books, or whatever. If they like each other, and one of them says they like, say this particular TV programme, the other one almost dives on top to say they liked it even better. Then the first one agrees and, before you know it, it's like that children's game where you put one hand on top of the other to make a tower of hands. No one wants to be the one to say, well, it was okaaay, if everyone else thinks it's the best thing on TV. I mean what are you missing then that everyone else is loving? Anyway, the programme we watched was okay enough for us to watch episode after episode until eventually I woke up in the cold with Ginger's hair stuck to my cheek and a crick in my neck.

I nipped round to Diane's before Ginger woke the next morning. The timing wasn't ideal because it was too early for her to be going anywhere and I didn't get to see her but I was happy just being near her for a while.

'You were up early,' said Ginger when I got back.

'I was out getting some bits and pieces for the picnic.'

'I thought we'd already packed everything?'

'Come on, hurry up and get dressed or the day'll be over before it even starts,' I said, busying myself with the kettle so she wouldn't ask me what I'd bought.

We didn't get on the road until after eleven. 'So what,' said Ginger, 'what's the hurry?' That's the kind of thing my dad would have said to my mum, resulting in a frosty silence in the car until we reached our destination. I just shrugged and said at least the roads would be quieter as it was well after rush hour. Ginger played about with the radio for a bit before finding the station she liked, and settled back in her seat to watch the roads go by. We didn't talk much but it was nice, a comfortable sort of silence that lets you know you're not alone but you can go and think your own thoughts without being rude.

The beach at Croy was empty, as we'd anticipated. The skies behind it stretched out, grey and murky, threatening a downpour. I glanced at the back seat to see what sort of jacket Ginger had brought with her – her denim-look anorak with no hood.

'I told you to bring a waterproof,' I said, indicating my own bright red rain mac, very similar to the one I'd seen Diane wearing – we even had the same taste in clothes.

'That's my jacket Wendy. I've only got one jacket.'

'You'll need to stop shopping for all these lipsticks and buy a new jacket instead,' I said. I looked up at the clouds again and sighed. 'Oh well, we might get lucky, maybe the sun will come out.'

She'd already opened her door and was stretching her legs. 'Come on,' she said. 'We're at the seaside Wendy!'

She slammed her door shut and ran down to the deserted beach, her hair streaming behind her in the wind. I watched her and laughed.

'Wait for me,' I called then ran after her, pulling on my rain mac on the way.

The rush of the waves and the salt on my lips roused my senses, reminding me of days long forgotten when I'd run the length of the beach, chased by Dad, and followed by Mum, pulling her hair away from her face and laughing. I faced down the wind and followed Ginger to the rocks. We found loads of great stuff that day: pebbles like jewels with their shiny hard edges; whole pearly seashells unbroken by the fierceness of the waves or walkers' boots trampling on them; foreign coins, dusky brown with age; and as many shards of blue and white pottery as we could carry.

'Look at this one Wendy,' called Ginger, standing by the edge of a rock pool close to the water's edge. She held up a small triangle of duck-egg blue shell, achingly pretty and almost too fragile to touch. 'Isn't it beautiful?' she said, looking up at me with eyes that were round and sparkling like a child's.

'You're beautiful,' I said, then raised my hand to my mouth to stop any more words coming out.

She lifted my hand away from my face and took it in hers. Her fingers were very cold, as she placed the shell in my palm.

'For you,' she said. 'For bringing me here.'

The wind whipped round our faces making them red and

numb. Ginger's hair was like a mad whirlpool of colour, and her eyes were shining. We stood there together for a few moments till I said, 'Come on, are you hungry?'

'We left the sandwiches in the car,' she said.

'Never mind them. You've got to have chips at the seaside. It's the rule.'

Ginger's smile grew even broader, like she couldn't believe her luck. 'It's the rule,' she repeated, laughing. 'We've got to have chips.'

On the way to the chippy, we stopped to look in the window of the Oxfam shop. I followed Ginger's eyes to a striking jacket hanging at the back of the display. It was deep beige, almost orange, and looked like it was made of soft suede. The collar was yolk-coloured fur.

'That's lovely, isn't it Wendy? Who gives stuff like that away? For free?' She stared in the window. 'It looks so cosy.'

'Come on,' I said, grabbing her hand. 'The least we deserve is a warm jacket.'

Later, we sat on the shingle, throwing pebbles and shells into the waves. I stared at the water lapping the shoreline and drifted into a daydream about Diane, Ginger and me all on a day out together. Maybe we'd trek up a snowy mountain path, and it'd be one of Ginger's good days like this one, her brilliant orange hair would be streaking behind her as she ran, laughing and throwing snowballs, her green eyes shining. Diane would be striding along in her classy red mac, older and wiser and leading the way, and Ginger and me would follow on like the von Trapp children marching behind the beautiful Maria. We wouldn't care about the weather because—

'The rain's getting heavier Wendy,' said Ginger, pulling up

the fur collar of her new jacket to keep her neck warm against the wind. Returned to Ginger and the beach, I watched as she leaned her head to one side so that her cheek was resting on the fluffy material. Her hair streamed into her mouth and when she pulled it out it flew into the air. Her cheeks were grazed red with the wind and her orange jacket shone. She was a blast of colour, like the flames of a fire, roaring and crackling. That's all she needed, I thought, someone to tend her and make sure she burned into life. She smiled at me then turned and looked up into the rain, her mouth open to catch the drops on her tongue.

The light was fading and the seagulls were pecking desperately at the damp shingle. In summer I could imagine this place teeming with screeching toddlers, exhausted parents and aspirin-white grandparents snoozing on towels. But now there was only us.

She turned to me, her face pink and healthy for once, her eyes gleaming in the pale light. She pointed to the thin crescent of silver moon above us, its light casting the shadow of the rocks on the damp sand.

'Look at that Wendy. Even the moon's come out for us. Hasn't this been the most perfect day?'

Not quite perfect because Diane wasn't with us but I didn't say that. 'Yeah, perfect,' I said. 'But we'll need to make a move now Ginger, or it'll be midnight before we get home.'

'I want to stay here for ever,' she whispered, but she gathered her jacket around her and stood up. 'Thanks for this Wendy.'

'You're welcome,' I said. 'It suits you.'

'No, not the jacket. I mean yes, the jacket but also, this.' She waved her hand at the slow lapping waves, the sounds of the gulls in the night.

A grizzly rain started again as we got back to the car and, by the time we reached the motorway, it was pelting down, my wipers flashing across the windscreen to keep up. The road ahead was slick and dangerous.

'What a downpour,' I said, taking my eyes off the road for a moment and turning to Ginger. She was sound asleep, her new jacket wrapped tightly around her, her hair falling over her face and dripping orange into its yellow fur collar. She was snoring softly. I smiled, and turned up the heating to make sure she was warm enough.

Later that evening, when I went to hang my jacket up at home, I reached into the pocket and felt for my blue shell. I stroked its smooth surface and placed it on the table next to my bed, in front of the red frame with Mum's picture and the love heart frame which now contained a photo Irish Mary had taken of Ginger and me, standing in front of my bus in the sunshine. I just needed to get one of Diane now and all the people I loved would be within my reach.

22

EARLY NEXT MORNING I WAS back at work and wiping the inside of the windscreen when I heard the rapping on the door of the bus. It was Irish Mary, with Terry, Myra and a couple of the others standing in a huddle behind her under three huge umbrellas.

'I can't move till quarter past,' I said, 'but come and sit on the bus to keep dry. I'll put the heating on.'

'Aw thanks Wendy, you're a gem,' said Irish Mary as she and the others shook the rain from their brollies and traipsed onto the bus.

'No wee helper today, Wendy?'

I shook my head. 'Just me today,' I said. 'Where are you all off to?'

'Up to St Columbas for a coffee morning. For St Andrews Hospice.'

'By the way Myra,' Terry cut in, 'did you hear about poor Maureen McGraw?'

'Who?'

'You know Maureen, she was at school with your Sandra?'

Myra looked at her blankly.

'You do, her sister Gail was the lollipop lady for years outside St Johns?'

'I don't know her,' said Myra, shaking her head.

'You do, she and her man moved to the new estate behind Scotmid?'

'Listen Terry, I definitely don't know a Maureen McGraw.'

Irish Mary chipped in. 'You do Myra, she won the lamp at the last St Patrick's night?'

'The one with the green shade?'

'That's the one.'

'Why didn't you say, of course I know that Maureen. What about her?'

'She's dead.'

'What? She can't be, not after she won that lamp!'

'She is though. She got run down by the van delivering morning rolls to The View, poor woman.'

'What a shame.'

The women were quiet for a bit then Terry said, 'They've started a collection for her. It's only been going three days and they've already raised nearly £300.'

I turned round in my seat and said, 'A collection for Maureen? The woman that's dead?'

'Yeah,' said Terry. 'She was very popular, more than that Gail one anyway, the kids could hardly get across the road before she'd put the stick down and gone back to her fag on the wall.'

'But . . .' I said, 'what could she possibly need £300 for? She's dead.'

Terry's smile faded a bit and Irish Mary said quickly, 'It's for a bench Wendy.'

I must have looked unconvinced because she added, 'With a plaque. To commemorate . . .'

'Where she was run over by the bread van. Right,' I said. I mean, it wasn't something I'd want but maybe I'd got the wrong end of the stick as usual. I turned back in my seat and started the engine to begin my shift.

There was a light rapping on the glass of the door and I opened it again. 'Morning Kevin,' I said. 'You're in luck, I was just about to leave. Your seat's free.' I waited till he'd sat down and leaned his face against the window before I drove off on my first circuit of the day to Bellshill and back.

I was walking home after my shift finished when I got a WhatsApp from Muriel saying writers' group was on that Monday. At first I wasn't sure whether I wanted to go back – I'd hardly written anything all summer because I'd been so busy with Ginger and doing up the house. But I decided to go in the end because I'd have hated to disappoint Diane if she ever asked to see what I'd been writing and I had nothing to show her.

Henry was back. He was wearing one of his natty blue suits and a pastel pink tie so I gathered everything was fine with him again.

'Hi Henry, are you and Joseph—'

Muriel cut me off with a smile and her hand on my arm. 'Henry's back in charge Wendy, which is great because we've all missed him, haven't we?'

'Well . . .'

'Yes, we have. So are there many submissions this week Henry? Maybe we should just make a start?'

I looked round the group. As well as Henry and Muriel, there was Reginald, half asleep and propped up against the jackets but there all the same, Sophie, looking pale and oddly still wearing her beanie hat even though it was warm in the bar, and a new guy I'd never seen before, who looked to be in his mid twenties or so. He was slim, dressed in a fringed suede jacket over an ice blue shirt, and his long legs were draped round the bar stool. A small smile played around his lips and he had the eyelashes of a cabaret star. Joseph was nowhere to be seen, which didn't worry me. Before I could ask who the new guy was, Henry was back in his routine.

'Order, order, let's get the meeting started, lots of submissions to get through. This evening, I think we'll start with a story from our new member, er, correct me if I've got this wrong but I have you here as Bounce?' Henry looked up for confirmation and we all looked over at the boy, who smiled softly back at us in the dim light of the pub.

'That's right. My real name's Rick,' he said, and paused before adding, 'O'Shea.' He raised his hands in apology and smiled again.

Muriel clapped her hands together. 'Very good,' she said. 'We won't forget that in a hurry, will we Sophie?'

Sophie shook her head and frowned a little as she tried to work out the joke.

'Okay, Bounce it is,' said Henry nodding vigorously. 'Please.' He held out his hand to indicate that he should start reading.

Bounce took off his jacket and stood up to read his story. I sat back with my eyes half shut, preparing myself for the usual crap first-time members gave us at meetings.

The story was about a young couple called Paul and Liam who met in a small village pub in Kinsale in Ireland. Their love was a secret so they met in this deserted old cinema, sitting at the crossroads but set back behind the road and hidden in bushes.

Bounce's accent was Southern Irish I think, beautiful and soft, so low we had to lean forwards to catch what he was saying. As he was reading, he pushed back some of his black hair from his face, highlighting his deep green eyes, set far apart on his face, and his thin mouth, which barely seemed to open to form the words. The light from the bar shone behind him, framing him like an angel, and I shot a quick look at Henry, who was staring open-mouthed.

The story continued. The villagers found out Paul and Liam were seeing each other and vowed to run them out of the very place they'd been born and raised. But then Paul's father overheard them talking together and realized that love is just love, and always something to be cherished rather than a reason for violence. He persuaded the rest of the townsfolk to give their blessing and it all ended happily ever after. Not the most believable storyline ever but you had to hear him read it. He was just so . . . convincing, you were rooting for the young couple regardless. I glanced again at Henry, I could tell he was in Kinsale, picturing himself in that gloomy cinema with Paul or maybe Liam, the more handsome of the two.

When Bounce had finished reading he said, 'And that's the end. I was bananas drunk when I wrote it, like. I hope ye all will tell me the truth anyway.' He sat down and pulled his glass of white wine towards him, lifting it and taking a small sip.

Muriel got in first. 'Well, I thought that was just beautiful, really. I loved it, wouldn't change a single word.'

'Agreed,' said Sophie softly, and I could tell she was thinking how crap her own attempts at writing love stories had been in comparison.

I said it was great to welcome another real writer to the group.

The others looked at me and I added quickly, 'In addition to all the real writers we already have here.'

Henry cleared his throat but it didn't seem to work because his voice was still husky when he said, 'That was very good indeed Bounce. How long did you say you'd been writing?'

Bounce shrugged. 'For ever. Haven't we all?' He laughed and said he was glad we'd enjoyed it.

Henry moved on to the next piece, a poem about the transience of icicles by Reginald, and we all sat back wondering how we were going to compete with Bounce.

After all the submissions had been read and critiqued, Bounce asked us if anyone wanted a drink.

'Oh, we usually just buy our own Bounce, seems fairer that way when we're not all here every week,' said Muriel, reaching down for her purse.

He insisted though and headed to the bar with our order. Henry watched him for a moment then said he'd go and join him 'just to help him carry the drinks back'. We all watched as Henry stood close to Bounce at the bar and the two laughed together, heads close.

Muriel smiled. 'Looks like he's over that business with Joseph then.'

Sophie sighed.

'Never mind Sophie,' I said. 'He was never really for you, was he?'

'I'm sure I don't know what you mean, me and Henry are just good friends,' she said, taking her glasses off and laying them on the table.

'How are things anyway Sophie?' said Muriel. 'Everything okay?'

Reginald was snoring softly in the corner but Sophie eyed me to indicate that I was listening.

'Oh it's fine Sophie. Wendy's one of the girls, a regular, aren't you love?'

I was surprised by that but nodded and said to Sophie, 'You'd feel a lot better if you took that hat off. You must be boiling.'

Sophie sighed and reached up and pulled off her hat.

My mouth gaped open. 'What on earth happened to your hair?'

'It's called a buzz cut. I needed a change so I thought . . .'

'You thought you'd chop off all your hair? You look like—'

'An edgy supermodel, you're right Wendy,' said Muriel quickly, patting Sophie on the arm. 'And anyway, it'll grow back before you know it.'

Sophie blushed. 'Don't worry, I know it looks hideous. I just thought a change would do me good, shake things up a little.' She glanced over at Henry again. 'Anyway, I'm better off without men, I've decided.'

I thought the problem was she couldn't get a man but I might have got that wrong so I said nothing.

'Oh don't give up on them altogether,' said Muriel. 'My Bobby's always been a good man, especially when he's sober. He was a rock when my Angie died, I'll tell you that. Don't know how I'd have coped without him.'

Sophie waved her hand as the boys came back over, clearly she'd had enough sharing for one night. 'It's fine Muriel, honestly. Thanks for asking though. And you Wendy,' though I hadn't asked anything at all.

We all had another drink, and even Reginald woke up long enough to tell us how much his dead wife, Elsie, would have loved being with all us 'young folk'. At one point Muriel put her arm round me and referred to me as 'our Wendy here', and it struck me that maybe I was getting things right at last. I wasn't doing worse than anyone else in the group at least, and I was definitely doing better than Britney Shears over there. I had my best friends Ginger and Diane, as well as all my friends from the bus. And there I was drinking the beer my new friend Bounce had bought me, and joining in the conversation with my writers' group. It had been just over a year since Mum died and things were finally looking up for me.

23

Diane Weston retweeted
Award-winning novelist @diane_weston presents a host of
new Scottish talent as well as reading from her own work
@WriteNow @CCA_Glasgow Thursday 25 September @
6.30pm. Tickets available here . . .

ALTHOUGH GINGER AND ME had been busy all summer, Diane
hadn't been far from my mind. I still sat on the hill watching her
house and catching little glimpses of her going about her day at
least a couple of times a week, depending on my shifts and what
Ginger and me had planned. She'd let her hair grow over the
summer and it now reached well past her shoulders and swung
about as she got into her Fiesta, or bent down to trim her pink
rose bushes. I think my favourite outfit was a yellow polka dot
dress I'd seen her in two or three times. It reached just below
her knees and was cinched in at the waist, making her look like
Doris Day or one of those other glamorous actresses from the
olden days. I was glad I'd started taking binoculars because it
meant I could see every detail of her appearance, even down
to the cork wedged heel of her sandals and the little silver bells
dangling from their straps.

It was a tweet she sent just before the Write Now festival that convinced me I should go to her event, even though it was at the Centre for Contemporary Arts, which is not a place I ever imagined myself visiting, certainly not on my own.

Like many things in life, nothing about the act of writing is improved by doing it in a posse. You don't need others to lift you up. Write what you want, go where you want, do what you want. #WomenWriters

It was amazing how in sync we were and how many times she'd tweeted exactly what I needed to hear at exactly the right time. I tweeted back that I was looking forward to seeing her at Write Now and kept the phone propped up against the sink as I did the dishes, and in front of the TV as I flicked through Netflix, so I wouldn't miss her reply. I wasn't disappointed – she liked my tweet three hours later, and a quick check through the other forty-seven responses revealed that she hadn't liked them all, in fact she'd only liked twenty-nine of them, so I knew she was genuinely pleased I was going along to support her.

I was still quite nervous going into Diane's event but it turned out the CCA was really just a café with books piled up on wide glass counters, and huge, black and white canvases of nothing much on the walls. Even though no one spoke to me, there were lots of people on their own like me so I felt okay.

The event was billed as a 'new writers' showcase' so, as well as seeing Diane, I was interested to compare the work being showcased with my own and gauge where I was on the scale of completely crap (Reginald, say) to absolutely brilliant (Diane and Raymond Carver, for example). I hoped I was nearer the brilliant end but it's very hard to tell when your writers' group is full of amateurs who may or may not be giving you their honest opinions.

The place was packed so I was pleased to grab an aisle seat on the front row when the guy who'd been sitting there got up to hang up his jacket. He glared at me when he came back to take his seat but I kept staring at my brochure till he swore under his breath and went to find a seat further back.

I spotted Diane standing at the edge of the stage, waiting to come on. She looked nervous, clutching a bottle of water and her book. I wanted to tell her it would all be fine, they'd love her, but she was distracted by an old guy with a head like a potato. I vaguely recognized him then realized it was the same guy I'd seen at her house a few times, sometimes cutting her grass or washing her car. I thought it was weird that her handyman would come to one of her literary events but that's how popular she is – who wouldn't want to come and hear her perform?

I didn't like the way Potato Head kept talking to her and ruining her concentration, though. At one point he even put his hand on her arm and, being as polite as she is, Diane didn't shake it off or look annoyed. I really admired the way she handled people, I bet people came up to her all the time, getting into her personal space. I felt like decking him though, who did he think he was, touching Diane's arm like that. He was standing close enough to her that he was almost whispering in her ear, I could see Diane's hair moving slightly with his breath. She was trying hard to smile but she wasn't answering him. Just as I was wondering if I should go up and ask if everything was okay, the lights went down and Diane walked onto the stage.

I leaned forwards in my seat to make myself even taller than usual in the hope she would spot me and wave.

I have to say she'd outdone herself on the outfit front. In honour of the Scottishness of the festival she was wearing a tartan pinafore, cut off just above her knee, and a little tammy with a red pompom at an angle on her head. I thought she looked adorable and a great ambassador for Scotland. But, famous as she was, it seemed like the costume made her unrecognizable to some people in the audience because as she sat down, someone called out, 'Hey, if it isn't Fran and Anna, gaun yerself darling,' and lots of people laughed. I could feel my face burning and I turned round and shouted, 'Her name's Diane,' which made everyone laugh even louder. Diane blushed almost as red as her tammy so I could tell she was pleased I'd called them out for being stupid.

Diane talked first about what she called the Scottish writing scene, and I made a mental note to find out where that was. She spoke brilliantly about new voices, and finding your rhythm, and the exciting literature coming out of Scotland. I could have listened to her all night but unfortunately she had to let some of the new voices come out and be heard. They were okay, I suppose, though in my opinion once you've heard one poem on the struggle for Independence and identity, you've pretty much heard them all. I shuffled about in my seat, waiting for the last new voice to shut up so that we could hear from a professional writer at last.

It was worth the wait because, when Diane finally got to read, she chose a passage from *This Girl's Life* which had struck a particular chord with me. It was about the day the girl's father missed her race at sports day and, when he did turn up, he was so drunk she didn't acknowledge him because she was ashamed of the way he smelled and how his voice was much louder than everyone else's. Later, she was more ashamed for feeling that way and gave her dad the silver medal she'd won to show him she still loved him.

I forgot about everything else and just lost myself in Diane's words. It reminded me that books are the only things that matter, and Diane's voice made everything better. No razzle dazzle, just the words and her voice reading them. It's deeper than you might expect for such a petite woman, and confident, like she was leading a choir. The sound seemed to come from her stomach rather than her neck, maybe writers get training in how to read because she was really very good at it. Her voice reached into me, touched a small, sad place in my heart that I hadn't been aware of all summer. Her words were beautiful so I'm not sure why I was crying by the time she'd finished. The studenty type next to me, in her chunky cardigan and earrings that reached her collar, was tutting and muttering about putting Diane off, but I ignored her and dropped my wet hankies in a little pile in front of her seat.

Diane said she would take questions from the audience and I wriggled about in my seat, mortified, as people asked lots of questions about how she actually wrote the novels – as though she'd share her process with them – and where she got her ideas from. I tried to exchange glances with her to let her know I understood how frustrating this must be for her but she was too busy concentrating for us to make eye contact. I raised my hand to ask a sensible question, writer to writer, but she didn't see it. Or maybe she wanted the people who were just there as fans of her work, rather than writers, to have a chance to ask their questions. It was a mistake though because the questions were all crap, especially some about structure and voice from one girl who started off by saying she was studying for an MLitt at Glasgow, like Diane had any interest whatsoever in that! But Diane was very kind and answered them all patiently, which was one of the reasons I admired her so much.

She thanked us and left the stage while an old guy came on and said Diane would be signing copies of *One World* in the foyer. I grabbed my jacket and dashed out the room so I could be first in the queue. Everyone else must have had the same idea because by the time I reached the foyer, there was already a queue of thirty or so people, and I couldn't even see Diane for the crowd.

Over the next twenty minutes or so, I watched as people queued to meet Diane. When they got to the table where she was sitting, they'd talk to her for well over the time it took for her to sign their book. It was one of the things writers had to put up with, hangers-on, people who become fascinated with what they write but make the mistake of thinking that, just because they get to know a writer's characters intimately, that makes them friends with the writer. Poor Diane.

I practised my greeting as I waited. 'Hello,' I whispered to myself then shook my head. 'Hi, how are you?' Or maybe: 'Hi Diane, long time no see.' No, that wasn't right either. Maybe just a wave and 'Hey there,' Christ no, we weren't in an American sitcom, get it together Wendy. Just 'Hello Diane,' and a slight raising of my right hand, that was the best approach. I practised that a couple of times then became aware of the girl who'd been sitting next to me earlier standing a few feet away, nudging the guy who'd given me his seat and smirking.

I couldn't wait to see their faces when they realized I was friends with Diane.

My legs were shaking a bit as I got closer to the head of the queue and I kept smacking my lips together to try and stop my mouth from drying up too much for me to talk. When it was my turn to move forwards at last, I raised my hand and said, 'Hello Di—, oh shit . . .' my rucksack had fallen off my shoulder and I'd tripped over the strap. I'd fallen forwards and staggered into the table in front of Diane, knocking a pile of books off the end.

She half stood, half supported herself on the squinty table as I set myself upright and tried to straighten out the table.

'Sorry about that,' I mumbled, my cheeks warm, and getting warmer as I heard muffled laughter in the queue behind me, and an assistant ran forwards to pick up the books.

'Don't worry at all,' Diane said, smoothing down her pinafore and sitting back down. 'Could've happened to anyone. Are you okay? You didn't hurt yourself as you fell, I hope?' She smiled such a warm smile like she was really pleased to see me that I forgot my embarrassment and said, 'No, I'm fine, honestly,' and hoiked my rucksack back up onto my shoulder, and flicked my fringe.

There was a pause as I looked down at Diane, hardly able to believe I was standing a hand's breadth away from her after a whole summer of watching her from a distance. She'd taken off her tammy, her skin was glowing, and the light reflected off the little round lenses of her glasses.

She coughed and said, 'So – can I sign a copy of my book for you?'

'What? Oh no, thanks, I've already got your book. It's me,

Wendy. I told you how much I'd loved your book when we chatted in your garden. Remember? Wendy, from Twitter.'

Diane frowned slightly and took off her glasses and looked up at me. 'Wendy, right, yes, of course. Well, thanks for coming anyway, I hope you enjoyed it.'

The assistant called, 'Next,' and Diane smiled over my shoulder.

'Yes, I did, it was fascinating,' I said, panicking then and forgetting all the clever things I'd planned to say. This wasn't going as well as I'd hoped, and I was worried that Diane would see me for my unlikeable, unremarkable self and not the interesting and witty person I wanted to be with her. And I couldn't believe I'd forgotten to bring the coffee cake I'd baked and wrapped in tinfoil for her. What kind of friend turns up empty-handed, and on a special occasion like this too. She'd think I didn't care about her at all. It dawned on me I might have offended her by not buying another copy of her book so I grabbed one from the pile in front of her and said, 'Actually, I'll take another copy please, for . . . a friend.'

'Sure, okay,' said Diane, putting her glasses back on and opening the front flap of the book. 'Who shall I make it—?'

'Wendy,' I said quickly. 'Just write "For Wendy".' I smiled and tried doing the half closing my eyes then opening them really wide thing that Ginger did with boys she liked. I tossed my hair a bit but was too worried my rucksack would fall off my shoulder again to do it as enthusiastically as Ginger did.

Diane glanced round the room like she was looking for someone. 'Right,' she said, handing me the book. 'There you go Wendy. I hope . . . your friend enjoys it.'

She looked beyond me to the next person in the queue but I couldn't bear for it to be over so soon. I yanked my phone out of my pocket and said, 'Would you mind?' and before she had a chance to reply, I leaned across the table so that my face was inches away from hers and took a photo of us both.

'Thanks so much,' I said, delighted to have thought of it.

'It's . . . well, you're welcome. I don't . . . usually do photographs, I mean people don't generally ask for them,' she said, looking at the assistant who stepped forwards and asked if everything was all right.

'Everything's brilliant,' I said, giving her a big smile and putting my phone back in my pocket. 'Thanks so much.' I turned back to Diane who was rubbing her hand across her forehead and biting her bottom lip. She was obviously fed up of having to make small talk with all these strangers, and I wished I could wave a magic wand and make them all disappear so Diane and me could go to the café and drink frothy coffee and talk for hours about characters and plotlines and the books we were reading and—

'So if you could move along, thank you.' The assistant was directing me towards the door.

Just before I left, I turned back and saw Potato Head standing a few feet away from where Diane was sitting. She kept looking over at him, as though she wasn't entirely comfortable with him being so close to her. He approached her desk and actually put his hand on her arm. I was wondering whether I should go back over and ask her if everything was okay when she whispered something in his ear, and he looked up and over at me. He held my gaze for such a long time that I had to look away and concentrate on putting my new book in my bag. By the time I looked up again, he was gone, and Diane was still busy signing books.

It had been an incredible night! Diane's reading had been just as wonderful as I'd expected but to have her defend me, like a real friend, when those folk in the queue were all laughing at me, that showed how deep our connection had become. I jumped on my bed and clicked on the photo of us posing and smiling together – I loved the way Diane had tilted her head so it almost touched mine. I propped the phone up against the pictures of Mum and Ginger, then lay back and shut my eyes. Sure enough, when I sat up and opened them, the first thing I saw was Diane looking back at me. Once I got it printed out and framed, I'd see her smiling at me every morning as I woke up to start my day, and that made me happier than I'd been for a long time.

I wonder now whether I just didn't deserve to be that happy because it was after that perfect evening with Diane that everything began to unravel.

Bad Times for Ginger and Me

24

IT STARTED WITH GINGER'S cat dying.

I was drawing up to Bay 4 at the depot when my phone rang. It had been a long shift and a busy one as people were already hitting the shops for Christmas even though we were still in October. Most people were nice and polite but there were the usual idiots who thought it was funny to try and jump on without paying, or worse, cause trouble on the bus shouting football chants or swearing at my regulars, which is something I don't allow. I wasn't in the best of moods when I answered the call from Ginger, telling me her cat had died.

'Did you call the vet?'

'No, I didn't call the vet Wendy, what's he going to do – bring back her spirit?'

'Sorry,' I said. But I wasn't really sure what she wanted me to say. If the cat was dead, there wasn't much to be done was there? But she was crying which wasn't like her so I knew she was upset.

'How did it die?'

'She. Her name's Nina Simone, Wendy, I told you that.'

I was sure I would have remembered if she had but she was too upset to argue with. 'Sorry. How did . . . Nina Simone die?'

'I don't know. I found her like that. I'm not sure of her exact age but we've had her for years. That guy Mum left with the first time, said he was some sort of musician, he left her with me. Uncle Tam said it was a pussy for a pussy, I remember.'

There was a pause. 'Did you give them your old pussy?'

'No, it's . . . never mind Wendy. The point is, me and Nina've got through things together. She's a survivor like me.'

'But I thought you said she'd died?'

She hung up on me.

I tried calling her back when I got home, and again the next day, but she wasn't answering. I decided to drop in on her after I'd been to Tunnock's. But as I walked back along Main Street, it seemed a shame to be that close to Diane's house and not to sit on the hill for a while first.

I put the brown bags with my steak pie and the carrot cake I'd bought for Ginger on the grass beside me and took my binoculars out of my rucksack. I was in luck because, as soon as I looked through them, I spied Diane coming out of her house. She was wearing her red mac and carrying a small blue and white bag with 'Support Scottish Museums' printed across it. A couple of minutes later, the Bald Wonder, hanging about like a bad smell as usual, came out of the house. They spoke for a few minutes before she got into the car. I tutted as he stooped down to fasten her seatbelt for her – like she couldn't do that for herself – and then shut the door. After Diane drove off, I was winding the cord round my binoculars and getting up when I realized Baldy was still standing in the garden. He walked slowly over to the wall nearest the hill and looked up in my direction. I froze, and dropped the binoculars to the ground. He put his hand up to his forehead, shielding his eyes, and stretched his neck so he was peering up the hill. I scrambled backwards into the clump of trees behind me and crouched there for a few moments before pelting down the hill on the other side and round the back of the station. Afterwards I was annoyed at him for making me feel I'd done something wrong. Diane was the one who'd told me to sit on the hill and admire her roses for inspiration so I wasn't going to let Potato Head stop me from taking her advice. And anyway, anyone was allowed to sit in a public space.

I was still out of breath by the time I reached Ginger's house. It was mid afternoon by then and the place was quiet, as it always was when I was there. It was hard to believe it was the den of iniquity she claimed it was after dark. She talked about people she'd never seen before coming and going, the fights flaring up so fast she hardly had time to flee to her room, the violence and screaming, the police rapping on the door at two in the morning, strangers spilling onto the street like vomit. She said sometimes she put her head under her pillow and screamed into the mattress. She had a lot of pent-up rage I think, I suppose it had to come out some time.

But the flat was quiet as a church that day, and so was she. Either her uncle Tam was at Fran's or he was still sleeping off a hangover somewhere else in the house. Ginger was lolling on top of her frowsty, unmade bed, hardly speaking. She looked tired and every time she yawned I smelled her breath, sour and unpleasant as my mum's had been towards the end.

'I've brought you some carrot cake,' I said, and she took it off me without looking at it and tossed it onto the bed beside her.

The room was cold and dark as ever, despite the late autumn sunshine outside. There was a pile of dirty clothes in the corner, and an empty Pot Noodle carton on the chest of drawers.

I thought it was best to avoid mentioning the cat so I picked up *Elmer Goes to the Circus* and suggested we do some reading. Ginger rolled her eyes.

'Not today Wendy, please. I can't be bothered. I hardly got a wink last night with the noise and sitting up against my door in case . . . anyone came in. I didn't even have wee Nina for company.'

'Come on,' I said. 'You were doing really well last time. We're nearly on the last page and you've read practically all of it yourself.'

I handed her the book and she took it off me reluctantly. She opened the first page and I waited, propped up against her bed with my back to her. She didn't start reading.

'Come on, Ginger.' I turned round in time to see a large tear drop onto a picture of Elmer and his cousin making their way through the jungle. I couldn't see her face, it was shielded by her hair, so I got up on the bed beside her and sat as close as I dared.

'Has . . . something else happened, apart from the cat?' I asked, wondering whether I should put my arm round her shoulders, which were shaking. The room was so cold I could see my breath as I spoke.

'No, it's just . . . What am I doing – reading bloody stories about Elmer the elephant that I should have been reading at eight years old, never mind fifteen.' She swung round to face me. 'And I'm not stupid you know Wendy, I just . . .' She threw her hands in the air then dropped them to her sides hopelessly.

'I know you're not Ginger and, believe me, this is only the start. We'll get you reading these short words then we'll move on to harder books. In fact, do you know what, I think if we finish this one today, we should start on books for your age group next week. We can go to the library and see what they recommend. Diane says—'

'Oh your precious Diane. I might have known she'd have to be brought into it sooner or later. And who the hell is she Wendy? Some book writer you don't even know. Half the time you're sitting outside her house, too scared to go and knock on her door. It's—'

'Wait,' I sat up suddenly. 'How do you know I've been outside her house? Have you been following me?'

She went red and pulled her hair in front of her face. 'Of course I haven't been following you!'

'But then . . . how do you know about her house?'

'I don't know what you're talking about, you're focusing on the wrong things as usual. You told me she lives in one of those huge sandstone mansions. But be honest Wendy, you really only see her when you pay to hear her talk about her books. What kind of friendship is that? You're kidding yourself on even more than me!'

'Is that right? Well, I think you'll find I'm the one who's in a writers' group and writing stories and poems that everyone thinks are excellent.' That was pushing it a bit but I was angry enough by then to say whatever I liked. 'And I'm the one whose life is on the right track Ginger, getting out and about and . . . and going places. I was at the CCA a couple of weeks ago. Diane and me had a photograph taken together, that's what good friends we are. I'm not like you, stuck in this room, not even getting dressed half the time.' I could feel my heart accelerate and my blood pound. Who did Ginger think she was, saying nasty things about my relationship with Diane? Diane was the best thing in my life, I had learned so much from her about writing, and how my voice needed to be heard, and how my opinion was as valid as anyone else's.

I was starting to wonder what I was doing there. Summer had been brilliant – I'd never have done up my house without Ginger's help, and we'd had loads of fun – but lately her moods were getting so bad, I wasn't sure I even wanted to be her friend any more. I stood up angrily, but got my foot twisted in her dirty laundry and fell back onto the bed.

Ginger flounced off the bed, throwing the book behind her so that the edge of it struck me on the side of my face. I cried out and raised my hand to my face, where the hard edge had sliced a thin paper cut all the way down my cheek. When I brought my hand back down, there was a line of blood striping my palm. We both looked at it in shock.

'I'm sorry Wendy, I didn't mean—'

Before she could finish there was a tap at her door.

She looked over but didn't open it.

The knocking grew louder then we heard Roddy's voice. 'Are you in Ginger? It's me, your uncle Roddy. I've got something for you.'

Ginger and me looked at each other but didn't move. The door opened slowly and Roddy's fingers – fat white worms like larvae – curled round the wood.

His chubby yellow face appeared at the door, followed by his lumpy frame. He was wearing a loose blue shirt with a dark wet circle under each arm and you just knew he'd smell like a docker's boxer shorts. He smiled when he saw Ginger standing there then slitted his eyes in disappointment when he saw me sitting on the bed, my hand cradling my bleeding face.

Ginger dropped her head so that her hair covered her face.

'This is my room Roddy, you're not allowed in here,' she mumbled.

'Sorry sweetheart,' he said. 'I just wanted to give you this. Something I got for you special, to say sorry for . . .' He glanced over at me and his lazy eye drooped a bit further, 'Well, sorry for . . . disturbing you last night. I'd had a few . . . Anyway, here, take it, don't mention it to your uncle Tam, eh? This is just between me and you.'

He held out his hand and I could see the muscles moving under the sallow skin of his forearm, the veins twisting as he reached over. He handed Ginger a small package, I recognized the wrapping as coming from that same shop she got me my lipstick from. Ginger took it and said nothing, didn't even look at him.

'Right, well, your uncle Tam's nowhere to be seen so I'll head off, eh? No need to mention I was here.' He glanced over at me again. 'Have you no home of your own to go to? Seems like you're here as often as she is these days.' He looked me up and down, muttered something under his breath, then left the room. A couple of moments later, we heard the front door slam and Ginger's shoulders fell as she relaxed onto the bed beside me.

'He was in a good mood today,' I whispered, as though he was still lurking outside the door, listening. 'What's that for?'

She threw the small package to the floor so that it landed amongst her dirty clothes and told me how much she hated him.

I sighed. I moved a bit closer to her and noticed the unwashed smell of her hoodie, her hair smelling like hair not shampoo, and the way she was sweating, really sweating like she'd run for miles, even though the room was so cold I couldn't take my jacket off.

'What was he doing in your room last night? Is that what's wrong with you today? Why do you put up with it Ginger? Just tell him.'

She looked up at me and laughed. 'Tell him what? Tell him he can't come and put his arm round me, sweating onto my shoulder, and tell me how pretty I'm getting, how grown-up. Tell him he can't twist my hair round his fingers and kiss my cheek with his slimy lips and breathe all over me with his boozy breath that smells like meths. Tell him he can't drop his hand down then drag it till it almost . . . but not quite . . . reaches my tits. Tell him he can't lean against me and rub himself all over me till I feel like I can't breathe, that I'm going to gag and puke. I can't tell him any of that Wendy, I can't because this is the price I've to pay for living here. Do you still not get it – I've got nowhere else to go, this is all I've got.'

'But, your uncle Tam?'

'Couldn't give a monkey's and anyway, Roddy knows too much about what goes on here for Uncle Tam to cross him.'

'You mean, his business?'

Ginger stood up and snorted. 'Yeah, his business Wendy, that's right.'

She sat down again and said in a quieter voice, 'Look, it's fine, okay? Most of the time, it's fine. This is just the price I've to pay to live here.'

I thought there shouldn't be a price on a woman's body and even if there was, it wasn't Ginger that should be paying it, it was her mum for leaving her behind.

'I'm sorry Ginger, I didn't mean those things I said. Still friends?' I held my hand out towards her. She didn't take it but she nodded and said of course we were.

I didn't say any more because I could tell she wasn't in the mood to listen. She was only fifteen and she'd been treated badly all her life, that's what people forget when they shake their heads over what happened and say they can't believe what she was capable of. Most people are capable of anything when their backs are shoved against the wall, it's just that most people don't have to put up with the crap hand Ginger was dealt. I still love her, regardless. You can probably tell that.

25

THOUGH WE'D MADE UP straight away, I was still angry with Ginger the next day for saying all those things about Diane and me. Diane had become one of the most important people in my life, the things she said about writing and how women mattered had helped me so much, and it was time to let her know that.

I walked down the Holm Brae in my jeans and T-shirt, my rucksack on my back, enjoying the fresh air on my bare arms. Even though it was late October, a pale sunshine was peeking through the clouds and there'd been no rain all morning. One of my dad's favourite jokes if anyone new to Scotland complained about the weather was to reply, 'Wait a minute.' Even Mum used to laugh at that one. Sure enough, by the time I crossed over the motorway, a gentle smirr had cranked itself up to a downpour and, by the time I stood on Diane's front doorstep, water was dripping from my fringe and my rucksack was stained and heavy with rain.

'What on earth—'

'Hi Diane, it's me, Wendy, I hope you don't mind me calling by.' I talked quickly, partly so I would remember to say everything I had prepared and partly because I was so wet I was worried she'd just tell me to dash home and dry off. 'It's this poem I've been writing, I've been sitting in nature and everything like you said but I'm still struggling with it and I was thinking about what you were saying at the Write Now festival – you know about rhythm and pacing and I thought maybe you could help me? Your advice is always so helpful,' I finished in a rush, flicking my fringe out of my face and spraying Diane with water. 'Oops, sorry.'

She took a step back. 'I really don't think—'

'It's just what you were saying about everyone's voices needing to be heard and me keeping on writing and everything. Oh, and I wanted to give you these.' I pulled out the now squashed and soggy box of Tunnock's teacakes from the side pocket of my rucksack. 'Don't worry,' I said, wiping the rain off the cellophane and pushing the corners of the box back to right angles, 'they'll still taste good. They're my favourites so . . .' I trailed off then, shivering a bit as the rain from her porch roof leaked onto my already sopping shoulders.

She hesitated, then took the bashed box from me and said, 'Look, you'd better come in out of the rain for five minutes.'

'Thanks!' I dived into her hall, my eyes everywhere, marvelling at the height of her ceiling and the white ceiling rose round the chandelier, and the brilliant clock hands on the wall that pointed to 3D Roman numerals that seemed to be suspended a few centimetres from the wall itself. A large canvas print of a cherubic boy took up most of the space on the opposite wall.

'Wait through there and I'll get you a towel,' she said, pointing to the front room I'd gazed into so many times from up on the hill. Being there felt like being inside a dream, and I walked in a slow circle trying to take everything in.

My eyes landed on the huge colourful painting on the back

wall I'd often admired from outside. It was exactly the kind of thing the Centre for Contemporary Arts should have had on their walls in my opinion, much better than those drab colourless things they had all over the place. Up close, I could see that what had appeared as swathes of colour from far away were actually made up of millions of tiny dots, each placed so close to the others that they gave the impression of forming one vibrant block of colour. It was mesmerizing.

'I love your painting,' I said to Diane as she handed me a navy striped hand towel. I took off my rucksack and sat it on the back of her couch.

'Thanks,' she said, her eyes following mine to the canvas. 'I love it too, it's a Larry Poons. Not an original of course.' She laughed.

'Of course,' I repeated, laughing with her.

'Do you know him then?'

'Uh, no, I don't think so. Is he local?'

She smiled then shook her head. 'I'm not even sure he's still alive to be honest.' She swept her hand in front of the canvas and I saw her nails were a bit longer than usual, and painted deep orange to match her T-shirt. Her silver charm bracelet slid up her forearm.

'But I love his use of colour, something so brave about it, isn't there?'

I looked back at the painting. 'Oh definitely,' I said. 'I was just thinking the same thing myself, really brave.'

'Anyway.' She turned to me and pushed her hair behind her ear, revealing a tiny amber stud in her earlobe. 'I'm really pleased you're writing Wendy, I meant it when I said that the world needs to hear different voices, but I'm not a poet you know.

Have you thought about joining a writers' group? I was in one for years before I published my first novel and the feedback from other writers was so helpful.' She hesitated then went on, 'And it's a great way to meet people, you know, friends with similar interests.'

I thought about telling her that she must have struck it lucky with hers because mine were a bunch of amateurs but I didn't want her to think I was being negative so I put my head on one side like I was considering what she was saying.

'In fact, wait here a moment and I'll jot down the details for a group that meets at Bellshill Cultural Centre. The number's in my phone upstairs. You dry yourself off and I'll be back in two ticks.'

'Great, thanks.'

As soon as she left, I put down the towel and wandered further into the room. There were more framed photos of the child model from the canvas in the hall, these ones in colour and at all different ages. The wall of books made Diane's living room look like the authors' rooms you see in magazines, and it was crammed with interesting knick-knacks and objects that didn't seem to serve any purpose. My eye was taken by a tiny turtle that was sitting in front of a tall vase of lilies. It was covered in green and red mosaic tiles and one eye was just a black line so that it looked like it was winking at you. I ran my fingers over its smooth porcelain shell and turned it over to read 'Made in Caen' on the bottom of it. I loved every inch of it and, before I'd even had the thought, I went back to the couch, unzipped the small side pocket of my rucksack and stuck it in there. As I picked up the towel again, I noticed Diane's beautiful scarf with the red poppies that she'd worn the very first time I'd met her in Waterstones. It was curled up softly beneath the towel and I looked at it for a few seconds before picking it up between my thumb and forefinger, as though I might break it. It was silky to the touch and when I let it brush against my cheek I could smell the flowery, summery smell I always associated with Diane. I closed my eyes and took a deep breath in. Imagine having this beautiful thing next to my skin when I slept at night, it'd be almost like having Diane there beside me. I couldn't help myself, I unzipped the rucksack again and shoved it in there, on top of the turtle.

'It's fine, I'm sure but . . . thanks,' Diane was saying into her phone as she walked back into the room.

'Okay,' she said to me. 'Here it is.'

'Mm-hmm?' I said quickly, swinging my rucksack back onto my back.

She handed me a yellow Post-it with a phone number on it and I marvelled at the perfect tiny numbers, written by Diane's own hand.

A door slammed at the back of the house.

I looked at Diane and I swear I saw her shiver as she heard the footsteps coming up the hall. It was Potato Head, who was never far away it seemed.

'I was only round the back. Everything okay?' he said, putting his hand on her arm again, in that rough way he'd done at the CCA. I wondered whether I should say something when Diane looked over to me and said, 'This is Wendy, Michael. She just popped in for some information on a writers' group.'

I saw the look pass between them but he recovered himself enough to ask whether I was staying for a cup of tea.

'Oh Wendy's just leaving,' Diane said quickly, and I really felt for her that she couldn't have friends to visit without clearing it with him first. I glared at him and said to Diane that I would definitely look up the group and thanks for her help.

I stood there. We all looked at each other in silence for a moment or so.

'So,' she said. 'Good luck with it all then. No doubt I'll be picking up a copy of your book in Waterstones some day.' She laughed but I wasn't fooled, anyone could see how uncomfortable she was. I was beginning to wonder just who exactly this Michael character was and what kind of hold he had over Diane. I gave him a look like the ones Joseph used to give me at writers' group and accidentally on purpose bumped against his shoulder with my rucksack as I left the room. I called back to Diane that I'd see her soon but she didn't reply.

As I walked back up the Holm Brae, the rain stopped and the perfect arc of a rainbow appeared, as though in honour of Diane. Things hadn't gone exactly as I'd planned but still, the bond between us was getting stronger with every meeting. It had taken me a long time to find my soulmate but now that I had, there was no way I was going to mess it up.

When I got home, I laid her scarf carefully across my pillow so that my face would be against it every night, and positioned Caen the Turtle on the mantelpiece, next to the shield my dad had given me. Now every time I looked up from the TV, Caen winked at me and made me smile.

26

THE NEXT DAY, THE rain started again, the clouds were heavy with water and even the air was damp. My house had a sour smell, despite all the fresh paint, and I noticed water pooling on the lino in the bathroom as I got out of the shower. I stepped over the foamy puddle and thought about going straight back to bed. I was feeling sad as I'd liked a couple of Diane's tweets, and even added a response to something she'd posted about whether we need prologues in novels or not – obviously we do, how else will the reader have any idea what's in store for them – and there had been no response from her. Not even a like. Did she not realize that even a simple like, which would take her half a second, would have made the difference between me having a great start to the day, or just going about my business miserably? Sometimes I wonder if anybody really appreciates the effect they have on others and how much simple kindness, that might take no effort at all on their part, can matter to another person. But by the time I was having my Ready Brek, I remembered how busy she was and knew she'd reply as soon as she had a moment to herself. After all, I'd been in her house, we'd chatted about art, and I'd dried myself on the same towel she used to dry her own skin. Of course she'd reply when she had the time.

Ginger came round the back and knocked on the door loudly, her face peering into the glass panel as she knocked. I'd hardly seen her in the past few days since our big fight at her house, and to be honest, the way she'd been acting recently, with her bad moods and the way she seemed a million miles away half the time, I hadn't missed her much. She could see me through the glass though and called out, 'Wendy, are you going to open the door? Hurry up, it's pouring out here.'

'You're up early,' I said, as she shook herself out like a dog in my kitchen.

'Yeah, well, couldn't sleep. There was a party at ours last night, Uncle Tam's coupon came up, a five-team accumulator, so they were all smashed. Roddy was there too,' she finished flatly, eyes to the floor.

I didn't know what to do for her so I offered her breakfast. 'Do you want some Ready Brek?'

She made a face and looked around the kitchen. 'Any bread for toast?'

When I gave her the toast, I said we'd need to hurry as I was on an early shift.

'You make great toast Wendy,' she said, each bite leaving teeth marks in the thick butter. 'Can I ride with you today?' She wiped the crumbs across her cheek.

I thought about saying no because I was in trouble over that already. 'Okay,' I said in the end, because it was hard to see my best friend sitting there shivering with dripping wet hair, and devouring toast like she was half starved. Who else was going to look after her if not me?

The bus to Hamilton town centre later that morning was dead. My regulars were all away on their annual seniors' trip to do their early Christmas shopping at the MetroCentre in Newcastle, and even the young mums who were always desperate to get their kids out the house and entertained by someone else for a couple of hours must have thought this weather was just too much. After four stops, we hadn't picked up a single customer.

'God, this is boring,' said Ginger, flicking her hair forwards and examining individual strands for split ends.

'Yeah, well, sometimes you get shifts like this. I wouldn't be out either if I wasn't working.'

I was pretty bored myself. Driving through the slow-moving traffic, windows steamed up, the windscreen wipers brushing back and forwards in front of my face hypnotically – I could feel my eyes drooping.

'Wendy!' cried Ginger, and I swerved just in time to avoid the bin lorry taking a right ahead.

The driver beeped loudly and angrily, and his colleague in the passenger seat gave me the finger.

'Christ's sake Wendy, size of that, how could you not have seen it coming?'

I signalled left, slowed down and parked at the side of the road, slightly short of the next bus stop, which I could see was empty.

'You okay?' said Ginger, leaning forwards in her seat, her face wrinkled with concern.

'I'm tired that's all, you're not the only one who didn't sleep much last night.'

I got up from my seat and stretched my back, yawning.

Ginger cleared a circle of condensation from the window with her sleeve. 'Look Wendy,' she said. 'We're right outside the shopping centre, let's go in for a bit. Go on.'

'No, I can't just leave the bus here,' I said. 'Don't be daft.'

'Oh go on,' she insisted. 'We haven't had anyone on the bus all morning. Who's going to know?'

I looked up the empty bus and then ahead into the still empty bus shelter.

Ginger could tell I was wavering. 'Go on,' she said again. 'You only live once, you know.' She was smiling up at me, the happiest she'd been all morning.

'Okay then,' I said. 'I could do with stretching my legs. But only ten minutes then we'll need to get this bus moving again.'

'Yessss,' said Ginger, grabbing the jacket we'd bought in Ayr and skipping down the steps of the bus. I looked at the bus stop again, making sure nobody was waiting on the 63, then put on my own anorak and followed Ginger.

Not surprisingly, Hamilton's shopping parade was also very quiet. The piped music, low artificial lighting and lack of shoppers gave the whole place a funereal feel. I shivered. I wasn't in the mood to look at clothes and shoes, or whatever else they were selling.

'Let's just go back to the bus Ginger.'

'Oh, not before I have a look in some of the posh shops. Come on Wendy, you said ten minutes.'

I was starting to panic a bit by then. I knew Mr Laverty wouldn't approve of me parking up the bus mid-shift for a shopping trip no matter how quiet it was, but I also wanted to keep Ginger happy, so I trailed after her as she marched to the escalator, saying as sternly as I could, 'Ten minutes maximum Ginger, I mean it.'

She stopped outside one of the posh shops on the first floor. I peered into the window, wondering if this was the kind of shop where Diane bought her flowing gypsy skirts and colourful tops, but all I could see were shop dummies in tweed coats and hats with feathers, posed so they looked like they were pointing to an invisible sky. I was just about to say to Ginger how ridiculous they looked when I saw she'd already gone inside.

She was talking to a tall, slim woman with impossibly clear skin and straight, blonde hair that I knew would smell of apples. She had a nose long enough to look down.

'Can I help you?' the woman was saying. She seemed to be speaking through that nose, in a tone that suggested she had no intentions of helping Ginger with anything at all.

'I'm just looking,' said Ginger, her eyes darting round the pale grey and white space, so unlike the shops either of us normally went into for our clothes.

I could see Apple Hair's nose twitching as she took in Ginger's grey Lonsdale sweatpants and jumper, the cracked Adidas on her feet and the dirt embedded under the fingernails of both her hands. Even her new jacket, which we'd both loved so much, seemed to scream second-hand and not good enough in this place. I don't know why she kept it on as the atmosphere in the shop was cloying and heavy, although Apple Hair had a sweater draped round her neck too so maybe it was just me. I also noticed she was wearing shoes but no socks so she wasn't really in a position to judge Ginger's clothes choices.

'I'm afraid we won't have anything here that will suit you. Could you please—'

'I'm just having a look', said Ginger again, staring Apple Hair down in the way she must have done at school when the older kids had tried it on, mistaking her skinny frame and passive face for an easy target.

Apple Hair stepped back quickly and looked around, unsure whether or not to call for the security guard.

'Excuse me, could I try these on?' called a woman from the other side of the shop.

Apple Hair looked over then back at Ginger, who was now standing in front of a rail, fingering the expensively smooth material that hung from it.

'These, if I may?' called the woman again, holding up a pair of tweed flares.

Apple Hair couldn't resist the prospect of a sale. She clicked her tongue as she took a last look at Ginger and me before dismissing us and turning to take the tweed trousers through to the changing room for the woman to try on.

'What are you playing at Ginger?' I hissed at her. 'There's nothing in here that you'd like.'

'So what?' said Ginger. 'I'm just letting her know, we've as much right to be here looking at stuff as anybody else.'

She carried on riffling through the dresses on the rail, one falling to the floor as she swished it roughly with her hand.

'Only looking,' she was muttering to herself. 'Can't even look now, is that it? Ginger and Wendy aren't welcome here. Not wanted is that it?' A young woman and her mother circled past us in a wide arc and left the shop. I could see them looking over their shoulders as they reached the safety of the first floor lift. Ginger could too, and shouted after them what were they looking at.

'Right that's it, Ginger, I've had enough. Let's get out of here.' I pulled her arm and dragged her out of the shop.

As we reached the door, she turned and shouted something incomprehensible to the women openly staring at us from the back of the shop and gave Apple Hair the finger. She broke into a run, and I followed on behind, watching as she collided with the other shoppers meandering along the first floor and tripped over her trainers as she escaped into the freedom of the street.

'For God's sake Ginger, what happened in there? Why were you acting like that?' I cried breathlessly as we leaned against the bus, the rain still coming down in sheets.

Ginger's eyes and nose were starting to redden. I could see the pools forming in her eyes and tutted.

'Don't start crying now, that's the last thing we need. I don't know what's wrong with you today but I'm taking you home right now. I don't need this, honest to God I don't.'

I marched onto the bus, and waited till she was slumped back in the front seat before I drove off. I watched her in the rearview mirror as she sucked on her locket and twisted her hair round her fingers, staring out the window and humming to herself. This was definitely one of those times when I wondered whether my friendship with Ginger was worth all the hassle, and whether I would have been better concentrating my energies on Diane. But later, when Ginger laid her head on my shoulder and said she was sorry, she didn't know why she did things sometimes, it was just that why shouldn't she go to a nice shop and have nice things like everybody else, I knew I couldn't leave her on her own. We were friends now, and we had to look out for each other. Perhaps if I'd known then the price I'd have to pay for being friends with her, I might have told her she couldn't stay with me again that night. I might have sent her back to face the music with Uncle Tam and Roddy and all the rest and, who knows, things might actually have worked out better for her than they did. But I know I can't keep going over old ground like that, I'd go crazy.

27

MR LAVERTY RAPPED HIS hands on his desk and didn't look at me for a few seconds. I glanced up at the wall behind him and saw that Miss July, aka Kelli, had been replaced with Miss October, who was called Bobbi. What was it with these little girl names? There were never any grown-up Margarets or Yvonnes in the world of calendar modelling it seemed. Bobbi liked canoeing so at least that was something different.

'Wendy!'

'Sorry, yes, you were saying Mr Laverty?'

'I was saying that if you're sure you don't want a union rep in with you, I'll just go ahead and tell you what I need to say.'

I waited.

'Wendy. I tried to explain to you last time you were in my office that we simply can't have our pals riding along on the buses with us as we drive. It's not . . . you just can't do that. As for stopping the bus and nipping into the shops for half an hour—'

'It was more like fifteen minutes,' I said. 'If that makes it any better.'

'No, it doesn't Wendy as you well know. You're really not leaving me with any choice. You've already had an oral warning so now you're on very shaky ground indeed.'

'Mr Laverty,' I said. 'I understand I've broken the rules but the thing is, Ginger's my friend and she was really in trouble that day. I had to let her ride with me on the bus because she's got no one else. I couldn't just leave her, could I?'

'On the contrary Wendy, not only could you have left your friend to look after herself that day, you had a duty to do so. You are contracted to drive our buses according to your shift rota and following our company rules, rules which clearly state you cannot carry non-fee-paying passengers, or make unauthorized stops.'

'But Mr Laverty—'

He stood up and raised his hands in front of him, making a gesture like he was patting the air. To calm me down, I suppose, which was even more annoying because he was the one doing all the shouting while I was just trying to explain myself.

He sat back down again and sighed. 'I'm afraid you leave me with no choice Wendy but to suspend you without pay. I want you to go away, think about your position with this company, and whether you really want this job. We'll talk again in a couple of weeks.'

'Mr Laverty—'

This time he just raised his hands in front of him like a policeman stopping the traffic. I knew when I was beaten so I said thanks for the time off, and left his office.

On my way across the yard, a couple of the lads stopped me and asked what had happened. I nodded back in the direction of the manager's office and told them I'd see them all in a fortnight, I'd been given leave.

Jim blew a low whistle and shook his head. Big Alex just waved vaguely in my direction. Although we weren't friends like Ginger and me, they were all great guys and I was pleased they'd miss me.

The first few days off work passed quickly and I was actually glad to have some time to myself. I told myself I'd have more time to go and sit on the hill outside Diane's, and I could catch up on my reading too, maybe even do a bit of writing. I hadn't submitted anything to writers' group for a few weeks, I'd been so busy with Ginger and work, so maybe now was the time to get back to it. I also decided to tackle the kitchen, the only room in the house Ginger and me hadn't redecorated yet, apart from the toilet. Ginger hadn't been round since the day she'd made me stop at Hamilton shopping centre, but I didn't need her help anyway. I cleared out the cupboards – there were spices in there from five years ago! – bleached all the surfaces and fronts of the units, scrubbed the cooker, which was remarkably greasy considering how little I cooked, and finally lifted the old lino. The slime and dirt underneath turned my stomach and I was glad when the fitter from Carpetright appeared.

It was a very nice guy called Ben who laid my new flooring. I knew his name was Ben because he and I had a great chat together all the time he was putting down the laminate. As Saanvi had taught me, I showed lots of interest in him by asking about his job, if he liked it or not, where he lived, if he lived on his own, where he went at the weekends, his hobbies. I was very thorough as I offered him tea and the Tunnock's teacakes I'd bought in specially and, while he was finishing off the floor, I went and put on some of my plum lipstick, to make the most of myself. When the job was done, he stood up, stretched his back and said, 'Do you live here on your own?'

I nodded and his smile grew bigger. 'Well, what do you do on a Friday night then yourself?'

I thought about it then answered truthfully that I normally

stayed in and wrote stories or read books, that sort of thing. He hadn't heard of Diane, he said, which I found hard to believe, but maybe it was true she was a writer that women liked more than men.

'Would you fancy coming out with me one Friday night? We could . . .' he scratched his nose '. . . leave the books behind for the night and go to the dancing maybe?'

I looked at him, puzzled. 'I would never prefer dancing to books,' I said. 'Never have. I'm probably not a party person.'

'Oh. Maybe just a drink then?' His smile was starting to fade and he looked at the cooker rather than me as he asked.

I smiled. 'I don't think so, but thanks for fitting my floor. It looks really good.' I stamped on it to emphasize how much I liked it.

'Okay then, well, maybe see you around one of these days. You know where I go anyway . . .' he trailed off, looking round for his tool bag.

I handed it to him. 'Oh I doubt it. Like I said, I don't go out much. Thanks again,' I said, hustling him out the door and down the path.

Then I had a thought. 'Ben,' I called after him.

He spun round and said, 'Yeah?' smiling hopefully.

'Here, take one of these Tunnock's teacakes with you. For after your dinner.'

Saanvi loved my new floor when she popped in that Wednesday. 'I must say Wendy, this house is coming on in leaps and bounds. Your floor's lovely.'

She followed me back into the living room, and we sat down. She tapped her pen against her folder and raised her eyebrows.

'Everything else okay?' she said. 'You don't seem as pleased with yourself for getting your kitchen all ship-shape as you should be. It's really impressive what you've done with the house in the last few months you know.'

I nodded, not sure what to say because it wasn't the house that was bothering me. Something a bit awkward had happened the day before.

Even though it was only Tuesday, I'd decided to head down to Tunnock's and treat myself to a steak and kidney pie. It wasn't forecast to rain but I could see the low clouds gathering like a blanket over the playing fields behind my house so I ran back upstairs to get my anorak with a hood. Diane's poppy scarf caught my eye and since I hadn't seen her for a couple of weeks, I thought it might be nice to have her smell close to me all afternoon as I went about my business. I tried knotting it at the front the way she had worn it but that was impossible, then I tried tucking it into my jumper but that just made me look pregnant. In the end, I looped it over my shoulder once like the stripey scarves I'd seen the students on my bus wearing. I felt like a different person with the poppies floating behind me as I marched down the Holm Brae in the sunshine, and I was aware of the people in passing cars admiring my sense of style.

Main Street was busy, the cars flowing like a river and the people dotted about on both sides. I was thinking that even though it was supposed to be a punishment, I was glad not to be working as the buses would be crowded. I dashed across the road when I saw a break in the traffic, not looking towards the pavement on the other side. I ran straight into her, and her bag fell onto the pavement, a small flowery notebook and her phone spilling from its open mouth.

'Diane! I'm so sorry, I wasn't looking where I was going.'

We both bent down at the same time to pick up her stuff then she stopped suddenly, and sat back on her heels.

'Wendy, is that my scarf?'

I fell back and landed on the pavement. The red poppies were floating treacherously between us. I grabbed the scarf and pushed it into my anorak.

'What? No, this is . . . this is my scarf that my dad brought me back from . . . one of his trips.'

She looked at me, still hunkered down behind her bag, her lips a thin line and her eyes trained on the edge of the scarf poking out from the neck of my anorak.

'It looks very like the scarf I bought on our last trip to Normandy. And it's funny, because I was looking for it the other day, and it seems to have gone missing.'

My cheeks were on fire, my mind racing like the computer at the library. I'm not sure what I said exactly but I garbled something about how I'd look for one just like it for her since she liked it so much and could I help her gather her things together since they were still lying on the pavement between us.

'No, thank you,' she said, picking herself up then reaching down for her phone and notebook.

When we were standing facing each other she opened her mouth to say something else then an old guy with a fierce-looking Rottweiler said, 'Excuse me,' and pushed past us. I raised my eyebrows at Diane in a *some people* look but she just pushed her bag up her arm and said she had to be going.

'Okay. I've been thinking about calling that number you gave me for the writers' group in Bellshill. I . . . haven't done it yet though.'

She gave a tight little smile, said, 'Goodbye Wendy,' and walked down Station Hill towards her house.

'I'm sorry about banging into you,' I shouted after her, but she just kept on walking.

'Wendy? Everything okay?' Saanvi was still sitting in my living room, waiting for me to talk to her. 'You were miles away there. I was asking if you'd had a good week? Have you been going out, meeting new people?'

Saanvi's face was so kind, her smile warm and wide, that I was tempted to ask her advice about what had happened and how I could make things right with Diane. But then I remembered I'd have to tell her I'd taken the scarf and I thought maybe she wouldn't approve of that. It was such a small thing – just a scarf, Diane had so many beautiful clothes, I didn't even think she'd miss it – but judging by the way she'd acted on Main Street, I think that might have been a mistake. I couldn't tell Saanvi though, she'd be disappointed in me and I couldn't bear that after I'd been doing so well. I'd have to find a way of making things right with Diane – we were soulmates, a wee thing like a scarf was hardly going to come between us!

I plucked at the arm of the sofa, and told Saanvi I was just looking after myself, my appearance, and definitely getting out and about, as she'd advised.

She was happy about that, I could tell, and I was relieved she was still pleased with me.

'That's great Wendy, you've really made progress these last few months.'

I nodded noncommittally, and bit my top lip.

'And I can tell you're feeling better within yourself, aren't you?' Saanvi was leaning forwards hopefully so I nodded my head a bit more vigorously.

She folded her notepad over, and dropped it into her satchel.

'Now. Anything else you'd like to talk about Wendy before we call it a day? Work going well is it? No issues there?'

Again, I wasn't sure she'd understand the complaints procedure at work, or appreciate that I had it all under control, so I just nodded and said, 'Everything's great. Do you want more tea?' getting up to put the kettle on. 'I've got milk,' I added so she'd know all was well.

As she was leaving, she said again, 'Keep doing what you're doing Wendy, getting out and about, meeting new people. We all need people in our lives, a support system. Not just you, everybody needs that.' She smiled at me and told me to take care till next week.

I know she was trying to be helpful but, sometimes, I think that if Saanvi hadn't tried so hard to make me like everyone else, with friends and a social life and club memberships and all that sort of stuff, I'd still be just driving my bus and daydreaming about Diane. None of this would have happened. Not that I blame Saanvi, not at all.

28

BY THE SECOND WEEK of my suspension, things were going quickly downhill. I didn't leave the house for days after that business with Diane's scarf, not even to go and sit on the hill, and I didn't speak to Ginger at all. I didn't answer any of her calls, and I didn't text her once. I knew it was wrong, and that she'd be worried about me, but I couldn't help blaming her for all the bad things that were happening. I was starting to think she was jinxing me. I heard her at the door a couple of times, knocking as hard as she could and calling out my name. She was like a cat desperate to be let back into the warmth, but I ignored her and stayed under the blankets thinking about Diane as my mum's old clock radio played miserable songs on a loop. I didn't even make it to writers' group. But then I grew tired of black tea and the bread was finished so I couldn't make toast. Sighing, I made myself get out of bed and put on my fleecy hoodie over my pyjamas. I slipped my trainers onto bare feet and headed to Naf's on the corner.

I don't know why my mind turned to alcohol, but I suddenly felt the urge to drink something stronger than I was used to. I'd never really been a drinker – even though I had lots of reasons to drink. Most people who are children of alcoholics are not fans of the thing that robbed them of their parent, and I was no different. Plus I'd never had friends to go drinking with before the writers' group. I'd seen plenty of people staggering out of pubs and stumbling their way across the road, heading for home. The saddest ones were those who reminded me of my dad, middle-aged men gone to seed, their faces russet red and noses bigger than they should be. They'd pull their jackets to them, or often be in their shirt sleeves, whatever the weather, and mutter urgently to themselves as they wandered by. I'd lost count of the times Dad came back to me and Mum in that state, and Mum would quickly pack me off to bed while she 'dealt with Dad'. I'd lie under my princess duvet, counting backwards from a hundred and clutching Squirrel or whichever soft toy was in favour that week, and listen for the low rumbling, followed by the crashing of plates and the oversized pepper grinder falling from the table, then the allegations and counter-attacks. The silence that followed was almost worse. Because then I'd imagine one or other of them – I'm not sure which one would have been worse – sprawled face down on the kitchen floor, one of the big chopping knives sticking out of their back, while the other sobbed quietly against the hum of the fridge. This same scene played out before me time and time again and, although it never actually happened, that didn't make it any easier.

I shook my head and pulled down a half bottle of vodka and a four-pack of lagers from the top shelf, and shoved them into my basket. I grabbed a pack of Scotch eggs for dinner and headed to the counter to pay.

I opened the vodka as soon as I got home and poured a thimbleful into my only clean glass. I downed it in one, standing up beside the sink.

'Christ, how can anyone drink that?' I thought, then poured another and this time added some Diet Coke, which made it slightly more palatable. I looked about for a plate to put my Scotch eggs on but gave up and took the bag with the eggs and my glass of vodka through to the living room.

I switched on Netflix and started flicking channels. After a few minutes' searching, I settled for a documentary about a painter called Francis Bacon. You might not know him because he died in Spain a long time ago, at least thirty years, and I'm not sure he was a big hit with the art world even at the time. I knew about him from reading Diane's book. That's what I mean about her being one of these people who are talented at everything. Not only did she write brilliant, heart-stopping fiction but even her biographies were a cut above everyone else's. Maybe even more than *Elizabeth*, I loved the way *Expressive Expressionism* took you right into the world of the people she was writing about. I didn't know anything about art before I read the book but of course I devoured it since it was one of Diane's and anyway you didn't need to be into art to become engrossed in these people's lives the way Diane told their story. They were a group of painters all working round the same time – a pretty miserable bunch by all accounts – and one of them was Bacon. I'd never even heard of him before that book but he was my favourite of all the painters she mentioned. I liked the fact that he didn't give a damn what other people thought of him. According to Diane's book – and she is well respected for her thorough research so I know this will be accurate – he thought nothing of going to a party on a Monday night and not leaving till the Wednesday, and once he won some money gambling in Monte Carlo or somewhere and he used the money to rent out a house for a month-long party and only went home to London when the whisky ran out. He also had a great love affair, with one of his young models I think it was, so I could understand the way his mind worked. He thought life was nothing except what we feel, and I agree with that, same as Diane did in the book.

But the documentary was nowhere near as interesting as Diane's book. Not enough focus on him as a person and too much attention on his pictures which, surprisingly, were not as great as I expected the way everyone talked about them. Very samey if you want my opinion and not exactly uplifting. Of course, I'm a writer not a painter so I'm not claiming to know much about it. I was just about to switch channels when a sudden movement in the kitchen caught my eye. I saw Ginger's face peering through the window of my back door.

She saw me too and started waving madly. Her nose was red in the cold autumn air and her jacket with the fur collar was zipped to her chin. She was holding a bag in her hand, high in the air and pointing to it. I could see Enzo's Fish and Chips blazoned on the side so I got up to let her in.

'Jesus Wendy, I thought you'd gone and died on me, I haven't seen you for a fortnight.' She took off her jacket and hung it over the back of one of the kitchen chairs.

'You all right, or what?' she said as she turned to face me.

'I'm all right,' I said. 'Just trouble with work, nothing important. It's good to see you,' I said, smiling at last, and I realized it was, it was great to see her in fact, and I led the way through to the living room and told her to sit down.

She spotted the vodka bottle. 'Are you drinking?'

I nodded, blushing a bit. 'I've been having a sort of rough time.'

She waited.

'Well, are you going to offer me some or not? Look, I've brought chips.' She laid the steaming bag on the table, and opened it. The chips smelled amazing.

'I'll get you a glass. Or a cup,' I added over my shoulder as I went back into the kitchen.

'Whatever,' said Ginger, as she settled back on the good sofa, a large chip in her hand. She didn't say it but I knew she'd missed me. Her eyes never left me as I went to the kitchen and back, and she sat as close to me as she dared after I'd handed her a mug of vodka and Coke. She watched me drink my vodka and she drank me in.

An hour later and we were giggling like the schoolkids on my bus at half past three.

Ginger tapped the rim of her cup and made a face. 'Why do people drink vodka? It's rank,' she said, tossing back the rest of hers and pushing her cup towards me for a refill.

'I know, we'd be better with just the Coke. All this vodka's doing is making the Coke taste bad.' I handed her another cupful and refilled my own glass.

'So where have you been then Wendy? You practically disappeared off the face of the earth these last couple of weeks.'

I sighed. 'Just been a bit down that's all. I mean, what's it all for, eh? You go into work every day, always on time, your customers love you – I know for a fact Irish Mary and Myra and Terry and all the rest of my regulars'll be missing me, Big Alex and Jimmy and all that lot never speak to them, not a word beyond "Show us your pass missus" – you do all that and for what? They can get rid of you as soon as you put the teensiest, tiniest step out of line.' I gulped more vodka and made a face as its sour sweetness hit the back of my throat.

'Is it just work then? I thought . . . I thought maybe I'd done something wrong, maybe you didn't want to be pals with me any more.' She looked at me from under her eyelashes, her cheeks red with the unaccustomed vodka, her lips chapped and her thin shoulders at her ears. Suddenly, I felt bad at how selfish I'd been, refusing to see her for days. I knew by then she needed me like a sister.

'No Ginger, you didn't do anything wrong.'

'Sure?'

'Positive. You're the one thing that keeps me going. You and Diane, that is.'

She shrugged off the mention of Diane, and sat back, balancing her cup on her knee.

'Do you remember when you were a kid, Wendy, and everything seemed possible? You could be anything you wanted to be?'

I wanted to tell her she was still a kid but I didn't interrupt her.

'Do you know what I wanted? When I was about ten or so, maybe, what I really wanted when I grew up was to work in an office and have my own house somewhere near the station, you know those big houses down there?'

I stiffened, wondering again if Ginger knew that was where Diane lived, and if so, how? She'd driven by with me on the bus and helped me take some photos of the garden in the summer but I'd never told her it was Diane's house. It crossed my mind again that she could have followed me, gone back there on her own even. And it struck me that, much as I liked Ginger, she was something of a loose cannon. I'd never seen her behave as she had in the shopping centre that day before I got suspended, but now I wondered if that's how she really was and if, when she was with me, she was on her best behaviour. She was speaking again.

'But by the time I was twelve or so, I realized I wasn't hoping for that any longer. I can hardly read for God's sake . . .'

I sat forwards to say that she was almost there, if she'd just come with me to the library sometimes, keep trying, but she shooshed me with her hand and kept talking, swirling her cup round and looking at it as she did so.

'No, I know that sort of thing isn't for me. No one's going to take me on to work in an office, how could that even happen, and if I can't get a job I'm never going to be able to afford my own house, never mind shop at Marks & Spencer and go to Benidorm or, I don't know Paris, maybe, on holiday and have my own car and . . .' She sat back, exhausted with naming all her mundane yet, to her, impossible desires. 'Oh Wendy, what's going to happen to us?'

I thought about saying I had a job and a house so we weren't really the same but I didn't have the heart. I scrunched up the chip papers that were lying on the table and took her cup off her.

'Come on, I think we've had enough for one night.' I hesitated. 'Are you staying?'

She looked up at me. 'Can I?'

'Of course,' I said. 'We're friends aren't we? Put the lights out.'

We slept till late the next day, and I woke up starving in a way I couldn't remember feeling before.

'Christ's sake Wendy, I thought Uncle Tam's house was bad but there's not so much as an egg, never mind a sausage in this fridge.'

I walked into the kitchen, enjoying the sensation of the cool, smooth laminate under my bare feet, drying my hair as I did so. I joined Ginger in front of a fridge so empty it whistled at us. 'Right,' I said. 'Let's go out for breakfast.'

Ginger's face lit up like I'd offered her a weekend break in Prague, and she told me to get dressed quickly then, she was starving.

The rain started as we made our way to The View. It was only five minutes from my house but we had to run the last part of the way to avoid the worst of the downpour. Ginger took a table by the window and I went to the counter to order.

'Say what you like, you can't beat a square sausage, can you Wendy?' she said, as she sunk her teeth into her sausage sandwich, doorstep bread with margarine thick enough for her to leave bite marks.

I laughed. 'No wonder you're putting on weight Ginger,' I said, pointing to her belly which had a distinct curve to it these days. Her face dropped when I said that though and I couldn't bear to upset her so I added, 'But it suits you. Here, pass me the ketchup.'

When we'd finished our second cups of tea, we left the café just as it was busying up with lunchtime trade – the road workers, the shop assistants from the retail units round in the industrial estate, and mums with buggies – all enticed in with the smell of coffee and all day breakfasts.

'Shall we go to Aladdin's for a bit? We haven't been in for ages,' said Ginger, turning round and walking backwards so that she was facing me rather than where she was going.

'Alright,' I said, thinking I might as well enjoy my time off while it was being forced upon me.

We strolled past the Shelter shop and Abbie's Nail Salon, dipped past the queue outside Subway, and avoided the dead-eyed punters coming out of Paddy Power. Ahead, we saw a small crowd of people gathered round the entrance to the arcade. We could hear shouting and saw two female police officers, one on a walkie talkie, patrolling the outside of the group.

'Come on,' said Ginger. 'Let's check this out.'

'Ginger,' I said, wary she was going to cause trouble, but she was already at the edge of the crowd, working her way into the centre.

'Ginger,' I called again then, sighing, I followed her into the crowd.

I couldn't believe my eyes.

There, standing in their damp anoraks, their Scotmid bags at their feet, were Irish Mary, Myra, Terry and about half a dozen other people I recognized from my bus. They were holding up homemade placards, a couple with the paint still dripping off the bottom of them, and chanting, 'Give Wendy her job back,' 'Give Wendy her job back,' over and over. I stepped a little closer to the women and read their placards. 'Bring back Wendy,' 'We want Wendy,' 'Save our buses, give us back Wendy.'

'Wendy!' shouted Irish Mary, spotting me in the crowd. 'Everyone, here she is. This is our friend Wendy, and we want her back on our bus.'

Terry put her arm round me and said, 'We were at the bus station yesterday Wendy, giving them our demands. It's not right, we don't want any of those arseholes taking over our bus service, they don't even give us time to get our bums on the seat before they're racing off, am I right Myra?'

'You are,' agreed Myra. 'Don't you worry,' she said to me.

'We've written to the *Bellshill Speaker* and the *Hamilton Advertiser* as well. We'll not take this lying down, you just wait.'

Suddenly Ginger grabbed one of the placards and she started shouting louder than everyone else, 'Bring back Wendy, bring back Wendy,' to the cheers of Irish Mary and the rest.

I didn't know what to say. I thought I had no friends till I met Ginger and Diane, but maybe that wasn't true, maybe Nuala Brennan and Mikey Sanderson and all the rest had been wrong after all and I wasn't the weirdo they said I was. Maybe I could even be one of those people that are good at life.

By the end of the week, I'd had an official letter from Mr Laverty, on bus company stationery, telling me my position 'remained open' and to get in touch with him directly if I was still interested in working with them. I was back on the early shift, taking Irish Mary and her beautiful cronies to dance class, by the following Tuesday. Okay, October hadn't been the best of months for me or Ginger but Saanvi had taught me that coping with the ups and downs of life was what being an adult was all about. I was confident things would look up again for Ginger and me – but maybe I underestimated just how hard it is to keep your life on track.

Saving Diane:
Where Everything Went Wrong

29

ARMED WITH MY NEW positive attitude, I decided it was time to go back to Diane's and get our relationship moving in the right direction. I would explain what had happened with the scarf and we could start getting to know each other properly. It was unfortunate that I'd told her the scarf was mine because, thinking about it afterwards, I realized I should have said, 'Oh sorry, is this yours, I must have accidentally put it in my rucksack that day I was at your house in the rain, and I've got so many scarves I didn't even realize.' That would have been totally believable I think, whereas the only option I'd left myself with was to take back her original scarf and say it was another one I'd found for sale on eBay and bought for her because she'd admired mine. That wasn't as good but it could still work, I thought. I was rehearsing my lines all the way there, my armpits prickling every time I thought about saying them out loud.

I looked round at the garden as I waited on Diane's doorstep. It had changed since the last time I'd been there. It was still as beautiful but in a different way, more golden now than pink, the rose bushes bare and vulnerable. The smaller trees had grown spindly and there was a mush of brown and yellow leaves on the grass. I could see nut-brown conkers strewn across the path.

I missed the fresh washing hanging out in the back garden and wondered how she dried her crisp white sheets in the winter.

The door opened and I swung round to see Mr Potato Head standing in the doorway in his flannel shirt and chinos.

'Hello,' he said. 'Can I help you?'

I don't know if I was imagining it but I thought there was an extra edge to his voice, an even more unfriendly tone that didn't bode well.

I looked past him into the warm hallway. 'Is Diane home? I've come to give her a new scarf I bought for her. On eBay.' I held up the poppy scarf in my hand.

He looked at it for a moment then reached his hand out to take it from me.

I snatched it back. 'I'd like to give it to Diane. Is she in? Tell her it's Wendy.'

'I'm sorry Wendy, Diane's not home at the moment. I can give her a message though if there's something you'd like me to pass on?'

I didn't believe him and, to be honest, I wasn't sure he should have been in Diane's house without her permission. So I said that to him.

He laughed and said, 'I'm Diane's husband. This is my house too.'

For a moment, I was so taken aback I didn't know what to say. I tapped the palm of my hand on my leg and looked back towards the garden, as though expecting Diane to appear any moment.

'Look.' He was speaking again. 'Diane is far too nice to say this herself but I can tell you she doesn't really appreciate people just turning up at her door uninvited.'

I stepped back as though he'd winded me. 'What? You can't . . . you can't say that. Diane and me, we're writers, she helps me with my writing, she invited me to join a writers' group . . .'

He started talking in a different, softer voice, as though to a child, but I still didn't like what he was saying. 'She suggested you join a writers' group so you could get support and meet friends. It's . . . look, I don't know what else to tell you. Just, please don't keep coming here.' He made to close over the door and I panicked and stuck my foot in the space between the door and the frame.

'Now look here,' he said again, his foot trying to force away my own. When he couldn't move it, he reached out for my arm and grabbed it roughly. I had a sudden flashback to the times I'd seen him grabbing Diane's arm at the CCA, and again at her house, in exactly the same way, and I jerked his hand off me.

'No, you look,' I said, leaning forwards so that my face was close to his. I was at least a couple of inches taller than him and I saw him flinch as I towered over him. 'Just tell Diane Wendy was here and I'll be here whenever she needs me, right?' I took my foot out of the door and he watched, saying nothing as I laid the scarf neatly on top of the welcome mat. I turned and walked out of the garden, pulling myself up to my full height, and refusing to turn round even though I knew he was still watching me.

I bent over to be sick as soon as I'd turned the corner at the top of Station Hill then pelted up the road to the safety of my house.

Back home, I tried to calm down by sitting at the kitchen table and writing Diane's name over and over on Mum's best, thick letter writing paper. It soothed me to see the navy blue letters cover page after page, and I experimented by putting hearts over the 'i' for a page then a tiny filled-in flower over each 'i' on the following page. By the time I'd covered six pages with her name, I felt calm enough to think about what had happened with Chrome Dome and the outrageous things he'd said, and what I should do next.

One thing was certain – I couldn't let Diane, with her talent and her stories and the way she championed invisible people like me, be bossed around and told who she could and couldn't see by anyone, and certainly not by that insignificant husband of hers.

It occurred to me I should check Twitter in case she'd sent a tweet that was meant for me to decode, or even a DM. I grabbed my phone from my bag, muttering, 'Come on, come on,' as I tried to load her profile page. Nothing came up.

'What on earth—?'

I tried again. Nothing. I was getting worried – could he be stopping her from trying to contact me? Shakily, I typed out '@diane_weston, it's me Wendy, is everything okay?' and pressed send. An error message appeared on the screen. That's when it dawned on me – he'd blocked me from seeing her account. I slammed my phone on the table, the pages covered in Diane's name swooshed to the floor, and I wished more than ever that Mum was there to tell me what to do.

30

I HARDLY SLEPT THAT NIGHT, I was so wound up with anger and frustration. Suddenly it all made sense – he was controlling her! I could have kicked myself for being so stupid. He'd been mistreating her all this time and I'd been too busy hanging out with Ginger and being absorbed in my own problems to even notice. All these months I'd been benefiting from Diane's help, and now she needed me. Of course I knew Baldy had been lying. There was no way Diane would have said she didn't want to see me, and I was beginning to understand just how much of a hold he had over her, who she saw, where she went, probably even what she wore. All those times when she didn't tweet for days, he wasn't letting her! And now he wasn't letting her tweet at all. I had to help her, she needed me.

I was perched on the hill by eight the next morning. I sat far back against the trees so I couldn't be seen from the house, and set out my flask and binoculars by my side. It was bright but icy cold, and there'd been a light snowfall overnight, the soft, powdery kind that makes everything quiet and still. Diane's garden looked really pretty that day – the stubby grass had silver tips of frost that sparkled in the sunlight, and the big oak tree looked sadder bereft of its leaves, but still tall and strong. The house itself had a shuttered look, thick, striped curtains drawn across each of the downstairs windows, and the front door locked tight. The station had been empty too since it was Saturday and too early yet for the shoppers. All was peaceful.

My flask was empty and the cold seeping into my bones when Diane emerged from the house around one in the afternoon. She looked harassed in that way young mothers sometimes do. You know when you see them in supermarkets, pushing a baby in a buggy, dragging a screaming toddler behind them, and trying to work out if they've got enough cash to pay for the stuff they need? Their faces all red and shiny with sweat – they'd smell of onions if you got close to them – and their eyes blank with tiredness and the sheer boredom of it all. That day, Diane looked like that. Her normally sleek hair was tied back in a loose, low ponytail but more of it was hanging sloppily round her collar than in the band itself. She was wearing some kind of old anorak rather than her stylish red mac, and her brown cord skirt looked crushed and stained. She was carrying two empty plastic bags which swooshed lightly round her legs in the cold wind, and when she took her car keys from her pocket, she immediately dropped them on the slippery driveway.

I watched as she called back into the house. Then he came out, the bald wonder that never left her alone. He picked up the keys and said something to her. It was probably an insult or a put-down, that's how these men work, chipping away at women's self-esteem till it's all they can do to leave the house on their own. She said something back to him but I could tell she was annoyed by the way she flicked her fringe and stood back as he opened the car door for her. I noticed she didn't even linger to wave him goodbye, just started the car quickly and sped away from him as fast as she could.

I stayed where I was for another couple of hours. Even though my fingertips were nipping and I'd run out of tea, I didn't want to go home. It was so peaceful sitting on the hill, watching over Diane's house and thinking about things. I spotted a half melted miniature snowman at the bottom of the hill, looking sorry for itself as its carrot nose drooped. It was nothing like the snowmen my dad used to make. He'd make a proper face with rock eyes and a perfectly curved stick for the mouth, and he'd always finish by winding his own tweed scarf round the snowman's neck. He'd been a good dad, no matter what Mum said, it was just losing his job and the drinking and the way things had worked out, but he didn't deserve what happened to him.

Dad might have been down on his luck when we left, but the last time I saw him, I had to look really closely into his eyes to check it was actually him.

I was walking back from Naf's with Mum's *Hamilton Advertiser* and a pint of milk, jiggling the coins in my free hand. I heard shouting from under the railway bridge and saw the usual group of men, a couple slumped against the slimy wall, while the three causing all the noise stood grouped together near the grass verge. Mum always told me to walk past fast as I could, never to acknowledge them, and certainly not to stop, so I wasn't sure what to do when one of them broke away from the rest and called after me. I would have ignored him and carried on walking except I realized he was saying my name. He knew me.

'Wendy,' he said softly, as he approached, his too big shoes flapping against the concrete slabs that separated the bridge from the main pathway. He seemed to be wearing too many clothes for the weather, I had the impression of many layers – jumpers beneath cardigans, beneath an old anorak, all covered by a vaguely familiar, but now rotting tweed coat.

'Wendy,' the man said again.

I stopped. Swallowed a couple of times. 'Dad?' I said, my voice not my own.

He was close enough for me to smell his unwashed clothes and another smell too, like disinfectant or methylated spirits or something. A scab the size of a penny was healing underneath his left eye.

What people don't appreciate is the humiliation. Dad told me it's really humiliating to be out there shaking a cup, twenty-four hours a day, but you do it to survive, that's all. That's the only thing that matters and, after a while, he said, you don't even care when they shout at you to get a job. He said he always knew he wasn't a bum, he was a human being, a father, but that he'd lost his job at the wrong time and, well, that's how he'd ended up. Apparently they found him under that old railway bridge at the end. Blue cold, stone dead and without anything other than the clothes he lay in, that's what Mum told me. But I don't think that's how the police put it, I think they were gentler with her.

The tears felt hot as they ran down my frozen face and I wiped them away with my sleeve. I shook away the images of Dad, reminding myself he was gone and that it was Diane's husband I was angry with, he was the one making me raw and unstable. I could feel my edges blurring again after all the work I'd put in to get better at life. I knew I should leave but I stayed where I was, watching the windows darken mid-afternoon and the house become sadder in the fading light. Diane hadn't come back and there was no movement inside the house.

I jumped as my phone rang and Ginger's name flashed across the screen. I hesitated before answering because being friends with her by then was much harder than it had been at the start. The last couple of times I'd seen her, all she'd wanted to do was sit in her bedroom wrapped up in her old duvet and moan about how awful everything was. But when I'd ask her what was wrong or if I could help she'd just bat me away like I was the one annoying her.

My phone kept ringing though and I had this image of her, locket between her lips, praying that I would answer and be pleased to hear from her. I knew how that felt. And anyway, Ginger was my best friend, I had to look after her when she needed me.

I pressed the accept button. 'Yes,' I said, eyeing Diane's house, silent in the dark. 'Yes, it'd be good to see you. Just wait there, I'll be home in ten minutes.' I stood up on unsteady legs, my knees creaking from kneeling so long. Of course I was still worried about Diane but sitting there in the cold was achieving nothing and I was relieved to be heading back to the warmth with Ginger for company. I heaved my rucksack a bit higher on my shoulder and headed up the hill as the moon hid behind the clouds.

31

THE MISUNDERSTANDING WITH THE police happened not long after and the funny thing is, I had no intentions of going to Diane's house that day. I'd had such a nice time with Ginger the day before, just talking and eating Tunnock's teacakes on her bed. There was no one else in and she was the most relaxed I'd seen her for weeks. I couldn't help comparing it to how things were with Diane and me. I know it wasn't her fault and Chrome Dome was stopping her from seeing me, but I was starting to wonder how much I was actually accomplishing by sitting out there on the hill. I thought maybe I should take a few days to really think about how I could help Diane.

I brought the bins in early, and the sodden moss from my front grass was still clinging to my trainers. The house was cold, and there was a smell of neglect or loneliness, or something anyway, that couldn't be covered up no matter how much fresh paint I applied to the walls. I tried putting on a couple of bars of the fire in the living room but there was something wrong with it, or the electricity wasn't coming through, I don't know. I put my anorak back on and sat in the corner of the sofa, biting my lips. I was kind of depressed to be honest, which I suppose is why I didn't really think it through, didn't see how it would be, from Diane's point of view that is.

I'd been watching her house almost daily, ever since I'd realized how controlling her husband was and how much Diane needed me to look out for her. I could see her moving about in there, folding laundry in her big warm kitchen, arranging flowers in a waisted glass vase she kept in the front room with the magnificent painting, sitting at the table, no doubt thinking about characters and plots and books, same as me. Maybe it was because I couldn't connect with her on Twitter any more but, lately, she seemed sort of distant from me. I was having trouble understanding how I was going to save her, if she didn't at least meet me halfway. I know she was a famous writer and she had to be careful who she got close to – who knows what these people wanted from her – but it was almost as though she was trying to keep the distance between us. How could I help her if she wouldn't let me in?

And I know this is unlike me, but I was starting to have my doubts about my own writing. I'd been working on this piece about love for so long – and I don't mean the usual clichés about warmth and sex and cuddling and all that, no, I mean finding someone who would share things with me, like the washing. I had this dream about Diane asking if she could wash my jeans for me, they looked worn and dirty at the knees and please could she launder them for me because, you know, sometimes people forget, love can be just that – wanting to bake a coffee cake for someone, or asking them if they're warm enough, making them feel clean and safe and looked after. Anyway, I was trying to write about that but I knew it wasn't working. We know, we writers, we *know* when it's not working. Oh, I don't mean the writers at my group, with their stories about Glasgow characters and poetry about water smooth as glass and whatever, I mean like me and Diane and Raymond Carver, we know, we get this feeling in our bellies when a piece just isn't working. That's when it occurred to me – this was something I should ask Diane about, it was entirely legitimate for me to go and say, 'Look Diane, writer to writer, how do you make a piece work? Make it sing so people read it and go, Christ, I feel *exactly* like that, that's what *I*'ve been trying to say all along and there it is, all explained perfectly for me.' She'd nod her head, understand the problem right away but it'd be too much for her to explain in five minutes so she'd ask me in. And this time, *he* would be nowhere to be seen, he wouldn't be able to pretend she wasn't in or that she didn't want to see me. It'd be just Diane and me. I'd join her at her scored old kitchen table, we'd both sit at the same side of it, maybe have a glass of wine, or a cup of tea and homemade shortbread. She'd ask me if I was warm enough and I'd say yes thanks and then we'd start talking. She'd talk through her writing process, in her soft voice, I'd need to lean in to hear her properly and maybe our knees would touch and I'd jump back a little because I'd never felt anyone's skin pressing hard against mine. She'd keep talking, pretend she hadn't felt the intensity of the bond between us, because despite her attention-grabbing outfits and the way she could command an audience, that's just her public face, like an armour she puts on to protect herself. In real life, she's quiet like me, we're shy and introverted like writers are. We'd talk till the light faded but we wouldn't want to stop. We'd talk and talk about how our stories needed to be heard.

That's how I imagined it in my head, but it didn't work

out like that and sometimes, honestly sometimes I started to wonder how much Diane really wanted to be saved.

When I saw her pulling up in the driveway in her wee red Fiesta that day, she looked so tired. Tired and unhappy, pale like a vampire with her hair twisted round her head, like she'd forgotten to brush it for a week. I mean, what else could I have done?

I could tell just by the way she was dressed that things were getting on top of her. No sign of her lovely colourful skirts or rainbow striped T-shirts, her beautiful red mac was all stained and ripped at the back, and her plain blue dress was as dirty as Ginger's jeans. I knew there was something wrong. She tried to tell me her car had broken down and she'd had a terrible day and what was I doing at her house again but I saw through it. I was very patient with her, though I can see now that I shouldn't have told her I was watching over her and not to worry, because I think that's really what made her call the police. Then I tried to explain to them how ridiculous the whole thing was. 'We're both writers, tell them Diane,' I said to her and reached out to touch her arm. The police officer, a thick-waisted brute of a man, snapped my hand back and told me if I tried anything else like that, they'd have to arrest me. I glanced over at Diane, willing her to tell them the truth about us but she didn't. I'm not going to lie, I was hurt by that but, thinking about it later, I could see that we were right outside her house and if the bald-headed idiot had been in, the consequences for Diane later on might have been grave. She did tell the police just to let me go, no harm had been done, so I think that was as much as she could risk saying. I could tell that I'd need to stop sitting outside her house for a while though, till things died down and got a bit easier for her.

It wasn't even my day to see Saanvi but she came by that evening anyway. She said she was disappointed in me, and that made me really sad. I'd been trying so hard to please her and do all the stuff she wanted me to do to fit in and have friends and things, and now I'd gone and upset her.

'I'm sorry,' I said. 'The whole thing was misrepresented. Not by Diane,' I clarified quickly in case she thought I was dropping Diane in it. 'By the police. You know what they're like, to women especially?' I glanced up at her shyly, trying to convince her we were in this together.

She wasn't having any of it. 'No Wendy, I don't know what they're like. All I know is, you're very lucky this . . .' she glanced at her notes, 'Diane Weston woman is not pressing charges. You understand you can't keep going to her home, don't you? It's not . . . that's not how we make connections Wendy. People don't like to be spied on like that, however well intentioned you are.'

She sighed and rubbed her hand across her forehead. I was interested to see the spot above her nose didn't wipe off, I wondered what material it was made of and whether she had to reapply it every day. I realized she was still talking.

'. . . Wendy? I mean really, what were you thinking?'

For a moment, I was tempted to tell her about how my relationship with Diane had developed into a real friendship, maybe more. I could tell her about the connection we'd had from that very first meeting at the signing event in Waterstones, how she'd remembered my name out of everyone in the crowd, or that day at her house where she'd actually said that the world needed to hear my stories. *Mine*. How she'd had the same childhood as me, even down to having a dad she loved but who preferred drinking, and all that that entailed. About the connection we had through her books, how we saw things in exactly the same way, the love hearts she sent in response to my tweets, the photo we'd had taken with our heads almost touching, all of it.

I could see she was waiting for me to reply, but something stopped me from saying all these things. I don't know whether it was the sight of her scritch-scratching the details of my life into her folder, or the way she glanced at her watch every so often when she thought I wasn't looking to make sure she didn't overrun our hour, but I suddenly understood that Saanvi was only here because she was paid to come and make sure I was coping; she might seem nice but she wasn't my friend, not like Ginger was anyway.

I shrugged and said, 'Sorry, you're right.'

She sighed and leaned forwards, her hand on my arm. 'It's okay Wendy, we all make mistakes. Just . . . keep going to your writers' group, see your friend – Gloria, was it?' She checked her notes. 'No, Ginger. Keep seeing Ginger, get out and about and enjoy life Wendy. I'll see you again next week.' She hesitated. 'Everything will work out, you'll see.'

I smiled. She was right about that because I'd made up my mind – I knew who my real friends were and I wasn't giving up on Diane. She was my soulmate, and not Potato Head, the police, or even Saanvi could come between us. Our relationship was too precious for that.

32

WORRYING ABOUT DIANE ALL the time was hard but, in a weird way, it did make me concentrate more on my writing. I couldn't go to her house for a bit after that misunderstanding with the police so I poured all my energy into my stories. I thought about all the things she'd said about telling my own story and how my voice was important, and the connection between us was at its strongest when we were both engaged in the same task of writing. I didn't see her at all for the next two weeks yet I felt so close to her, it was as though her hand was guiding mine as I added each new paragraph to my story.

I was quite nervous as I walked down the stairs to The Drury, wondering if all my hard work was about to be ripped to shreds. I spotted Bounce and Henry at the bar, Henry practically glued to Bounce's shoulder and beaming that smile people have when all they can think about is this new person who suddenly matters more to them than everyone and everything that's gone before.

'Hi Wendy,' called Muriel from our usual table. 'I've saved you a seat.'

'Thanks Muriel. Hello Reggie, hi Sophie.' Reginald nodded at me, half asleep as usual, but Sophie looked up from her phone and smiled from across the table and waved like we were friends. I was pleased to see she was letting her hair grow back and she'd put gel or something in it so she was beginning to look less like GI Jane.

'Here,' I said. 'This is for you.' I handed her the copy of *Britt Ekland's Book of Natural Beauty* that had worked so well for Ginger and me.

'Britt Ekland?' said Sophie, turning over the book in her hands. 'Who's that?'

'She was an eighties porn star I believe but don't let that put you off. She knows what she's talking about when it comes to beauty.'

'Well, thanks,' she said, glancing at Muriel.

'You're welcome,' I said. 'She's very good on French manicures and you might want to check out chapter five first, the bit about how men like to run their fingers through women's hair. That could be why you're struggling to get a man.'

'Thanks Wendy,' said Muriel quickly. 'Have you met our two new members? This is Sarah and . . . Tony, was it?' She indicated the two artsy types in double denim, sitting close together at the top of the table. I nodded but didn't bother getting too enthusiastic as they probably wouldn't be back the following week. If they were, I'd say hello then.

My palms were damp as we waited for Henry to begin proceedings. The piece I'd been working on, a new story that showed *my* voice and *my* experience of the world, which Diane had said was important, was finished and I'd submitted it for review. The other stuff I'd brought to writers' group had never gone down that well. Of course I knew a lot of that was down to most of the group not knowing what they were talking about but, if I'm honest, maybe those other pieces weren't quite as good as I thought they were at the time. I knew a lot more about writing now, and I'd learned so much from Diane, especially about taking your inspiration from the people around you. The group might hate my story but I knew I'd carry on loving it anyway.

I rubbed my hands down my jeans and waited till Henry had cleared his throat and the new guy had stopped clinking the ice cubes together in his Irn-Bru before I began. I took a deep breath, and tried to make my voice as confident and loud as Diane's had been when she was reading out her stuff at the CCA.

I'd written about my bus, about the people I see there, day in, day out. I wrote about Irish Mary and her pals, and their zest for life, about the silent nuns who wait at the bus stop with their pale faces upturned as they savour every sliver of freedom and fresh air, I described the strange boy who lopes onto the bus every Friday, wearing a motorcycle helmet and goggles which he never takes off, about the young woman who comes on carrying a huge bag full of the things she doesn't want her alcoholic husband to pawn while she's out, about the tired mums heaving buggies onto the bus, wishing they could walk swinging their arms instead, about the schoolkids' banter and the way they treat each other, about Gorgeous Kevin and how he hunches over the whole left side of his body to hide the puckered, burnt skin of his face and neck, I wrote about the folk that come on my bus with the exact change counted up in small coins like they've had to save for the journey, and the ones that are wired for sound at six o'clock in the morning, oblivious to the real world, too busy starring in their own private movies. I knew them all – their names and their nicknames, the days they got on the bus and the routes they travelled, the things they told me, and what I overheard others saying about them. I was part of their world whether they noticed me or not, and ours was the story I wanted to tell.

When I was finished, I sat down and took a long drink of Diet Coke. I didn't look up into the silence but I could feel everyone's eyes on me. I'm not sure why but suddenly I felt like crying, and I might have done if Bounce hadn't spoken up.

'Wendy, that was beautiful,' he said.

'Really?' I looked up at last.

'Really. So filled with empathy and understanding. Tender in an odd way, and completely non-judgemental.' He looked at me quizzically. 'Unexpected, given the material you usually read.'

'I suppose so,' I muttered, not sure if that was a compliment or not, but I knew Bounce was a real writer like me and if he thought it was beautiful, that was good enough for me.

'Well,' said Henry, wiping the beer off his top lip with the back of his hand. 'You've certainly come on in leaps and bounds since you joined us Wendy. You might want to polish that one up a bit and submit it to this year's *New Writing Scotland*? Okay, who's next? Oh, can someone wake up Reginald, it's his piece on the uplifting season of spring next.'

And he moved on to the next piece, but that was fine because they liked mine. I could tell, they really liked it, even Henry. And if it did get published in the *New Writing Scotland* book, that would make me a proper, published author – just like Diane.

I was glad I had something positive to tell Saanvi about on her visit that Wednesday.

'That's great Wendy, seems like you've found a real talent there. Well done.'

I blushed but I was happy she was pleased with me again.

'And I love your new suite,' she said. 'You must be delighted it was delivered in time for Christmas? Speaking of which, shall we talk about your plans?'

I looked away and fiddled with the seam of the cushion. I wasn't sure yet what I was doing for Christmas. Ginger wanted me to spend it at hers but I wasn't sure what Uncle Tam would say about that and, anyway, I didn't even know if I wanted to celebrate at all. I'd spent hours the day before searching for the perfect card for Diane, then a lot more time writing, editing and rewriting my message. In the end, I realized there was nothing I could say that could express my admiration for her and the concern I felt for what she was going through, so I just wrote 'For Diane, From Wendy x' on the card and S.W.A.L.K. on the envelope after I'd sealed it. I had to creep into her front garden in the dark to drop it through her letterbox, after that business with the police, and it felt so wrong that I was the one sneaking around while Wanker Potato Head was in there in the warmth.

Christmas was just one more headache I didn't need, and I really wished the whole thing would go away. It's not like it was a particular problem because I'd be spending it without Mum. I'd hated it for years.

The last Christmas when my mum and dad still lived together was horrible. Mum had been buying in provisions for weeks, so she wouldn't have to pay for it all in one go, but every time Dad or I went into the fridge to pull out a delicious sausage in bacon, or a puff pastry stuffed with prawns, her radar would go off and wherever she was in the house, she'd be in that kitchen, slapping our wrists and telling us no, we had to wait till Christmas Day. Still, there was a festive spirit in the house, an air of anticipation that good things were coming, which made a change from the usual gloom and despair clouds settling overhead.

Our Christmas pantomime trip to the Kings was ruined because Dad whistled under his breath when he saw the price of the tickets and Mum said why shouldn't we have what everyone else had, '*even* if he *still* wasn't working,' and then refused to talk for the rest of the evening. By Christmas Eve, everything was unravelling. The plan – Mum's plan, that is – was that she would finish work early and get changed for Mass, which we'd attend together 'as a family', she said sternly, glaring at Dad, who was still in his pyjamas and fluffy socks, reading his paper. When she left for her afternoon shift at the chippy, Dad and I had strict instructions to clean the place from top to bottom so that when we came back from evening Mass, we could put up the decorations together and 'sing in Christmas'.

I started in the kitchen, as I'd been told. I scrubbed the surfaces and mopped the floor, avoiding the fridge full of goodies for fear of my life. I kept glancing through at Dad to see whether he had started on the living room but he remained in the same position near the fire, idly turning the pages of his paper, which he'd surely read by then.

Half an hour later, I was finished and went through to tell him I was going upstairs to clean the toilet. His paper was lying open on his chair. He was gone.

When Mum came home at six, he still wasn't back. She pursed her lips but said nothing as she tonged her hair and sprayed Cinnabar on her wrists and rubbed them together.

At seven, she said, 'That's it. We can't wait on him any longer or we'll miss Mass. Come on Wendy.'

I glanced at her sideways during Mass, trying to tell whether she was happy – as the hymn-singing and smiling at neighbours and mothers from my school suggested – or whether she was boiling and frothing, ready to erupt. I suspected the latter.

I feared the worst as we walked up our street and saw that our house was in darkness. Dad was still out. Mum said nothing but took off her coat, told me to hang mine up and come and help her put up the decorations. We dressed the tree in almost complete silence, the occasional sipping of Mum's sherry the only sound. At half past eleven, she told me to brush my teeth and go to bed.

I hesitated then asked in a quiet voice, 'Will Dad be here soon?' scared she would shout at me for asking but feeling an urgent need to know Dad was safe and would be back in time for Christmas.

She sniffed and put down her thimble of sherry, which I knew she wouldn't refill even though there was an almost full bottle on the sideboard behind her.

'He always comes back, doesn't he?' She added, 'More's the pity,' in an almost-whisper as I left the room. She must have had second thoughts though because, as I was halfway up the stairs, she shouted me back and held out her arms to me. I ran into them and breathed in the Cinnabar covering the lingering smell of her shift at the chippy.

'Don't worry,' she said. 'Look, I've put the carrot out for the reindeer and a wee drop of sherry for Santa Claus. He'll be here tonight. And Dad'll be here tomorrow for Christmas. You just go up to bed now and get to sleep as quick as you can. He won't come when you're awake, you know,' she called after me as I bounded up the stairs. Of course at twelve I didn't really believe in Santa any more and I suppose Mum must have known that so I'm not sure whose benefit she was saying those things for. It cheered me up anyway, especially the way she was so sure Dad would be back.

I don't know what time he got home in the end but he was slumbering on the sofa when I got up to open my presents. He might have been there all night as his face was yellow with tiredness, his eyes sunken in his cheeks, and he was still wearing his tweed coat. He looked startled as I jumped on him and shouted, 'Merry Christmas Dad, look, he's been!'

Mum stood in the doorway, smiling a thin smile while I unwrapped my presents. Dad had taken off his coat and mumbled, 'That's nice,' at each gift I showed him.

Christmas lunch was served cold and unappetizing at one on the dot. There were no other guests, and I could tell Mum and Dad weren't talking so I kept up an incessant chatter about nothing in particular while the gravy congealed in the middle of the table. Later in the afternoon, Mum shouted, 'Ta-dah,' and made a production of coming out of the kitchen with the silver tray full of all the little Christmas goodies she'd been hoarding for weeks. But now that we finally had permission to eat them we were too full to enjoy them, and the pastry landed in my stomach like a bullet. Dad ignored them completely and poured himself another glass of wine. He'd been drinking steadily since before lunch and each time he reached across to fill up his glass, Mum glared at him but said nothing. He glared back, raising his eyebrows and daring her to comment.

After Mum and I cleared up for the second time that day, we

watched a James Bond movie together, Mum tutting every time the Bond girl came on in her bikini, Dad sinking further and further into his chair, his only other movement the refilling of his glass from the whisky bottle he'd placed on the floor beside him. I could hear the clock ticking behind me, and smell the turkey bones Mum had simmering on the cooker for stock.

I started yawning and said I'd go to bed now, thanks for a great day. Mum softened for the first time that day, and asked which present was my favourite, and whether I'd really had a good day.

'They're all great,' I said, smiling broadly. 'It's been lovely. Best Christmas ever,' I added, looking at a point somewhere above her head.

'Well, I tried my best,' said Mum, with one more glare at Dad, whose eyes were closed and mouth open now, his head cocked to one side in a way that looked likely to give him a painful crick in his neck.

I shut my bedroom door tight, putting my desk chair in front of it as though that would somehow help to dampen the noise. It started as soon as I switched on my globe light. Her high pitched accusations, his low, grumbling, couldn't-care-less responses, thuds and clunks as furniture was knocked aside and decorations set asunder. It reached a crescendo with Mum screaming, 'That'll be the last Christmas you ever ruin, you hear me?' and the door slamming when he'd had enough and gone back out into the night.

Thinking back to what Christmas had been like when I was younger, I figured Christmas at Ginger's couldn't be any worse, could it?

33

I DIDN'T SLEEP MUCH ON Christmas Eve because I was too busy wondering what the following day would bring for Diane. I had no idea how other people celebrated but I hoped, for the day at least, that wanker of a husband would be nice to her, maybe even buy her a gift, though of course he'd have no idea of the kind of thing she liked. If I'd been in charge, her day would have been as magical as she deserved. That big clock in her hallway would chime at midday and wake us up. We'd have slept late because we'd have been at Midnight Mass with all our friends the night before, but I'd get up first and wake her with warm croissants which I'd made myself, and huge strawberries, which would be round and lush even though they were out of season, and of course fresh, strong coffee served in one of those duck-egg blue coffee pots you see in magazines. We'd lounge for a bit, talking about the books we were reading – and the books we were writing. Diane would be wearing . . . well, something colourful and floaty anyway, her hair would be mussed up but still beautiful and her skin would be glowing after all the strawberries, and also with happiness. We'd exchange gifts of books and she'd love the one I'd chosen and wrapped so carefully for her, and I would be delighted with mine, by an author I'd mentioned in passing that

I admired and whose name Diane had stored away for exactly this reason. We'd spend the day curled up on one of those comfy leather sofas, surrounded by ornaments and tasteful Christmas decorations, before having a late Christmassy themed supper, with mulled wine and walnuts maybe, or chestnuts, prepared by me. It was only what she deserved, and I tossed around in the twisted sheets, keeping my eyes pressed shut so I wouldn't have to wake up and leave it all behind.

In the end I got up around five-ish, shivering in the blue light and cupping my hands round a mug of tea for warmth. I peeled a black-skinned banana and ate it on the sofa in my anorak, waiting for it to be time to go to Ginger's house.

I'd never been to anyone else's house at Christmas so I didn't know what to expect. I went round there at half past nine because I knew cooking a turkey took hours and I was knocking for ages because no one else was up yet.

'Wendy, you're early,' said Ginger, answering the door in her jogging pants and T-shirt. Her eyes looked bruised with tiredness and her hair was stringy.

'Happy Christmas Ginger,' I said, lifting the bags with the dinner stuff. 'Get dressed and we'll start cooking.'

We spent most of the day in the kitchen. It took us a while to clear the surfaces and wash the dishes tottering round the sink before we could actually cook, but I don't know what Mum complained about. It's not that hard to put a giant bird in the oven and peel a few potatoes and carrots. Like most of the stuff Mum was unhappy about, I think she'd let it get all out of proportion.

Everything was ready to serve at one o'clock. By the time Uncle Tam and Fran came out of their room at three, it was mostly overcooked but no one seemed to mind. Looked like the delay was Fran's hair. She'd clearly given herself some sort of home perm as there were little black bubbles over her forehead and round her ears. I avoided Ginger's eye and neither of us commented on it as Fran gave her hair delicate little pats with her palms. She didn't have the look I'd have thought someone like Tam would go for but what do I know about what men like. Maybe a tight perm is more attractive than I think, and at least it would stay in place in a draught.

They were deep in discussion about some business deal as Ginger and me prepared the starters.

Fran said, 'There's no point in huffing about it Tam. If they want the stuff delivered to Arrochar, that's what we've got to do.'

Tam silenced her with a glare that was magnified by his thick glasses and jerked his head in my direction. I busied myself fanning out the melon slices so they wouldn't think I was listening.

'We need to get it there by early January at the latest. What do you suggest?'

'Maybe getting off your lazy arse and passing your driving test at last?'

It seemed odd that a businessman like Tam couldn't drive, perhaps he was driven everywhere and, of course, most of his business was conducted from home.

Ginger and me put down the plates and sat next to each other. Tam and Fran just carried on talking.

'Well, what about cutting Roddy in? He could—'

'No way. This is the big one, he's not getting any of it.'

'He could do a driving job for you though, does nothing else,' mumbled Ginger, looking at her plate.

Tam slammed his palm against the table. 'Keep out of this

Ginger, you hear? And not a word, not one word of what's discussed here goes back to Roddy, got it?'

That seemed an odd way to treat a business partner but I didn't know anything about business, maybe keeping secrets was the key to Uncle Tam's success.

When Ginger didn't answer, he leaned across the table and hissed again, 'Have you got that?'

Ginger nodded, then looked up and said, 'Me and Wendy could do it.'

'Don't be so ridiculous, we need someone to take the stuff up there in a car.'

'Wendy can drive.' She paused then added quickly, without looking at me, 'She's the oldest in her year, passed her test first time.'

I nodded. I wasn't sure why Ginger was volunteering but she'd been so miserable lately that if taking her somewhere in the car could cheer her up, I'd definitely do it.

'What age are you exactly Wendy?' said Fran.

'Never mind that. You can drive? You've got your licence, I mean?' Tam spoke directly to me for perhaps the first time that day.

I nodded again. 'I'm a pretty confident driver,' I said, thinking I should be when I drive for a living but, taking Ginger's lead, I guessed he didn't need to know that. 'Is it a company car I'd be driving?'

'Oh yeah,' laughed Tam. 'It'll be the company car. Better get it insured for a new driver, eh Fran?' They both laughed but I don't know why because insurance is a pretty serious thing, we did a course on it at work.

'Right, well that just might work,' said Tam, smiling properly for the first time since he'd sat down. 'What the hell's this? Melon? I don't eat fruit for dinner, where's the turkey?'

I gave everyone a plate full of turkey and trimmings and sat down again. I was so tense my back didn't touch the back of the chair and my armpits felt itchy beneath my sweatshirt. I waited for their verdict. No one said anything, they all just ate until Fran pushed her plate away saying she couldn't eat another thing and Tam agreed, with a burp. But Fran must have seen my eyes round with anticipation because she sat forwards again and said, 'That was brilliant Wendy, I didn't know you could cook.'

'I can't. Usually. I looked up the recipe for turkey online. And for baby carrots. They were cooked in butter.'

Ginger scraped her knife against her plate and said nothing.

'Pudding?' I said, getting up again.

By the time we'd finished the black forest gateau, Tam and Fran were well on their way to being drunk again so they were happy, and Ginger and me were satisfied we'd done well. Fran was making kissing noises at Tam and he had his arm round her shoulders, telling her how much he loved her.

'Shall we do presents now?' I said, pushing my chair away and reaching to the floor for the bag of presents I'd brought with me. Everyone round the table looked at me.

'I'll start.' I gave Ginger an ornamental chipmunk in a Santa hat that sang *Silent Night* when you pressed the little button under its stand. I could tell she loved it because she kept it sitting in its box in her bedroom for ages afterwards so that it wouldn't get dirty or broken. Fran was pleased with her box of scented handkerchiefs with a thistle design. 'Because you're always sniffing,' I said, as I gave it to her.

'Am I?' she said, with a sniff. 'Well, thanks.'

I hadn't been sure whether to buy anything for Uncle Tam but then I saw the perfect present for him and just had to buy it.

'What is it?' he said, peering at it through the thick lenses of his glasses. A small smear cast a shadow on the left one.

'Present,' I said shyly, kicking my heels and looking at the floor.

'Is it . . . a diary?' He turned the book with its leather-look cover over in his hands.

'It's a Filofax,' I said, blushing. 'For your business appointments and things.'

Tam glanced at Fran and cleared his throat. 'Well, that's great, thanks. Did we get Wendy something Fran?'

Fran glared back at Tam and pulled at one of the stiff little curls above her ear. We all waited in silence as she looked round then said finally, 'Yes, we got her . . . um, just a minute.'

She came back into the room and gave me a box with Lynx Africa shower gel and deodorant.

'Thanks!' I said. It smelled lovely.

The door went and we heard footsteps coming up the hall. Tam jumped up, then relaxed when Roddy came into the kitchen. His head was covered by a beanie with the word Mackenzie scrawled across it. He had week-old stubble up his cheeks though his chin was oddly bald and vulnerable. He was smoking the end of a cigarette, his stubby fingers brown with nicotine, and no nails to speak of.

His eyes glinted off each of us in turn, resting for a moment on Ginger, who had crossed her arms defiantly over her chest and tossed her chin upwards in his direction.

'It's all happy families here, isn't it?' he said, sliding into the chair next to mine. The smell of drink was strong on him and

I stood up and started picking up the dirty plates. 'I'll have a beer if they're cold,' he said to me.

I hovered beside him with the dirty dishes in my hand, saying nothing.

'All right Roddy?' said Tam, standing up awkwardly, his skinny thighs pushing against the table. 'Let's leave the girls to the dishes and get some drinking done.'

Fran and Tam stumbled out of the room. Roddy sat for a few seconds then, with a last glance at Ginger, followed them through to the living room.

'Sausage supper tits,' hissed Ginger under her breath, my presence and the fact I was staying overnight making her confident. We fell back laughing as Roddy slunk out the door, his greasy hair in his face.

'Oh, don't make me laugh any more Ginger,' I cried, hugging my knees to my belly. 'I'm so full, it hurts.'

The next morning, I woke up at eight, the early morning brightness hurting my eyes. The house had still been shaking with music and the high pitched laughter of the very drunk when Ginger and me had fallen asleep around four, fully clothed, on top of Ginger's bed. I looked down at her and saw she was still sleeping, her eyes tight shut and her lips pouting like a baby's. I moved her hair away from her face and behind her ear, and noticed the patches on her scalp had returned. The skin above her ear was dry and flaky and completely bald. I touched it with the tip of my finger, and she turned a little and shook her head but she didn't wake up. I sat up and wondered what to do.

The rest of the house was like a graveyard – one that had been desecrated by partygoers. There were half empty bottles of whisky and gin, and endless upturned bottles of beer and scrunched cans of lager like meteors, lining the floors of the hall and the living room. The kitchen was a hellhole and I quickly shut the door on it. I decided to go home which, looking back, may have been the point at which everything started to go wrong.

34

AS SOON AS I GOT home, I took out my tablet and started making notes for a new story for writers' group. The group really liked my last story because it was set in Scotland, and filled with realistic characters they could relate to, so I decided to stick with the same approach. My new idea was about a really busy detective agency, based in Viewpark, whose speciality was international jewel theft. The twist could be that it was run by two old women, one who always wore a tweed hat – a clever nod to Sherlock Holmes even if only Bounce, who was the group's other real literary connoisseur, would get it – and one who was the real brain behind the enterprise, saying nothing but digesting all the clues and solving the crime before the other woman had had her tea. Maybe I could even name the characters after my friends on the bus, I bet Irish Mary and Terry would be thrilled to be in one of my stories. I was just about to google 'diamonds from Monte Carlo' when I heard knocking at the front door.

'Have you lost your key again—?' I said as I opened the door, but it wasn't Ginger.

'Merry Christmas Wendy!'

I'm not sure if I was more dazzled by the sheen of fresh snow covering my grass, or by Muriel's shocking pink fake fur coat.

'Do you like it?' said Muriel. 'This is my Christmas present from Bobby, he outdid himself this year.' She twirled round on my doorstep, singing, 'Ta-dah,' and almost knocking over poor Sophie, who was standing next to her, stamping her feet against the cold, her breath coming out in little puffs like she was smoking. Her hair had grown back fluffy like a toddler's, but it was long enough to curl round the edge of her collar now, so I was pleased she was taking Britt's advice on board.

'Have you come to see me?' I said, which seemed likely since they were standing on my doorstep but also unlikely because no one ever came to see me at home, except Ginger.

'We have, Wendy, and we come bearing gifts.'

Muriel held out a small, beautifully wrapped parcel, tied with gold ribbon that curled into a frothy centrepiece on top of the box.

'You bought a present for me?' I said, taking the box from her hesitantly in case I'd misunderstood. But she nodded so I untied the ribbon and tore the plush red paper, saying, 'I haven't got you anything.'

'Don't worry about that Wendy, that's not why I give my friends gifts. Do you like it?'

I turned over the bottle of Cinnabar in my hands.

'I remembered you said it was your mum's favourite, I thought you might like it too?'

Before I could answer, Sophie held out her parcel, a larger, softer package, wrapped in greaseproof paper with what looked like a white rosette on top.

'It's a lemon drizzle cake,' she said, blushing.

'Thanks,' I said, opening the paper and sniffing the springy, yellow sponge. 'It looks like the one I get from Tunnock's, only less professional.'

'Well, I . . . made it myself. As a thanks for . . . being a good listener and a good friend.'

I looked at her in surprise and tried to think of something just as nice to say in return. 'I'm sure I'll love it,' I said. 'Some people don't like cake that's all dry round the edges but I quite like a bit of crunch. Thanks.'

I stood there with my packages in my hands, the second time in two days I'd received gifts from someone other than my mum, and wondered what to do next. Afterwards I thought maybe I should have asked them in as they hung around for quite a few minutes even after I'd said thank you another couple of times. Finally, Muriel said, 'Right then, I guess we'll see you at writers' group after the holiday,' and she and Sophie sort of shrugged at each other and walked back down my slushy path.

'Thanks again,' I called after them, then, 'I like your new coat,' as they disappeared down the street.

I spent the rest of the day writing. After dinner, I cut a chunk of Sophie's cake and wrapped it in tinfoil to keep for Ginger. I cut myself a slice and sat on the new couch, setting a cup of tea and the cake beside me. I ran my hand across the smooth leather and glanced round at the clean, fresh walls, my coasters on the table, and my mum's purple rug in front of the glowing fire. It occurred to me that I was happy – comfortable in my own home, content in my own company because I knew I had friends I could see if I wanted to, and happy to be writing. *And* the cake wasn't actually as bad as it looked, which I would tell Sophie next time I saw her since she'd been so nice to me.

I felt a bit guilty as I realized I'd been so engrossed in my own life that I'd hardly thought about Diane and her problems all day, so I scrolled through Twitter for any mentions of her. Someone had tweeted they'd been lucky enough to see a proof of Diane's new short story collection, though why they'd need evidence of it I don't know. Diane's own account still wasn't working properly and I was wondering whether I should contact Twitter about it when Ginger appeared at the back door, blood on her cheek and her eyes flashing.

'What happened to—'

She pushed past me. 'Where were you Wendy? Why did you go when he was still there, sleeping it off, right next to me?' She was screaming now. 'In the bedroom right next to mine, do you understand what I'm saying Wendy? And Uncle Tam was so fucking out of it after all the booze and everything else, he was nowhere to be seen, didn't even hear a thing . . .'

'Was it Roddy? What did he do to you? I'm sorry Ginger, I never thought . . . I didn't realize things were this bad.'

'Liar! You knew, I told you.' She was pacing the living room, her hands in her hair and then pointing at me accusingly, her face streaked with dirt and tears.

'But you were asleep, I didn't want to wake you. I'm sorry Ginger, come on, you can stay here tonight, we'll stay up late and watch YouTube. I've got lemon drizzle cake.'

That seemed to calm her down a bit because she sat next to me on the sofa, the smell of her sweat mingling with the new leather. She was breathing hard through her nose, the hair round her face damp. I stared at her trainers and saw that water had seeped into them and stained the toes. I was about to ask her if it was still snowing out when she turned to me suddenly and said, 'Can I trust you Wendy?'

Her eyes were huge, her mouth gaping as she waited for my reply.

I pursed my lips, careful to say the right thing, not wanting to upset her more. 'Of course you can, we're friends,' I said, then added, 'What do you mean, trust me not to tell a secret, or . . . ?'

She gave a strange smirk and reached into her pocket, bringing out a small package wrapped in one of the handkerchiefs I'd bought for Fran.

'Does Fran know you've got—'

She tutted. 'Never mind that Wendy. Look.'

And that's when she showed me the gun.

I jumped back as though it had already wounded me.

'Don't worry, I won't shoot you,' she laughed. 'Do you want to hold it?'

I looked at it, hardly able to believe I was looking at a real gun. I mean, you see them a lot on TV, and you read about them in books, lots of detectives have them, especially in American novels, and they don't seem that scary, more like part of their uniform, something they have to have like their thick leather belts or their aviator shades. But in real life a gun is not a friendly object. It was so small and trim in Ginger's hand, but all I could think about was its power to kill a person. It was quite beautiful in some ways – the handle part was tan wood and looked smooth to the touch. There was a large silver screw in the back of the handle and a seam along the metal that almost cut the handle in two. The barrel of the gun was about six inches long, black and sleek except for the scores and nicks along its surface, I didn't want to think about what had caused them. I screwed my eyes up and read the letters BAC and some numbers engraved into the metal, the last two of which had been scored out.

Ginger held it out to me and I hesitated, then took it from her. It was lighter than I imagined guns would feel.

'It's Russian,' she said. 'Cool isn't it?'

It was very cold to the touch and I passed it from one hand to the other, wondering how such a thing had ended up in my house in Birkenshaw.

'It's called a Makarov. That's the make of it.'

'Whose gun is it?' I whispered. 'Where did you get it?'

'Roddy got it for Uncle Tam, he paid eight hundred quid for it. It's been sitting at the back of the lock-up for months. They hid it beneath a crate of old dinner plates but I found it.' She watched me examine it for a bit then said, 'I don't know how many bullets are in it.'

Suddenly, I felt as though I was going to be sick and I threw the gun back at Ginger.

'For God's sake,' she said, as she leaned over to catch it. 'Be careful, it might go off.'

'What? So it's definitely loaded?' I cried. 'For God's sake Ginger, what are you even doing with a gun?'

She pushed her hair back from her face and spoke through tight lips. 'I realized something last night. No one's going to make sure I don't get hurt – except me. But no one can come near me now, I've got this to protect me. I'll protect you too Wendy.'

I took a deep breath. 'Listen to me. You need to put that gun back exactly where you found it, as soon as you get home. We don't need guns to protect ourselves, I won't let anything bad happen to you. We'll do that job they wanted, right? We'll take whatever it is up to Arrochar like your uncle Tam wants, make him realize he doesn't need Roddy like you said. Maybe you could even tell him what's been happening . . . and he'll tell Roddy to stop coming round. Then we can . . . well, I don't know what we'll do next but we'll figure out something, right? Nothing bad's going to happen. I promise you, Ginger.'

35

A WEEK LATER WE WERE driving up the M8 to Arrochar, the boot of Mum's old Micra just about big enough to accommodate the oversized suede travel bag Tam wanted us to take to his business associates up north.

'What's in it?' I asked Tam, as he placed the bag very carefully into my boot. His glasses made his eyes big as coins, and he peered into the boot, making sure the bag was stowed safely.

'Just items that need to reach their destination undamaged and as quickly as possible Wendy,' he said. 'Don't worry yourself about what's in the bag.'

'Stock?' I said, not at all sure what this would be as I still wasn't clear as to the nature of Tam and Roddy's business. It must have been something valuable though by the way Tam was acting.

'That's right,' he said. 'Stock. Exactly.'

He walked back round to the front of the car where Ginger was sitting hunched up in the passenger seat, the furry collar of her jacket pulled up to cover most of her face.

'You not speaking this morning?' he said, but in an offhand way that suggested he didn't care whether she ever spoke to him again.

She muttered something I couldn't hear and he didn't reply.

'So, you're to call me as soon as you get to Loch Fyne, have you got that? Use the phone I gave you, not your own mobile, that's important.'

I nodded and told him not to worry, we were perfectly capable of dropping off a bag, however important the contents. He pushed his glasses further up his nose then looked to the ground, shuffling his toe along the icy pavement.

'Yeah well. Keep in touch,' and he stepped away from the car as I got into the driver's seat. I turned the key and as the car eased away from the street, Tam came running after me, waving his arms. I braked suddenly and waited for him to catch up with me.

'You're not to speak to anyone on your way, understand? No one, I don't care who it is – you don't say what you're doing, where you're going, nothing. And you don't let the bag out your sight till you drop it off, right? You remember I told you that, do not leave the car unattended, not even for a piss break. Understand?'

'Yes,' I told him impatiently, wondering if all businessmen were as precious about their stock as he was. 'I promise, we'll take good care of your stuff, don't worry.'

'Yeah, well you'd better, or . . .'

Ginger looked up and we both waited on Tam finishing his sentence.

'Or . . . well, you'd better, that's all.' With that, he patted the back of the car and turned on his heel, back into the street.

'Ready for our road trip?' I said to Ginger, trying to cheer her up.

She nodded, and we were off.

'I need to pee,' she said, less than twenty minutes later.

I sighed. 'For God's sake Ginger, we've only been driving five minutes. Could you not have gone before we left?'

'I did. Plus, I feel sick, I think I'm actually going to be sick.'

I looked at her. This was the first time I'd seen her since she'd showed me the gun and I really wanted to ask her whether she'd put it back in the lock-up without anyone finding out but I didn't want to make her feel worse. She gave me a smile that was more of a grimace and I blinked at the whiteness of her teeth. Perhaps it was just against the sickly green of her face but her teeth looked preternaturally white, like the inside of a skull. I imagined if I rubbed my fingers across them, they would squeak. I shook away the image and told her we'd stop at the next services we came to.

As I was driving, it struck me that this was the first time I'd ever been on an overnight trip with a friend. Just me and a friend driving together in the sunshine. It was a shame Ginger wasn't feeling well because otherwise this would have been a beautiful day for our adventure. A crisp, bright January morning, with the hope of spring just round the corner, even as the frost was melting on the ground. The roads were quiet and the car was snug and warm. The sun was blinding as I turned off the motorway into Dumbarton Services and I began to wish I'd brought my sunglasses.

I stopped directly in front of the services and looked at Ginger.

'Maybe you'll feel better after you've been sick,' I said.

'Maybe,' she said, opening her door and waiting for me at the entrance. 'Are you not coming in?'

I shook my head. 'I need to stay with the bag, remember? We're not allowed to let it out of our sight.'

'Oh, him. Are you still going to do what he says even when he's not here to see you?'

I shrugged. 'Don't need the toilet anyway, we've only just set off.' I took a tenner from my purse and nipped out the car to hand it to her. 'Here, get us both a coffee.'

I watched her as she came back out of the services ten minutes later, my coffee cup in one hand and a bottle of water for herself in the other. Balanced between her arm and her hip, she carried a package from the doughnut shop. No wonder she was putting on weight, I thought, noticing for the first time that she was no longer the straight up and down pencil shape she'd been when I'd first met her. Her hips were rounding out and her boobs seemed to be getting bigger. Lucky her, I thought, mine had stopped growing when I was fourteen.

'Okay?' I said, as she sat down.

'Yeah, I was sick as a dog, but I feel better now. Must've been that roll and sausage I ate for breakfast, you never know how long food's been hanging around in our house.' She bit into a jam doughnut.

'Want one?' she said, offering me the bag.

I shook my head and tutted. 'You'll get spots from all that sugar,' I said, and started up the engine.

'Can I put the radio on?'

'Course. Be careful with the knob though because it . . .'

The dial for the radio fell to the floor.

'. . . comes off in your hand if you're not careful.'

'Sorry Wendy,' said Ginger. 'What about I-spy?'

'Okay,' I said. 'You can go first.'

'I spy with my little eye,' she sang, then looked around her for something to say.

'Got it,' she said, snapping her fingers. 'Something beginning with BF.'

'Inside the car or outside?' I asked.

'Inside.'

I looked over the dashboard, round my feet then round Ginger's. I glanced into the back of the car but could see nothing. I made a face. 'Are you sure it begins with BF?' I said, not wanting to make her feel stupid but wondering whether the fact she still couldn't read that well also meant she couldn't spell.

'Yup,' she said, pleased with herself for foxing me. 'Want a clue?'

'Go on.'

'You're very close to it.'

'Ginger, the car's tiny, I'm very close to everything that's in it.'

'No, I mean, really close.'

I looked about me again, moving my feet and checking underneath. The car swerved slightly.

'Watch the road Wendy!'

'Okay, I give up. What's in this car that starts with BF?'

'Best friend,' she said, laughing and punching my arm. 'Best friend, that's you. See – close to it because it *was* you.'

'But Ginger, that's . . . oh, okay, I suppose so,' I said, not wanting to spoil her lifted mood.

'We are best friends aren't we Wendy?' She looked at me shyly, her fingers touching the bald spot at her forehead which was getting bigger again.

'Course we are,' I said, looking over my shoulder to switch into the fast lane. 'You, me and Diane.'

'Ppff.'

I looked at her. 'What's that supposed to mean?'

'Nothing.'

'No, go on, say it.'

'Well, there was the small matter of her calling the police on you for being at her house. I don't know what kind of friend would do that to their best friend?'

I squirmed a bit in my seat but shook my head. 'I should never have told you about that, I knew you'd misunderstand.'

'Not much to misunderstand Wendy, she—'

I slammed my hand on the wheel and she jumped. 'No, we're not talking about this any more. I know you don't like my friendship with Diane, but she is my friend, same as you are. We've got this special connection, and not just because we're both writers.'

Ginger was looking out of the window, refusing to meet my eye. I reached over and touched her knee. 'Look, Diane's going through some stuff at the moment, she's not . . . her life's not as different from ours as you think, and . . . she needs me right now. It doesn't mean you and me aren't best friends too though.'

She didn't speak again till we passed Loch Lomond.

As we turned the corner where the stretch of water came into view, we both gave an involuntary intake of breath. Say what you like about Scotland and its crappy food and its drinking culture and whatever else they say about us, but there's one thing they can't take away from us. There's no country in the world more beautiful than Scotland. With the sun glinting off the water, the trees swaying on the banks and miles and miles of greenery as far as the eye can see, what could beat it?

My mum never thought so. When Dad was working and we had holidays, every year they'd have the same row. He'd want to go north, as far up as we could, to Ullapool and Achiltibuie, to breathe in the untainted air, walk the beaches and explore the misty hills. She could breathe as much Scottish air as she wanted all year right here in the west of Scotland, thank you very much. She wanted to go to Spain, or France maybe, and drink fizzy ice-cold water in pretty town squares with a clock tower and roaming black cats, and locals who would tell you all about the history of the place. She might even attempt some of their foreign food, paella was supposed to be lovely. Her eyes would be shining and far away as she described the scene, Dad's eyes would be rolling and winking at me.

When I thought about Mum and Dad, I couldn't help wondering what drew them together in the first place. They were just so different in every way, how they looked at the world, everything. And then I thought about Diane and me, and I was astonished by how similar we were, and not just because we were both writers. We were also both strong women, we worked hard and saw the world in the same way. You'd only have to read, say, a passage from Diane's biography *Elizabeth* to see exactly what she thought about arrogant men, and she was writing before all this #MeToo stuff. She'd never jump on any bandwagon just to go with current opinion, no, she had her own opinions and she was not afraid to air them either. I suppose that's why I'd got so frustrated with her about the way she dealt with that man she'd somehow been persuaded to marry. Not that he was any sort of husband to her, not in the real sense of the word, he didn't love her or support her, not the way I did. They didn't even sleep together. I'm guessing.

Anyway, my dad hadn't been a bad man like the man Diane was shackled to. He was just, maybe, I don't know, weak or something. But he had loads of good qualities too. Once he took me camping, when I was very young, just me and him. It was a September weekend and we drove to Ardluie, which is quite near Loch Lomond come to think of it. He pitched our tent while I danced around, gathering sticks and finding odd-shaped pebbles which I kept presenting to him as he worked.

'Great, sweetheart,' he said. 'Lovely,' hardly looking as he hammered in the tent pegs.

When the tent was done, we went swimming in the lake. It was dusk, too cold to swim really, and my legs and arms were covered in bumpy gooseflesh.

'Come on,' he called from further out. 'Get your cozzie wet.'

I held my breath and ducked into the freezing waves, my feet lifting from the sandy bottom and my hair rising up like seaweed.

Later, we had sausages on thick white bread and bananas with a flake in the middle, all cooked on the fire. Dad's face was flushed with the heat of flames and the red wine he was drinking from a big flask he'd brought. By bedtime, his teeth and lips were black with wine and I had to stop him from stumbling into the charred remains of the fire pit.

'This has been great, sure it has Wendy?' he said, leaning on me as I helped him into our tent.

'Brilliant, Dad,' I said. 'I don't ever want to go home.'

There was a rustling sound beside me as Ginger reached into the bag for another doughnut. She smiled at me and memories of Dad were replaced by the realization that this trip with Ginger would be every bit as good as my trips as a child, maybe even better.

Half an hour later we passed the Tarbet Hotel and took a left to Inveraray. There was a sharp buzzing sound.

'What's that?' I asked Ginger, who'd been dozing for the past ten minutes, her head against the window.

'Wha'? What's that noise?'

We looked round the car. 'It's your uncle Tam's phone,' I said, swerving a little as the road narrowed and I almost drove into the grass verge. 'That phone he gave me as we were leaving. Pass me it over, would you?'

Ginger reached into the back and found the chunky black phone at the bottom of my rucksack.

'Hello?' I said. 'Hello? This is Wendy.'

'How's it going? Are you nearly there?' I stiffened; it was Roddy.

'Where's Tam? How did you get this number?'

'Never you mind asking questions, I'm Tam's partner and I'm asking you if the stuff is safely with you?'

I wasn't sure what to say. Tam had been quite clear that Roddy was supposed to know nothing about the delivery, but he did have the number of the special business phone and he did work with Tam so maybe I'd got it wrong as usual. His thin voice grated in my ear so I answered quickly to get rid of him. 'Yes, we'll be there just after four. I'm driving now so I need to go. What?' I looked over at Ginger. 'Yes, she's here. Yes, wait a minute.'

'Roddy wants to speak to you,' I whispered to Ginger, my hand over the phone. I held it out to her.

She pursed her lips then took it off me, holding it away from her like it was covered in germs.

I heard Roddy's muffled voice on the other side so I knew he was saying something but Ginger looked straight ahead and didn't answer for what seemed a long time.

'It's the same as I told you. Arrochar,' she said finally.

I kept my eyes on the road.

'It's up to me,' she hissed at him before cutting him off and throwing the phone on the back seat. She didn't look at me, sat fingering her bald patch and scratching her chin.

'What's up to you?' I said. 'What did he want?'

'Nothing,' said Ginger.

'Ginger, do you think we should tell Uncle Tam about—'

'Don't make something out of nothing, Wendy. Let's just do our side of the bargain and get home,' she said, batting me away. 'Any more doughnuts?'

I thought about saying we'd already broken our side of the bargain by telling Roddy but I didn't have the heart. I shook my head as she offered me a doughnut, knowing it would stick in my dry mouth. A low pressure headache was starting to throb behind my eyes, a feeling of unease rising in my belly. Our big adventure up north was turning out to be less fun than I thought it would be; I couldn't wait to get back home.

Ginger shuffled down into her seat and closed her eyes after she'd eaten two more doughnuts. I carried on driving for another twenty minutes or so, until we passed Loch Long on our left, the white hotels and squat holiday cottages rising up behind the gleaming water.

'Let's get out and stretch our legs for a bit,' I said. 'Ginger. Ginger!' I shook her awake and she rubbed her eyes.

'Are we there?'

'No, nearly though, I'm just going to get out the car for a bit, are you coming?'

'S'pose.'

We wandered along the shingle, the only people in view for miles.

'Now this is more like it. Isn't this beautiful Ginger?' I said, lifting my face to the thin winter sun.

'Yeah,' she said. 'Anywhere's better than Viewpark, let's be honest.'

'You seem awful down today Ginger. Is there something wrong?'

She looked towards the water, her eyes filling with tears. 'It's just . . . it's . . .'

Suddenly a large white labrador appeared from the trees behind us, bounding along the pebbly beach like there was no place better in the world to be. Ginger brightened immediately and ran after the dog, following it to the water's edge.

By the time I caught up with her, she was rubbing the dog's coat while it shook itself off all over her. I was about to tell her to stop getting so wet but her face had lit up for the first time all day, there was pure joy in her eyes at being with this big, stupid, fun-loving pup out in the fresh air. I said nothing and watched them play together, all the while looking around me for the dog's owner. When no one appeared to claim the dog, I told Ginger reluctantly we'd better head back to the car.

'Actually, I've just realized we've left the bag on its own all this time. Come on Ginger, we need to get back to the car.'

I was fumbling in my pocket for the car key as I marched up the shingle but Ginger was still faffing with the dog.

I turned back and shouted at her, 'Come *on* Ginger, leave the dog now, we need to go.'

She was kneeling beside the dog with her arms wound round its neck. 'But what if no one comes to claim him? What if he's on his own here with no one to take care of him? Oh Wendy, what if he's hungry?'

'Not our problem,' I said angrily, walking back now to Ginger. I grabbed her by her arm and pulled her to her feet.

'Ow, that was . . . Wendy, leave me alone, you can't—'

The dog was barking madly now and insinuating itself between Ginger and me, almost like he was trying to protect her. I stopped then, what was I doing, hurting my best friend.

'Ginger, I'm sorry,' I said, dropping my hands to my sides. 'I didn't mean to pull you, it's just . . . the bag . . . and your uncle Tam will be angry if it's not delivered on time, and . . .'

Ginger was quiet then and started walking back to the car. 'It's okay,' she said. 'I'm used to it.'

I stopped and looked at her. 'Don't say that Ginger, please. I'm not like them. I didn't mean to grab you, I'm sorry. Okay?'

She nodded. 'It's fine.'

When we reached the car, I checked the bag was still stowed safely in the boot, then we drove on.

'Last leg,' I said to Ginger, and put Mum's old Micra into gear.

Just before we reached the service station Tam had told us to phone him from, we passed a McDonald's. I saw Ginger's head swivel as we passed it and knew she wouldn't give me peace till we stopped.

'You must be hungry too Wendy. I'm—'

'Starving, I know,' I laughed, slamming the door shut behind me and following her in.

We stood at the counter and I said, 'What are you having?' When I turned to look at Ginger, she was beaming.

'Wendy,' she said, her eyes sparkling, 'I can read everything on this menu. Every single thing.' She laughed again and came up close to me. 'This is brilliant, I can read the whole board.'

I smiled back. 'Things are looking up for us Ginger, just you wait.'

We were standing outside the service station with five minutes to spare. Tam called the new mobile at four o'clock and gave me exact instructions on where to leave the bag.

'Are you sure we've just to leave it? I mean, will the clients not want to say hello?' I asked, twiddling with the zipper on my anorak as I spoke to him.

'Listen to me Wendy, and listen carefully. You leave the bag exactly where I say, at exactly the time I give you, and you walk away immediately. Do not stay to check the bag is lifted, and for Christ's sake do not hang around to say hello to the client as you put it. Do you understand me?'

It seemed like an odd way to do business but he was the expert. I paused, wondering whether to tell him about Roddy's phone call but he sounded angry already so I just said, 'Fine,' and threw the phone back into the car.

Thick clouds were gathering overhead and the gunmetal grey of the sky indicated a downpour. I took a deep breath then said to Ginger in a bright voice, 'Come on then, let's do as Uncle Tam says.' The sooner we got this done, the sooner we could go home and everything could get back to normal.

36

WE STAYED OVERNIGHT AT a pub guesthouse Fran had booked
for us. It was a bit depressing with lots of brown swirls on the
floors and Artex on the walls but we were so tired by then,
we didn't care. We'd left the bag beneath the second from the
end dumpster in the Asda car park, texted Tam the minute
we'd done it and driven straight here. All the driving was
beginning to affect me now, and my eyes were half closed as
I looked round the low ceilinged bar. It reminded me of an
old aunt's living room when I was growing up. Far too many
velour chairs littered the room, some tables had as many as
ten empty chairs packed round them, like all the party guests
had just upped and left. We were the only people eating, the
rest of the customers were mainly old men with flat caps and
sideburns, nursing half drunk pints of ice-cold lager and nips
of whisky to chase them.

'Is that nice?' I said to Ginger, as she finished the last of her
sausage and mash. She nodded and pushed her plate away.

She cleared her throat and looked round the room, her tongue
constantly flicking at whatever was lodged in her back teeth.

'Everything okay now?' I asked. 'Feeling sick and stuff
I mean.' I pointed to her stomach which still looked bloated.

'Yeah,' she said. 'I really only feel sick in the mornings.' She looked at me. 'Probably because I wake up hungry?'

'Yeah,' I said, doubtfully. 'I suppose so.'

The truth was, I was getting a bit tired of Ginger's increasingly frequent bouts of sickness and how tired she was all the time. It seemed like she was becoming less fun the longer I knew her, and sometimes that made me a bit resentful. After all, I was choosing to spend time with her that I could have been spending looking out for Diane. But Ginger smiled at me then, a big beaming smile that reached her eyes, and I promised myself I'd be more patient with her. Even though I was preoccupied with serious concerns about Diane's welfare at that point, I still had to be patient with Ginger. She'd been my best friend for months by then and had done loads of nice things for me. I had to be there for her even when she wasn't feeling great, that's what friends did.

I listened to her talk for the rest of the night, nodding and patting her arm whenever her voice wavered. She missed Nina Simone she said, and I nodded. I'd forgotten all about the cat. She was worried about the dog too she said.

'What dog?' I finished my coffee.

'Sandy. That's what I called him, I don't know his real name, if he even has one. Sandy from the beach today at Loch Long.'

'I can't believe you're still thinking about some strange dog. You know he'll be fine, probably sitting at the feet of some young boy or girl who loves him to death as we speak.'

She brightened then. 'Do you think so? Oh, I hope so, I'd hate to see him left out in the cold.' She sat back and took a sip from her Coke. 'Oh, that's good Wendy, I'm glad Sandy's found someone,' as though my word on the matter was enough for her.

We went to bed about ten and I lay there, sweating and twisting in the scratchy sheets, dreaming strange, mixed-up dreams about Diane being chased by Roddy who was holding an oversized gun and shouting that all women writers should be shot in the neck. I got up exhausted at six and waited for Ginger to stir.

The phone was ringing out as soon as we got into the car. I'd left it lying on the back seat overnight and there were twenty-seven missed calls.

I reached to pick it up and Ginger grabbed my arm, saying, 'Don't answer it.'

I shook her hand off impatiently. 'What do you mean, don't answer it? It'll be Uncle Tam, raging with us for not taking the phone in with us last night. We need to speak to him some time.'

'Do we?' Ginger's face looked terrible. Her cheeks were scooped out and even her nose looked pinched. I could tell she hadn't slept and I'd heard her being sick again before breakfast.

'Okay,' I said quietly, as though to a very young child. 'Let's switch the phone off for now, and just head home. We can do any explaining we need to do when we see him. He'll understand we left the phone in the car, don't worry.'

We drove home without speaking, the only noise in the car the sound of Ginger's locket clacking against her teeth. I shivered as the rain bashed against the windscreen, and turned up the heating as high as it would go.

We reached Viewpark by early afternoon, just as the rain had exhausted itself to a slow, grey drizzle. I parked right outside Ginger's house.

She didn't make a move to get out of the car. I turned to face her.

'Do you want me to take your bag up for you?'

She didn't answer.

'Come on Ginger, we need—'

There was a pounding on the window at Ginger's side, and Tam's face loomed over us, his eyes huge behind his glasses. His knuckles thumped against the glass and he was shouting something we couldn't hear inside the car.

Ginger shrank into the fur of her jacket and started shaking. I rolled the window down and Tam stuck his face in and shouted, 'Where is it? What the fuck did you do with it?' He grabbed Ginger's collar as though he could pull her out of the open window. Ginger screamed and Fran came running down the path.

'For Christ's sake Tam, not in the street. Wait till we get into the house.'

She pulled his arm, he flung her off but stood back from the car and put his hands on his knees, breathing heavily. His glasses had steamed up but we could still see his eyes blazing.

'Right,' he said finally. 'Get out of the car and follow me inside. Now.' He grabbed Fran and the two of them started to walk back up the path.

I looked at Ginger. 'What shall I do?'

'Drive,' she whispered. 'Just drive Wendy.'

I took a last glance in my rearview mirror and saw Tam half turn and run towards us as I started the engine and the car shrieked away from the kerb.

'Get back here, get back here right now. Oh, you're dead, you hear me? When I catch up with you, you're dead . . .'

I couldn't understand why Uncle Tam was so angry and his words were whirling round in my head so that I could hardly concentrate on the road. I swung into the wrong lane on the roundabout at Tannochside and a young guy in a blue Peugeot stuck his head out the window and shouted at me, 'Where the hell did you learn to drive ya noob?'

Ginger didn't say a word till we got back to my house.

'We dropped off the bag in the right place didn't we Wendy? We dropped it exactly where they said at exactly the right time,' she said, all in one breath, spinning round the room, her movements small and jerky.

My mind skittered to keep up with her. 'Yes, of course we did. You know we did. Look, you need to calm down a bit Ginger,' I said, taking her by the shoulders and leading her into the living room.

'We never touched it did we?'

'We never touched it, apart from taking it out of the boot to leave it where they told us. What can have happened to it? Maybe the clients weren't told the right place to pick it up, it was a bit weird leaving it in a car park.'

She waved me away. 'That's how they do things Wendy. We kept our side of the bargain, didn't we? They can't be angry at us.' Ginger's eyes were huge with fear, her hair swirling about her head.

'Yeah, of course we did—' I stopped, as something occurred to me. 'What about Roddy? He knew, Ginger, he knew about the stuff and . . . we told him where we were dropping it. Could he have taken it, maybe, I don't know, forgotten to tell Tam he was picking it up for the client instead?' I shook my head. 'We should never have told him Ginger. Why did you tell him anyway, Uncle Tam was so particular about not telling anyone, even Roddy.'

'He knew something was happening. And it's not that easy to say no to Roddy. I should know.' She sank back into the sofa, looking tiny against the big, slithery leather cushions. Her face looked clammy, and I imagined if I touched my finger to her cheek it would come away with the soft gluey sound of sellotape peeling from a wall.

'You look exhausted Ginger, go and lie down on my bed for a while, sleep it off. Everything'll be fine when they've all calmed down a bit.'

'Okay,' she said. 'Do you want to come and look at the stars for a while with me?'

I closed my curtains and lay on the bed while Ginger paid yet another visit to the toilet. She came and joined me, curling into me like a little puppy, snuggling into my belly for heat. Pretty soon she started whimpering like one too so I kept patting her and making shooshing noises like I've seen people do in American movies. I could feel her hot forehead pressing into the wall of my belly then she raised herself up and her lips were at my jawline so her breath puffed upwards towards my ear. Soon, we breathed in and out together – deep breaths, long and hot, like we'd already slipped into the dead of night. I patted her some more and, despite everything that was happening, felt as calm as I had been for a long time. I could see why people kept dogs as pets, even though they were an extra responsibility.

I waited until I was sure she was asleep then picked up my trainers from under the bed and crept out of the room. I felt a bit bad about leaving her, I could see she was really worried but, to be honest, she'd always been a drama queen and I was sure things weren't as bad as she made out. After all, apart from Ginger spilling the beans to Roddy, we hadn't done anything wrong, in fact we'd done them a favour driving the bag all the way up to Loch Fyne in the first place. Diane, on the other hand, had real things to worry about and I had to check that she was okay.

The grass was too squelchy to sit on and a soft evening mist hung low on the hill, casting shadows on Diane's house. I stood by the trees at the top of the hill and pulled out my binoculars but I couldn't see much. I peered as hard as I could when I thought I saw Diane in her kitchen but then, nothing. I stood, shivering and stamping my feet for another hour or so until the front door opened.

I almost dropped my binoculars when I saw her.

She was wearing a long yellow coat which made her look golden and ethereal as she strolled across the drive, her hair gleaming. But all I could focus on was her left arm, tied up in a sling so that she had to hold it at a right angle to her body, her fingers curled round her waist. She'd tied a yellow scarf round it to match her outfit as though it was just an opportunity to add a fashion accessory. No doubt she'd have some story about how she'd tripped on the ice, or banged against a door, but I wasn't fooled. My eyes scanned back to the house and, sure enough, there he was, slithering through the front door like a slug, leaving an oily trail behind him. I could feel the anger pulsating deep in my skull and I vowed that would be the last time he hurt her. Although Diane couldn't see me, I like to think she knew I was there, watching and protecting her from afar, ready to rescue her when the time was right.

My heart was still pounding after they'd driven off in Diane's little red car. I ached with the worry of all the stuff Diane was hiding – hurt feelings, slights, living a lie with that man, not to mention broken bones, bruises, bleeding, God knows what. Seeing her injured like that convinced me that I had to rescue her soon before he took her over completely.

It was as I was trudging back up the hill to my house that the solution hit me – Diane would need to come and live in my house with me. By the time I crossed over the motorway bridge, oblivious now to the cold, I was already running through plans in my mind. I'd arrange the date with her, maybe an evening she knew he'd be out, or during the day when he was at work, and I'd sit outside in my mum's Micra, the engine still running. She'd tiptoe out fast as she could, with a couple of suitcases – just her clothes and essentials, we could buy other things when we needed them – and jump in beside me. We wouldn't talk much on the way to mine, we'd just be happy in the knowledge we were together and she was safe. We probably wouldn't be able to stay in Uddingston for very long afterwards, it was too close to her husband, but we could go to France, or the Lake District, or America. I hadn't thought too much about the future yet but we could go anywhere as long as we were together.

My heart sank a bit as I thought about how to break it to Ginger but after all, I thought, Uncle Tam was bound to forgive her for getting one single delivery mixed up, and she still had her mum too in a way; Diane and me only had each other.

'Ginger?' I called out in the yellow downstairs hall. 'Ginger?' But I could tell by the deep silence that the house was empty.

Ginger had gone.

37

GINGER TURNED UP AT my house again the following evening, her face bruised and bleeding, and we didn't even speak as I ran the bath. It took a long time for the water to be hot enough. Ginger knelt on my fluffy old bath mat, staring at the water as it gushed from the tap. Slowly, she leaned over to the side until she was lying on the floor in a tight ball, her dirty hair streaming over the edge of the mat. She didn't say a word as I curled myself behind her and we lay there together, like an oyster in its shell. I was conscious of my long limbs wrapped round her clammy jeans, mud and grass still clinging to the bottoms of them. I kept making shooshing noises and running my palm down her damp hair till it was sticking to her head. She felt weightless, and she was cold, quivering like a tiny bird.

It wasn't easy to get her jeans off her, the damp denim clung to her skin, and she was still trembling with cold. 'Come on, come on now,' I kept whispering in the same voice I'd used to my mum at the very end. It was only when I tried to pull her baggy sweatshirt over her head that she stopped me. Her eyes met mine, they were terrified, flashing through the steam.

'Come on,' I said again. 'You'll feel so much better after a bath.' We tussled for a bit then she went limp and I pulled her top over her head. My eyes rested on her swollen belly and the blue veins drawn across her heavy breasts and I drew in a breath. She raised her chin and looked at me for what seemed like a long time.

'Oh Ginger,' I said and put my arms round her. Together we swayed by the side of the bath until eventually I helped her into the warm water.

She lay back in the bubbles, her eyes closed, the tears still managing to squeeze out beneath her eyelashes and streak her cheeks. Her bloated tummy rose from the surface, like a smooth boulder mid-stream.

Downstairs, I put on all three bars of the electric fire and brought a chair through from the kitchen. I told Ginger to sit there and keep warm. She was clean and dry and smelled of shampoo, but she was already shivering away from the wet heat of the bathroom so I pushed her chair even closer to the fire.

I brought in Mum's old Victorian hairbrush with the pearl handle, the one she kept for show on her dressing table, and started to brush Ginger's still damp hair. I used long, slow strokes, starting at her parting and reaching all the way to the tips. I bit my lip as I saw the patches of her pale, tender scalp. It made me gentle with her as I brushed her hair. As it dried, the curls sprang tightly back into place and her shoulders dropped as she began to relax at last. I stood behind her and, looking down, I could see she had shut her eyes and I felt her warm back pushing into my belly. Her shoulders were level with my breasts and, as I breathed, her shoulders pushed into me then away, then into me again.

'That's the end of it now Ginger,' I said, as I carried on brushing her hair till it became electric. 'We'll go round to yours tomorrow, early while they're all still out of it, take what you need of your stuff, then we'll decide what to do next, okay?' I bent closer to her face so that my face was practically touching hers. 'Everything's going to be okay Ginger. I promise you.'

I stopped brushing her hair and helped her over to the couch. I sat next to her, but not touching, and although I didn't ask any questions, she started to talk about Roddy, the things he did to her.

'But how does he get away with it? What about Uncle Tam, or Fran? Why don't they stop him?'

'Like they care. Anyway, he creeps into my room, late at night mostly, after a drinking session, when everyone else is either out for the count, or gone home. He's this close to me' – she pushed her face up to mine till there wasn't even a hand's breadth between us – 'his tongue's all furry and sour with coffee, and he puts it into my mouth. Right in till I think I'm going to gag.'

I felt like gagging myself and I wanted to tell her to stop but she was talking as though I wasn't there, as if the words were just flowing out of her and she couldn't stop them. 'His hands are everywhere, here' – she grabbed her own breasts – 'and here' – her jutting clavicle – 'and . . . and here' – she indicated her poor, tender pelvis. 'It's like he's stabbing me between my legs, but I can't get up, can't see what he's doing, just the pain of the knife spearing into me, over and over.'

She pressed her lips together and looked up at me. 'Don't say anything else,' I wanted to say but the words wouldn't come. I touched her hand and she flinched.

'And he's so heavy Wendy. So heavy against me, pushing and shoving his weight against me. And it feels like I'm underwater, I can't breathe in case my skin breaks and I'm torn wide open.'

337

'Stop Ginger!' I said suddenly. 'Please.'

We were both silent for a moment or two, tears pooling in Ginger's eyes and dripping onto my new couch. My fists curled up at my sides and I slid them back and forth along the smooth leather beneath me. The thing people don't understand about Ginger is that she might have looked tough, and talked a good game, but underneath, she was vulnerable and others took advantage of that. She was only fifteen for God's sake. Not much older than I was when Dad died so I know it's a difficult age, and that's without predators like Roddy, feeding on you like maggots on a corpse.

'I've been a terrible friend to you Ginger, I see that now.' She shook her head. 'No, it's true, you told me things were bad for you and I did nothing to help. But I'm telling you now, it'll never happen again, I won't let it. We'll get your stuff tomorrow and you're coming to live with me.'

She swung round to face me. 'Do you mean it Wendy? Oh, why would you want me? I'm useless.'

'No, you're not. Neither of us are. You and me, we're going to do something special, you'll see.' I shifted back a bit in my seat. 'And Diane too. Well, I haven't worked out yet how that's going to happen but I know all three of us can be together. Everything will be okay, just the three of us against everyone else.'

'Promise?' she said.

'I promise.' I smiled at her. 'And now I'm going to make us a cup of tea.' I needed one.

When I got back to the living room, Ginger was sitting forwards on the couch, sucking her locket and rocking slightly.

'Wendy, I've got something to tell you.'

338

I gave her her tea and sat forwards with her, bracing for the next bombshell.

'I went back to the house to tell Uncle Tam about Roddy, how he must have taken the bag. But . . . he didn't believe me.'

I blew on my tea.

'Do you understand what I'm telling you Wendy? Roddy set us up. He took the stuff and now he's letting us take the blame.' Her words came out in a rush. 'And I told Uncle Tam and he had it out with Roddy but he said he knew nothing about it, how could he, Tam had told him nothing and what the fuck kind of business partnership was that. And then they both turned on me, Uncle Tam was spitting when he shouted at me what an ungrateful bitch I was, and his eyes were like a wolf or something, he was that angry. And he was shaking me Wendy, like this, pushing me by the shoulders. He was so angry.' She indicated the long cut above her eyebrow. 'I had to get out of there, I thought he might kill me.'

'But even if Roddy did take the bag, could your uncle Tam not just resupply it? If the customer still wants it, I mean?'

'Oh Wendy, it doesn't work like that. These people . . . they're not . . . they're not like the customers on your bus, you can't reason with them.'

'What's going to happen then? Do they want their money back? Maybe we could help pay some of it back, get some money together from . . . somewhere.'

'Where are we going to get that kind of money from? Anyway, it's too late for that. They're after Uncle Tam now, threatening all sorts, so I ran away as soon as I could. They don't know where you live but Wendy, they're threatening to come and find you too.'

'What have I got to do with their business? How can I help?'

'Christ's sake Wendy, don't you get it? These people are animals, they'll stop at nothing, and Roddy's blaming the whole thing on us.'

She was talking so quickly her words were tumbling over each other and I was having trouble following what she was saying. 'Well, I suppose this is the kind of thing Uncle Tam's got that gun for,' I said, trying to cheer her up by making light of it.

She wouldn't look at me, stirred her tea vigorously.

'Ginger. You did put that gun back, didn't you, where you found it? You wouldn't . . . Christ, what am I saying? Of course you wouldn't.'

Ginger shook her head and ran her fingers through her hair, thick clumps of it coming away in her hand and falling onto the carpet. I could tell she was too exhausted to talk any more.

'Look, let's sleep on it. Tam doesn't know where you are so just stay here and we'll make a plan in the morning okay? No point getting all worked up at this time of night. Everything will be fine.' I nipped upstairs for an extra blanket for her and told her to sleep.

I couldn't sleep. I lay in bed thinking about what she'd told me and I began to suspect that maybe the stock we'd been delivering for Tam hadn't been entirely above board, legal I mean. Between that, needing to do something about Ginger's predicament and, most importantly, the urgency of Diane's problems with her husband, I knew I had to act fast. Taking Ginger along had not been part of the plan but I didn't see what else I could do. I wondered if she could come with me, maybe even help Diane carry more of her stuff to the car, then we could all drive off somewhere away from Uddingston immediately, never mind lying low in my house for a while. But where would we go, maybe Diane would know somewhere, some place only she knew about, maybe an old cabin that she used for writing. Yes, that was it! My mind was whirring with possibilities and escape plans so that I couldn't sleep at all. Although it was still too dark to see, I got up and put my clothes back on, ready for action.

I tiptoed into the living room so as not to wake up Ginger, but she wasn't there. I lifted the blanket from the couch as though she could somehow be curled up there like a stray cat, but only the shiny leather sofa lay beneath. I stood looking round me wondering if she was hiding somewhere in the semi-darkness of the room but of course she wasn't. I couldn't think where she'd gone – I knew she couldn't go back to her uncle Tam's house so where else could she be?

In the kitchen, I stood at the back door for a while, peering into the darkness, trying to work out what the moving shadow was at the end of the garden. The wind lifted suddenly and the shadow sprang back and cracked so loudly I jumped and banged my elbow against the fridge. I realized it was only the door to the shed, flapping in the wind and catching against the wall. I peered again into the gloaming but there was no one in the garden.

I wasn't sure what to do next. I thought I'd calmed Ginger down but she was gone again. No matter how many times I go over the events of that night and the following morning in my head, I still don't know if she'd made her plans already, if she didn't trust me to make everything okay like I said I would. If only she'd waited, let me work things out. Things could have been so different.

I switched the kettle on and stood waiting for it to boil. Suddenly I snapped the switch back to off and grabbed my anorak from the back of the chair. I made my mind up in a flash – I had to get to Diane's, the time had come for us all to leave.

38

THE HOUSE WAS A GRAVE when I got there. It was still black as night and, from my spot on the hill, I could just make out the branches of that old oak tree swirling around in the dawn wind like giant spider legs, shimmying against the blackened windows at the front of the house. Almost right away, things started to feel weird. I had a sense of foreboding or anxiety or something. I could almost see it in the air in front of me. That feeling you get in nightmares, like dread, fear of everything changing so that life can never be the same again. My gut was pulling downwards and my scalp itched.

I stayed where I was, just watching the house for an hour or so, trying to stay calm and think things through. The wind died down and quietened the daybreak. It was still and silent, apart from the steady drip of rain as the first light of day approached. My breath steamed in the air and the ground was hard with yesterday's frost. I knew it was time to make my move. I crept closer to the house and crouched behind the thick bough of the tree.

I had this idea I'd peep in the windows first, sneak a glimpse of Diane going about her lonely morning before I let her know I'd come and everything was going to be okay. I stepped over the rose bush nearest the door, my foot sliding across the frozen mud, and propped myself up on the window sill. I couldn't see anything at first – the rain was getting heavier – but then I saw her at the back of the house. She was spotlit by the ultra-bright strip light on the ceiling so that her image was reflected in the back window and there were two of her moving gracefully around the kitchen. How warm and cosy her kitchen looked, with its mugs and long wooden table and brown eggs in a thick bowl by the cooker. My nose was practically on the glass as I struggled to see it all.

Her poor arm was still bound up in its sling so she was moving slowly as she took a carton of milk from the fridge and poured it into a glass waiting on the table. I knew she was thinking about themes for her next novel, or maybe a twist in the current story she was writing. We writers never stop thinking about our work, it's part of us. I knew that about Diane and she accepted it as part of me.

I saw Diane turn and shout into the air, and then he appeared, the wee boy from all the pictures and photographs I'd seen in her house. He looked about eight or nine, wearing light blue pyjamas, hair mussed up like he'd just got out of bed, and his hands outstretched for the milk. Diane reached over and ruffled his hair, whispering something close to his ear that made him smile.

My chest was a spool of thick, jute twine, that was being pulled tighter and tighter, I couldn't get a breath, the shock of what I was seeing whipping against my face along with the rain. I calmed myself as the boy sat at the table, showing Diane something in a book. Okay, I thought, okay, so she's taken pity on a wee boy because he's lonely like us. Maybe

344

a budding writer too, wouldn't be surprised. Maybe he could even come with us, then the boy could be a brother for Ginger's baby. Saanvi was always saying how we all need lots of people around us, so maybe the boy would make it all perfect.

But then that husband of hers came into the room, stalking into the kitchen like he owned the place, in his dressing gown and slippers, his big, bald head shining. I nearly fell from my spot because he walked over and kissed Diane! She had her good arm round his waist, laughing and looking up at him, putting on a show. He pushed her shoulders down so that she had to sit at the table and went over to the kettle to make her tea. As though she wasn't capable of doing even that herself. He brought her tea over and they sat down together like . . . they were a family or something. They were laughing and warm in the kitchen, I was out in the bushes with my hair plastered to my head. No, this wasn't right.

Minutes later the man and the boy left the kitchen while Diane sat on, flicking through the paper, sipping from her mug. More time passed and I watched her wave goodbye to the man and kiss the boy's head. I jumped off the ledge and crouched on my heels behind the tree as they came out of the house and drove off in the car, leaving Diane alone.

I looked across the street and towards the station. By this time, I could hear the rumble of cars heading down Station Hill towards the car park and, if I peered a few hundred yards across the road, I could just about make out the silhouettes of the office cleaners and the road workers in their yellow high vis vests standing at the platform. I had to move quickly before any more people came and—

'Wendy!'

I fell to the ground when I heard Ginger call my name. I turned and saw her ghost staring back at me. The bronze street lights bounced off her skin, draining the blood from her. Dark bruising framed her face so that the centre was like a fossil peeking out of the dirt, her hair plastered down like mine by the rain, and I could see her bald patches gleaming like silver coins in the early morning light.

'What are you doing here?' I hissed, as she stomped across Diane's beautiful silver lawn, her red trainers thudding on the frost hardened ground.

She didn't say anything as she approached me but I could see something had changed in her, hardened or transformed or something, her eyes projecting a look I couldn't read.

It was all wrong, Ginger being here like this.

'You can't . . . you can't be here. This is Diane's house, this is my place, do you hear?'

Ginger laughed and put her hand to her hair, feeling her way round her scalp in a vain attempt to make the clumps of damp orange hair cover the bald patches, which I could see now covered most of her head. She licked her lips which were thick and pulpy, then coughed as she tasted whatever that brown stuff was that was sticking to her mouth and face. The right-hand side of her body was smeared in brown gunge, like she'd just stepped out of the sewer.

'What happened to you Ginger?' I whispered, though I wasn't sure I wanted to know the answer.

'Nothing happened *to* me Wendy. For a change, I was the one making things happen, doing stuff that made them sit up and take notice. For once in my life, I was in charge.'

'What . . . what have you done? Ginger, what's that in your hand?'

She half smiled and curled up her hand, waving the other one in an ah-ah-ah gesture as though we were playing a game. She raised her chin, and I could see that the streaks of brown, or was it red, reached all the way from her chin and down her throat. The zipper of her jacket was open, its once soft collar matted and stained, like road kill round her neck. At last she turned her hand palm upwards and I saw the gleam of the gun, its smooth wooden handle and the gaping hole of the barrel.

She jerked her right shoulder and said, 'Roddy tried to take the gun off me but I wouldn't let him. He dodged me and I ended up getting hit in the shoulder.' She winced. 'Typical eh, the likes of Roddy will always get away scot-free, there's nothing I can do to change that. But listen Wendy, it doesn't matter any more. It's time for us to get away. Just you and me, do something special, like you said.' She cradled her tummy which seemed even more swollen than it had been the night before.

I glanced towards the house, where Diane was still sitting at the table, drinking tea and smiling at whatever she was reading, a perfect tableau of the writer at rest, completely unaware of the drama unfolding outside. I tried to stay calm. 'Why don't you give me the gun Ginger, and I'll keep it safe?'

'Don't worry about the gun. It's just for protection,' she said. 'Because they're all liars Wendy – Roddy, Tam, my mum, the lot of them. We can't trust anybody except each other, you must realize that by now?'

She was coming towards me and I was pressed further into the bush. I looked around me but there was nowhere for me to go.

'But what about Diane?'

'Forget about Diane! Who is she anyway, what does she mean to us? The hell with her, look where she lives, in this mansion with her family. She's not like us Wendy, we're different.'

'I'm like her,' I shouted. 'I'm a writer, same as her.'

Ginger laughed so hard she slipped as she came towards me and the gun fell out of her hand.

I raised my hand to my mouth and screamed, stumbling as I pushed her away from me so that we both fell back onto the grass.

The front door opened and Diane poked her head out. 'Hello? Is there anybody out there? Who's there? Oh, it's you, what are you—'

Ginger and me both sprang to our feet at the same time and reached for the gun which was lying between us like a landmine. I knew I had to get to it first to stop Ginger from doing something stupid but she lunged faster than me and her index finger was already curled round the trigger when she slid on the frost, her left trainer kicking the gun and spinning it round to face her.

The gun went off.

Ginger staggered backwards, fresh blood blooming like a rose across her chest. She thudded onto the white grass, limbs flailing and her eyes and mouth black holes, like a girl in a Francis Bacon painting. As she fell, the gun skidded across the ground, and landed with a clatter on the doorstep in front of Diane.

'Ginger!' I cried, running towards her. 'Oh God, please be okay,' I whispered as I leaned over her, smoothing her hair back from her face, and trying to gather her up from the cold ground, my hands sticky with the blood from her chest. Behind me, I could hear Diane on her mobile, shouting, 'Police, police, please it's an emergency, there's been an accident.'

In my heart I knew already that it was too late for Ginger. I turned to Diane, and watched as her knees buckled and she crumpled on the doorstep.

And That's How I Ended Up in Prison

THERE'S A SMALL WINDOW AT the back of the cell and most days this week we've seen snowflakes like fat white moths floating in soft diagonals across the glass. My mum used to say snow in January was a good sign, it meant a long summer, but I'm not sure if there's any science behind that. Other than that, the cell's pretty desolate. It's cold in the mornings and icy at night, and there's a smell of damp from the nasty blue duvets on the bunks. Well no wonder, the sheets haven't been changed in the three weeks I've been here. The cell smells like my house used to smell, before Ginger and me did it up.

I never imagined prisoners would have so much time on their hands. I thought they were all forced up at sunrise to eat lumpy gruel, maybe spend a few hours sewing some mail sacks, and then march round a compound for a bit with a hundred other women. Honestly, it's nothing like that and I do feel some of the prison series on TV have misled us a bit. You spend 80 per cent of the day on your own, twiddling your thumbs and whatever else you fancy twiddling, wondering how you're going to pass your time till they release you. Or find you guilty and throw away the key.

Of course, you do get cellmates. In fact, there's a heavy

turnover in cellmates on remand, certainly in my cell. The first woman I shared with was called Demi-Lee and she never stopped talking. Sometimes that was annoying but she did tell me some good stories, like the one about her mum who was the wart woman.

'Why did you call her that?' I asked.

'That's what everyone else called her because she could get rid of people's warts.'

'Was she a doctor?'

Demi-Lee snorted from the top bunk. 'Nah. It was just a way of earning some extra cash. Folk would come to the house, bring their kid maybe, God love them, sometimes their hands would be covered.' She made a face and cupped one hand over each finger of the other hand in turn to indicate the size of the warts. 'My mum rubbed pieces of silver on them and they had to bury them in the garden.'

'Wow, and did the warts just disappear?'

She propped herself up on her elbow and looked at me. 'Are you taking the piss?'

'What do you mean?' I said. 'Did she not cure the warts?'

Demi-Lee waved her hand. 'Sometimes the warts went away, sometimes they didn't, but they'd paid my mum by then anyway and me and my sister used to watch where they buried the ten pence pieces and spend them on pickled onion crisps.'

I wanted to ask her more about how the silver superpower worked but she'd already moved on. She never talked about anything for very long before returning to her favourite subject – her wee princess they'd taken away from her.

'I never used when she was with me, *never*. She was my wee angel, the only thing keeping me out of prison.'

'But you're in prison,' I said.

She leaned over the edge of the bunk and shot me another look, her face close enough for me to see the shrivelled scabs round her mouth.

'I shouldn't even be here,' she said, 'that's the God's honest truth. It was self-defence Wendy, if I hadn't stopped him, he'd have beaten me half to death. They're saying my temper's out of control but you can tell by speaking to me I'm not like that, can't you?'

'Could you not just have called the police?' I asked. I was going to tell her about this article I'd read in the *Hamilton Advertiser* that said they prioritize domestic abuse situations, but she said, 'Right, that's it, fuck's sake,' and jumped down from the bunk with her hairbrush in her hand and clobbered me with it before I got the chance. They moved her the next day when they saw my face so I never got to hear the answer.

The last girl was called Audrey. She was thin and jumpy but we got on great. She spent most of her time pacing up and down the cell like she wasn't sure what to do with all her nervous energy. I asked her if she wanted to make soap figures with me, but she said no. She wasn't one to jabber on, but neither am I. She was only in for shoplifting, she said, but she didn't get bail because she's been convicted for the same crime so many times before. She stole mainly Lynx and razors, that's the stuff people want. She'd get a tenner for the razors and sell the Lynx for a pound each. Her patch was the lane behind Buchanan Street, she'd sell the stuff, score, then do it again.

'It's snakes and ladders isn't it?' she said, sitting down at last and swinging her legs from the top bunk. 'Up the ladder and down the snake, do it again, and again, till game over.'

Even though her hair was very short, she still managed to have a good inch or so of dark roots at her parting. She said she was twenty-five but she looked younger, too young to have had three daughters and to have lived the life she described.

She stood trial last week and was only given a year's suspended. I'm really pleased for her even though it means I'm on my own again in the cell. Most of the time, I just lie on the bottom bunk and think about stuff. About Ginger mostly, and how things could have worked out differently.

People keep going on about the gun as though she was trying to kill people with it or something. She wasn't, she was trying to protect herself, and me, she just went about it all the wrong way. The Ginger I knew was kind and generous and funny and thoughtful. She was the best friend I ever had, and I'm even including Diane when I say that. If you really want to talk about who deserves to be punished, what about Roddy, all those things he did to Ginger. It keeps me awake at night thinking about how he hurt her and I didn't stop it. And how he's still walking around going about his business while Ginger's not ever coming back. All that potential, all that love she had to give, it's all gone. I didn't know being someone's friend would be this hard.

I don't like to think too much about Diane although sometimes I can't help it because you can't just turn off that sort of love overnight. But the things she said that last day at her house, and the things she said to the police about me! It was like she hated me, or worse, like she didn't even know me at all. One thing I will say, when she came to the door that morning, before she saw Ginger and it was only me, this beautiful look of recognition passed across her face and I knew, I knew then that if I could have got to her sooner I would've been the one sitting there with her at that kitchen table. We would've drunk tea in the morning and wine at night and talked about books and writing and just . . . just ideas . . . all day, every night. She wouldn't have wanted anyone else, and nor would I. Ginger would have had to deal with that because it would have been just Diane and me. Telling our stories to the world.

I mean, when does reaching out to your soulmate become a bad thing to do? Of course I can see why telling her about that dream I had – where she was sprawled on her front step with treacly blood seeping through her hair and her eyelids flickering like bats, and I was the only one who could save her – I can see why that would have frightened her. Specially when the gun was lying there right in front of her, and Ginger's body was going cold on the grass behind us. And I do understand now that I shouldn't have gone to Diane's house that day to make her come with me immediately. She'd had years of being badly treated by that man so she needed time to understand that everything was going to be okay, that I was there to save her. And most of all, I should have known that Ginger would follow me and mess it all up the way she did with everything else in her life. But, like I said to the police, I'd never harm Diane. I loved her.

When I opened my eyes this morning, I saw the sun coming up and the cell was filled with an almost invisible pink light. Spring is coming and things are looking up for me. Mr Cameron came yesterday with the good news that they've dropped the stalking charge and as long as I agree to some ridiculous conditions about not going near Diane, or her house, they're going to release me and let me go home. I wasn't as surprised by that as he seemed to be because, despite her behaviour the day I was arrested, I've

357

always known it was only a matter of time before Diane told the truth about our relationship and how close we were.

Saanvi hasn't been in touch while I've been here – I bet no one thought to tell her where they took me – but I'll call her as soon as I get out. I hope she won't be too disappointed in me because I was only doing everything she told me to do to make friends and connections and open up to people. It's not my fault if Diane misinterpreted the situation and the police wouldn't listen to me. And I haven't forgotten all the stuff Saanvi taught me about getting better at life – making plans and getting out and about, meeting new people. When they let me out, I was thinking I could go to Buchanan Street, have a cappuccino in Greggs then wander along the road and see if I can see Audrey. I could help her to sell some Lynx, and maybe even offer to babysit her children, and make the kind of connection Saanvi's always on about – except this time I'll do it right.

And my time in Polmont hasn't been a waste. I've been able to do loads of reading, including Diane's latest short story collection, *Pondlife*. Now I'm going to be honest here – because I know Diane appreciates honesty more than people just saying how great she is all the time – I wasn't absolutely won over by the stories in *Pondlife*. For one thing, there's a reason books are mostly about sex and not much about having children – I would have liked more about Gordon and Fiona, and less about wee Fraser and his first day at school – though I admit likening the toad's eye to a splintered river rock is classic Diane. For another thing, for no apparent reason, the story titles were all in small letters. I found that really annoying, maybe that's just me.

But I also picked up a book by a writer called Ali Smith the other day. Maybe you've heard of her, she's Scottish too apparently. Now *she* can write. In fact, I can see loads of similarities between her writing and mine, especially the way she goes off on a tangent and makes you think you're reading about one thing but actually it's something else altogether. I love that! I'm planning to go to one of her book signings when I get out, there's a few things I could share with her about dialogue and ways of setting out your work so that the reader engages with it right away. We'd have a lot in common I think, with us both being writers.

Acknowledgements

Sincere thanks to:

My editor, Katie Seaman, and assistant editor, Becky Jamieson – for your insights, passion for the characters and their story, and meticulous editorial direction, which vastly improved the writing.

Sophie Buchan, Rhian McKay, Kate Oakley, Sarah Lundy, Claire Brett, Dawn Burnett, and all at HQ – because you are the best team in publishing.

Cathryn Summerhayes, Lisa Milton, and all the fabulous Primadonnas – for making the world as it should be.

Claire Mannion and Alison Gray – Claire, for reading not just one but two early drafts, and Alison, for supporting my writing from the beginning, thank you my friends.

Women writers everywhere – because 'your story matters and only you can tell it'.

ONE PLACE. MANY STORIES

Bold, innovative and
empowering publishing.

FOLLOW US ON:

@HQStories